Contents

Characters

Micky likes to have long showers.

Holly is Micky's big sister.

Leah and **Cam** are Micky's best friends. They like watching Super Snoop cartoons.

Stupid Cat is very stupid, but very friendly, too.

Smart Cat is pretty smart.

An Hour Shower

Written by Jenny Pausacker

Illustrated by Kelvin Hucker

sundance

A Haights Cross Communications Company

🐕 a black dog book

Published by
Sundance Publishing
P.O. Box 1326
234 Taylor Street
Littleton, MA 01460

Copyright © text Jenny Pausacker
Copyright © illustrations Kelvin Hucker

First published 2001 by
Pearson Education Australia Pty. Limited
95 Coventry Street
South Melbourne 3205 Australia
Exclusive United States Distribution: Sundance Publishing

ISBN 0-7608-4990-0

Printed in Canada

Chapter One

Mad Holly

It was breakfast time at my place.

Everything was the same as usual.

Mom was drawing while she ate breakfast.

Stupid Cat rubbed against her hand,

and Mom poured milk on his head.

Then my sister, Holly, on her way

to the bathroom, tripped over Smart Cat.

Then someone screamed.

That was unusual.

I looked up to see what had happened.

Smart Cat zoomed out of the bathroom,
shaking water off his fur.

My sister, Holly, came zooming after him,
in her bathrobe.

"Cold!" she howled. "The water's cold, Micky.
You had an hour shower, didn't you?
You used up all of the hot water."

I had an hour shower once.

Two years ago. And I said I was sorry.

But Holly never forgets anything.

Chapter Two

Looking for Clues

Holly took the last banana for breakfast.

It wasn't fair. I like bananas, too.

"I have to go to school now," she said.

"We're having a math test,

and I don't want to be late.

But I'll get you tonight."

When Holly says she'll get you, she means it.

I needed help. Fast.

So, I asked Leah and Cam to help me
find out where all the hot water went.

"Great," Cam said. "We can be detectives.
We can be just like Super Snoop on TV."

At lunch, the three of us
went racing back to my place.
Mom was still working at the kitchen table.
She had ink on her fingers and ink in her hair.
She even had ink on her face.

Leah had her Super Snoop magnifying glass.
She inspected the dried ink spots all over Mom.
"I don't think your mom is the culprit,"
she said. "She didn't use the hot water."

"What about Micky's sister?" said Cam.
"Maybe Holly was worried about her test.
Maybe she walked in her sleep.
Maybe she had an hour sleepwalking shower."

So we looked for clues in Holly's room.

It was a mess.

Math books and clothes and banana peels
were all over the place. If she walked
in her sleep, she would've tripped
and fallen flat on her face.

As we headed back down the hall,

we heard a strange sound from Mom's office.

BOING!

"What's that?" Leah squeaked.

I grinned at Leah.

"That was a *BOING*," I said.

"That's the noise the computer makes
when Mom turns it on."

But when we pushed the door open,
the office was empty.

Chapter Three

Leah's Idea

The computer was buzzing, but there was
no one in the room.

Two mysteries in one day!

It was getting kind of spooky.

"Ghosts!" said Leah.

"Aliens!" said Cam.

I turned the computer off.
Smart Cat jumped up on the desk.
"Meow!" he said.
He hit the start key with his paw.
BOING!

"Cool," I said.

"Smart Cat's learned another trick.

It looks like we've solved one mystery,

but we still need to solve the shower mystery."

Leah snapped her fingers.

"I've got an idea!" she said.

"The faucet! What if the faucet dripped
last night, and all of the hot water ran out?"

Our faucet is on the side of the bathtub.

It has a long lever.

You push the lever up to turn it on.

Then you push the lever down to turn it off.

It doesn't drip.

I pushed the lever up to show Leah.

Smart Cat heard the water
and came speeding in.
He jumped onto the bathtub.
He patted the lever with his paw.
The water went off.

"That's it!" I shouted.
"I know what happened."

Chapter Four

Cam's Idea

Just then, Holly walked in and frowned.

The water was running down the drain.

"You think you're really clever, don't you?"
she said. "You haven't solved the mystery yet.
Okay, so Smart Cat turned the faucet off.
But who turned it on in the first place?"

I looked at Leah, and she looked at Cam.

Cam went racing out.

He came back with Stupid Cat.

Stupid Cat is very friendly.

He rubbed against Cam.

He rubbed up against Smart Cat.

Then he rubbed up against the faucet

and pushed the lever up.

The water started running.

Holly frowned harder.

"Stupid Cat turned the faucet on," said Cam.

"He had an hour shower!"

"All right, Micky," said Holly.

"You and your friends solved the mystery."

Leah and Cam and I slapped hands.
"Great detective work!"

PRAISE FOR THE KNIGHT

"*Novice Dragoneer* is d building and resonant ch who fell in love with Tam

—Django Wexler, author of *The Infernal Battalion*

"Engaging, inventive, and compulsively readable, *Novice Dragoneer* serves up adventure after adventure of our determined, clever heroine, along with plenty of surprises. Highly recommended."

—Howard Andrew Jones, author of *For the Killing of Kings*

"One of the most consistently interesting writers."

—Charlaine Harris, #1 *New York Times* bestselling author of *A Longer Fall*

"An excellent fantasy coming-of-age story. . . . Ileth's journey leads her to places of wonder, but also sorrow and loss, and how she copes with the challenges is where the storytelling of E. E. Knight shines."

—*Booklist*

"If you enjoy fantasy, dragons, training, and a wonderful young heroine, I suggest you read this book."

—The Reading Cafe

"If readers like dragons and magic, there is plenty to enjoy here."

—SFRevu

"Delightfully entertaining. . . . Fans of magic school stories will especially take great pleasure in it."

—The BiblioSanctum

BOOKS BY E. E. KNIGHT

The Dragoneer Academy series

NOVICE DRAGONEER

DAUGHTER OF THE SERPENTINE

The Age of Fire series

DRAGON CHAMPION

DRAGON AVENGER

DRAGON OUTCAST

DRAGON STRIKE

DRAGON RULE

DRAGON FATE

The Vampire Earth series

WAY OF THE WOLF

CHOICE OF THE CAT

TALE OF THE THUNDERBOLT

VALENTINE'S RISING

VALENTINE'S EXILE

VALENTINE'S RESOLVE

FALL WITH HONOR

WINTER DUTY

MARCH IN COUNTRY

APPALACHIAN OVERTHROW

BALTIC GAMBIT

DAUGHTER
OF THE
SERPENTINE

A DRAGONEER ACADEMY NOVEL

E. E. KNIGHT

ACE
NEW YORK

ACE
Published by Berkley
An imprint of Penguin Random House LLC
penguinrandomhouse.com

Copyright © 2020 by Eric Fisch

Library of Congress Cataloging-in-Publication Data

Names: Knight, E. E., author.
Title: Daughter of the Serpentine : a Dragoneer
Academy novel / E. E. Knight.
Description: First edition. | New York : Ace, 2020. |
Series: Dragoneer Academy ; 2
Identifiers: LCCN 2020011326 (print) | LCCN 2020011327 (ebook) |
ISBN 9781984804082 (trade paperback) | ISBN 9781984804099 (ebook)
Subjects: GSAFD: Fantasy fiction.
Classification: LCC PS3611.N564 D38 2020 (print) | LCC PS3611.N564
(ebook) | DDC 813/.6—dc23
LC record available at https://lccn.loc.gov/2020011326
LC ebook record available at https://lccn.loc.gov/2020011327

First Edition: November 2020

Printed in the United States of America
1 3 5 7 9 10 8 6 4 2

Cover art by Dan Burgess
Cover design by Katie Anderson
Interior maps by Eric Frisch
Book design by Kristin del Rosario

WURM FRONTIER

THE RARI COAST

The Borderlands

DAPHIA

Torland

Jotun

The Freesand

Stavanzer

The Cleft

The Serpentine

THE GALANTINE KING'S PROTECTORATES

Sammerdam

Asposia

Antonine Falls

River Tonne

Tyrenna

GLORIAN COAST

THE GALANTINE BARONIES

The Scab

Reester (recently lost)

The Vale Republic
in the year of Ileth's draft
1966

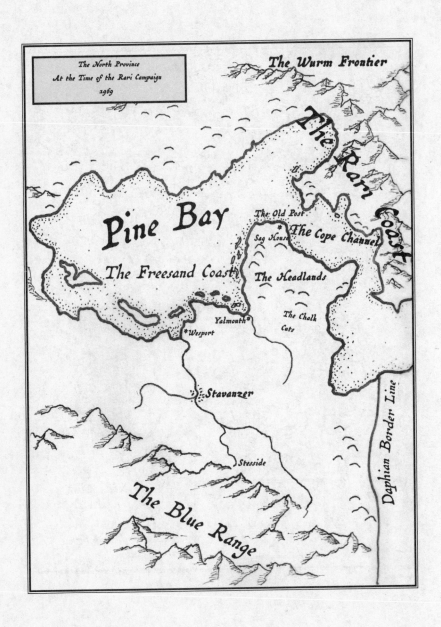

The North Province
At the Time of the Rari Campaign
1969

The Wurm Frontier

The Ram Coast

Pine Bay

The Old Post

*The Cope Channel

Sag House

The Freesand Coast

The Headlands

The Chalk
Cuts

Yalmouth*

*Wesport

Stavanzer

Daphian Border Line

Stesside

The Blue Range

For Larry,
My second father. A teacher. A movie lover.
And a guy who would have stayed up with me
all night playing coup.

DAUGHTER OF THE SERPENTINE

The ten-year-old girl stood in the roaring surf. Windborne sand pelted her and she had to squint to keep it out of her eyes. She felt small and frail against the two teenage boys hunched to either side of her, the boys all gangly limbs and wet, shaggy hair. The three held on to a flat-bottomed rowboat, which tried to escape at the pull of every receding wave.

"You wanted this! You begged, Ileth," the Captain said, his voice booming over the gale blowing off Pine Bay as he drank in her discomfort.

Ileth, the second-oldest girl in the Lodge now, had in fact begged to join the boys in their seamanship training. Girls never went off to sea, as the few orphaned boys in the Captain's Lodge on the Freesand Coast were always trained to do, but she'd asked and asked, carefully and only when the Captain was in his better moods, until he finally relented. "Maybe these scuts'll try harder with you around," he'd said, looking at the Chakl twins, three years older than Ileth. They'd been at the Lodge since they'd lost their father to the Rari pirates at seven and their mother disappeared from the Freesand shortly thereafter.

Ileth had pleaded for secret reasons. While she didn't mind learning about rigging and lines, how to claw close-hauled against the wind, or how to measure depth with a pole or a weighted line, her true intent was to learn proper map reading and navigation. She had a dream, a

dream so secret she never let a word that might hint at it escape her lips. To fulfill it she had to know how to use a compass and how to measure distance traveling by sea or land, so that in four years she might leave the Lodge in pursuit of it.

She'd always been an active, athletic sort of girl given to climbing and exploring, and the Captain shrugged off her odd request as Ileth's restlessness, wanting to be out and about rather than cooped up with the other girls. The other girls didn't much like her. The Captain, in their view, played favorites and Ileth was a favorite. Then there were her stutters and halts that dampened their spirited chats over the work.

Today was a real challenge, one he'd evidently been saving for a suitably stormy fall day. Ileth and the boys were to take a small boat out in the surf to Dragonback Reef, running a line to imaginary sailors shipwrecked on the reef. The danger of the Dragonback was anything but imaginary; an old fishing boat mast still pointed skyward from a wreck just the previous winter, and there were older fragments of boats, line, and canvas still caught in the jagged above-tide protrusions of the reef.

The would-be sailors stood barefoot in the cold surf. The Captain said you might as well tie bricks to your feet as wear boots if you go overboard or capsize, possibilities that seemed terrifyingly likely to Ileth as she watched the little rowboat lift and fall.

"This is just foul weather. Barely a storm," the Captain said, from the warmth of a boat cloak, thick woolen scarf, and sealskin boots. His charges were already soaked through, the boys in thin shirts and woolen vests that left their arms free to row and Ileth in an oversized boy's shirt that hung so low it could almost be called a dress over her holed woolen hose.

The surf didn't agree and roared back at him. To Ileth, the waves looked like hands reaching for her, and she held extra tight to the side of the boat when one attacked the beach through them.

Ileth looked at the little rowboat dubiously. She knew enough about small craft now to know that the flat-bottomed little thing, ideal

for poking around in the shallows checking the cages for crabs and lobsters, would slew all about in this water.

"The Dragonback's only bad on the other side. She's sheltering you in her arms, like," the Captain said, as his three trainees looked out at the surf blasting against it.

Nothing to do but get to it. The boys held the boat steady while Ileth got in and fitted the tiller and readied the rope to be paid out. Then they ran it out as deep as they could find purchase and jumped in on the upsurge of one of the breaking waves.

The twins, Avar and Trad, rowed like mad, leaning in and pulling in unison, bracing themselves on the rower's bench. The flat-bottomed boat was pushed this way and that by the surf and wind; the Captain had probably chosen it because it would be difficult to handle properly unless they worked as a team. Ileth did her best to keep the boat pointed at the reef, bow into each wave.

They were in the worst of the surf now, and a wave pulled the boat sideways and swamped them. It was all they could do to stay onboard. Avar took the oars while his brother bailed. Ileth helped as best as she could, using Avar's storm hat, bottom cold in the flooded boat with the tiller clamped under her armpit. They just got her bow into the next wave, a credit to Avar's rowing.

Two more waves and they were into the more sheltered waters close behind the reef. The currents around the reef were confusing. Ileth and the twins shot orders back and forth.

"Boathook. We forgot the boathook!" Trad, the meaner of the two, shouted. "You should have said something, Ileth!"

She ignored him. The stern spun round as the boat was pulled away by some current and Ileth spotted a sandy patch among the rocks of the reef. It was just a short distance—

Ileth's body decided for her. She had the rest of the line in her arms anyway, ready to hurl it on to the reef. She launched herself at the sandy spot.

It was a dangerous thing to do but she didn't have to swim, and her

free hand felt the wet sand as soon as she went into the bay. Her fingers were numb from the cold, but not so numb that they weren't able to find purchase on a rock as she scrambled up onto the Dragonback. Ileth had always been a good climber. She ignored the surf pounding the other side of the rocks and made it to the broken mast, quickly tying the rope about it with a solid mooring knot.

The boys didn't have time to cheer her; they were pulling for the rope stretching back to the Captain on the beach. Most of it was submerged, of course, but in a real rescue now would be the time to set up a winch on shore so that sailors could be pulled safely through the surf.

The Dragonback! And she was atop it!

Ileth pressed against the sheltering rock, staying out of the wind and surf. It was one of those talismans, a sign that one day she'd make it to the Serpentine. She touched objects that made her think of dragons—a turtle's back whose rugose patterns reminded her of scale, a bit of polished whalebone like a dragon-tooth, assuring herself with each contact that the dream would come true.

Avar joined her on the rocks. Between waves he whooped defiance at the heavy surf striking the other side, like a warrior safe from enemy arrows behind a stout wall.

Ileth, always interested in stories behind things, cast her eye about the bits of flotsam and wreckage the reef had collected. Her eye was drawn to an odd mass of canvas and wrecked barrel, when she realized, to her horror, that a stark white arm was sticking out of it.

"There!" she shouted. "A dead body."

The boys handled the worst of it while Ileth held the boat against the reef. Somehow they got the body out of where it and the wreckage were stuck and lashed the "rescue" line about its torso. Avar worked the line in a figure eight around the shoulders and chest of the man—it was a man, Ileth could see now—and from there it was a fairly simple matter to return the boat to shore and pull the corpse through the surf.

The Captain took over from there, hauling it well up onto the beach. It was a horrible, bloated thing. The face was a ruin where scavengers had been feasting on the most tender and accessible flesh. Even

now, Ileth could see hopeful crabs looking at the meal from the surf. Trad threw a rock at one.

"Fisherman?" Ileth asked. She found herself looking out of the corner of her eye at the bloated body. It helped, for some reason.

"He's escaped from the Rari," the Captain said. "Look, he's missing all his toes from his left foot. They made a neat job of it. See that, lads. Makes it hard to run. Guess he could still swim for it, though, on those kegs. Wonder if there were others with him?"

"How did he make it all the way to the Freesand? The Rari coast is on the other side of the Headlands," Avar said, gesturing vaguely at the high hills on the coast east of them, invisible at the moment in the rain.

"Could have died at sea and been carried by current. Could have slipped off a Rari ship. They're bold these days, they sail all over the bay, and aren't above going after a fishing boat that ventures too far out."

Ileth scowled out at the bay. Despicable. Even countries at war didn't molest each other's fishermen. But the Rari were mad for slaves.

"Well, now you've seen death, lads, raw and gone cold. And Ileth. Not fit for paintings, but it's just as much a part of life as a mother suckling her babe. Help me get him into canvas so the crabs don't have him before we can see him turned in and properly buried."

Ileth wondered what desperate fate drove this man to risk Pine Bay at this time of year, with more ways to die on a couple of kegs than he had fingers and toes. This man hadn't been following some secret dream. He'd run away from something. Something bad enough to make him brave crossing Pine Bay on a raft, in fall.

There were worse places than the Captain's Lodge.

A LENGTH OF WHITE CLOTH

"In coup, as in life, preparation is sovereign."

—IOW HEEM JEET, *A MONOGRAPH ON THE GAME OF COUP*

1

Ileth, a sixteen-year-old with a list of possessions as short as her not-at-all-famous name, arose quickly her first full morning as an Apprentice to the Dragoneers of the Serpentine. Having a bucket of cold lake water dumped on her head gave her no choice. It left her sputtering in her rope bed.

"Tail-er! Tail-er! Tail-er!" chanted an assortment of her fellow dragon-dancers, apprentices, and wingmen with nothing better to do that predawn than make some noise. They rattled old cowbells, banged tin trays against each other, shook coins in bottles, anything to increase the racket in the tight confines of the Dancers' Quarter.

A blanket enveloped her head and strong arms lifted her. She squeaked in alarm as they carried her out of the Quarter and into the passages of the Beehive, the cavern-laced mountainous rock that housed the Serpentine dragons and the throng of humans attending their needs.

She'd been warned the previous night that there was some sort of ceremony to endure for being the "tailer"—the last of a year's novices to cross the threshold into apprenticeship at the Dragoneer Academy. She'd even turned in wearing her day clothes and kept her boots handy, but her boots were presumably still waiting, forlorn.

One of the party amused themselves by tickling her feet. She'd

never liked being tickled, even as a child, and lashed out and felt her heel connect with something bony with a satisfying *thump*.

"That'll teach you," a male voice laughed.

"Galba's Anchor, she's strong!" one of the wingmen said as Ileth struggled. "What do they build these dancers out of, ship's cable?"

The racket quieted. She picked up the oily, metallic scent. They were passing through one of the dragon levels—and then she felt the breeze of outside air on her legs.

The blanket came off and a trio of muscular wingmen—she knew they were wingmen by their sword-belts buckled over their sashes—righted her and set her on her feet. The noisemaker racket and jeers broke out anew from the crowd surrounding her. She was at the landward end of the Long Bridge, a wide two-span thoroughfare that itself would be a wonder worth a trip and a painting to remember it by, were it not sandwiched between the towering hump of the Beehive with its famous lighthouse and the Pillar Rocks. The Pillar Rocks loomed overhead, standing like gigantic mushrooms at the end of the peninsula that was crowned by the Serpentine fortress. It was still early enough that the lighthouse's beacon caused the clouds overhead to glow and the bridge lamps formed little halos in the moist air of the predawn.

A drizzle washed over the party, but no spirits were dampened.

The assembly, such as it was, surrounded her. All the faces watched her, with the anticipation of a crowd expecting entertainment.

Ileth didn't care to be at the center of attention, particularly a crowd. It brought back memories of the children in the Freesand village circling around her to taunt the stuttering lodge-girl in the thrice-handed-down dress and homemade clogs.

When she'd tried to find out what sort of ceremony she, as the tailer of the draft of '66, would undergo, she'd just heard a few hints about a "crossing" or a "bridging." Well, if all they wanted was for her to cross the Long Bridge, she'd comply. She'd done it hundreds of times in worse weather than this.

She looked down the alley of youths. She saw a glint of scale in the

mouth of the gaping entrance to the Beehive. At least one dragon was either restless or bored enough to come see what all the noise was about.

Were they going to whistle as she walked back to the Beehive? Turn around and bare their bottoms? Ileth saw the snowcap hair and porcelain complexion of Santeel Dun Troot standing with her sister dragon-dancers in the crowd. It was hard for her to imagine a rich Name like Santeel lewdly waggling her backside like a seven-year-old at a window overlooking a busy street.

Vareen Dun Klaff, the bluffest and apparently the senior of the wingmen, addressed her: "You're lucky, girl. Privilege of sex, you get chaired across the bridge." Dun Klaff was an officer in the Guard. She'd sometimes run into him in the Beehive, when he was going about on watch, checking the bored sentries at the entrances to see that they were awake. The two others with him were very much alike in size, manner, and hair, each with a carefully tended forelock curled above the eyebrows.

The big wingmen stood aside to reveal a litter, perhaps some noble's relic from before the Republic. It had been retrofitted with a toileting stool, the sort of thing that would be set up over a sanitary ditch on a campaign. Some comic artisan had found humor in fitting out the litter with its curved golden armrests and a small, but plush, blue velvet backrest for such prosaic use.

"Your noble chariot, lady," said another wingman, not one of the trio who carried her, as a few of the apprentices hooted. She also knew this one's name, Rapoto Vor Claymass. He wore a tailored Guard's uniform and a pair of boots that would be the envy of half the dress uniforms in the Serpentine and was good-looking even dripping wet, as though the distinguished Name and enormous family estates and securities weren't enticement enough. One might criticize the ill-conceived mustache, a broad smear across his upper lip that turned down into two fanglike triangles at either side of his mouth in the fashion popular with the wingmen of his draft, as he didn't quite yet have the robust facial hair to carry it off properly, but the rest of him was turned out to an artist's ideal of a dashing young dragonrider.

He and Ileth had a history. The minor, ridiculous scandal around their kiss and a few fumbling intimacies in a stable stall resulted in her being booted from her lodgings with the other respectable Serpentine Academy girls and sent off to the dancers.

Someone in the crowd suggested that Ileth ride him across the bridge, and a back-and-forth of suggestions for positioning rippled through the group.

The ribald jests died down as she stood there, silent, her hair a wet tangle and her soggy charity-case clothes flattering only the Republic's ideal of thrift.

The chair looked filthy. She wondered how exactly it was used between tailers. Also, a lot of the mob about her carried bundles and little baskets. She wouldn't bet her only pair of boots that the bundles and baskets were full of flowers and trunk-sachets. It seemed likely that she was to be pelted by old bread husks, fish tails, apple cores, and walnut shells while aloft in the chair.

"As a young lady, you will be carried in all state and dignity back to the Beehive," Vor Claymass continued. "Symbolism suffers, as you live there already, but it's the tradition."

"It's the closest any of us are likely to come to a victory parade up the Archway," Dun Klaff said. He had the air of a youth who was agreeable as long as he got his way.

"No one's going to be throwing flowers," one of Dun Klaff's companions said. This one had a thick gold ring on his finger with a knuckle-spanning flattened design, big enough to make an impression on a wax seal. Ileth had more pressing issues at the moment, but she felt like she could remember who he was if given a moment of quiet to think.

"What do . . . what do the b-b-boys have to do?" she stuttered. She'd had an obstinate tongue since her first word, she'd been told. Half the elders in the orphans' lodge where she'd been raised insisted it was from an unfortunate topple off a table as a small child, with the other half claiming it was a judgment for her dead mother's sins.

"They run a gauntlet," Signet Ring said. "Everyone tries to get one

good whack in as you pass." Ileth had never seen this Serpentine tradition performed. She'd spent much of her novice year abroad in Galantine lands tending to a captured dragon from the late war.

"Ileth's being difficult again," Santeel Dun Troot said. Her observation gave other tongues freedom to wag.

We're never getting rid of this idiot, are we?

She's struck. First dragon she ever worked on died that very year, and then there's that dragon that flew to the Galantines.

The Galantines were preferable to having Fishbreath responsible for you.

Never did fit in.

"I'll . . . I'll run-run the gauntlet," Ileth said. She had exactly one set of outdoor clothes, and she didn't want to have to scrub all day to get whatever was on that chair out of them. She hitched up her skirt, anticipating the need to run.

Santeel Dun Troot gave a scandalized squeak.

"Ileth, just get in the chair," a round-faced girl named Quith said. They had been roommates when she first came to the Serpentine. Quith had the best memory for gossip and connections Ileth had ever known. "Please!"

A couple of the boys set to hooting again.

"She wants to run?"

"I say yes. Let's have sport!"

The three wingmen who'd carried her in the blanket put their heads together and had a quick conference. "All right, anything to get out of the wet," Dun Klaff finally said. "Vor Rapp, form ranks!"

Vor Rapp—that was it, not that it mattered much to a fresh-minted apprentice. The wingman with the big ring surveyed the double line of apprentices. "Remember, you blighters, back only! Strikes to the front are interference and I'll have the ears of anyone who strikes her head. No tripping, either!"

"Oh, I'm done," Santeel said. "This is turning into a comedy. I dislike comedies." She moved off on the bridge toward the Beehive.

Ileth tested the wet footing on the bridge with her bare feet. Just as

well they hadn't given her time to get into her boots. She could run better barefoot. She gathered up the hemming of her overdress and pulled it through her legs where she could hold it at her waist. It would be awkward, but better than stripping off into her shirt and sheath. Her first year at the Serpentine she'd challenged an aging apprentice who'd tormented her to a duel and fought him in her sheath and had been forever after introduced as *This is Ileth, the girl who fought Gorgantern in her sheath, remember?*

"All you have to do is make it to the other side of the bridge," said Vor Claymass. "We'll keep it fair."

Ileth could still see the dragon watching from the entrance tunnel. All she had to do was run to it. Maybe the ceremony was symbolic, after all. "I-I-I don't suppose you were your draft's tailer."

"It was a near thing, but no."

At the last moment Santeel, who was alone in her walkout of the performance, rejoined the throng at the far end of the gauntlet. She narrowed the gap at the far end, where most were already leaning far inward to get a better look at the action at the other end.

"One-two-three and UP!" called Dun Klaff.

Ileth jumped off like a flushed fox, running between the arrayed lines of apprentices. The vast majority were boys and young men, of course; the Serpentine Academy was overwhelmingly male.

The excitement of running brought its own exhilaration. She never got a chance to run just for the fun of it, not since she left childhood behind with the onset of puberty. She was in fair condition for it; the prancing and leaps and turns of being a dragon-dancer kept the muscles and nerves in tune.

The blows, such as they were, were halfhearted and most didn't even make more than a show of trying to hit her. A few pummeled her with whatever they had in their sacking, and she was right in her guess, it didn't feel any heavier than stale bread or fish tails.

Dun Klaff and one of his companions padded just behind, playfully urging her on with snaps from the damp blanket that had been over her head. Only the noise of it reached her. Signet Ring ran on the

outside of the gauntlet, keeping ahead and watching for misplaced blows or tripping.

No one aimed for her head, though a few mistimed their swings with their bundles and struck her front. A few tried to swat at her buttocks. The near misses and halfhearted strikes only served to urge her on.

Off-balance thanks to the burden of her wrapped overdress, she dodged and bobbed as best as she could in the spirit of the tradition. She'd made the right decision, better this than that filthy litter. And it would be over in a few more seconds . . .

The crowd at the end had closed off the gauntlet in their eagerness to watch. She marked Santeel Dun Troot and decided to fling herself between her and the boy next to her. If Santeel was bowled over that was just too bad.

Something caught her below the knee. She tripped.

The rest was a blur. She managed to right herself somewhat and get off one more stride and plowed into the press, one arm held up as a guard in front of her face. Bodies crashed into and around her with an assortment of grunts, *ooofs!* and squawks. Elbows and knees battered her from head to calf and she felt her shoulder strike Santeel hard.

Finding herself on the ground tangled up in two boys and Santeel, Ileth rolled to her feet. She stood at the Beehive end of the Long Bridge. She'd done it, made it through, now a full apprentice (albeit the tailer) in the eyes of the Serpentine.

She came up smiling and smoothed her skirt as the others who'd fallen with her sorted themselves out and picked her up.

"Stars, Ileth, you're bleeding," Santeel said, alarm widening those doeish eyes in her delicate, doll-like face.

Ileth put a hand to her cheek.

"Just above your eye," Santeel supplied. "Right eye."

Ileth's hand went up and came down bloody. Very bloody.

The scrum broke up quickly. Nobody wanted to be bled on.

"Terlich, it's those damned bracers of yours," the other wingman said, running up behind. "Don't you ever take them off?"

A thick-shouldered apprentice in a uniform that looked like he'd sewn it himself held up his leather-wrapped forearms. Bands of metal closed them, there were attractive lines of stitching, and a green dragon scale had been set in each. The scale had been chosen for its high ridge.

Terlich examined his bracers. "Wasn't me! Not a drop of blood on it. I was down by her legs."

"We'd better wake Joai up and get that attended," said Dun Klaff, who'd been just behind. He still had her blanket that he'd been using to thrash her; she'd have to ask for it back.

Santeel pressed a handkerchief to Ileth's eyebrow and guided Ileth's hand to it. Trust a Dun Troot to go to a ragging party on a rainy morning with a clean handkerchief concealed on her person. It still didn't hurt much; she felt the assorted bashes from the end of the gauntlet and scrape from the fall more.

"Thank you," Ileth said.

"I'm so sorry," Santeel said.

Ileth looked about for the broken glass or whatever she'd fallen on, but there was nothing obvious about. None of the women about her had rings or bracelets that might have cut her. Odd.

Ileth tore away from the group and tottered to the far end of the bridge under one of the lamps. A little blood dripped on her worn, patched, and pilled shirt. She'd have to soak it, along with Santeel's delicate mouth-wiper. The pain arrived, fierce and hot. She cursed.

"Now you can put on your sash, apprentice," Dun Klaff said, leaning over the rail next to her. He was still cheerful, and she found it oddly likable that her bleeding all over everything hadn't dampened his spirits.

"Thank you, sir—"

"Call me Vareen, Ileth. I'm so sorry you were hurt."

"Thank you, sir."

"Santeel is to blame for this. Shouldn't have happened."

Ileth looked over at Santeel. The third forelocked wingman, the biggest of the three, was talking to her, and Ileth could see from her

face that she wasn't enjoying his conversation. "What's Santeel to do with it?"

"She did lean way out and block you at the end there. You would have made it clean elsewise. I could hardly keep up with you, and I won foot-races as a Blacktower boy."

Was he trying to get her to dislike Santeel? They were fellow dancers, fellow apprentices now, and while they weren't natural allies, they'd always been shoulder-to-shoulder when one of them was threatened by anything outside their circle. But then he was in the Guards, and there was something of a rivalry between all the cadets in the Guards and the dancers.

"I decided to r-run the g-gauntlet."

He had the sense to change the subject. "Where is your sash, by the way? Does Santeel have it? We should end this by putting it on you."

Ileth felt her heart fall and some of her triumph dribbled out onto the stones of the bridge along with the blood from her eyebrow. She'd known since coming the long, hungry way to the Serpentine that apprentices in the Dragoneer Academy—which wasn't much of an academy, but you did learn about dragons one way or through constant labor—she'd known that apprentices wore a white sash. Most had two, in fact, an everyday one and a more formal one for dress occasions.

"I . . . I don't-don't have one . . . yet," Ileth said.

"Can she borrow mine?" Quith asked. She and Santeel approached, having recomposed themselves from the exertion of the gauntlet.

Vor Rapp pointed at her waist with signet ring finger. "Put it on her."

"Oh, Ileth," Santeel said. "I suppose you've no money for one."

"I only have the one, so I need it back," Quith said. "Please don't get blood on it."

Quith's sash was made of what looked like cotton, doubled and stitched into rugged channels. It wasn't a quality white, like Santeel's, more of an ivory. Quith started to show her how to knot it, but Ileth's fingers knew their business.

Santeel held the handkerchief to the wound while Ileth tightened the sash about her waist.

"I'm supposed to put that on you the first time," a gangly boy put in. His eyes were wide, staring at Ileth's bloody brow. "I was the tailer of the draft before yours."

"Oh. We didn't know," Quith said. Santeel sighed heavily.

"Just as well," the former tailer said. "You need that closed up."

"Cer-ceremony over?" Ileth asked.

"Ileth ran bravely. I'm proud to be in her company, tailer or no," Vareen Dun Klaff said. Rapoto Vor Claymass left off studying the ground around Ileth's fall and looked at him sharply. Ileth realized she was still holding her skirt up, as though ready for another run. She let it drop. "If you find difficulty in one subject or another, send for me. I was in charge of the tailer party—you being hurt is my responsibility."

The Serpentine was a fortress the size and population of a small town, and as a dancer she didn't mix with the others. It would be good to know a few wingmen. "Thank you, sir."

"I'm glad to know you, Ileth," he said, a rather elaborate and old-fashioned way of affirming a new acquaintance. He gave a short bow, which Ileth retuned with the usual feminine bob. "Get that cut looked at right now. Have you signed your apprenticeship contract yet?"

In that matter, at least, Ileth was prepared. "Not yet, but I was told I should visit the archives."

"Good. Well, all the luck in the skies to you."

Dun Klaff nodded and moved away, halted, turned, and handed the wet blanket back to Ileth. He and his two companions fell into step as they walked away.

"Congratulations, apprentice," Rapoto Vor Claymass said. He gave her wound a careful look and departed.

Santeel approached her again.

"Sorry about your handkerchief," Ileth said, folding it so a fresh side could absorb blood.

"My mother always made me carry one," Santeel said. "She hates the 'girl without a hankerchief' trick."

"That Vareen is nice," Quith said. She and Santeel had been oathed in as novices with Ileth. "Nice manners. Best of his draft, I've heard."

"Don't give him another thought," Santeel said. Quith fairly danced lest her one and only sash become soiled. "He fancies himself a poet. If he promises to write *grand verse* with you as the subject, don't take it too seriously."

Ileth, who wasn't educated enough to know *grand verse* from chalked alley scrawls about copulation, shrugged as Quith took off the borrowed sash and inspected it for bloodstains.

"Never knew Dun Klaff was interested in you, Santeel," Quith said as she knotted her sash. "You and Vor Claymass seem certain—"

"Could we perhaps keep Ileth from bleeding to death?" Santeel said tightly.

Quith pursed her lips. They started back across the bridge toward Joai's little house tucked in the corner where the fortress wall met the Pillar Rocks. Joai served as sort of an emergency nurse, cook, and mother all tied up in one heavy-pocketed apron.

Quith glanced around the bridge. "You know, if it wasn't the bracers on that oaf Terlich, what did cut you? There's nothing sharp about the ground, plain pave-stones, no cracks or buckles."

"Some idiot probably put a rock in their sack of rotten eggs," Santeel said.

"Still, we should report it to Master Traskeer."

Santeel stiffened. "Report it? It was an accident."

"I think someone tried to hurt Ileth," Quith said. "Blind her, even."

"Why?" Santeel asked sharply.

"So she has to leave the Serpentine. You know. Traskeer and his talk of odds. One less competitor for a dragon saddle."

Santeel adjusted Ileth's head gently so the wound would have to fight gravity. "First comedies, now dramas. You go ahead, report your suspicions. See what it gets you."

"'Suspicions,' she says! With Ileth bleeding all over like a stuck pig."

Santeel wiped the drizzle from her face. "You're probably half right. Whoever did it is worried about a bad note in Traskeer's index. There are only so many wingman slots. If I were one of those boys, I wouldn't

want to admit I'd hurt a fellow apprentice. Especially in a ragging stunt."

Traskeer. The new Master of Apprentices. Ileth hadn't met him yet, but she'd already heard he was just as much a dragon in spirit as any living in the Beehive.

2

The gash, washed out with stinging vinegar and then duly and painfully closed by a set of three silver pinch-pins just above, on, and below her eyebrow, throbbed painfully the first day, burned the second, and became an annoying itch on the third. It was a jagged sort of wound, something that looked more like a fishing accident—Ileth had seen plenty of those growing up on the Freesand Coast. It reminded her of a red sliver of moon, bisecting her eyebrow. The silver pins holding it shut gave her a bizarre appearance ("the silver helps keep the scar small," said Joai, as she inserted them with the same fast, deft skill that she used to dress a chicken). The pins going in hurt more than her receiving the wound in the first place, but of course anticipation of pain made everything worse.

Ileth had been sworn to return the solid silver pins and then released to her rope bed.

Examining Joai's work in Santeel's very fine mirror, Ileth decided she'd make a good sorceress on a stage with that metal in her face. It made her look fearsome and even a bit mad. She would play the sort of exotic, damaged beauty who would briefly tempt the hero from his righteous path. She'd seen two plays since coming to the Serpentine, sponsored by the Masters and dragoneers and put on by the novices and apprentices of the Academy. The stories weren't much, men engaging in heroics or villainy, women presented briefly as rewards or

hazards, with the odd motherly figure giving out good advice that was ignored or a curse that came to full, horrid effect by the play's end. Ileth reckoned she now had a face fit for hazards and curses.

Ottavia, the Charge of the Dancers, excused her from dancing duty and practice fatigues for five days, as she'd been cautioned against activity that might reopen the wound. She soon felt well enough to visit the archives to be *signed and sealed in*, as the Serpentine phrase had it. She was tired of lying in her rope bed reading borrowed novels chronicling the tragedies sunk into the hearts of young aristocrats.

She rose early for the long walk to the other end of the Serpentine.

The archives were housed in a basement catacomb with an old temple above. Even the stonework in the walls, great blocks that must have been an enormous problem to move about and lay, struck her as strange and unlike anything else in the Serpentine. But it was dry, immaculate, and lit about as well as human design and an ample supply of fat lamps in polished reflectors could make it.

Master Kess, the archivist who reminded Ileth of an old gray statue, pitted and weathered, must have been expecting her. He had her contract at hand and placed it on a reading table. You had to stand to read anything in the archives; Master Kess didn't believe in indulgences such as chairs.

A pair of novices sweeping the floors and dusting moved off to give them privacy. Ileth took in the first page. She'd *oathed herself in* to the service of the Serpentine as a novice in her first days, and that oath held until she was no longer a dragoneer. Or she died. The apprenticeship contract was a formal promise from the Academy that she'd have a place here. She looked over the first words:

"I (*lorca*), the undersigned, understanding the consequences and proven *ampetis azu releem*, do attest in the presence of legal witness affixing seal . . ."

The Contract of Apprenticeship to the Academy of the Serpentine went on and on like that for a full page that was the size of a placard, in elaborate lettering with each thick-stroked black letter edged like a

sword and cornered like a temple as though the whole weight of a civilization stood behind them. Mysterious Hypatian legalisms crawled through it like worms in a freshly turned spring field.

After she finished her study, silently buzzing over the arcane phraseology that meant nothing to her like a bee skipping over a weed to move on to the next flower, she raised her face to the archivist. "Done," she said.

In the light of the reading lamp, the Master Archivist's pockmarked face also looked fit for curses. "'Done' is a carefully chosen word. I can be 'done' reading a book or 'done' falling out of a tree."

Ileth had a young lifetime of being careful with her words because they had such a tough time getting out properly.

"It looks worse than it is," Kess's apprentice said. He struck Ileth as fidgety, or perhaps he just seemed that way next to Kess, who stood like one of the old columns holding up the temple floor above. "It's a fancy way of saying the Serpentine Academy will own you for the next six years."

"You're lucky, Ileth," Kess said. "In the time when the man I apprenticed under was himself an apprentice, the contract was entirely in Hypatian. You had to be able to translate it to the archivist's satisfaction to prove your education. That was before the Directory's legal reform. These days even—ahem!—indifferently educated souls such as yourself are apprenticed here and we make allowance in deference to republican sensibilities. Not that the old lot were that much better. According to the way old Heem Halveth told it, half of them would memorize the translation until they had it down by rote. Seems to me it would be easier and more useful just to learn your Hypatian from a tutor as a boy."

Ileth didn't give a fig about his opinion of her education. She thought about men like Hael Dun Huss, standing here as a spotty teen, reading over the phrasing and wondering if he'd make a good apprentice. He'd probably stood right at this table. It was a great hunk of stone like an altar and seemed likely to have been here two thousand years ago, never mind fifteen or twenty.

"Shall I take you through it?" the apprentice asked. He kept glancing at and then looking away from the pins holding the scar shut around her eyebrow as his fingers fluttered nervously toward the contract. Ileth worried that he'd knock the inkwell over and spoil it.

Ileth nodded. She was also nervous, just better at hiding it. Her stutter would be bad if she spoke. She felt out of her depth in all the elaborate lettering and legalisms.

"Paragraph One, establishing the parties, their competence to make contracts, and the fact that this contract comes under Assembly Law and traditions of the old Diet, which is to be in effect in any and all Provinces, Districts, and Cantonments of the Republic should any matter relating to it arise. Paragraphs Two and Three, the Dragoneers and Dragons of the Serpentine being under General Commission from the Assembly to protect the citizens of the Republic, their property, mail, trade, and reputation, take on as an apprentice at the Academy you, established above, for a term of at least six years so that you may one day serve as a Dragoneer if so appointed. Paragraph Four, you promise to obey any and all lawful orders from any or all superiors according to the ranking and traditions of the Serpentine even at risk of your life, with you having the right to give evidence to a Jury of Honor if you believe one or more orders from a superior unlawfully jeopardizes the Republic or your honor. Paragraph Five, the Serpentine through its Academy will provide you with food and shelter and certain specific tools needed for your duties, and will issue any allowances, inheritances, or incomes as provided for according to terms originally arranged by family, commission, or contract for the purchase of uniforms, arms, and other necessities. Paragraph Six, you shall have the Apprentice Password allowing you through any gates and doors of the Serpentine according to their practices of curfew, holiday, and mercy-leave . . ."

He droned on through the other fifteen paragraphs, the rest being legalisms about priestly rights at burial and storage of property, assorted dooms that would befall her if she deserted, disobeyed orders,

or intentionally caused harm to the dragons (the apprentice said that while the word *intentionally* didn't appear in the contract, in every case of an actual jury being assembled regarding harm to a dragon, intention figured largely in the arguments so it was traditionally considered an element of the contract, and therefore he added it), and finally added that in the event of a state of war, the contract would be considered extended until such time as peace was reestablished or the Republic had no further need of her and issued a written release.

"We usually still have the apprentice read the final paragraph aloud before signing," Kess said. "But if you'd rather not, I understand."

Kess had been present when she'd been sworn in as a novice, when they had to read off their oath. The entire assembly of dragoneers and apprentices had witnessed her embarrassing, stuttering performance.

"I'll—read it s-silently," she said. She felt the weight of the moment. She enjoyed the sensation, something like the feeling of a good tool in your hand and a challenging job ahead.

Ileth wondered if anyone backed out at the last moment. Probably very few. Only those who'd lasted through a novice year (or more, in her case), where you could be thrown out for minor infractions or just judged unsuitable for service with the Dragoneers, were offered an apprenticeship. She traced it with her finger as she read:

Knowing the consequences of this action, on my honor I pledge myself, in body and mind, to the Dragoneers of the Serpentine, the Dragons they serve, and our Republic that they jointly protect.

She signed. Just the name *Ileth* seemed inadequate, but the only additions to her name were from the Galantine aristocracy and wouldn't do for a document of the Vales and its Republic.

"Better add your place of birth," Kess said.

That was another problem. She wasn't at all sure of the circumstances of her birth. But she'd grown up in a lodge in the Freesand, the coastal area of the North Province, so she added *of the Freesand.*

"There," Ileth said.

The apprentice scattered some drying sand on the document. "We

have other papers for you, in your role as that late dragon's assignee," Kess said.

As far as the Academy was concerned, she was formally enrolled as an apprentice. But she had other business in the archives. There were some documents to sign, more legalese, relating to the death of the elderly dragon, who apparently had books or scrolls on loan to different regions of the Republic. "The Lodger"—as she'd known him—had turned over management of these oddly named volumes to her as one of the executors of the estate. Her signatures authorized the locals to maintain the collections. She only glanced at the documents, thick with Hypatian phrases she didn't understand, but they had piled up while she had been on her enforced residence in Galantine lands.

All the while Kess's apprentice kept glancing at her eye.

"It doesn't hurt m-much, if you're wonder-wondering," Ileth said.

"You're that girl who is always getting into fights," he said.

"J-just one. A duel," Ileth said. "I l-lost."

"Did you start swordsmanship or—"

"It looks like it's healing," Kess said. "She doesn't want to talk about it. This is an important day for her, Gowan. Stop spoiling things."

Ileth forced a smile. "It was a silly accident. Joai pinned the wound closed."

Every time I see that scar, Ileth thought, *I'll remember the day I became an apprentice.*

"You're the tailer of sixty-six, right?" Gowan grimaced and lifted his white apprentice belt. It had a faint brown stain that had survived many washings. "I was first of my draft. Sixty-one. They just threw wine on me. Said it was supposed to be blood, but they were too drunk to catch a chicken. Well, first or tail end, we're equal now."

"Congratulations, apprentice," Kess said. "Fate see you standing before a dragon one day, chosen as a dragoneer." Something in the practiced tone made Ileth believe the archivist thought it unlikely.

She bobbed. The cool, quiet archives seemed an odd place for such a ritual, with a couple of novices eyeing her jealously as they dusted, but the Vale Republic ran on contracts, stamps, and seals.

"Ileth, do you have your own affairs in order, just in case your service requires that greatest of sacrifices?" Kess asked. "I tell all my apprentices they should have a testament as to burial and property."

Ileth stared at her Galantine boots. The laces had broken in several places and been retied. The bootmaker made good boots but supplied her with poor lacing. "I—I expect to be buried with all my property."

Kess's face twitched. Ileth wondered if she'd seen the briefest smile in the history of the Serpentine or if it was just a nervous tic. "Well. That always kills the mood, but you'd be surprised how few even consider such things. You'll find we lose one or two a year, even without war. More in a plague. You should go along now to Master Sel—Master Traskeer, I should say—and report that you've been signed into the rolls. I wish you well in the next six years and then a rewarding assignment as wingman."

Ileth steeled herself. Traskeer was the new Master of Apprentices. Selgernon had resigned as a matter of honor after the affair with the egg theft and the flight of the dragon Fespanarax, as one of his apprentices had taken part in it. She'd heard from Quith that there was some back-and-forth about his resignation not being accepted but Selgernon forced the issue. The general opinion from those who'd met Master Traskeer seemed to be that the change was for the worse.

She nodded.

"If at any time you are doubtful about a point in your contract, you may examine it here," Kess said. His apprentice had shifted his furtive stares to her overdress. It was a shapeless, ill-fitting thing and she didn't have much of a build to fill it, so she wondered what he was looking at.

She checked the hooks and loops holding it closed. "Am I . . . am I mis-misaligned?" Her little white dragon-scale novice pin was on. Some apprentices and wingmen still wore them; some didn't. Ileth liked hers, and it drew attention away from the worn overdress and lately helped keep it closed where a button was missing.

"No," Gowan said. "Your sash. Traskeer will rake you for it, if you're

not in uniform." His hand mechanically checked the knot on his own white sash as if worried it had loosened.

"Don't . . . don't have one y-yet. I don't suppose you have a spare?"

He shook his head.

She'd already found out sashes were hard to come by. Former apprentices dyed theirs to match the "colors" of their dragoneer when they were promoted to wingman. The wealthier even ceremonially burned theirs at a feast, or laid them into storage with camphor to keep moths away in the hope that one day a family member would follow in their footsteps. A few gave them away to close friends for good luck. Ileth had only been close to one apprentice who made wingman. She'd married a rich Galantine and vanished.

She nodded, thanked them for their help in her halting fashion, and left the pair in their catacombs-without-temple.

The Captain who owned the Lodge where she'd grown up had once told her that in the Republic, legal contracts protected more hides than shields and parrying blades. Now she was protected by that fence of words printed with those sharp angles and razor-edged lettering, and ensnared by it at the same time. She'd joined the Serpentine because she loved dragons, but it was also an escape from the life laid out for her, where the best she could hope to be was some lady's maid or cook or maybe a wife to a fisherman—a lodge-girl probably wouldn't even get one who owned his own boat.

She'd kept herself alive and hopeful in the Lodge by collecting every scrap of information, every story she could of the Vale Dragons and their Dragoneers—which wasn't much, as they rarely visited the Freesand. She'd indulged in youthful fantasies about taking part in great deeds, righting wrongs, flying medicine on dragonback to snow-choked villages, or carrying a message that saves the day, making bandits and pirates fear the wrath of the people of the Vales . . . vague thoughts ripened into whole processions of elaborate fantasies. Silly, perhaps. But they'd kept her dream alive until she was old enough to act to bring the dream to life.

But she'd passed through that creaky little red door at the side

entrance and discovered that the Serpentine wasn't about making her dreams come true. The Serpentine, like a great dragon uncoiling itself, revealed itself to her in all its power as a complex machine built for the purpose of keeping its dragons well fed and healthy and its dragoneers trained and ready to be of service. The Captain had once told her that it was sailors who worked to keep a ship alive, not the reverse as most landsmen thought, and the Serpentine turned out to be sort of a ship in that way. Through endless toil, people kept the dragons alive and the dragons kept the Republic alive.

She'd come to love it, just as the Captain loved his ships. Even if she played only a small part, dancing—*sweating* would perhaps be more accurate—to keep a dragon diverted and content until it nodded off to sleep.

Feeling a new sense of ownership and responsibility—odd how words on paper had that effect—she went to the Masters' Hall to meet Traskeer and report in as an apprentice.

The Masters' Hall is at the "up" end of the Serpentine in a collection of buildings that greet visitors passing through the front gate. The Serpentine's buildings are a jumble of styles built up over the course of some three hundred years. Or more, depending on which scholar you ask. Parts of it jam up against the wall and run against each other like someone who has put on a great deal of weight but not purchased new clothing that fits. One edge of it meets the great cobblestoned plaza where the Serpentine holds market days (which Ileth never had coin to enjoy), revues, and festivals in good weather. Much of the up end was still a mystery to Ileth; she knew the names of the little features, "Turkey Run" and "Hanging Court" and "Ragged Alley" and "the Slide," but had only the vaguest of ideas of who lived in which or the Serpentine business that was conducted therein.

The Masters' Hall is one of the newer buildings; she'd been told that only the Great Hall where dinner was served each night—to those who could get away from their duties in time to dress—with its astonishing cast-iron stoves and the latest in brick ovens was more recent. What had been the Serpentine's graveyard had been partially

relocated to new consecrated ground so a proper hall with proper grounds could be built and matters that had long been neglected—conference rooms, a library, and a map room—could be established.

She heard a distant cry as she approached it and turned to look back toward the down end of the Serpentine where the dragons lived.

In the sky above the lighthouse that stands at the rounded peak of the Beehive, a pair of dragons—whether they had riders was difficult to tell at this distance—swooped and turned around and around each other in a sort of paired sky dance. After watching them for a moment, Ileth judged that they probably had saddles and riders, as the dragons took care not to turn too tightly or invert themselves in their dives. Ileth had just enough aerial experience to appreciate the thrills and fun in the evolutions above.

She stifled a sigh as she turned to the Masters' Hall.

The "old" graveyard stands next to the Masters' Hall, where some of the first Dragoneers of the Serpentine lie buried under monuments. She wondered if any of the Masters were bothered by the daily reminder of death crowding about their doorstep as she passed. It sent home Kess's talk of sacrifice.

She reported her presence to the day-page, who in turn reported her presence to a clerk, who appeared and reminded her that she'd forgotten her sash, and after Ileth issued another apology for not being in uniform, he gestured for her to follow with a warning that Traskeer would rake her for the omission. He took her past the meeting room and map room—Ileth liked maps but it was kept locked and she'd never had a reason to be taken in—and upstairs. Two boys wearing white dragon-scale novice pins with recently bloodied noses glared at each other from opposite ends of a bench outside the Master of Novices' door. By pure muscle habit she turned toward Caseen's office before checking herself. She heard the voice of Caseen, the Master of Novices, from the other side of his door. "If you'd like to remain here . . ."

Ileth wished they'd promoted Caseen to Master of Apprentices.

She'd always felt comfortable with him, even when he was displeased with her, which was most of the time.

With a few quick steps she caught up to the clerk, who ignored the bloody-nosed boys and took her down the black-and-white diamond-tiled hallway to another door and another bench. She eyed his apprentice sash hungrily and tried to work up the nerve to ask him for the loan of it.

"Master Traskeer is momentarily out," the clerk said. He jerked his chin in the direction of the privy she knew stood by the wall and departed before she could form her request.

So much for asking him about the sash.

She sat on the bench and looked through the very good glass of the window facing the plaza. An apprentice she only recognized by his shaggy hair was sweeping it with a tiny hand-broom. A punishment, obviously. He had good weather for the duty.

She didn't have to wait long. A figure appeared from a door at the other end of the hallway. His long trip down the corridor past Master Caseen's office allowed her a look at him out of the corner of her eye. She didn't want to do anything as rude as stare as he approached.

Traskeer was an unremarkable-looking man, perhaps a little on the short side—but then in her time in the Serpentine she'd learned that very large dragoneers were the exception—with sparse hair cut into a ring of bristle about his ears and the back of his head. He had a slightly sad face and indoor skin. He wore the traditional simple black plain-clothes of a Republic commissioner and a metallic-colored sash that might be called coppery or bronze depending on the light. His sash didn't have tassels on it like the other Masters, but then he was new to the position; maybe one was still being made for him.

He hadn't bothered to take his skullcap for his visit to the privy.

She rose to her feet when he came within the distance where if they both extended their arms they could touch.

"You must be Ileth," he said. He was the sort of man who was hard to read. He didn't look either pleased or displeased to meet her, just a

little fatigued. "I'd heard you were injured in the tailer—*ahem*—ceremony. Signed into the rolls and officially one of the Academy's apprentices, I take it?"

She bobbed an acknowledgment.

He invited her inside his office. The layout was very much like Caseen's: door to his private chamber; a small fireplace—unlit at this time of year; a leather-topped desk with a locking drawer and cubbyholes beneath for books and scrolls and maps. The chairs all looked borrowed from other rooms. A bare candle-holder rested on his desk, unlit. Unlike Caseen's office, he had a little gable window set into the sloping ceiling admitting some light. The shelves above the hearth and the case for books were both empty and smelled faintly of polishing oil. The only personal items in view were a gaming board with a design of interlocking hexagons in a beehive grid and delicate, elaborately carved pieces, most about the size of her thumb, save for a pair of very large ones on either side representing dragons. The dragons were true works of both craft and art, carefully sculpted so they would fit on their base without tipping. The gaming board was built into a case that probably held the pieces when moved. It aroused her curiosity and she was about to ask about it when he spoke.

He gestured to one of the mismatched chairs and she sat. "No sign of a malevolent turn to the wound, I hope?"

He had a faint accent, like those she'd heard on the Galantine border. But then most everyone in the Vales sounded odd when you came from the opposite side of the Republic, and the Vales were famous for sheltering outcasts and oddities—even criminals, sometimes—from other lands.

She stammered that the wound was healthy and closed.

He leaned in close enough to get a good look and she heard him sniff the wound, at least trying to be subtle about it.

Apparently satisfied with her affirmation that the wound was of no further concern, he introduced himself as the new Master of Apprentices. He didn't have any distinctions to his name, at least that he chose

to reveal to her. She liked that about him. Some men bludgeoned you with their titles. "I would offer you a card of introduction, but the titling still claims my late role at the Assembly. I await correct ones."

"I'm not from the sort of house where people traded cards," Ileth said. Some of the novices were card collectors; she remembered them passing about cards of young men they favored during her first weeks as a novice. She might even have been jealous. Now she just appreciated the peek into a different world of social rituals. In the Lodge the Captain's roustabouts didn't hand out cards, they called you by your most prominent physical feature and slapped you on the buttocks when you brought them drink or a light for their tobacco.

"That injury troubles me, now that I see how extensive it is. Quith thinks someone tried to blind you."

"Quith likes to . . . likes to . . ." How could she put it? Her mind flipped through the books of letters she'd studied. "She likes to add drama to incident."

"Still, it's odd. That's no fingernail or scrape against a cobblestone. You've no idea what made the cut?"

She shrugged.

"I don't consider that gesture appropriate for this conversation. Answer me."

Ileth stammered out an apology and something about it all happening very quickly and there being a tangle.

Happily, he didn't comment on her stutter. Just for that she was inclined to like him. "If you have an enemy who'd draw your blood, it's my duty to know about it," Traskeer said. The word *duty* landed hard. Dragoneers took, and used, the word seriously. She repeated her denial. "It's in the nature of people to form factions. Especially young people. I'll have no groups at enmity with each other in the Serpentine. People who feel themselves outcasts are preyed upon by our enemies, as that bad business with the eggs illustrated. I spent a lot of time with my predecessor talking about where we went so wrong with the Duskirk boy."

Ileth had never felt part of any faction, or excluded from others, but then she wasn't naturally social and the dancers were isolated from the daily routines of the up end.

"I hope the next six years will be happier and less eventful than your prolonged novitiate and late entry into apprenticeship. You'll stay with the dancers, I expect."

He expected wrong, but she didn't want to directly contradict him. "I—I'm here to be a dragoneer, sir."

"Of course you are. There are many ways to serve as a dragoneer."

"I . . . I aspire to wear a sword and pauldron, sir."

Traskeer's eyebrows went up. He excused himself for a moment and went to his chamber. He returned in a moment with a sort of case made of wax-stiffened canvas or thick paper, she couldn't tell, held closed by a string and a button sewn to the case. He extracted what looked like letters and a few notes.

"Forgive me for not having this ready. This is your index file," he said, scanning it. "Anything of significance relating to the training of the members of our Academy goes in here. Each apprentice has one. Some here complain about all the paperwork but I find it useful; I am one who considers a quick note in ink superior to the most detailed memory."

He thumbed through the pages within, extracting one. "Charge Ottavia in her letter recommending your apprenticeship says you have the makings of a great dragon-dancer."

Having assured himself that his memory on the matter was sound, he relaxed. "I'm afraid I have a great deal of catching up to do. I've been posted the past four years at the Assembly. I was already there by the time your draft was sworn in. I don't know half the apprentices here." His voice broke a little as he spoke. Ileth suspected he was exhausted or sick but hiding his weakness. He did seem pale for a dragoneer in summer, at this altitude.

"I . . . I'll be happy to help the dancers as much as I can. I had a little flight train . . . flight training, and s-still s-served as a dan-dancer."

"Dragon dancing is of keen interest at the moment in Sammerdam,

Zland, and so on. Between Ottavia's exhibitions and those paintings by Heem Tyr, experienced dragon-dancers can nest themselves up nicely. You could make a good living as one, or teaching it. Ideally, you would remain here as long as you're fit to perform. You wouldn't grow rich, but the life here is rewarding in its own way, as I hope you've come to believe."

She had, but she still wanted to fly. She had a taste for it now.

"My intent is to b—is to be paired with a dragon."

The corner of his mouth turned down.

"The math doesn't favor you. You must have some math to get in here, so I'll set the numbers out 'even, clear, and accurate' as the sovereigns in the counting houses put it. With your signature this morning, the Academy has six hundred seventeen apprentices here and carrying out their duties at other posts. Four are away for extended sick leave and their return is questionable; two seem likely to die. Eighteen more have been called home by family request and have their apprenticeships formally suspended. Few of those are likely to return either. So that is five hundred ninety-five apprentices competing for the very few wingman slots that vacate with our thirty active dragons. Typically, each dragon has a dragoneer and one to three wingmen, depending on the inclination of our dragoneers. Some of our dragoneers refuse the bother of training wingmen, like that Borderlander fellow who wrote you perhaps the shortest letter of recommendation in Serpentine Academy history. In peacetime, a wingman slot opens up at most every three months or so, so in your six years as an apprentice, if we remain at peace, that's twenty-four chances of promotion and you, a girl, and even worse, a girl of no Name, and still worse yet, a girl of no Name without patronage or political influence, are competing against nearly six hundred others. Many of our apprentices come from influential families with representation in our government, who can be made grateful and interested in the Serpentine's place in the Assembly's priorities by having their young men promoted. I won't bore you with the difficulty we have at the Assembly in obtaining the vast sums required to maintain the dragons, though without the

Thirty our Republic would stand all the chance against the Alliance of Kings of a fat worm dropped into a carp pond. Your chances of success are so small they're not much worth considering, you see?"

Ileth fought to remain still. Her body trembled, nevertheless. She'd thought this interview would be her first step toward a dragon saddle.

He kept his hands comfortably folded in his lap as he talked, shoulders relaxed, face indifferent. It didn't come across as the mask of a card player hiding the strength or weakness of his hand. Perhaps he was simply a man without anything that could be called feeling.

"Galia—did it."

The rather sad eyes lifted from the file folder on his desk. "Galia. Who was she, again?"

"Wingman under . . . under Hael Dun Hu-Huss."

"Oh, yes. She married some Galantine while you were there on that Fespanarax difficulty, yes?"

Ileth nodded.

"I remember now. Marked as discharged with prejudice. I think Dun Huss had an interest in her. A particular interest. A lot of it came out in the jury's inquiry. Found her in the gutter in Sammerdam or something, do I have it right? I understand she was exceptional in every respect: athletics, navigation, so on. Superb artist, too, she had a very successful apprenticeship with the aerial surveyors, I believe. Yes, that was it, survey drawings. Well, I suppose you could try to follow her example, but I still think the numbers are hard against you."

"Are the numbers that d-d-different fr-from when you did it?" Ileth burned under her tongue's betrayal of the fact that she was upset.

"I came in right after the Second Alliance war. If you know your country's history, that was a desperate one. There were openings. A great many, sadly."

"Openings didn't mean you'd become a Master. There are even fewer of those than there are dragoneers. There's a story there, I'm sure."

She had hoped she could draw him out. Most men his age were only too happy to talk about their lives. At length. "True," he said, not taking the bait.

"Did you let the chances against you bother you?"

"I was young. Men can take a chance and survive a catastrophe. Worse for someone like you."

Ileth set her shoulders. "I want my chance. My-my chance to become a dragoneer like Annis Heem Strath." Ileth had met her and sat on the silver dragon Agrath, when she was a child.

"I, in turn, am obligated to give it to you. I warn you, you'll be disappointing more than me. Ottavia is every bit your superior in this as well, and her letter makes clear how much she and the dancers need you. You'll be a servant with two masters. That makes for one very tired servant and two frustrated masters."

"That's m-my problem, sir."

"I expect you'll satisfy neither of us." Even this was delivered with a flat tone, as if he were dictating and expecting scribes to copy him accurately. Traskeer was the least animated man she'd ever met.

As it was a statement rather than a question demanding a response, Ileth just did her best to meet his gaze. As usual, she failed and looked away.

"Why do you dislike me so?" she asked, and felt like kicking herself as soon as the words escaped. Stupid, girlish sentiment. She was sixteen!

"Dislike? Like and dislike have nothing to do with it. If you must know, I believe I like you. It has nothing to do with taste, either. I've just found, in my years, that there are two basic sorts of men. Or women. But I find it fairer to judge the female apprentices by male standards. With you it's easier to forget your sex, as you carry yourself like a man.

"There are two basic sorts of people. Those who try to change their situation for the better, and those who look around and seek out villains to explain life's many, many disappointments and spend the rest of their life crying on the proverbial stump assigning blame.* I believe

---

* *Go cry to a stump* is an expression used to dismiss a complainer in the Vale Republic.

very strongly you are the first type, rare in your sex and rarer still at your age. The running away to join the Serpentine proves it, but there are other instances. Your attempts in the Baronies to acquire silver for that Fespanarax. However, I must set aside any feeling about you to coolly and contemplatively judge your chances here."

Almost the first lesson Ileth had learned arriving at the Serpentine was that they chose odd ways of testing a person. Nor did you know you were being tested. Maybe this was another test—tell her she would fail to see if she would try all the harder to succeed.

"I understand, sir," she said. "I still believe I can do both. I know the rhythms of the Serpentine now. The apprentices mostly work in the day; the dancers are most active at night. We have dancers like Santeel Dun Troot who are doing both."

It was like talking to a salmon laid out on ice at a fishmonger's. Finally he spoke: "Very well. The method at the Academy is simple. Over your six years we will rotate you through different roles you must have in order to properly care for dragons in peace or war. Through this, we learn that some of our apprentices turn out to be so skilled in one area or another that we let them remain under the instruction of a Master for the rest of their time here. Others move on, once they've demonstrated an understanding of the required techniques. On the one hand, generalists tend to make better dragoneers, but on the other, great talents in a field that can only be done on dragonback, like your friend Galia's reconnaissance sketches, require that they serve in the air. There are always some who don't seem to fit anywhere, and we do our best to give them something useful to do for the remainder of their apprenticeship that will allow them to earn their keep once on the other side of the gate."

"If I . . . if I may, I'd like to start with rotation in the Guards, sir." Every wingman at her tailer ceremony had been in a Guard uniform, even Rapoto, who never struck her as military of mind or inclination.

"We don't expect young ladies to rotate through *that* duty. Sword fighting and so on."

Ileth hardly knew one end of a weapon from another. She'd felt the

need to improve ever since she'd faced Gorgantern across a dueling square. "Not even young ladies who carry themselves like a man, sir?"

Traskeer shifted uncomfortably. "You will be busy enough with training during the day and your dancing at night. You seem an active young woman. Sentry duty is dull, physically and mentally. I speak from experience."

Ileth saw a cracked window in the shut-and-barred door to her being a dragoneer. Getting into the Guards, somehow, would distinguish her from the other young women.

"We need good dancers, Ileth. We don't need girls pretending to be men pacing a watch."

Ileth liked to think of herself as the kind of person who gave others a fair chance. Few enough gave her that consideration. But she was forming a dislike of Master Traskeer. Maybe it was just his way of seeing what an apprentice was made of. He looked thoughtful.

"Still, if you're set to model yourself on Dragoneer Heem Strath, you could hardly have done better. I knew her somewhat and her and her dragon's death was a great loss. Welcome to your apprenticeship in the Serpentine Academy, Ileth of the Freesand."

He didn't quite smile, but he had an air of contentment, like a man who has finished a good meal.

"I am . . . ready to start."

"I want to make one more matter clear to you. Your novitiate is over. I am indifferent to all events, both good and bad, that took place during it. To me, you are a blank sheet of paper, identical to every other new apprentice. Others, such as Charge Ottavia and our esteemed Master in Charge, are under no such prohibition, of course, and probably will let what they know of you influence their decisions. I look forward to filling that blank sheet of paper with work and behavior that brings honor to your name and that of the Serpentine Academy."

At this, Ileth smiled. A fresh start! *See, you should give people a few chances.* She blinked away tears and resolved to prove herself to him. "Thank you, sir."

"Before I give you over to your first Master and assign you to a

rotation, I have a little task I'd like you to perform. Consider it a commission."

Ileth stiffened. In the Republic a commission was an important duty.

"Sir?"

"Almost anyone here is capable enough of solving an existing problem if they understand the nature of it. Fires must be fought. Dragon is injured, consult a physiker. Barrel of fish is spoiled, find out what went wrong in the salting or smoking and dump the spoilage in the hatchery or crab bed. Relief didn't turn up at your watch post, report it to the officer of the watch and remain on duty until properly relieved. A novice in his second week knows that."

Ileth wondered if he'd ever fought an actual fire. The Captain in her lodge taught every child to ring the alarm for all you were worth if there was a fire and summon help. He drilled them like one of his ship's crews.

He leaned forward a little, the first show of animation she'd seen in his face brightening his expression. "What's much more difficult is discovering that a problem exists before something goes wrong. Spotting the loose slat in the henhouse before the fox creeps in, noticing the unbolted stall before the horse wanders off, to use a couple of moss-grown phrases. Do you understand?"

"Y-yes."

"Do you know Vyenn well?"

"I've never . . . never b-been. L-looked at it, from the cl-cliffs, of course."

"Is that so? Never? Not a shopping trip on an open day?"

Ileth pursed her lips and blew out a short puff of air across her fingertips, a gesture in the north that meant one's purse contained nothing but air—lack of money. She instantly regretted it. If Master Traskeer didn't like shrugging, what would he say about that?

"Ah. Well, that's to your credit in my personal index file. It means you appreciate that small change makes a big difference, as my mother used to say."

He paused for a moment, studying her. Had she looked pained when he said *mother*?

"So now you have the excuse of orders for a visit. Go into Vyenn. Don't wait for the next market day; use the password for the gate. It's *honeycomb* this quarter. But be sure to be back by dark; the apprentice password is no good after dark. Find something wrong in Vyenn. The town's large enough that there must be something amiss. Assess it for the Serpentine. You can impress me by drafting a remedy."

Ileth must have looked confused. "Do you understand?" Master Traskeer added.

"Yes, sir. Do you . . . do you mean like a crime? Something for a j-jury?"

"A crime would definitely impress me. Report back to me by the week-over on whatever you find. Written report. Comprehensive."

"I understand, sir," Ileth said.

"You can draw paper, quill, and ink from the clerk downstairs to present your commission's finding. The writing room is strictly quiet and there are plenty of high desks, but some prefer the map room as the lighting is better."

"Thank you, sir."

"Before you go: I'm sorry if I poured water on your inner fire earlier. Organizing training rotations was not my dream when I oathed in as a novice, Ileth. But when you are offered a better title, take it. I never saw myself as Master of Apprentices, but had they offered me Master of Stores and Sanitation I would have said yes with my next breath."

As he seemed more at ease now, Ileth decided to ask him about the board. It was the only personal item in the office, after all. "May I ask a question?"

"Of course."

"That game board. What is it?"

"Coup. I take it you don't play."

"No. I've never seen a board with that sort of woodwork. It's very pretty."

"It adds another level to piece placement, which is why I prefer the

six-direction board rules. Coup goes back to Hypatian times. I think it was first played on a board with peg-holes and wooden stakes, and then a square board—rather like the black-and-white tiles you see in this hall. The honeycomb layout adds entirely new layers of maneuver."

She wondered if he chose the apprentice passwords, and if *honeycomb* revealed something of his oh-so-carefully-guarded self. She studied his set with new interest.

He showed off the carved—but sturdy-looking—pieces, picking up a little figure in a tall helmet and cuirass. She looked at the figures, white and black, each resting in its own six-sided space.

"The pieces, have you seen them? Infantry, cavalry, artillery, fortification, captain, dragon. All the pieces are expendable, unlike Court where if you lose your king you lose the game. Also, unlike Court, your array can vary slightly by taking either captains or fortifications. Some players like more fortifications, or all fortifications; others take captains. I prefer the classic balance of one captain and two fortifications recommended in Heem Jeet's study of the game."

"Whoever made your pieces was an artist."

He put his spare captain back in its velvet-lined compartment. "Some players buy elaborate figures and go to great trouble to paint them.

"Of course you don't actually need pieces to play. You could do it with a board drawn on paper and coins or buttons or what have you. I once saw some prisoners in a road camp using teeth as pieces. Well, except for the dragons. Those were whittled out of wood."

"May I see the captain?"

"Of course."

Ileth examined the little figure. He had a blank, unreadable face, rather like Traskeer.

"My set has separate fortifications and captains. I've seen sets where if the piece stands one way, it's a captain, turn it over and it's a fortress, but I think a captain with a great flat head doesn't have as nice an aesthetic as this banner."

He wasn't such a cold fish when discussing his game. Interesting.

Traskeer continued: "I've suggested before that all the apprentices should learn coup. They have them play at military academies, I understand. Gives you an instinct for concentrating or relocating your force at need, advantages and disadvantages of mobile and static warfare."

"The dragon is magnificent," Ileth said, leaning in to examine it.

"Speaking of mobile . . . Thank you. I confess, I bought this set because of the dragons. Some sets just have flames as the dragon—carving a decent dragon is a lot of work—but I don't see the point to owning a good coup set unless it has a beautiful dragon. But then, given our calling, a certain passion when it comes to dragons is to be expected."

Something like human enthusiasm had definitely crept into his voice as he held the pieces. Ileth saw a crack in the man's wall under his use of *our*. "Would you teach me?"

"Perhaps once I'm settled in. It's a good way to spend a winter evening. But I doubt you'll have the time to learn to play well."

"Winter it is, sir."

"Well, we both have duties at the moment. We should be about them."

Ileth bobbed. "Thank you, sir." Was she finally free of this man and his one-thing-mores? Perhaps not, he was frowning at her attire.

"Oh, and Ileth, I don't want to see you again without a sash. Obtain one while you're in town. Borrow money if you must. A short one that you can tie simply. I don't care for girls who go about with a braided sash or back-bowed knotting, wide folded silks, triangle drops, that kind of thing. Simple is best for an apprentice. You are dismissed."

Ileth left his office enervated. He wasn't at all like Caseen, who, even when he was displeased with you, gave the impression he was somehow on your side. She had a sense already that if she'd dropped over dead in his office, Traskeer would have made the proper file notations and put her folio wherever the letters regarding dead apprentices go before calling for her body to be removed to whatever pauper's grave was currently open on the mountainside.

There was still a good deal of morning left. If she went back to the

Quarter, Ottavia would put her to mending, sorting, and airing of dance costumes. Even if she wasn't allowed to exert herself, Ottavia wouldn't let her idle.

Who knew when another chance would present itself? She would go into Vyenn!

3

In the Captain's Lodge, the Captain always made sure his charges had full bellies when expected to spend the day outside exerting themselves. The "Captain's Crew" was a ready source of extra labor when it came time to shock and bundle oats. Ileth decided she should eat first if she was going to spend the rest of the day exploring Vyenn.

She crossed the market plaza to the Great Hall with its great sloping roof and couldn't resist glancing at the gate beyond with its arch of dragon wings. She hugged her knowledge of the password to herself. Ileth, the stuttering girl from the Captain's Lodge in the Freesand whose basket the baker would fill with old rolls with a few new ones on top because they thought her an idiot, *Ileth* had the password to the Dragon Gate!

Her steps became strides as she entered the Great Hall. As it was still summery with the weather fine, the doors stood open to the air.

The Great Hall only served an early-morning meal for those who had the time and appetite for a hot breakfast and then a satisfying dinner, but one could usually scrounge something to eat at any hour, given that the Serpentine never truly sleeps.

Her footsteps echoed in the unaccustomed emptiness of the interior.

Half stonework, with huge blocks of granite for flooring and

topped with thick ship timbers, roofed with nothing but fireproof dragon scale and blocked glass to let in light: one couldn't help but be awed by the space, set in the shape of a great camp tent. Hundreds upon hundreds of bodies could be assembled within should the complement be gathered for an address—only the open-air theater in the center of the Serpentine where she'd been *oathed in* at fourteen seated more—with the shape of the roof amplifying the sound from the speaker's pulpit so that all might hear.

Enemy war banners and memorial battle flags representing victory hung from the ceiling, another source of pride. As a novice, she'd been told you could ask any wingman the story behind each and hear it, but Ileth found that not to be the case generally. Arms, armor, and other odd accoutrements of battle—like a special saddle with a back brace that had allowed a wounded Charge to fly into battle and keep his dead body seemingly upright and invulnerable in the Hierophant's War, before the founding of the Republic.

She passed a few boys from the new group of novices, each with his bright new bit of white dragon-scale brooch, scrubbing the flooring stones with small, stiff brushes. Punishment for leaving anything at their eating place, she suspected. Breaking the habits of those raised with servants to do everything was the first order of business upon entry into the Serpentine.

Clusters of novices and apprentices with their tutors occupied the better-lit tables near the windows. The Serpentine Academy provided no formal education, but the families of those enrolled sometimes sent, hired, or pooled resources to bring in tutors. The Serpentine boasted a few scholars on the rolls, so the "Academy" part of the title wasn't the humbug it seemed to most of the youths enrolled after a full day's labor at the washtubs or flushing out the sanitary sluices without once taking a book off a shelf or hearing a lecture. Ileth had yet to formally meet these sages. They certainly didn't give lessons on Hypatian declensions.

Ileth, having no family or sponsor paying her way, hadn't had the benefit of lectures in grammar, Hypatian, religion, math, rhetoric, the

natural, theoretic, and applied sciences and all the rest. Until now, she'd only felt the want of education socially, where her fishing-town northern manners sometimes made her feel as conspicuous and unwelcome as a rat on a banquet table. Her peers mentioned books and plays she'd never heard of, discussed characters and situations that meant nothing to her, or quoted moral instruction and examples that showed individual guidance from a family priest. But then all the plays in the world didn't help you find an infestation of scale nits, even if they made you more philosophical about the grubby work of exterminating them.

She went to the serving counter. There was a bit of breakfast milk left in a pitcher. She rarely had a chance at milk, as the dragons didn't care for it. She poured it on some cold oat-and-fruit mash and grabbed an end of a hunk of cased meat.

With no one around to reprimand her on her table manners, she bolted her food and returned to the pleasant summer air.

It was a quiet morning. She heard faint whistle blasts from farther out in the middle of the Serpentine; someone was giving the new draft a hard time in the fields, probably. She approached the gate.

The night she'd arrived at the Serpentine, muddy, wet, and bleeding from a slip and fall on a slick rock concealed by a puddle, there'd been a watch above, and sure enough, a man in the uniform of the Serpentine Guard stood above. She knew that the uniforms—attractive and not at all of the plain republican style of the rest of the Vale's soldiery—were much traded about by those who didn't have the funds to purchase one especially for their turn.

"Look here," she called, using the one Serpentine Guard expression she knew.

The Guard turned. He was on the craggy side, probably a long-service soldier no longer fit for marching up and down mountains and retired to the dragon fortress to add discipline and experience to the youngsters.

"I'd like to pass through the gate."

"Officer of the watch!" he called.

A boy in an ill-fitting man's uniform emerged from a doorless shack huddled under the stairs up to the gate. The shabby construct could only with the greatest charity be called an "officer."

Ileth recognized him. She'd met Apenite Sifler Heem Streeth her very first day in the Serpentine, in Joai's house when he barged in on her bath. He'd grown taller but was still mostly limbs and ears and runny nose. She wondered if they still called him "Sniffler."

"Thank you, Barstel, return to your duty," he called up to the watchman. He'd gained a man's voice since she'd last spoken to him.

"Ileth, isn't it?" said to her, taking off his fore-and-aft cap with its colorful little officer's cockade. "We were oathed in together."

"You were the first of our draft to make apprentice, uhh, s-ir," Ileth said. Only after the words came out did she realize she'd hardly stuttered; the words had come out almost naturally. Usually that only happened when she swore hard enough to turn her lips blue. Maybe it was that she still remembered him as a dusty, sweat-streaked little monkey, wide-eyed at her nakedness.

"And you're the tailer. Not your fault, I understand, stuck in the Baronies. Still with the dancers?"

"Yes, but I have a few days off for wounds taken." Only after she said this did it occur to her that it was strange that this boy was interested in her career. There were a lot of odd things about the youth. Judging from his name, he came from a renowned family, but his uniform looked like odds and ends from the discards. As she looked at the droopy cuffs, she marked ink staining his fingers.

"Paperwork keeping you . . . busy?"

Sifler followed her gaze. "Oh, that? No, I had a session with Choppers this morning. Had to write an essay about honor while he timed me. Made a mess of the inkwell."

"I'd like to read that." The corner of his mouth turned up and he straightened.

"Would you? Well, I'd like your opinion." He scuttled off before she could say she didn't have time to look at it right this morning and

returned with two closely written pages. "Here's the fair copy. I was inspired by the essays of—"

He had a very good hand. She liked it better than Santeel's or Ottavia's even. "I wish I had time to read it now. But I'm out the gate today and pressed. I have the password: honeycomb." She passed the pages back.

"That's not the password," Sifler said.

"But . . . Master Traskeer . . ."

"I'm just ragging you up, Ileth. You should have told me you were in a hurry. Of course it's the password. But you only need it to come back in. That's the Serpentine in brief: easy to leave, hard to get in. Follow me."

He took her over to the gate, lifted a heavy hook out of the fitting, and slid part of the decorative, interlaced metal gridwork of the gate open. Though she was by no reckoning tall, she would still have to dip, and step over the gate bottom, to get in.

As she passed through the gate-within-a-gate, beneath the great metal dragon wings arcing like two great fans above the gate, shading those beneath (or perhaps sheltering those firing crossbows and meteors down at attackers), he reminded her to be back by sunset. "I could be your brother and still wouldn't let you in, not after dark. If your business takes you late, find lodgings in town. Shall I log you out on orders?"

Lodgings. She didn't have a fig to flip.

"It's sort of a . . . a commission from Ma-Master Traskeer."

He smiled a shy smile, which made him look even more like a boy playing in his father's uniform. "I shouldn't keep you then. Carry on, Ileth."

As Ileth walked down the very good road from the Serpentine to Vyenn, she examined it with fresh eyes. Vyenn was the northernmost large town on a line of river traffic that extended south all the way down to the river delta on the Blue Ocean. It clung close to the lake and then grew out over it on wide piers, people above, boats below. A

stone wharf extended farther than the farthest buildings south of town, with barges and what in the Freesand would be called "coasters" tied up along it, though at the moment there didn't seem to be water traffic coming or going.

The town itself was colorful, the roofs in good repair, paint and whitewash everywhere. Splashes of green filled every gap between buildings, where there were gaps, sometimes just big enough to hold a single tree. Almost every building had window boxes bursting with flowers or what were probably herbs and vegetables. On the side away from the lake, an old wall stood, or the remains of one, anyway, as the town had outgrown it in long years of peace, though there was still a substantial hedge and a roadside ditch at the end of town that served as a polite warning that you were about to fall under the jurisdiction of Vyenn's watch.

She knew Vyenn had a watch because they sometimes returned drunken dragoneers and wingmen to the Serpentine, but whether they had uniform hats or coats or were just an assembly of the more vigorous citizens whistled up when there was trouble (as was the practice in the Freesand) she didn't know.

Halfway down the road she turned around and looked back at the Serpentine. The low, thick walls girding it appeared much more imposing from below the steep sides of the peninsula. She could just see the tops of the Pillar Rocks and the Long Bridge where it joined the Beehive. All but a few decorative spires of the jumble of buildings at the up end were invisible. The Beehive with its lighthouse atop looked a little more angular from this side, where it sloped down to the lake, and less like a half-buried melon the way it appeared from up by the gate (she'd heard it called a "flame-topped teat" by less reverential apprentices).

All around the Skylake were picturesquely steep mountains with bits of snow clinging year-round in the more sheltered areas. You could get lost in the detail of just one, examining the slides of fallen rocks and the treeline and where bits of greenery had established themselves in improbable-looking crevices. She congratulated herself again at the

extraordinary old view from a new vantage point. She was lucky to have found a place in the fortress. If she were an artist, she could set an easel down just about anywhere in this inspiring valley and get a picture out of it.

Out over the lake another pair of dragons, or perhaps the same pair from earlier, were flying, one just below and behind the other. The one beneath was making some effort to match the one above. Ileth thought for a moment and then remembered hearing that was how messages were passed between aerial dragons: one dragoneer dropped a weighted line, and then the message was sent down on a little tube attached to a ring. The one below had to not get struck about the head by the end of the line, catch it, and then release the message-case. Tricky work.

The dragons separated. She hoped for the trainee's sake that the message-case hadn't been dropped into the Skylake.

Renewed in her pride at living as a dragoneer in one of the most famous landmarks in all the known world, she entered Vyenn for the first time with head high and a confident smile.

The first house she came to at the edge of Vyenn belonged to a tobacconist. A sign hung over the door, well-painted (the Vales were full of aspiring artists; the most famous painters in Zland and Tyrenna commanded fabulous, or infamous, sums—depending on who was doing the creating and who was doing the paying) and depicting a relaxed, reclining dragon with soothing smoke coming out of its nostrils. The proportions were all wrong; it had a snakeish body and tiny wings, but real dragons were mostly wing jutting out of mountains of muscle at the wing joints and rear limbs and had tapering necks and tails. Odd for a shop with dragons in daily view, but perhaps the owner wanted something fanciful.

She supposed she could submit a report critiquing the art and pointing out all the anatomical errors and try to pass it off as a joke. She doubted Traskeer would be amused.

Ileth only knew two roads in Vyenn from conversations about town. One was called Broad Street and the other Wharf Way running

the length of the town north–south. She knew that the Serpentine's moneyed and respectable females visited Broad Street when in town; the wharf was considered disreputable, having little to offer unless you were looking for a grog shop. It was obvious which was which. They divided at a small triangular travelers' shrine where those entering or leaving town could leave an offering, in either hope or gratitude. The road to Broad Street was the better of the two; heavy loads had rutted the road up from the wharf.

She'd seen enough ships in her young life, growing up in the Freesand, but very little of towns with more than a shop or two and a few necessary artisans, so she tried Broad Street. Other streets and alleys branching off it led up the slope to the old city walls, some small and crowded, others wide and inviting.

The town smelled like horses, to her nose long used to the dragon-air in the Beehive. Horses and cooking smells and summer sunshine on wet soil full of growing things.

There weren't many people about on Broad Street, but then it wasn't a market day in town so the street was practically deserted along its long, gently bending length. She heard the faint sound of children shouting and playing from the streets and alleys of the one she walked upon. Broad Street ended in the south at what looked to be a temple or meeting rotunda.* She expected to see more boatmen, but maybe there was some unspoken social order that kept them to the wharf. She did mark a pair of Serpentine Dragoneers, out of uniform save for their bright sashes, riding leggings, and black boots, idling at a table sitting at the edge of what looked to be a beer garden where they could watch what little was going on in the street. They were shaded by trellises grown summer-thick with flowering creeper. The dragoneers nibbled on something crusty and dripping with cheese, each with a potbellied mug of what she guessed to be the local ale. One was

---

* Like most places tracing their culture back to the Hypatian people on the other side of the Inland Ocean, the Vales prefer round structures or arenas for religious and public structures and spaces and rectangular ones for private or commercial use.

dark and youthful; the other had white hair and a deep tan that made it difficult to guess his age, but certainly older than the other.

The younger she knew by face but not name, though she knew his dragon; the other she'd never seen before. Of course, dragoneers were constantly posted in different parts of the Vales, and about half the dragons could be expected to be out at any one time. Made them easier to feed. If all thirty were crammed into the Beehive overlong they'd soon run out of fish and mutton. And tempers would erupt with the crowded-together males, no matter how hard the dancers worked.

She shifted over to the boardwalk on their side of the street to pass close. It wouldn't do for an apprentice to ignore a pair of dragoneers. But she didn't want to press herself on them either; Ileth was unsure of how their connection was handled outside the walls of the Serpentine.

The dark-haired dragoneer she just knew by face had been listening to the other talk. Ileth couldn't make out his words as she approached, as he had a low voice and his back was to her.

Next to the beer garden there was a rag room. She peered hopefully through the poor glass of the windows, hoping that she'd see a length of white fabric somewhere that she could trade her sheath for. It was good material with little wear and no holes. She could replace a sheath easily enough; there were always a few spare stained castoffs lying around the Dancers' Quarter. Someone inside was going through children's smocks, but whether it was the proprietor or a customer she couldn't tell.

She overheard the one she knew by face. "Still, it doesn't sound like any great difficulty, though the Troth preserve us if they ever get meteors. Routes west are secure."

"Trade routes out to the Azures and the Indigos don't matter a fig if we've no markets. Tea already won't pay for carriage. That's all gone, at least in a profitable sense, thanks to the Galantine Impounds. No Scab, no river. No river, no route to the Blue. No Blue, no Inland Ocean."

Ileth, who liked studying maps, sidestepped closer to the men and

mentally traced the route south and east he described. Though she'd never seen it, she knew that the Scab was a great red-walled fortress that sat on the river the Skylake fed at the south end of another big lake, with the navigable river that led up to the Antonine Falls at one end and the Scab at the other. She'd often heard it described as a "cork in the bottle" of the Tonne River. Vyenn rested at the northernmost easily navigable point, being a great artery to both the Blue Ocean to the south and the Inland Ocean far to the east. The Scab had been a point of contention in the long peace negotiations that ended the Galantine War, where the Vales lost both control of the fortress and access to the Blue Ocean. Now a Galantine Baron sat in the Scab and charged a fat premium on any trade along the river and impounded any cargo that couldn't pay his ransom.

"So you see it doesn't matter how easily things flow into the pipe if the exit is corked," the elder finished.

The younger jerked his chin at Ileth, and the two looked up at her. The white-haired man was very tan and fit, with shoulders like a blacksmith. Ileth thought his eyes shrewd. He looked more like a thick-skinned mountain shepherd than a dragoneer.

"Ha, girl! Felt like an escape from dragon-air, I mark," the younger said, noticing her. "Join us, cousin."

He took out his handkerchief and wiped a chair for her.

She couldn't help but smile at him. He was one of those sunny young men who went into the Serpentine as sort of a youthful lark. He possessed the trimmed, watered, and raked good looks she'd seen among young Galantine nobles. "You picked a fine day for an excursion. You should wear your sash in town, though, you'll get a more respectful tone from the locals."

"G-good m-morning, sirs," she managed. She was too far away to bob, so she paced forward and performed one.

The men rose to their feet. The white-haired one's face stayed hard, like he'd just had bad news. She didn't trust men who stayed intense, despite a beer and leisurely breakfast. The younger spoke: "You're the stuttering one: Fish-something?"

Ileth kept up the smile. "They . . . they used to call me Fish-Fishbreath when I—when I w-worked in the Catch Basin. Ileth, of the . . . of the Freesand."

"We've not formally met," the dragoneer who spoke to her said. He was very young, he must have risen fast. "I'm Velleker, Taresscon's dragoneer, though she flies but little these days, so I feel something of a dragoneer-at-large. This is Garamoff. He flies Nephalia. She's Taresscon's niece, and Garamoff had me as his wingman before I moved up in the late war."

Ileth knew Taresscon. She was one of the senior dragons of the Serpentine, analogous to Charge Deklamp. The two consulted frequently.

"Cousin, actually. Taresscon's cousin," Garamoff corrected. He had a clipped manner of speaking, like his words were having the door slammed shut behind as they left. He wore a green sash with silver lines set in it.

"Join us, Freesander?" Velleker asked. "Now that he's relieved himself of the burden of his stock market losses, Garamoff can tell you stories of the Channel Isles and the Indigos. He's blue-watered his dragon, which is more than most of us can say." Ileth wasn't entirely sure what that meant, but she knew from her upbringing among sea folk that blue water meant ocean out of sight of land. Garamoff didn't look pleased at the idea.

"I'm on . . . on an err-errand, you might s-say."

"Don't let the Gar's manner put you off," Velleker said. "He's always this way, even in the summer shade with good beer."

"Do join us," Garamoff said. He didn't exactly smile, but he pulled out the chair Velleker had wiped for her. "I've been away too long. Don't know any of the new drafts. I should remedy that."

As a freshly enrolled apprentice, she'd have to be mad to publicly refuse an invitation from a pair of dragoneers, one of whom was evidently senior enough to be away in some sort of far-off command. Someday one might be looking for a new wingman.

"Thank you, sirs," she said. "Pl-please don't think me rude if I—if I don't stay long."

She sat.

At the creak of the somewhat weather-warped chair, an attendant left off chalking a price change next to the open serving window. She made little effort to smile or move briskly. They were the only customers outside, after all. Ileth couldn't tell through the smoked glass of the establishment who might be within.

"Anything for you, miss?" she asked.

"No. No, thank you," Ileth said.

The server gave a nod whose brevity indicated what she thought of someone who'd sit in a beer garden without ordering anything and returned to her chalkboard.

"Ileth," Garamoff said, not addressing her, but speaking the name as though it jogged something. "You helped recover Vithleen's eggs. They promoted you to apprentice after that. Dun Huss mentioned you."

"One of the Serpentine's best, Fates keep him," Velleker said, toasting them both and taking a generous swallow of his beer. Garamoff joined the toast so mechanically Ileth wondered if he even took a sip. Velleker clanged his pot on the table and pointed to it. "Terrible on his wingmen, though. They all sicken, die, or quit. He expects too much. We're all just flesh and blood. Flesh and blood that gets used up fast as it is, when the bolts start flying."

Velleker didn't look at all used up; he looked as though he'd enjoyed a good breakfast and Vyenn's best ale.

When the beer was refilled and a tally scratched on the table with the chalk, Garamoff spoke again. "What happened to the apprentice fellow that helped with the theft? Hanged, or did the dragons burn him?"

"The jury of inquiry decided the dragon gave orders to him. They were never able to establish a direct connection between the boy and the Galantines, and of course the dragon's not around to testify what was ordered or promised. As, in the end, the eggs were saved and Vithleen returned to full health, they packed him off on a labor sentence."

Ileth had been friends with the boy, a lad named Yael Duskirk. They'd both worked in the Beehive and came from ordinary folk. She'd pleaded to the jury for mercy for him.

"So it's an egg year after all. You wouldn't know it," Garamoff said, looking up and down the empty street. A year where that rarest of events occurred—a clutch of dragon eggs were produced—was supposed to be an unusually prosperous one, good-omened.

Velleker nodded. "Good news for you, Ileth. They say it's lucky to novice on an egg year."

"I need it. I was the tailer."

Garamoff kept glancing at the line of pinch-pins going up her now-divided eyebrow. Velleker shrugged. "Let me stand you a beer. Tailer or no, you deserve a drink to celebrate your apprenticeship."

"I should be about my duties."

The dragoneers exchanged looks. Velleker shrugged and opened his mouth to say something, but Garamoff shook his head. "Then we mustn't keep you, errr, Ileth. Galantine name, isn't that?"

"That's what I'm told, sir. I grew up in a lodge."

She bobbed and left them to their beer and discussion. She popped into the rag room and learned that there was nothing white about, though a gray jacket with dark blue piping tempted her. She could do a lot with such a jacket. "White goes out as soon as it comes in, flower," the woman told her. "Try the Kingfisher's."

Ileth had heard of the Kingfisher's and thanked the woman and moved down the street.

A painted belted kingfisher marked the store. Ileth was a little in awe of the glass; the panels were almost as tall as she was, long thin ones that formed a sort of blister-gallery sticking out the front of the store. They had gold leaf painted in the corners. A fine gown stood on a sewing model. The material was so thin she wondered if it was silk. She fingered the thick channeled cording of her overdress.

The door opened. A man who had benefited from an excellent shave that morning beckoned her inside. She smelled the same sort of body powder Santeel used on him.

"Do you care for scent, dragoneer?" He wore a wig. Wigs marked one as someone who missed the fashions of the days when the Vales were under the king and his court. Ileth was only a "dragoneer" in the

very loosest sense of the term, but its use warmed her. "I have several individually distinct scents that can sweeten the air about you socially, or be placed into a handkerchief for working around the dragons. No? I happen to have just received a new batch of face powder. Not only does it conceal blemishes, and, errr, even the most obvious damage, it heals them at the same time. I'm prepared to offer you a special price for it, as it will work such wonders with your skin your friends up in the Manor will wish to know its name and where you acquired it."

"Oh, she's lovely, a treasure!" another male voice said from within. Ileth made out a figure standing near a worktable littered with material in the back. He had measuring lengths about his neck and a marking pencil behind his ear. "Invite her in here and let me get a look at her, such a graceful neck." He didn't say it lustfully, more like an art collector wanting a painting lit to advantage. "You have a fine carriage, young lady. Are you out of the Great Stair in Sammerdam? Asposis Academy for young ladies?"

Ileth knew very well that *lovely* wasn't a word that applied to her; she was more the sort who was told, "Oh, you're pretty enough" in an encouraging sort of voice.

"Thank you. You have . . . you have a v-very nice shop. But I only paused to admire," Ileth said, accenting in her thickest northern.

She'd learned why some in the Academy spoke warmly of the Kingfisher's. You didn't get much well-meaning flattery, or any kind of flattery, for that matter, up in the Serpentine.

She decided that nothing on the main streets would fulfill her commission.

The sensation of being on the hunt for something amiss in a town was as new to her as being fawned over in a shop. In the Freesand, as a girl, she'd always shrunk out of the way in passing. They were good people; she was a lodge-girl living on charity. In Galantine lands, on her rare visits to the Baron's town, she'd quietly followed instructions and tried to be the next thing to invisible, being something of a cross between guest and prisoner. Vyenn was larger than Wesport in the

Freesand or the Baron's village, and yet here she might be called, to use the Galantine phrase, *a person of significance*.

She tried the wide street that led to the old wall opening in the west. Like Broad Street it was paved with stones, at least to the old wall. The shouts of children grew louder. She followed the noise up the street toward the old wall and saw two groups of boys hurling dirt clods at each other. As the weather had been unusually dry, the clods exploded into clouds of dirt and dust in a boy-satisfying fashion, whether they struck boy, wall, or cobbled road.

"Turn the invaders back!" one of the taller boys shouted from a position atop a parked cart that showed no trace of horse or harness. He brandished a dented and tarnished serving platter as a shield, banging on it with a gardening trowel when he wasn't hurling dirt. He had a similar version of himself, no doubt a younger brother, feeding him lumps of dirt to throw.

Gradually, she distinguished the two forces. The group trying to force their way up the street were somewhat older boys, barefoot and mostly in canvas clothes and loose shirts such as the fishermen and boatmen she'd seen in the Catch Basin wear. They stuck tightly together in a disciplined wedge. Facing them were smaller and younger boys— no, there was a girl among them who'd sensibly put a metal bowl on her head to protect herself from the flying dirt, but her loose dress and long hair gave her away as she hurled clumps of pulled-up weeds—scattered in the alleys and atop a horseless cart defending their territory. The defenders wore shoes, for the most part, and a few of them had neckerchiefs wound and knotted about the throat. Definitely town-bred.

Ileth passed up through the crossfire and everyone stopped by seeming mutual agreement to catch their breath. And gather more clods of dirt.

"What's this?" Ileth asked the boy with the platter-shield in the commanding position on the cart. His brother hurried to refill the dirt clod supply from one of the rutted roads branching off from the cobblestones.

"The Boat-Rats have mounted a sally," the boy reported, mixing up his tactical terms, but the patter made sense to those involved. "I've called the Town-Cats to arms. No Boat-Rat crosses Broad, they know that full well." His face was well caked with grime.

"Rain and piss on the Town-Cats!" shouted a Boat-Rat. A clod flew and detonated near Ileth.

With the armistice broken, Ileth had to be quick as dirt clods flew with refreshed vigor. New Town-Cats arrived on the Boat-Rats' northern flank, and the older boys started a tactical retreat toward Broad but didn't give ground easily. A fusillade of clods proved to be too many for the Town-Cat leader to block with his shield, and he and his brother dived behind the cart as puffs of dust and pebbles exploded all around.

She left the battle and explored the area around the old wall. It proved to be a kind of informal park, though apple trees and an assortment of berry bushes had been planted all around the overgrown walls, with tended beehives keeping them company. The citizens of the Vales loved honey as much as they did their paintings and flower boxes.

The old fortifications looked safe enough and the bees had other business. She investigated a tower first but didn't like the look of the rotted wooden stairs, sturdy enough for the spiders inhabiting them but not her. She found a flight of stone stairs going up to the wall, ascended them, and enjoyed the view from there. Vyenn was a pretty town from this angle with the Skylake behind, though all the laundry fluttering in the breeze might be left out by a painter keen on selling their work. Enjoying the sense of being busy at nothing much, she decided to walk along the wall for a bit. It seemed a popular walk. The town or public-spirited citizens kept the wall path free from creepers and probing weeds.

On the other side of the wall were smaller houses, most with coops or pens and extensive gardens, not quite town and not quite country. Only along the lanes did they cluster together. South of the town the ground rose gradually again to a mighty cliff in profile at a distance,

perhaps two leagues* of lakefront away. She'd heard it called Heart-break Cliff.

An angry grunt sounded another stairway down, and she leaned over to look. Fallen leaves and growth had turned a sheltered exterior stairwell to a kind of bower. A tousle-haired youth with blood on his arms startled from where he bent over a bare-legged female form, and Ileth gasped.

She had something very wrong in Vyenn to report now.

Or perhaps she didn't. She gasped again and covered her mouth with her hand when she realized he'd draped a butcher's leather apron over the stairwell wall and the girl sitting up was half-dressed, very alive, and some mix of angry and embarrassed that Ileth had interrupted whatever was going on. The formerly prone girl half shielded her face with her hand, but one eye still glared angrily up at Ileth.

"Fly off, reeker. We're not takin' turns," she said.

Ileth had heard enough talk in the Serpentine to know that *reeker* was a Vyenn insult reserved for the Serpentine's people.

"I see the butcher . . . d-delivers. Is there a sp-special surcharge?" Ileth laughed. She hurried south along the wall.

"Did you hear that?" the girl asked the butcher's apprentice. "Did you? You going to take that?"

The boy said something in response that might have been "Serpentine priss" and added something in a soothing tone, but Ileth was too far away to make out much of it.

Parts of the wall had been pulled down south of town, and there looked to be nothing more interesting than a garbage heap and a gravel pit here, where the hills leading up from the lake became steeper and forested toward the cliff, so Ileth found a ruined spot where she could safely jump down from the wall. She turned toward the domed building she'd seen at the end of Broad Street, the only real landmark on the south side of town.

---

* A *league* in the Vales is the distance a formation of soldiers can march in an hour, roughly three miles.

The houses here huddled around narrow, twisting streets, probably the oldest part of town. Women were out at the public water basins with small children and such handwork as could easily be carried. They moved around the square, washing and talking and trading fussing littles. Some eyed her curiously, some nodded and smiled, and Ileth had a chance to roll a marvelously stitched canvas-covered ball that felt resilient—it was probably stuffed with cork or perhaps coconut coir brought from some far-off voyage on the Blue Ocean to the south—with a couple of the younger children who were using it to knock down empty thick green bottles they'd set up for that purpose in a blind alley. It was a fun game and the children were happy to have what amounted to an adult playing with them, but Ileth was no closer to fulfilling her commission than she'd been when she first set foot in town. She moved on to the temple.

The temple dominated the south end of town. The older residents sat about its steps or in the square before it, which had a raised pool in the center that was more of a slow, intricate trickle off a dragon head projecting from the pool like a sea serpent than anything that could be called a "fountain." *A gift for the people of Vyenn* read the legend on the pool and something in Hypatian Ileth didn't understand. A yellowish dog with a curled tail couldn't read the Hypatian either, but it didn't stop him from lapping up water before returning to run with two other dogs chasing about the square.

The older men watched her, some smoking from pipes, some sitting with amiable dogs equally elderly at their feet; some read or played cards.

A pair of beggars, husband and wife, claiming to be travelers going to the bedside of a dying mother, worked the assembly, such as it was. Ileth overheard some of the story: they had just sold their last spoons to get them this far but needed funds for their journey north. Ileth had no purse and was dressed as poorly as the beggars; in fact, her old bootlaces were in worse shape than the husband's, so they passed her after a single appraising glance.

Back on Broad Street, the only thing that interested her was a

music shop. They had a couple of music boxes in the window along with instruments and folios of sheet music. *INSTRUMENTS AND WINDINGS BOUGHT AND SOLD* read a sign leaning up against a small harp. She supposed she could sell the music box the old dragon had bought her before his death, though it would tear out her heart to do so.

As though summoned by her thoughts, an instrument tuned and then started to play back from the temple. She retraced her steps to the plaza and followed the sound around the fountain until she saw a bare-footed boatman seated on the ground with his back to the fountain with a flexible wheeze-box opening and shutting the hand-paddles with great skill. It sounded like two instruments playing together. He nodded up at her and she smiled in return.

Rather than greeting her, he changed up to a more sprightly tune. Dance came so naturally to her at this point that her feet moved before she was fully aware of it. She couldn't dance in boots properly, so she undid the laces and stepped out of them. The overdress wasn't ideal for dancing, but her arms could move.

It felt wonderful to dance for just the enjoyment of the act in the summer sun. No dragon glowering down at her as his nostrils opened and closed, and Ottavia wasn't here to correct her alignment; just music and motion and the fresh Skylake air.

She felt gloriously happy.

Another elderly couple set to dancing, facing the same direction with his right hand in her left, doing a simple folk dance, constantly turning to face a new direction together. Now and then the man would slip an arm behind his partner and pull her hip to hip with him for a fast turn, then release her to arm's length again. Ileth admired their grace.

Seeing feet move in courtly steps among the growing ring of watchers, she took the hand of one of the older gentlemen watching. He had an elaborately wound and tied neckerchief on his rather saggy neck. He just stood and turned, shifting his feet to the music (a little unsteadily as he tired) and she did the real work of dancing around him,

though he gave her hand a friendly squeeze when she reached the limit of her steps away as if to reassure her that she wouldn't pull him over.

The old man started coughing and the music and dance stopped.

He extracted a handkerchief and coughed into it. "Oh, girl, that does take me back. My lungs aren't what they were." He caught his breath. "Feet were willing enough, my wind gave out."

Ileth heard a few figs bounce onto the cobbles as the party broke up. She bent to retrieve only her boots; she couldn't bring herself to scramble for coppers on the ground. The boatman with the wheeze-box had no such reservations.

"Young lady," the old man with the elegant neckerchief said, "here." He held a silver coin in his trembling hand.

"Sir," she began.

"I know you weren't dancing for coin," he said, pressing it firmly into her palm. "I know a Serpentine girl when I see one. Back in my time, your favorite partner from the evening's dances, well, you gave her flowers as a thank-you. They sold them outside the assemblies, and it offered the perfect excuse for conversation. Now, as it's not a market day Teesa isn't here with her flower cart, but the next market day I want your promise that you're buying yourself flowers. Lots of flowers, so they fill your arms all the way up to that fine regal neck you keep so pretty and straight. A girl like you who dances so deserves them. Put them next to you as you sleep so's you get relief from dragon-reek and think of the lovely new memories your hand gave to an old man, an old man who hasn't had any new memories worth the thought in too long."

She looked around, feeling strangely guilty. No one watched the byplay but the boatman, who gave her a quick wink.

"Sir, it's . . . it's t-too m-much."

"Oh, I've enough to keep myself, just me these days, and I'll have no need of coin for my next stage. No. Take it. But for flowers, girl."

"Flowers," she said. Problems dissolved and plans rose to take their place. With a silver guildmark she could easily buy a pure white sash, nothing fancy, just sturdy, quality cotton such as many of the men wore, long enough to wind around her waist twice and knot, and have

figs left over to buy a great basket of summer flowers and keep her promise.

It would be fun. She'd never bought flowers in her life. She imagined what the Captain would say if she brought home flowers after being sent to the market for oats and milk.

Skipping back toward the Serpentine on Broad Street, she just spotted the Kingfisher's. She took the time to admire the sign. It had a very nice oval sign featuring a blue belted kingfisher hanging on an elaborate wrought-iron gibbet, or whatever the correct word was for the rail the sign hung from, Ileth wasn't sure. She could walk in there, a paying customer this time, and spend her time picking and choosing. The commission could wait.

She heard quick steps behind. She turned, a little alarmed.

The beggars from the fountain plaza bobbed in front of her. He was unshaven, with bright, hungry eyes; she was ragged and tired-looking and obviously footsore.

He spoke: "Miss, miss, begging your pardon, but I happened to overhear the exchange between you and that gentleman. Now a good deed's worth more than all the riches of the earth as the prayerbooks have it, and I memorized mine same as I'm sure you did, and hearing from your accent that you're a northern girl, well, me and my wife are in a hurry to get back to Stavanzer, but this is as far as the river will take us and we have to buy medicine here for my sick mother before going north again. That silver coin could mean life to her. We beg you to help!"

He did have a faint northern accent. Or was good at imitating one.

The copybook moralizing pulled at her. She'd neglected her rites and prayers since coming to the Serpentine, save on the odd feast day here and there when everyone else was attending to their souls by stuffing food in their mouths.

His wife looked at her pleadingly, silently mouthing *please-please-please-please* with her hand over her heart and bending a little in the old-fashioned obeisance of the plain to the aristocratic.

"A . . . a s-sick mother?" Ileth asked.

"I'm her only son, since my brother died in Reester at the hands of the Galantines defending the Scab. You know what that was like, being of the dragoneers, unless you were spared on account of youth."

They must have seen her receive the silver coin. How did they know she was with the dragoneers, if they weren't from Vyenn? Perhaps they saw her brooch.

"I'm sure . . . I'm sure she is a good woman. L-long l-life to her."

"That may depend on you."

"What was your f-favorite meal of hers when you . . . when you were a boy?" Ileth asked.

He flinched a little at the question and his brows furrowed. "My favorite meal?"

"Yes."

They both looked hungry. Perhaps some evil instinct prompted her to make them talk of food.

"I loved oat porridge poured over good sour toast," he said, bright eyes looking up. He licked his lips. "When we were too skint of meat, she'd soften it in hoof-broth gelatin. Gave them a lovely meaty mouth, the oats. Molasses she'd put on too. My brother and I worked all day on that."

Ileth relaxed. Porridge was common throughout the Vales, but around Stavanzer and Freesand in the north they made an art of it. They'd used the gelatin trick in the Lodge to add something like meat but cheaper. Pouring the oat porridge over toast was also something she hadn't seen outside the north.

She looked over her shoulder. The old man who'd given her the coin had his back to her, washing out his neckerchief in the fountain. "I . . . I have this. Take it."

"Oh, may the finest of fates find you and grant your wishes, miss. You can't know what this means. Blessings! Blessings on you!"

Ileth's plans for a bright new sash vanished as quickly as the coin. "I hope your—I hope your mother recovers."

Oddly, she felt lighter. The coin had felt like charity; maybe the old fellow had spotted her tied-together laces and decided to do her a good

turn. Childhood teachings also pulled at her. She never had sacrificed to make up for her lies at the Lodge before she left or her thefts of food on the trip south. Giving all she had in charity even when she was in need would cleanse her, if Directist teachings of her childhood had it right.

The silent wife hugged her—she needed a bath—and they departed, taking with them the promise of her new sash and the ghosts of her past sins against both the man who'd raised her and countrymen she'd robbed.

Well, money that came easily also left easily, the Captain always told her. And she still had the pleasure she gave that old fellow with the neckerchief. Silver couldn't purchase that gentle smile, his heartfelt words, or the brightness in his eyes thanks to the stimulating dance. That was another thing the priests harped on: your deeds counted to your credit more than coin. She thought about childhood stories of beggars' blessings. She'd done two good turns that day; maybe she could find a third person to help.

"You didn't give them money, did you?" a sharp voice asked.

A gentleman, or someone with the time to perfect his attire like a gentleman, glared at her from a bootmaker's that occupied a little slot of building between the Kingfisher's and a wine and oil merchant. The bootmaker had a measuring tape wrapped about his wrist so it dangled just a little; perhaps he was the proprietor. He had small eyes, and they surveyed her from hair to old boots.

"They aren't even from the Vales. Both wearing Galantine boots. I know Galantine bootmakers, always that extra decorative stitching at the back."

Ileth shrugged. People from all over the map washed up in the Vales, looking for a new name and a fresh start.

The man's eyes flashed angrily at that, but then he must earn significant custom from the young female Names in the Serpentine. He smiled. "You have to be more careful in Vyenn, miss. Even by day it's good to have a companion and keep to respectable shops and streets. A girl your age shouldn't be out alone, even on Broad."

"My duty in this case asks that I brave the risks of Broad Street." The street was as free of risks as it was of shoppers, as far as she could tell.

He put palm to breast, gave a curt bow, and returned to his leathers. She enjoyed getting away with a little insolence.

So much for shopping for a sash.

Still, she was no closer to finding anything wrong in Vyenn, other than that the boys who worked the fishing boats, barges, and coasters were at war with the town boys over a treaty about border lines. Would negotiating a peace treaty between the Town-Cats and the Boat-Rats satisfy Master Traskeer? She thought not. As she had the time, she turned down one of the short, narrow streets connecting Broad with Wharf. If a girl her age shouldn't be about Broad, who knew what peril lay on the waterfront. Perhaps she could find some actual boat rats.

She disturbed prowling cats in a badly drained alley between two warehouses, followed a splash of sun, and then she was on Wharf Way. Five paces farther east and she'd be off the edge of the wharf and into the Skylake.

There were no rats out that afternoon, and only a few people, as it turned out.

Scattered signs of commerce showed in the form of boxes, barrels, carts, and winch-fitted yards to handle them, but there wasn't any activity worth observing. The fishing boats were putting in, having unloaded their catch at the Serpentine. She saw why the boatmen's boys had time to battle it out with town children. The usual lake and river boats and barges stood tied up. Ileth, thanks to her time in the Freesand, knew idle, unloaded ships and boats when she saw them. Some captains or owners were taking time to scrape, repair, re-rig, and paint; others just sat at their moorings with that despairing look of an empty vessel.

There was a red flag flying from the mast of one coaster. Up on the Freesand Coast, that meant the boat was for sale, and she suspected the same was true on the Skylake.

She surveyed the establishments near Wharf Way and its extension

out onto the lake atop thick pilings. There were even what looked like houses built on one cheerfully painted pier, some with rooftop gardens or rigging for drying laundry. There were children about, mostly poking around the water from the edge of the wooden docks. Ileth indulged in a brief fantasy of having one of those narrow, upright homes, right out over the lake, a boat in its own little shelter beneath and a sunny space on top with flower boxes and a superb view of Vyenn and the Serpentine.

Perhaps, if vouchsafed a career with the dragoneers, she'd take her pension in one.

The rest of the establishments were traders, small and large, warehousing, shipping names, a ship chandler, a courier and guide service for travel about the Skylake or down beyond the falls. There were a few taverns, a cheap eating house with long tables, and a little tea and tobacco shop with smiling husband-and-wife proprietors, she guessed, amusing themselves inside with a game of cards. None looked as though they were thriving. Ileth didn't see a single customer anywhere save the taverns, where men had pulled chairs outside to nurse their ale in the summer air.

Ileth knew her way around boats and struck up conversation with those at work, asked a few questions, and did her best to make herself agreeable. Despite her hopes, nobody offered to sell her smuggled Galantine cottons or wines from the Hypatian coast.

There was discontent born of idleness among the boat-folk. River trade had dropped thanks to the Galantine control of the southern stretches of the river and the Scab. Boats and barges that would normally be bringing cargo back and forth from the Blue Ocean in the south were idle, or fewer trips were being made thanks to Galantine duties. Everywhere men were being put off, or paid only with promises, and it made for hardship.

Most blamed the Galantines.

"They'll impound your ship and cargo at any bad excuse," a mate on a coaster told her. He was supervising a work gang fixing a coaster's bottom; they had it up out of the water like a beached whale. "Captain

Vatkin had his whole ship taken because they found a Directist prayer-book on board, said he was smuggling in materials of a banned faith. The sailor who owned the book's sitting in the gaol. Sounds like they're chopping his head off or not, depending on if Vatkin pays a ransom."

"That's—that's piracy!" Ileth agreed, even if she couldn't come up with the proper name for the outrage.

Ileth had heard many such stories in the Freesand that brought the word to mind. The Rari pirates on the narrow channel where Pine Bay let out onto the Inland Ocean gobbled up entire ships and held the crew hostage for ransom. Shipping traffic out of the Freesand withered and died, save for a few fast, well-armed (and expensive) vessels that challenged the pirates and their cursed fast and handy two-masters.

"More ships will flag themselves Galantine and spare the trouble, you know," another old sailor said. His captain, it seemed, had sold his boat entire to the Galantines and he was looking for work. Today he had to settle for watching this mate's crew work the coaster's bottom. "I'm strong for the Republic, always have been. I'll starve before I bow every time some Galantine Baron rides by. But gods, those fools in the Assembly make it tough for a man."

The mate took off his flat sailor's cap and wiped his brow. The sun was hot now. "You dragoneers ought to put a good force together, get that whole lot of dragons together, and take back the Scab, that's what I'm thinking. Last time you fought 'em all wrong, little two- and three-dragon attacks. I saw 'em flying off. It's like slapping when the other guy's throwing punches and kicks. No wonder we lost."

Ileth had neither reason nor experience to argue with him. She let him get back to his repair work.

She couldn't find much at fault around the wharf, other than the general idleness from the decline in river trade—

Ileth stopped in her tracks, realizing her own blindness. The "problem" in Vyenn was all around. She'd practically waded through example after example. Cargos that should be headed downriver to the Blue Ocean and from there to the Inland Ocean weren't flowing. Entire livelihoods were being lost. She would have danced at the

epiphany, if not for the knowledge that the hard times endemic to the Freesand were about to spread here: poverty, foreclosure, people scraping out the barest of livings or selling everything at a loss to relocate and start over.

She turned toward the Serpentine, deep in thought. She left town hardly knowing she'd done so.

The husband and wife she'd given her silver guildmark to were at the little travelers' shrine on the edge of town. They broke her out of her reverie. She gave them their space to go through their devotions, though they both turned to her and made obeisance again. They lit and left a candle and moved off on the road to the Serpentine after thanking her again.

Ileth bobbed an obeisance. "N-no, thank you. Sincerely. I mean it."

The couple were puzzled by that but left the mad Serpentine girl alone at the shrine.

Ileth, having considered it at length, knew exactly what she owed them. If she hadn't given over her coin, she would have spent the afternoon bickering about the cost of white cloth in the Kingfisher's and possibly being talked into having them sew her sash, as they no doubt could do a better job. She might never have made it to Wharf Way and filed away the hundreds of little impressions of dying river trade that led her to a decision about her commission. She might have gone back to the Serpentine with nothing more to show for her time than a report on some attention being needed at the slow-flowing decorative fountain before the Commonist temple.

Such a stroke of fate should be recognized.

After collecting her thoughts and reviewing the rituals she'd practiced as a child what felt like two Ileths ago, she did her own obeisance at the shrine. The candle was still burning, and as the Captain used to say, any light would do, even one at a Commonist shrine. Using the Directist phrasing she'd been taught as a child—the one thing her mother had given her beyond a name of an old Galantine queen was the request that she be taught Directist prayers, where you

interacted with the gods without benefit of priests and sacred spaces—she asked that her crimes and offenses be forgotten, and that she be allowed to grow into a dragoneer at the Serpentine. She asked that she be given strength and wisdom to do her duty, care for a dragon and wear its colors, be known for brave deeds, one day have a name and reputation that was a credit to those who went ahead of her, and be an example to those who came behind.

She dreamed of doing something that would be written about in a book someday, be talked about after she was dead, even if her part in it was forgotten with her name. Should she one day have wealth, she'd use it to help people like the beggar couple. No, she was at a shrine with a candle burning, she had to be fully honest. She also wanted wealth so she could walk into any shop in the land and have the proprietor drop everything to attend her. She wasn't proud of those thoughts, but they had to be acknowledged because unless she admitted the bad parts of herself to herself, identified, numbered, ranked, and examined them, they could sneak around the edges of her motives and lead her astray. She asked for her stutter to be lifted, and if she was paying for some misdeed of her mother's with it, that soon her mother's fault would be forgiven through her daughter's good works.

Oh, silly girlish wishes, they were, but at sixteen she was still part girl, wasn't she? She was like a snake shedding its skin; the younger part remained inside while the older husk was shrugged off and replaced with something bigger and newer.

Feeling bright and cleansed—perhaps giving away the silver coin had carried off old guilt with it—she used her password and stepped back through the gate, exchanging courtesies with the new officer of the watch, a youth a few years older than Sifler bearing the green sash of an apprentice who'd completed all his rotations.

Inside the Serpentine, the late-afternoon heat hit its peak. Usually this sort of day ended with a quick, refreshing rain shower, but the unusually still air must have changed the pattern. A team of young men and boys were working; an ad hoc draft of apprentices and

novices sweated shirtless outside the stables. She'd heard that part of it was to be converted and expanded into a dairy, and there was a dusty piling of gravel and excavated dirt.

Curious, she circumnavigated the works. They still looked to be working on the foundation. The horses were out in the Serpentine's small paddock. Ileth walked over to one to make friends, but it didn't like the smell of her and it trotted off.

From the unaccustomed angle behind the stables she had a good view of the long, low, rectangular building that was the Dragoneers' Hall with its bright metal roof. It was one of the older pieces of the Serpentine, with a colonnade walk out front and gardens behind. The garden was built around a sheltered stone gazebo with an exotic sort of overly bulbous dome, unoccupied as far as she could see except for a pair of green boots propped up on the decorative wall of the thing. She walked into the garden—there wasn't a wall to keep anyone out, just a row of bushes—because she suspected she knew the owner of the green boots.

Before she reached the gazebo, and with a view of the garden entire leading down to the wall, she spotted the dragoneer she perhaps knew best in all the Serpentine, Hael Dun Huss, hanging laundry of all things. His face was shining with sweat. He was mostly out of uniform, but he'd kept his loose work shirt, not that different from the one she wore under her overdress.

As far as she knew, there was no prohibition against apprentices being on the grounds of the Dragoneers' Hall. It seemed so odd that so important a man would do his own washing that she felt compelled to aid him. He was the sort of man who was very easy to talk to, and even if you didn't throw your troubles at his feet and spoke of nothing but the weather, you usually felt better after.

"C-can I help, sir?" she asked her sun-pinked living shrine.

"Oh, hullo, Ileth," Dun Huss said, examining a seam with a frown. "No need. Just about done as is."

"You do . . . you do your own l-laundering?"

"I've done my own laundry since coming here. Keeps certain

reprobates from stealing my best shirts. Leave the bedding to the novices, though."

She heard a snort from the gazebo. "A blind man wouldn't steal one of those shirts. Your tailor should go back to his true calling of sewing flour sacks."

She would recognize Dath Amrits's accent and quick style of speaking anywhere. He was usually hanging about Dun Huss; when you saw one of them about the Serpentine, the other usually wasn't far away. Amrits sat up, rubbed his unshaven chin on his sallow face, and blinked the sleep out of his fishlike eyes. His teeth were wine-stained.

"Oh, this heat. Ileth, come over here and let me look at you. I've had enough of the stink of summer heat on men, I need a clean girl like you about."

"I warned you against roast pork and all those fried potatoes," Dun Huss said, examining a shirt with a missing button. He moved it to the end of the laundry line. "Change your diet with the seasons, man."

Dath Amrits vented gas with the indifference to company of a dragon. "Nonsense. Am I a cow to stuff greens in my face all day? Do me charity and bring me some cool water, would you, Ileth?"

Amrits had been pillowing his head on his rolled-up tunic, resting on one of the stone benches ringing the interior of the gazebo. It would be a nice spot for musicians, and there was an open paved area where people could dance. Or hang their laundry to dry. Ileth followed the walkway to a cistern, but it was empty thanks to a poorly patched crack, and there was no cup.

"You'll have to go to the Visitors' House pump, sorry to trouble you," Amrits called.

"Let him get his own water if he wants it, Ileth," Dun Huss said. "It'll do him good to move. He's been lying in the shade since breakfast."

"Your cis-cistern is cracked," Ileth said.

"I know," Dun Huss said. "There are dozens of repairs that need doing, but the Republic's in arrears. Again. We can't even get the roof

fixed. We're shaving expenses down and being more self-reliant about supply." He twitched his chin toward the future dairy barn.

"Ileth," Amrits groaned from the bench, his arm across his face to shut out the light. "Do be quick! I'm perishing here."

Dun Huss sighed over a stain that didn't come out in his underclothes. "Set an example for our new apprentice and perish quietly, then, with the quiet acceptance of fate that marks a true dragoneer. Why aren't you wearing your sash, Ileth, was there a problem in your promotion?"

A gaunt dragoneer in a patched-up set of scarecrow clothes with a quill stuck in his teeth strode out the back entrance of the Dragoneers' Hall carrying a washbasin. His bare feet made no noise as he approached the gazebo; he had a great deal of stealth for such a big man. Dath Amrits had no idea what was coming until the basin was poured on his head.

"Shaving water!" Amrits sputtered at the man Ileth had only ever heard called "the Borderlander."

"The piss-pot was empty," the Borderlander said through the quill clenched in his teeth.

Ileth knew these three to be old friends. They often flew out together on commissions; when one was absent on his dragon, the other two tended to be as well. They'd always been kind to her. She wasn't entirely sure why, but thinking about it in her rope bed at night, she often thought that Dun Huss did it because his personal code required him to be kind to everyone; the Borderlander saw her as a fellow northerner, a moneyless, nameless odd-one-out much like himself; and as for Dath Amrits, well, he was easily bored and she always seemed to be getting into difficulty in ways that amused him.

Amrits wiped suds out of his eyes. "What brings this?"

"Figuring and totaling. Your bellowing's making my writing go all spidery."

"How are the accounts?" Dun Huss asked.

"More or less, less and less," the Borderlander said, spitting the

quill into the basin. "The Charge can sign off on them tonight if he likes. If he doesn't object to my columns looking like a mountain switchback."

"He gets ornery because he has to take his socks off to do the math," Amrits said out of the side of his mouth, jerking his chin at the Borderlander.

"Gets it right, though," Dun Huss said, holding a shirt up to the sun. "The last time you handled the accounts, we had a financial panic in Sammerdam."

"Would help if you didn't turn in a whole quarter's worth of your dragon's expenses under the heading 'sundries,'" the Borderlander growled.

"But they do get turned in on time," Dun Huss said.

"We're all terrified of Old Bore, Ileth," Amrits said, arranging his wet hair. "He has a reputation for extreme behavior when vexed that nothing can account for, and the proof drips before you now."

The Borderlander asked about her injury. His eyes narrowed when she haltingly explained that it was just an accident when she fell into a tangle of people at the end of her gauntlet run.

"That's a gash from a weapon. A jagged weapon for ripping. Animal claw, serrated blade, could have been a broken bit of glass or hunk of shell."

"What?" Dath Amrits asked, standing up.

"It happened so fast," Ileth said. She told the story about the tailer tradition. "A bunch of us fell together. It might have even been before that; I didn't feel it, I was being knocked about so much running the gauntlet."

Dun Huss left his laundry and came closer for inspection. He made a noncommittal noise. "Accident or not, you're fortunate it didn't get infected."

"I'd say you had an enemy," the Borderlander said.

Ileth repeated that she couldn't believe someone in the Serpentine wanted to hurt her. But the fact that these three men thought her wound suspicious gave her pause. But who would wish harm to her?

Santeel Dun Troot? Santeel had been upset when she found out Ileth had been reporting on her progress at the Serpentine to her family, but Santeel wounded with words and wit, not a broken bottle-end.

"If I had, they'd have pl-plenty of ch-chances at me in the Beehive. No one had a weapon. One b-boy had a dragon-tooth on his brace-bracer. I might have caught on it."

Amrits turned away, losing interest, but the Borderlander just shook his head.

Ileth nodded. "I do . . . I do have one question. How do you submit a report about your find-findings in a commission?"

Dun Huss turned from his laundry. "A commission? From who?"

"Master Traskeer."

"He's a stiff reed," Amrits said, sitting down and pushing soapy water off the gazebo bench.

"Don't criticize her Master in front of her," Dun Huss said. "What did he ask you to do?"

"F-find a problem in Vyenn and report on . . . report on it."

"So he brought back that old chestnut," Amrits said. "He always did like filling up sheets of paper."

"What did you find?" the Borderlander asked.

"A blight on the window-box posies in the high street?" Amrits asked.

Ileth shifted her feet, wondering how to form it into words. "Idle-ness. Boats and barges at their moorings. Just rotting."

"The river's like a limb with a tourniquet at the Scab," the Border-lander said.

Ileth liked the Borderlander. He was so direct about everything. "It reminded me of the Freesand. The Rari killing off trade."

"Oh, yes, you grew up there," Amrits said. "Pirates and slavers both, yes?"

Ileth nodded. The Rari pirates. She'd seen one as a girl, when the Captain turned out the Lodge to watch a pirate being hanged. He hadn't taken them to the actual hanging, as that scene wasn't fit for young female eyes, but she'd watched him being pulled through town.

He must have been some person of importance because of his rich red attire, a warm rolled and channeled vest, though it was still wet enough to drip as he was hauled from the docks. His beard was also scraped and shaped and tended, cut into crisp, severe angles. The bracers and belts taken off him and displayed to the crowd had gold and gems, and he had a fine seal hat set into a stiff cylinder. He seemed amused by the crowd shouting at him more than anything.

She'd snuck out later to see his body, coated in tar to preserve it, though the tar hadn't put off the crows who'd made a mess of what tender flesh they could get at. Stripped of the fine clothes he was just a fleshy, tar-painted man with a beard dangling from a rope by a stretched neck. The sight was horribly fascinating, but it made her glad the Captain had returned them to the Lodge before he was hanged. For some reason she wondered whether they put the tar on him before or after he was dead as she snuck back in through the attic vent.

"Good choice. A dying town's a problem," Dun Huss said, bringing her back to the Serpentine sunshine.

"He wants my commission in writing," Ileth said. "I don't know how to begin."

"Here's a title: *A Presentation of the Findings of the Ileth Commission: A Town Going Ti . . . Belly-Up.*"

Dun Huss ignored Amrits. "Yes, he'll expect it on paper, unless he expressly ordered you to make a verbal report. Fair copy, or you'll get your ear chewed about it not being fit for the Republic, so labor over your handwriting and grid your paper faintly with a pencil beforehand. There's a good guide-grid in the writing room in the Masters' Hall you can use. Even an indifferent hand looks better if the lines have been precisely spaced."

"Aren't you rather giving his game away?" Amrits asked, lying down on the balustrade so he could dry in the sun. "He wants to burn in a lesson in his own miserable way, and if she puts it all in correct, you'll spoil his fun."

"An apprentice of the Serpentine has asked me how to do her duty. I'm going to do everything in my power to instruct her."

Amrits ran his tongue around his teeth under his lip in thought. "For my sins, girl, I spent a term at the old Horn and Drum in Asposis. Blacktower Military Academy for Boys. I only lasted a year before they kicked me out and the Wheezer sent me off to the Serpentine. I understand Traskeer went there as a boy too, before my time. They used to pound it into our heads that it wasn't enough to just describe a problem, you should present a solution."

"You were a flat-hat at Blacktower?" the Borderlander asked. Ileth thought it was the first time she'd ever seen him startled. "You?"

Ileth had heard of Blacktower. She'd listened to her fellow novices talking about which boys went there when she was first sworn in and lived in the Manor. It was a strict military school near the old court city of Asposis. "Blacktower Boys" were destined for high office and great responsibility; before the Republic, they had been called the King's something-or-other.

"Briefly," Amrits said with a wink. "It didn't take. Never developed the taste for being bent over the bombard and beaten the way some there do."

"Do you have any ideas for a solution, Ileth?" Dun Huss asked. "It'll look better if you suggest one."

For once she was ahead of Dun Huss. The Captain never let his charges tell him about a problem without suggesting a solution. "I think s-so. Don't know how to put it down correctly."

"I'll be happy to look it over for you," Dun Huss said. "Show it to me before you make your fair copy, if you like."

"Oh, now that really is cheating," Amrits said. "He's testing her."

"Remember when he came back when Sel resigned?" the Borderlander said. "Talked about too much chaff in the wheat, said we were overenrolled because we were setting up for a war that wasn't going to ever happen?"

"Let's not talk about that in front of an apprentice. Ileth, don't alarm your fellow apprentices. Master Traskeer expressed an opinion not shared by the Charge, the other Masters, or the dragons. Nobody's being cut for the sake of cutting."

"I'm no talker," Ileth said.

Amrits cleared his throat.

The Borderlander and Dun Huss both glared at Amrits. "What? Are you expecting a joke about the poor thing's stutter? My throat's closed up with dust and dry air, that's all. Ileth, quit taking forever about that water. A Dragoneer of the Serpentine is in need, girl."

The Borderlander made a move for the basin he'd dumped on his head.

Dun Huss stood. His laundry was already visibly dryer in the heat despite the lack of wind. Ileth savored the faint smell of his soap flakes baking in the sun. "Don't bother, Ileth, I'll get it. I must go in anyway and find if I have a spare button to fix this shirt. Go about your duties."

"And get that wound checked for black rot," the Borderlander said. "Anyone mad enough to want to tear your face up would be mad enough to dip the edge in something foul. It's too red around the top for my liking. Make sure he smells for sepsis."

The physiker's office was empty and his apprentice was out as well. A novice boiling out dressings said he'd been called into town on an emergency. Ileth wondered if one of the town or waterfront boys had taken a dirt clod to the eye.

That meant Ileth was first in line for soup in the dining hall. After soup, she walked back along the winding central road leading down to the Long Bridge and the Beehive that gave the Serpentine its name. The lavender was in fragrant bloom in the park. Some Guards were practicing with crossbows, shooting at straw targets drifting about the pond in the middle of the gardens. Ileth appreciated the small economy; a miss wouldn't ruin the bolt, though it meant wading about in the pond to retrieve it.

She heard a hail, saw a familiar figure waving as he hurried toward her. He became caught up in his braces, trying to put them on.

"Ah, there you are," Sifler said, straightening out the suspenders. "Saw you from the wall."

His tunic was unbuttoned, which was strange, and he was out of breath. "Sifler. You're not on watch?"

"No. Off duty. The walls are a good place for solitude. Saw you and wanted to have a word."

Ileth wondered if he'd been watching for her. He seemed tense, as though he'd nerved himself to confront her.

"Th-that's f-f-funny. I wanted to speak to you, too."

He looked nonplussed. Sometimes the old tricks were the best ones, ambushing the ambusher. "Me?"

She explained that she needed to turn in an official report, as an answer to a commission, but she didn't know how to organize it and her handwriting wasn't suitable for such a matter.

"You've heard about that, then?" Sifler asked.

"What?"

"That I make fair copies for money. You're the first girl to ask me about it."

"You make money with your handwriting?"

"Isn't that what we're talking about?"

"It is . . . it is now."

"Not much, especially to some of the Names here. Fates know I need it, though."

"I thought you had a great Name."

"I do, among the greatest, as I've been told constantly since I was old enough to pronounce it properly. There's just no money attached to it. I don't mean I'm written off or anything like that—the family's bankrupt. On the pile. Every debt collector and his dog has our Name in the book with a red line through it."

"I'm s-sorry. None of my business."

"I'm not ashamed; I didn't run up the debts. But I understand you're poor as I am."

Ileth wanted to hear where he got that understanding, but she supposed the boys gossiped too. Instead she asked, "Will becoming a dragoneer restore your name?"

"In the end, that's why I'm here. Or maybe I should say in the beginning. There's no business left for me to go into. The dragoneers are a last throw of the dice. Something may happen that will allow me to enter politics a hero, maybe even marry into money." He explained it with a cares-to-the-wind joking tone that reminded her a little of Amrits. Misfortunes were easy to shrug off when you lived with them your whole life. Or you got a lot of practice pretending such old wounds didn't ache.

She tried to share his joking tone. "One less m-mouth to feed, too."

"No, I'm it. I had a younger brother for three days, I'm told, but something got into his blood, and my mother got so weakened by the same thing that they couldn't risk more. She's been weak ever since." The cheery tone was gone.

If Ileth could do anything well in conversation, it was change the subject, a favorite tactic of hers. She did so.

"I did w-want to ask you about w-writing. I need . . . I need to improve mine."

"Well, our stars are aligned today, it seems," he said. "It's just a trick of working the quill or pen, if you have such available, and practice. Rather than just having me write it out for you, I could teach you."

"I can't . . . pay you. No money. We're shipwrecked on the same raft."

"Well, I do have a sort of offer of exchange. My proposit—my offer is this: I've never mixed much with women, you see. Not even my mother. I get a lot of chafe from the other fellows about it; they're very raw in their talk. For all the books, I don't know the first thing about women. You could make me a bit worldlier about such matters. But obviously it would have to be a secret."

Ileth froze. Was the little monkey asking what she thought he was asking?

She was about to tell him to jump the wall and get his experience with a sheep when a dragon-roar sounded from across the Long Bridge, muffled somewhat by the Pillar Rocks. It came up through the window galleries that let the sun in on the dragons' meeting Rotunda,

so loud that it startled the pigeons and gulls that infested the place there. They rose in alarm and a patrolling hawk swooped and took his chance at the sudden flurry of rising meals.

Ileth didn't see whether he caught one. She was too busy running for the Long Bridge.

She flew over the cobblestones of the bridge. Another roar sounded. She'd heard enough dragons being loud by now that she knew it was different from the first.

By the time she was in the passage up to the Rotunda ring, she'd left Sifler far behind. His suspenders betrayed him again.

The Rotunda where the dragons met, her troupe danced, and lesser humans looked down from the gallery above was a flurry of action centered on a triangle of fang and scale. A red she knew, a garrulous old dragon named Falberrwrath, had his *griff* down, snapping at a smaller, slightly younger but more muscular silver she didn't know. The silver kept rearing up on his hind legs, flapping his wings in Falberrwrath's face much as a human might slap another. Taresscon, the senior female of the Serpentine, made a third corner of the triangle, bellowing in Drakine but keeping out from between the jaws of the two males.

Ileth knew she was a favorite of Falberrwrath, not that it would count for a fig when a dragon's fighting blood was up. Some human females just made for more pleasing company to certain dragons; some mixes of scent and motion were extra soothing.

Ottavia and the dancers huddled out of the way with their musicians. Ottavia pulled her dancers toward a passage; if a dragon loosed a careless burst from its fire-bladder, she could lose the entire troupe and her with it in a blast. Grooms and dragoneers were similarly sheltering in alcoves and the passage off the Rotunda. Two other dragons, purple Mnasmanus and Taresscon, the senior female, had retreated up on hornlike perches midway between the Rotunda floor and the gallery, keeping out of the way as they called down in Drakine.

No, Ottavia didn't quite have all her dancers. Vii crouched between the two, her costume torn, a little blood running from her scalp.

Wide eyes filled with fear moved from dragon to dragon as she dodged lunges, hunting for a way out between the stomping feet and swinging necks.

The silver came down from his rear, lost his footing as a *sii** slipped, and Falberrwrath was on his neck in a jump like thunder. He managed to hold down the silver and open his jaws for a bite at the neck. If they rolled now they might crush Vii, who'd had to throw herself on her belly to avoid a wing.

Taresscon intervened at last, turning quickly, and with a swing of her tail she cracked Falberrwrath on the snout. He backed off—more importantly, stepped off the silver's neck—and the glare seeped out of his eyes. His gaze swept the room and he seemed unsure of himself. He gave a snarl as he looked again at the silver.

Vii took the opportunity to crawl away from Falberrwrath's *sii*, but in her fear or confusion she ended up nearer the silver.

The silver was back on his feet in an instant, *griff* rattling and wings rustling.

Ileth took her chance. She was sweaty from her run, after all, and she felt the heat trapped under her overdress. She took off for the center of the Rotunda, passing around the gap in the floor that led down to the flight cave.

"ILETH!" Ottavia screamed.

She put herself between Falberrwrath and Vii . . .

Ileth's Drakine was very limited; about all she'd learned to do was pronounce names correctly, use a few honorifics, and engage in the odd politeness. She fired off all three: "Falberrwrath, old hero! Be easy, now." As she got under his snout, she shrugged off her overdress.

Even she could smell the odor of the long day in the sun coming up off her body.

Behind her, she heard wings rustle and *griff* rattle. If the silver jumped, she'd never see her death coming.

---

* Drakine for the front limbs.

Taresscon said something in Drakine that she didn't understand; the dragons had to pitch their voices a certain way for humans to even make out the proper sounds.

"Falberrwrath, old hero," Ileth repeated. She didn't stutter when she spoke Drakine.

The red looked down at her. His nostrils widened, tested the air about her, then opened as he took her odor, suspiciously, like a cook checking a doubtful egg.

All the while Taresscon kept speaking, the modulations in her voice steady and even, like a chant, if dragons did such a thing as chant.

She heard the dragon snuffle behind her as well. Could one sun-baked girl calm him as well? She tried a careful dancer's turn to throw off more body odor, and saw the silver nudge Vii, who seemed stunned or paralyzed with fear, out of the way. Ottavia ran quick and light to retrieve her. "Falberrwrath, you never finished telling me about the Battle in the S-Snows."

Falberrwrath closed his lips over his teeth and glanced down at her. "What's that?" he asked in Montangyan.*

Both the males settled their wings. Their *griff* retracted.

Ottavia had Vii to safety in a flash.

Falberrwrath breathed deeply, listening to Taresscon. He said two more words in Drakine that Ileth recognized: *I will.* Then he retreated toward the dragon chambers below the Rotunda.

The dancers retreated to a trickle of water so Vii could be cleaned up. "That was a stupid thing to do, Ileth," Santeel Dun Troot said. She looked paler than usual. "You would have been mashed if they'd lunged at each other again."

---

* Unlike the rest of the Outlands west of the Inland Ocean, the Vales do not speak a Hypatian-derived tongue. The Republic has three languages in general use, but since the advent of the Republic, all military and government work, most business, and a great deal of social interaction is done in the dominant popular tongue, Montangyan. Its closest linguistic neighbor is the language spoken by some of the human enclaves from the northeast coast of the Inland Ocean, and a few scholars insist it is the last living tongue that has some elements of the vanished dwarf language, as there are old dwarvish expressions for contracts, deals, and payment terms sprinkled throughout.

"My hair caught on Fal's scale when he charged," Vii said, as Ottavia and the others looked at her injuries. "I can't stop shaking."

Ottavia, voice dull with shock, described what had transpired. It was a typical dragon formal meeting to hear news from the just-returned dragons from the west. There was an argument, and as the dragons weren't conversing in a manner that allowed humans to hear the words (Ottavia's Drakine was quite good; her musical ear made her good with languages), all she knew was that Taresscon called for an intermission to let tempers settle. The dancers came out to perform. Nothing out of the ordinary, especially when male dragons were crowded together and arguing. Suddenly Falberrwrath exploded, charging forward at the silver. The dancers and musicians fled, and Ottavia didn't even know Vii had fallen until she'd reached the passage, and then it was too late; the fight had started and Vii was caught up in it.

Taresscon spoke to the dragons and they ended their session in the Rotunda. They avoided the place where Vii's blood had dribbled, some making small groaning noises over the spot, others stepping around it the way you might avoid a spill on a floor. Dragons, for such famously savage hunters, could be funny about blood, their own or that of friends.

Taresscon called Ileth and Ottavia aside. The dragon settled herself down so that she could speak to the humans at their level. Her skin was a little loose in the manner of old dragons and Ileth dully watched the bones beneath the sagging skin move in sad fascination.

"I am sorry for that," the great old dragon-dame said in Montangyan. "That poor girl could have been killed. You know Falberrwrath. Docile. He's not so old that his mind—well, I will keep him away from other males. Ever since the business with the eggs he has been on edge. Falberrwrath is sensible now and will apologize to you all for shedding blood, perhaps on the morrow."

Ileth wondered what the fight had been about, but if anyone should ask, it should be Ottavia. Ottavia looked tired. Wearily, she asked Preen to take the dancers down to the Quarter and make them strong tea.

The green dragon turned her slack-skinned face to Ileth. She had

odd scales; there were a few white spots and blotches against the faded green. Ileth wondered if it was aging or just a coloration oddity like Mnasmanus's purple scales or the stripes on the Lodger.

"Ileth, you are Ileth, yes? Our gentle old Trother's friend? I remember you from his funeral. That was a brave gesture, just now."

"Was the silver hurt?"

Taresscon glanced back at the silver, who was being examined by the green dragon. "I do not believe so. He's young and interested in Nephalia, the dragonelle you see checking him for broken scale. He rarely gets to see her as they're posted out, she to the west and he to the south. When Nephalia became heated with Falberrwrath, he interposed, and before I could even blink *griff* were being rattled and the fight was on.

"I must now try to reconcile them. I hope one day to see you dance myself, I so rarely get a chance to enjoy your art. Perhaps in the winter we could visit, when the flying is bad and there's less to do."

Ileth promised she would. It never hurt to be agreeable to the dragons in the Serpentine. They were as much citizens of the Republic as their humans. Ileth remembered the Lodger going on about the uniqueness of that. He'd been a part of establishing that tradition, or law. Status. Whatever it was.

Back in the Dancers' Quarter, with Vii's torn scalp tended by a physiker and hot tea in their cups, Ottavia asked after Ileth's wound and if she felt well enough to return to her dancing. She left off her usual laments about being short of dancers but mentioned that she expected a batch of novices to join them soon. She'd heard that these girls had applied to the Serpentine Academy with the purpose of becoming dragon-dancers, having seen performances or paintings. She asked Ileth to help them with the first drills as they passed a silver bowl of nuts back and forth.

This was a bad time to have this conversation, but Ileth knew that the longer she put it off, the worse she would feel. "I had hoped, Charge . . . I had hoped t-to be able to do . . . to do more apprentice work."

Ottavia's lips disappeared for a moment as she set her mouth. "You *are* an apprentice, Ileth. An apprentice dancer. It's your specialty."

"I joined the Serpentine to become a dragoneer, sira."

"So did I, but I found my own calling," Ottavia said. "This is much better for you. As an ordinary apprentice, if your six years go by and you're not a wingman, well, out you go. You've told me you have no family to go back to, no expectations of marriage. Your apprenticeship ends with the dancers; you're hired on as a specialist to the Serpentine company, which means a quarterly income and pension. You may dance as long as you're healthy enough; the dragons don't care a fig if your hair goes gray or your teeth yellow. Shatha's going on twenty years with the troupe. She'll have money to travel, purchase a property, do whatever she likes when she retires."

"S-S-Santeel Dun Tr-Troot is dancing and apprenticing both."

Ottavia reached for her bowl of nuts, offered Ileth a handful, then chewed a few in thought. "She has a famous Name and is expected to rise. She'll succeed her way upward, or fail her way upward, or marry her way upward. She'll leave the Serpentine and go back to the security of that Name or take on a better one. People like you and I don't have the luxury of wasting our youth indulging our fancies."

Ileth bristled at the word *fancies* but guarded her tongue. Her Charge had never been anything but fair, even generous, in her acts. A quarrel about a word would not be worth jeopardizing that.

Ileth felt tears on the way. She'd only just made apprentice, and everyone was telling her she'd stop there? "I've wanted nothing but that since . . . since I was little." She blinked the tears back.

"Ileth, I'm sorry. Sorry. I shouldn't have said that. The troupe had a bad scare today. We'll talk later."

"Tomorrow sh-shall I—"

"Let's see how things look in the morning. I appreciate what you did with Falberrwrath. I know Vii does. Go to bed proud of yourself."

Ileth passed through to the sort of alley with their bed partitions where the dancers, other than Ottavia, of course, slept in a long row. Preen and two others were still up, having tea.

She accepted a cup and sat on one of the rugs that added some warmth and color to the Quarter. Shatha told the story of a dancer from her apprentice age who'd lost a leg in an altercation very like the one they'd just witnessed when she was knocked over and stepped on by a charging dragon, and another girl named Aylee who'd vanished— she'd been up late entertaining a dragon, the last thing the dragon remembered was nodding off into sleep as she danced, and no one ever saw her again. Some said suicide, some said murder, but she was still marked on the rolls as missing.

Shatha suggested that everyone get some sleep, and Preen picked up the tea things. Ileth looked in on the sleeping Vii, took a glass from beside her bed, and sniffed the contents—Ottavia's brandy. She helped Preen wash up the cups and infuser, neither of them saying a word, and she turned in.

Her body felt heavy in the rope bed.

The long day, begun in hope and ended in disappointment, weighed on her. What had started as a bit of necessary formality, signing herself in to the Serpentine, had turned into a labyrinth of difficulties. Except it was a labyrinth where she had to negotiate it by somehow taking both the right turn and the left turn or she'd fail. And no matter which passage she chose, there was failure. She knew what was coming, like the first faint tendrils of pain that promised a thundering headache. Her mind would pick through every horror she'd witnessed and carried about ever since, like the terrified eyes of the boy she'd lost in the rescue from the mining plateau in the Baronies when her grip failed, or the dead escaped slave she'd seen as a child, white and bloated after being pulled off the Dragonback.

Her life had turned into one of those stories where every time the hero strikes down one enemy, the body breaks and forms into two new ones.

She felt like crying.

Ileth didn't fight crying. She'd been told as a child to have her cry and then "get on." Getting on might be returning to the streets in the Freesand where the boys mocked her stutter as she tried to sell little bits of sewing

the girls in the Lodge had created (aromatic herb sachets with bits of prayerbook wisdom embroidered in were popular with fishermen's wives). Getting on might be apologizing to the Captain for whatever you'd done that had irritated him into cuffing you in the ear. Getting on might be going back to the laundry pot after you accidentally scalded yourself taking a boiled shirtdress out. But if the crying was relief, it didn't much help with the getting on. It just made her too tired. She'd found it more effective to fight the impulse to cry and use the emotional energy to get on, with maybe a little striking back thrown in. Like the time she put a generous dose of mineral oil in the Captain's bread dip.

On the other hand, it was bedtime. She was tired. A good cry would help her go to sleep all the quicker. But such was the state of her over-wrought emotions that the moment she gave in to the impulse, the tears wouldn't come. Instead she rolled over, again and again, in the bed she'd once considered the most comfortable she'd ever enjoyed.

If this was the life of an apprentice of the Serpentine, she wondered what she'd look like after six years of it. Gray-haired and gaunt, she imagined, a crone by her twenty-second year. Her tongue probed her teeth, checking for soundness.

She quit summoning sleep and got up. She decided to have a swim.

The Captain, for all his nastiness and flashes of cruelty, was right about a few things. He used to tell a story about how when he feared for the future—he was surprisingly open about some matters, one of which was being scared pale before every long voyage—he'd swim about in the chilly waters of the bay until he felt better.

He believed cold seawater built up the constitution and the blood and cured everything from skin blemishes to gout. Twice a week, winter and summer, his girls dutifully trooped down to a secluded sandbar and splashed themselves or swam, teeth chattering, while the Captain napped on the other side of a dune. Ileth, who'd been told she shared blood with the Captain, was expected to set an example and always swam, and while she never grew to exactly like it, she believed he was more right than wrong about its effects on health and mood.

She passed down through the kitchens, where a lone, tired-looking

apprentice cleaned and watched the embers in the bottom of the great grill where they cooked fish and joints for the dragons. The cooks were used to dancers showing up at odd hours in various states of dress and just nodded as she passed, grabbing a clean cloth from the rack above the sink. The dragons kept unpredictable schedules, staying awake for a day or two and then sleeping for up to a week, so the dancers who entertained them had to take meals when they could.

She walked from the kitchens to the now-empty and nearly light-less Catch Basin, where only a bored sentry on night watch stood guard. She knew he'd be joined now and then by the Guard officer and his escort, who tromped about through the Beehive checking on the sentry posts. Ileth looked at the scrubbed, empty gutting tables where she had done her first labor as a novice without the least regret. She even recognized her balky old gutting knife with the broken handle she'd repaired, shining in its hanging-place on the wall. Life was much better in the dancers.

Why shouldn't she be happy with them? It was a more interesting job than anything she'd been thought capable of growing up in the Lodge. You worked with the dragons, heard their stories and philosophies and confessions, which was more than the apprentices who labored in the up end of the Serpentine could say.

Refreshed by the thought that at least she wasn't gutting fish as much as by the air of the lake, clean of dragon-smell, she trotted to the far end of the wharf beyond the cave's mouth where it descended to the chain of rocks that led out to the old ruins of the lighthouse and guard tower that had once stood there. A wooden walkway still existed but wasn't much in use; it was a chilly, windy spot and she'd been told all the stonework and platforms were treacherous.

One of the dragons was out night fishing, gliding over the lake about a wing length above the water, eye cocked to the side, but the creature was too far away for Ileth to identify it. A quick dragon could get a few fish by just diving into the water with as large a splash as possible over them. The force of his impact would stun a fish, which could then be taken by mouth easily enough.

She double-checked to be sure she was out of sight of the sentry before stripping off her shirt—she took the precaution of weighting it with a rock, as sudden gusts of wind could come rolling in off the Skylake—and slipped into the glacier-fed lake.

The shock of the cold water woke her from toes to hair ends and she paddled vigorously, breathing deeply as she'd been taught to cope with cold water since childhood. It was a bit of a game to her, testing herself against the cold water, holding out as long as she could and then holding out a bit longer. She swam on her front, her back, her side, always keeping within the light thrown out by the Catch Basin.

When she emerged, she felt deliciously alive, glowing and tight-skinned. She wiped herself off with the kitchen rag. The air chilled and dried her and it was good to get back into her clothing.

She'd had an audience after all, as it turned out. The officer of the Beehive watch and the sentry lined the ramp up to the kitchens. She recognized the ensign; it was that wingman who'd been at the tailer ragging at the Long Bridge, Dun Klaff. Odd that he was just an ensign. Sifler, still only an apprentice and younger by a good few years, sported the same junior officer's cockade in his hat. Dun Klaff held his hands behind his back, looking stern, and she suspected he was concealing a spyglass, not that it would have done them much good, dark as it was outside. Heem Beck was with him on guard duty, and a younger apprentice from Ileth's draft.

She'd heard that the overnight guard shifts were either a punishment or a way to prove your desire to do the difficult and uncomfortable in your service to the Serpentine and, by extension, the Republic. She wondered which form his service took.

Ileth dripped her way up to them, wet hair wrapped in the cloth she'd snatched from the kitchen.

"Lots of hot water in the kitchen," Dun Klaff's friend, that Heem Beck, asked. "Why freeze your jigs off out there?"

"Good evening, Ileth," Dun Klaff said. They'd often passed each other in the dark when she was first a dancer, before her trip to the Baronies. He'd just been a sentry of the watch then. "Hard night

dancing?" His tone and smile suggested much more familiarity with her than he really had.

"Couldn't sleep," Ileth replied, too tired now to come up with anything witty. She did smile at Dun Klaff; the friendship of a wingman-at-large in the Guards might help her learn how to get into the Guards.

The lonely watchman who had charge of the quiet Catch Basin overnight joined the conversation. "By the Dragon Horn, I heard you finally made apprentice. Congratulations, Ileth. What happened to your eye, you brush against a dragon?"

She mumbled something about an accident, suddenly exhausted. Her body was finally tired enough to overcome her mind.

"Rum luck, Ileth, a botch at every new moon," the boy from her draft said, sounding as if he was quoting Serpentine gossip. She ignored him and moved off toward the kitchens and the Dancers' Quarter.

Ileth heard a clatter and looked over her shoulder to see the youngest Guard sentry's hat on the floor, and the youth protecting the back of his head with his hand, looking at Dun Klaff in shock. Dun Klaff's hat looked about to fall off too, and he was shaking his hand out as though it pained him.

"Are you mad, Klaff?" the sentry asked. "We're on duty."

"You've bent on her now?" Heem Beck asked. "You changed your tune about her right quick. Giving up on that Dun—"

"Straighten up, the both of you. You're in uniform, on duty, and I won't have contempt for any of the Serpentine in my hearing. Next post, march."

4

Ileth slept soundly in her cozy rope bed after the cold of the lake and awoke refreshed.

Her Charge informed her that there would be no calls for dancers from the dragons for the next few days. Adding to Ottavia's troubles, Vii was in the common room crying that she must leave the dancers. Ileth decided she would do laundry and offered to take a load of bedding up to the big washing troughs at the up end. There was always the chance she might find a scrap of something white fit to be turned into a sash.

Ottavia and the others were happy to fill a washing basket. Ileth told Ottavia that she'd call at the physiker's too, and have her wound examined. The pins might be ready to come out.

Taking her basket and eating a bit of smoked fish she'd palmed while passing through the kitchens, she set off through the winding passages out of the Beehive. The preserving salt in the fish restored her. She kept to the narrow, winding human routes. The wider rings where the dragons had their sleeping-shelves were faster, but there was always the chance that a dragon would order you on some errand.

Like most mornings on the Skylake, an overcast hung low, trapped between the mountain ranges girding the lake. Ileth had lived there long enough to judge that it was thick enough that it had perhaps a fig's flip of burning off or not in the summer sun. Otherwise they'd get rain

that afternoon, probably heavy, as rain at this altitude in the mountains almost always followed a hot day.

The laundry at the up end was, she understood, an old kitchen built into the thick harborside walls of the Serpentine near the crowded dormitories where most of the boys had their beds. She passed a few of them, yawning and scratching as they carried their little basins, soaps, blades, and combs for their shaving and grooming to the washrooms.

There were boys already hanging socks and undersheaths to dry when she entered. Quith looked up from a great steaming cauldron she was working with a stick about the size of an oar and smiled. Ileth hoped she wouldn't bring up her suppositions about her eye. She wasn't in the mood this morning.

Quith helped her find lye, and the mention of hunting up a sash led them to the pauper's bin while the bedding soaked. Nothing even close to white.

Seeing Ileth's disappointment, Quith shifted the conversation to lighter subjects and said she remembered Ileth as an early riser from their days together at the Manor.

"I like to get at it early too," Quith said. "You can have half your day's work done before breakfast and then help the novices or sit in with another group of apprentices. Most of the wingmen and dragoneers and such don't mind an extra person, if you're quiet. I think the dragoneers like to see someone eager to learn as much as possible, whether it's their duty or no."

Ileth had never thought Quith much of a striver. She might even have been the tailer of their draft if Ileth hadn't been marooned in the Baronies. Though she did like to be wherever news might be passed about. Maybe she'd matured.

She took Ileth over to one of the sewing tables and gave her some sensible advice about how best to make a sash, if she ever did find anything white worth turning into uniform.

Ileth checked over her shoulder. The boys had moved off to talk to another apprentice, just arrived with a full wicker basket. "As you . . .

as you're here, let me ask y-you: Who in our group is from . . . came from Blacktower."

"Blacktower. That's some very exclusive hunting ground. Ileth, didn't know you set your eye toward mar—"

"I'm not. I just n-need to know the right words for a . . . for a strategic matter. Someone from our draft."

"Well, there's Dun Treeth, but he's not at all bright. I don't think he learned anything there. I'm told Vor Claymass went there for a year when he was ten but his family pulled him back out. Oh, yes, you had that—don't know why I mentioned him now. There's that little Apenite Sifler Heem Streeth. Fair warning: his family's got nothing but the Name these days."

So little Sifler had gone to perhaps the most elite school in the Vales. That was interesting.

Ileth shook her head hard. "Told you, I'm not after a husband. I just need . . . I just need some help with military matters." She folded over where they'd cut and started on the seam, hoping Quith's capacious memory for connections could settle on someone else. She didn't want to mess about with Sifler in exchange for his help.

"Sifler is who I'd consult. First in everything. I'd say he's your boy, if you can get him to speak to you. He's shy, poor thing. I'm sure the others tear him to bits about being poor. You know, I think the boys are worse than us about that."

Ileth tried to keep her face neutral. You could learn a lot from Quith if you let her rattle, but she would sometimes realize she was going too far if you looked shocked or skeptical. "Then there's Vor Rapp, Roben's wingman, who's always hanging about with Dun Klaff and I've heard he's smarter than he looks. There's that other forelock, Heem Beck, but I don't think he'd tell you the time if he was standing next to a clock. Your best chance is Sifler, I think."

Ileth thanked her. Quith helped her with the bedding, and in a few moments they had it cold-rinsed and hung up to dry. If you could get her to stop the gossip, Quith was a good worker.

Well, the fates had something in store for her with Sifler, it seemed.

Perhaps she could find him on duty again after the physiker looked at her wound.

The physiker Threadneedle had practically a whole building to himself at the up end. It had a crazy collection of chimneys and piping, with the patched and whitewashed and sag-roofed look of a place that had at one time or another been meeting hall, dormitory, workshop, and storehouse, perhaps all at once. It probably had once had a nice view of the Serpentine grounds leading down to the Beehive, but the construction of the Great Hall had turned the view into something not much better than an alley. The physiker's residence was in a set of rooms up a flower-potted stair and the rest of it had been subdivided into examination rooms, sleeping areas for patients, a dispensary, a tool room, and the other necessities of medicine.

Ileth knocked; his apprentice answered and informed her that the physiker was at his breakfast. "He was out late last night. One of the watch tumbled down the outer Beehive stairs in the dark."

Ileth and those slippery stairs were old enemies. A boy had been killed on them her first year. The apprentice invited her to sit in a practice chair. It was a great heavy thing, more like a torture device than furniture, and had leather straps to restrain parts of the body.

Threadneedle's office was much like that chair, a strange mix of horror and science and herbology, with several lamps and mirrors with focusing aids to increase the power of both natural and artificial light. Objects and models and sharp shining devices rested in and on cases, bowls of silver and copper piled atop cabinets, and there was a sort of kitchen in back filled with glass jars containing powders and dried things that looked like mushrooms and tree bark and leaves.

There was a huge, fascinating print on the wall, an anatomy guide of a dragon rendered beautiful by an artist's ink. The dragon had been stripped of scale and skin so the muscle tissue looked like a butchery shop. Great care had been taken to add beautiful waves of precise lines.

Ileth asked about the lines, as someone had gone to great trouble over them.

The apprentice smiled and nodded. "You strike the heart of the matter, sister. Oh, the hours I've put into the study of this piece, adding names and direction to those lines."

Ileth was content to just nod and let him go on.

"There are some who hold that the seat of health rests in the brain and nervous system. My Master took me once to a symposium in Sammerdam where I heard a lecture from a very convincing learned man who presented his analysis of the liver as the supreme sovereign of the body, for it energizes the blood and must be supported by moderation in diet and drink. Then there are those who concentrate on the relationship between heart and lungs, the exchanges of new air for used that go on with every breath you draw and its distribution through the system.

"My philosophy is that we are constructs of muscle, for it is through muscle we animals thrive or fail. The bones give it a framework, the brain and nerves direct it, and the blood supplies it in ways known, guessed, and still to be revealed as our science improves. We are a fantastic system for directing and supplying our muscles."

This interested Ileth, as she used her muscles constantly dancing, and she would probably have described her body much the same way, except with shorter words.

"The next time you eat a chicken, observe the meat, the muscle tissue you are eating. Cut it one way, and the fibers separate as easily as you might open an envelope. Cut it across the fibers, and it becomes frayed rope, and equally useless. That is a great deal of the physiker's art, knowing how to operate upon a muscle, to extract, say, a highpoon from a dragon's left transverse apogrex, without doing so much damage to the tissue that the dragon will never fly again."

It was obviously going to be one of those conversations where Ileth would be looking up words later. She nodded so he might be encouraged to continue.

"You dancers are good examples; you're like deer, ready to run and leap and turn at an instant. So you know there is nothing that so instantly changes everything in your body than exertion, especially

extreme exertion. The muscles swell with blood as they are fed in accordance with need. The breathing becomes labored to the point it seems you cannot take in enough air, your body releases heat—some say this is due to chemical reactions—and the sweat comes to deal with that heat, and incidentally soothe our dragons. It is a shock to the system. I've heard some of the profession say that such shocks must be avoided; they point to sudden, painful deaths as reason for the heart and lungs not to be overtaxed. To never run, and to walk in such a way that you do not tire, to sit rather than stand in conversation. There's a doctor in Sammerdam who designed and sells this sort of apparatus that allows women to roll about in a little harness on rotating wheels, *to take the strain off the legs and limbs,* as he puts it, preventing them from being worn out by endless labors in keeping house, which robs them of their beauty. Or so he claims. Bah. Threadneedle swallowed that nonsense whole. He has a sister rolling about in one; she looks like someone tried to make a marionette out of a sack of potatoes. It's loss, not use, *loss* of muscle functionality that invites in decrepitude, which sets up housekeeping until it can invite its cousin death."

Ileth wondered what such a young man thought of his old fusspot Master Threadneedle. Ileth remembered him stitching up the wound she received in her duel. All the while he worked, he sang little songs to himself like a six-year-old girl getting dressed: *socks garter boots and laces, socks garter boots and laces* . . .

"The body saves energy where it can. Muscle that is not being used requires too many resources, food especially. Do you not have a great appetite after dancing?"

"We're always eating," Ileth said, agreeably. She was relaxed now. When she'd first sat in this terrible-looking chair she'd been nervous about all the shining, pointed instruments.

"Unneeded, unused muscle becomes a repository for extra fats and eventually withers. Same with dragons. Many of our troubles with dragons living together come from underemployment. A dragon alone will roam about, mimicking patrolling and hunting actions it would do in the wild, but when artificially put together like this they will fret

and fight. The Academy is very good at keeping you all productively busy. I've told them they should have similar duties for the dragons, but I'm in no position to effect change. Yet. It might relieve some of the tension with the Assembly. Society as a whole isn't that different from anatomy. Our brains, such as they are, are jealous of all the resources that go to the dragons. It was one thing when there was a king and they were a symbol of his throne's power and glory, and of course in the early days of the Republic we were fighting for our lives, but now with that Galantine defeat it seems unfit, unused muscle to be withered off."

Now that he'd turned neatly from anatomy to politics, Ileth lost interest.

Threadneedle's apprentice must have sensed it. He began a discourse on a study of the bodies of miners gathered after a tragic accident that killed them by the dozens and how there were many in their seventh decade of life almost indistinguishable from those in their third when the physiker entered. Threadneedle had bits of his breakfast on his shirt and picked at his teeth with a sliver of wood.

He was much as Ileth remembered him: potbellied, whiskered, and with little lenses such as those with failing eyes (who could afford them) wore on the end of their nose.

"You're the girl from that duel a draft or two back. Cut just above the hip in a duel. Bled a lot."

"The same," Ileth said.

The apprentice looked at her with new interest.

Threadneedle's eyebrows came together as he looked at the wound about her eye. "I'm glad I don't see much of you, errr . . ."

"Ileth," she reminded him.

"Yes. Ileth. I'm glad I don't see much of you. Most of the young ladies here have been brought up to ask for a physiker at every sniffle and cramp. It's nice to know some of you get by on your own. I hardly ever see you dancers. Perhaps young Gift here is on to something with all his advice about the tautening of muscle tissues."

He looked at his apprentice. "That reminds me. Make up a few Number Four draught packets for Falberrwrath and bring them to the

Beehive. Double-check that we have the latest on his estimated weight before you measure. Instruct the dragoneer Roben that he's to have one a night in with his wine and to be sure that he drinks it. Roben's the one with gold teeth if you don't know him. He should sleep and awake refreshed. I think those eggs being about to hatch is making him anxious."

"Yes, Physiker," the apprentice said, and disappeared into the kitchen area with all the jars, drawing a curtain behind him. Ileth heard jars being taken down.

"When were you injured?" he asked, turning her head to view the wound from different directions.

"F-four days ago. I was worried, it was so red."

"And the wound, it was cleansed?"

"Soon af-after, with vinegar, s-sir."

"Excellent. I've often told Joai that had she been born a man she would have made a fine physiker."

He tested a pin with his finger. She winced. He wiggled the other one, then looked close at the wound with the aid of a magnifying glass. When he pressed his nose close to her wound and took a deep sniff, she finally protested, as his belly threatened to squash her.

"Sir!"

"The nose is a better finder of corruption than the eye, dear. Be happy that your wound has closed without infection, considering it was closed with nothing but pins and sticky plaster. A small scar will probably remain but in someone your age it will fade so that powders applied with sufficient art will render it invisible. Your eyebrow will have a small notch, but the hair will cover it, provided that old Court habit of plucking them down to a thin line such as elegant ladies did in my youth does not return to fashion."

Ileth felt a painful pinch at her eye. Something rattled into a metal bowl. *"One is out, here's number two,"* Threadneedle sang.

"Your . . . apprentice is very learned," Ileth said.

"You are not the first young lady he's impressed. Sorry to dash your hopes; he would only be interested in examining the tone of your legs

if he were to find himself against them. If he ever marries, it'll be for her reference library, not a pretty face. I should like to send him on to the Greatyard, even for a year or two, and train another apprentice then retire when he returns, but the Republic's finances have bottomed and there's no money, and likely to be none anytime soon. I expect my pension's to be shaved next." He tested and then drew out another pin and Ileth winced.

Ileth wanted talk to keep her mind off the pain. "Your assistant, G . . ."

"Gift." She felt him pinch at the remaining pin.

"There's a story behind the name?" Officials in the Vales often reworked foreign names into Montangyan when adding émigrés to the rolls. It wasn't always laziness, some came to the Vales wishing to leave behind old troubles with a new name.

"Exactly. Orphan left on a doorstep. Not even of a rich house, a little crossroads farm. It's one of the things that keeps me believing in the Republic, even when the money dries up. Over in the Baronies, he'd be tilling soil, all that brain wasted. Here, well, we might finally get a worthwhile book on dragon anatomy. The one I have is in Hypatian and it's terrible. Thank the gods for Gurion the Anatomist from eighty years back. We have copies of his notes and sketches here." The silver pin clanged into a metal bowl on a little table near the heavy torture chair.

Ileth asked if he did the wall-spanning study, and the physiker nodded.

"You're done, uhh . . ."

"Ileth."

"Yes. Ileth. It's a beautiful wound. On a man it would give him a bit of dash. You, well, women have their own mind about things." He took out one of his sun-reflecting mirrors and allowed her to examine herself. The wound was pinkish save for the red spots where he'd just removed the pins and didn't look anything like beautiful, but then she'd never expected to get through life on her features.

Ileth rose to leave when the physiker rattled the metal bowl.

She turned on her heel and he smiled. "I forgot." She'd been warned of torments if she left the silver pins somewhere; she wanted to give the old physiker a kiss.

Threadneedle smiled. "I forget names and family connections at the Assembly. My tools, never."

As Ileth went out the door, she pulled up to avoid a collision with someone bound for the door. It was a woman swinging along quickly despite a wooden leg, and she stopped herself with a quick brace of the leather-capped limb.

She wore a silver sash and matching pauldron, but no sword, being in the Serpentine on ordinary business, and had an old, hard look about her, everything tarnished and worn down like a weather-beaten bronze statue. Her skin was red with wind chafe.

Scars on the dragoneer's face made Ileth's little rend seem like the nothing it was, with damaged and repaired skin drawing her left cheek tight that gave her sort of a smirk.

"Who are you?" she asked sharply, looking from her face to novice pin and back again.

Ileth bobbed. "Ileth, app-apprentice and dancer, s-sira."

"Where's your sash? Not hiding a pregnancy, I hope?"

"Sira?" was all Ileth could manage.

"Don't look shocked. You wouldn't be the first. Seeing you coming out of the physiker's with dress loose as a sheetcut sail."

"She was being treated for a gash above her eye, Garella," the doctor said from the door.

So this was Garella! There was only one female full dragoneer in the Serpentine entire. Ileth, somehow, had never encountered her or her dragon. They were posted somewhere south. The Serpentine seemed to be full of new faces lately: the tanned, white-haired dragoneer in the beer garden, and now Garella. She wondered what was going on.

"Ain't you proud of your sash?"

Ileth fought her way through an explanation that she'd just been promoted and hadn't acquired hers yet.

Garella finally noticed the wound above Ileth's eye. "I remember your name now. Dueling again?"

"Garella, I received your note," the physiker said. "Let's have a look at your back."

"Needs more than a look. Jab your knee in hard if you must. And don't kiss me off with a draught, drugs have never fixed *mlumm*."

She watched Garella stump into the office, wondering if she was looking at her own future.

Breakfast had passed in the Serpentine and the apprentices, novices in their new clothes and shorn hair, and the exalted wingmen were filtering in and out of the Great Hall. She circumnavigated the little clusters of the Academy and returned the silver pinch-pins to Joai. Joai was happy to get her pins back and pronounced her scar healthy, silver once again proving its sovereignty in keeping corruption out of a wound, and had Ileth breakfast on oat porridge, cold sausage, and yesterday's bread toasted over flame and smeared thickly with butter. Joai groaned a little as she picked up a tray of dirty dishes and Ileth jumped up and took it herself. Ileth asked if she had any white cloth about, even an old table covering or curtain would do. Joai chuckled.

"So you're too thin to come up with the price of cloth? Poor thing!"

"What'll happen to—happen to me if I can't come up with a sash?"

"You know this place by now, girl. Testing you all the time, even if the tests aren't proper Academy style with you standing in front of Masters reciting poetry in Hypatian or whatever they do at those gentlemen's schools."

"It's not a fair test. Were I rich, I could just go into Vyenn and have one made."

"And does that make them clever? Or tough? You learn a lot more climbing a mountain than you do standing atop one, girl."

Ileth chewed on a sausage and thought about that. Joai was right.

"There's tests for that lot too. Don't forget, you probably thought nothing of gutting fish all day. Some of these Toppy-Nameseys, why, they'd sooner take a slap than do manual labor."

Ileth remembered Santeel working in the chicken pens, cursing quietly to herself as she tried to get her boots clean again.

"Doesn't help me get a sash."

"I'd give you mine, but it went years back. Local boy from Vyenn. Thickest hair I've ever seen and brown eyes like a puppy dog. Poor local boy mixed in with all these rich swells, well . . ." She trailed off as she wandered through her memories. "Can't say if it was my soft woman's heart pulled at by those eyes or my republican politics, but it went to him despite me being so proud of it that it used to hang right there by the door in a glass case. Good glass, too, Elletian. Gave it to the Charge to keep his ribbon and star as it had no further use."

"Did he make wingman?" Ileth asked.

"Oh, yes. Killed over the Scab a couple years back and his dragon, Serenene, she was wounded and quit on us. Wasn't much of a wound, I hear, but quit on us all the same. I suppose a Galantine agent worked on her in all the confusion of the war."

Ileth must have had a question in her eyes, and Joai answered it.

"There's more than one way to win a war, flower. Which do you suppose is easier, killing a raging dragon, mad with fighting blood, or sneaking in and convincing it that it's throwing away its one precious life in this world in a human war that won't even be in a nation's memory in five hundred years?" She mocked a whisper: "*Where are you going to be in five hundred years, great dragon? Scale on some fortress roof and bones on a mantelpiece, or napping in the mountain sun with a belly full of elk?*"

Spies and sausage and porridge. Ileth crunched into her buttered toast as Joai talked, and then when she swallowed, she asked: "How did a . . . did a G-Galantine g-get to a dragon?"

"It's not like they come over in uniform, girl. You know the Vales, people show up from all points to start a new life. Easy to get an agent in. Sometimes they join up. We don't get actual turncoats too often, that's more of a thing you see in plays and novels, for all that that boy who used to sick up at the smell of dragons went for them. See, that's

the problem, all it takes is one act of conscience and you lose the turn-coat and the agent who recruited him both. No, the agents, they more pick up information like and put in a nasty word here and there where it'll be surest to lower everyone's spirits. Of course for all I know Puppy-Dog Eyes was their agent. He would have been good at it. Maybe he was doing the whispering in Serenene's ear and caught poetic justice on the crossbow bolts of his countrymen."

"I could be an agent, then."

"Well, you could be one; Caseen told me you spoke Galantine well enough, which is a strange knack for a girl who's poor as a pile of raked leaves to have, but then it would be dumb of them to let you go off and spend a year or more in the Baronies, knowing you'd be watched after that because you might turncoat on us. Because I'm sure the Republic has an agent or two giving reports on what's going on in the Ser-pentine."

"What, the dragoneers?"

"Lots of aristocrats—even if we don't call them that anymore—send their sproggies here. If someone wanted to put the king back on his throne, this'd be a smart place to start."

Their talk turned to lighter subjects and Ileth helped her with the washing and brought in more firewood. Joai said that she'd be glad of a young body to help out around her kitchen, if ever she grew sick of the smell of dragons.

With a full belly she went in search of Sifler. She suspected he'd be at the gate, on the wall, or doing his studies in the Great Hall.

She tried the Great Hall first and was rewarded. There were six or seven tutors in, some with groups of about ten, others teaching a single pupil. Caseen used to tell her that the Academy was that in name only, but many of the families wanted their youths to continue their formal education even while they trained to be dragoneers. She'd overheard lessons in the social graces, music, singing, Galantine, and more artis-tic endeavors. Sometimes when she'd had time to eat dinner in the Great Hall, she'd seen an artist filling in a rough sketch on a canvas of, say, the fishing boats in Vyenn's harbor from a paint palette, but then

there were many in the Vales who drew or painted just for fun. Art gave you something to look at when the weather was awful.

Sifler was there, off duty as his Guard's tunic was hung up on a wall hook near the bench where he sat with some novices. They were passing a book around; it appeared to be a history or a commentary, as Ileth overheard descriptions of how many thousand light cavalry something called the "Ironriders" possessed, and Sifler interrupted to mention that cavalry weren't of much use against a well-defended mountain pass.

She caught his eye and he excused himself.

"Ho! Ileth, we're deep in Forder's *Influence of Dragon Power on History*. Care to join?"

"You're a tutor?"

"More of a minder. I make sure they've read the texts and so on for Jellisween. He does history, military organization and method, leadership. Between guard duty and helping him, I skim by without paying a tuition. He's an old family friend to our Name. That helps."

Having a Name meant even when coin was short, the rough edges of life were smooth and cushioned. Well, no helping it.

"I wanted . . . I wanted to ask about"—her discomfort with the subject and her stutter combined to render her wordless—"your offer."

He led her away, his hands clasped behind his back. He didn't look particularly embarrassed. If anything, he was eager to talk about it.

"My offer is this: I'll help you with this report you have to write, phrase it properly and so on, show you a few formal composition traditions, whatever you need, and we'll work on your handwriting. Turn it into something a lady can be proud of."

Sifler glanced around and lowered his voice. "What I want in return is this: I'm utterly inexperienced with girls. Never mixed with them, don't know the first thing about them, beyond, you know, all the, well, all the biological processes and such. I've never so much as held hands. Through you I could get the amorous experience I need so the others don't chafe me up so much."

There it was. "You w-want me to let you . . ."

"You! Heavens, no! Not for a fortune, never."

Ileth was relieved, yet oddly put out by his alarm at the thought. Was her reputation that terrible?

"You see, Ileth, there's this girl in town. Do you know Caribet's?"

Confused, Ileth could only shake her head.

"It's not on Broad Street. It's not even on a street, it's up an alley, he sells paper and ink, envelopes, stamps, books. He doesn't buy books, though, the cheap bugger. I have several I'd like to sell."

Ileth had missed it on her reconnaissance. "So this girl is . . . is—"

"His daughter. She's quite pretty. I was thinking as she was about your age and class, except with the advantages of parents, you could advise me on how to attend her socially."

"No scars and a perfect little nose, I'm sure," Ileth said.

"Ah! Oh, you thought —"

"N-n-not exactly."

"Oh, well, that is funny. No, never. You wouldn't believe the blistering lecture we got when we came in as novices about keeping our hands and . . . our hands and . . . kisses off the ladies here." His face had turned bright red, Ileth had never seen anything quite like it. "Even you dancers. You know, some of the boys in our draft joined partly because they heard there was a troupe of dancers permanently attached as entertainers. You know, they thought they were for the dragoneers. Like a . . . well, one of those houses with people going in and out at all hours. Didn't know the dancers were strictly for the dragons. Some author of red-letter novels had been letting his imagination run away on him. I've never seen such disappointment."

Ileth was used to the attitude by now. Women who danced in public were considered disreputable at best. Conversely, they had a certain contradictory glamour to them, perhaps partly because of their reputation. High-born young men liked to appear in public with a dancer on their arm and enjoy the swirl of scandal. When the young men were done with them, they'd move on to older, richer men who showed public proof of their virility by being associated with a dancer, or former dancer, and so on, until they wound up quietly keeping one of the old

rakes company in his dotage. Not that that sort of thing went on in the Freesand. Old men showed their virility there by boating stripers.

"You mean to . . . to s-seduce her?"

"That's putting it too crudely. No, just social congress. I've floundered. She's wary of men from the Serpentine, I'm sure."

"No doubt," Ileth said.

"There's a bit more social life for apprentices, and the Guard have dinners and memorials and dances, and there'll be more should I make wingman. I should like to have someone I can partner with at dances and festivals and dine respectably with in her home at the family table. You're a girl; don't they want invitations, especially with a man in uniform?"

Sifler was still much more boy than man, but Ileth nodded. "Some. Some," she said.

"The gang in my bed-row, they're mostly hot air, I think, when they describe their, well, exploits. I don't mean to brag myself up or lie about her. But I think if I'm associated with a girl in town, if they see her with me at the Overwinter Ball and such, they'll leave off."

Once again, cutting down one problem seemed to make two rise up. How many comic stories were there about an inept man being aided in the wooing of a lady? Sifler must know that most of them ended with the would-be gallant disappointed. "Then I'll . . . I'll help you. But I must complete my—my commission first."

"Agreed."

"What must I do?" Ileth asked.

"Go and write down what you found as best as you can. Paper and ink not a problem?"

Ileth shook her head.

"You can give it to me anytime. Until the next week-over I'm on four-hour watches at the gate, past noon and the evening one that ends at midnight. If you've no objection to late work, we can look at it then."

Ileth returned to the Guard quarters that very night, just not for the purpose she intended. She was shaken out of a deep sleep by Santeel, with a crowd behind her. Ileth startled. "What? Is it Falberrwrath again?"

"Just get dressed. Quietly." Santeel had a lot of powder on her face and smudging at the eyes. Much more than she normally wore.

The troupe was dressed in ordinary clothes, all dark. Most had their hair wound up in cloth. All except Vii and Santeel, who were in dancing sheaths with cloaks thrown over them. Ileth put on her boots, broke the old lace and retied it. Ileth noticed that Vii also had made an effort to highlight her face with powder and smudge.

They allowed her a quick cup of tea to warm herself, as it was ready anyway. Ileth followed them out of the Dancers' Quarter. Shatha grabbed Ottavia's walking stick on the way out.

They threaded through the quiet Beehive, Santeel far ahead as scout, waving them forward.

"What's this about?" Ileth, now fully awake, asked Vii.

"Counter-raid. Been planning it for a while." Ileth choked back a laugh. "Counter-raid for what?"

"For that throng of wingmen and apprentices barging into the Quarter to run you across the bridge, of course. No parley, no formalities observed. They can't just shove into the Quarter like that. Especially not Guards."

"In uniform no less, the mutts," Shatha said.

"If this is about me—"

"It's about the sanctity of the Quarter, Ileth," Fyth said.

"Santeel is Chief of Staff and planned the whole thing under Shatha's approval," Vii said.

They crossed the Long Bridge in still air. It was a clear night. The lighthouse atop the Beehive littered the grounds with moonshine, strong enough to throw shadow. They moved cautiously past Mushroom Rock and left the road, moving along the interior shade of the walls, Santeel still ahead scouting.

Santeel ducked down.

"There's the main guard door," Shatha said.

Santeel returned. "Everything's as usual. Just like the Guard at the gate. Officer of the watch, sentry above the side door."

"Vor Claymass?"

"Where he's supposed to be, of course," Santeel said with a smile.

"Dancers!" Shatha said. "The plan?"

Everyone but Ileth recited: "Officer at his station. Sentry at the wall. Infiltrate. Chastise. Retreat."

Shatha smiled at Santeel and pointed with Ottavia's stick. "Your turn. It all depends on you now."

Santeel removed a cut lemon from her sheath and took a deep breath. With a swift, savage motion she tilted her head back and squeezed lemon into each eye. Preen winced; Fyth hid her face.

Santeel dropped the lemon and used an oath that Ileth hadn't heard since the Captain's Lodge. Someone gasped. "Bitch who bore me, that *stings*," Santeel said, rubbing her eyes with her fingertips.

After a moment she looked at them. Her eyes were already going red and tears streamed down her cheeks. She smelled a bit like lemon, but Santeel had a habit of rubbing cut lemons under her arms to freshen herself when she sweated, so that was nothing strange to those who knew her. "How am I?"

"Pathetically perfect," Shatha said.

"Officer at his station," Santeel said. She stood off, moved more into the open, and walked swiftly up the parade ground toward the Guards' garrison door at the side entrance. Vii gave her a moment, then followed. Vii had worn her most daring sheath and her body moved provocatively in its confines.

"Rapoto! Rapoto!" Santeel sobbed.

The troupe snuck closer under the shadows of the wall.

Vor Claymass shot to his feet from the officer's desk at the door. "Santeel!" He got his scabbard out from between his legs and ran to her, holding it clear.

"I have to talk to you," Santeel bawled.

"Santeel, you mustn't tell *him*," Vii pleaded. Vii was good at drama.

"Leave off, Vii."

"Gods, Santeel, whatever's wrong?" Vor Claymass asked, taking her hand.

"I—" She looked up at the wall. The sentry was looking down at

the action. Santeel pulled Vor Claymass away with the hand he'd put on hers. "I can only speak in private." She glared at Vii and led him off toward the gardens. They were on the other side of the Serpentine Road and a longish walk.

"What is that about?" the sentry asked Vii.

"Sentry at the wall," Shatha murmured.

Vii put her finger to her lips. She ran lightly up the steps to the sentry point. Watching her bounce going up the stairs, Ileth wondered if Vii had rehearsed.

Shatha waved the limber dancers forward. They scuttled low, like crabs, to the door.

"I don't know how you do it," Ileth heard the sentry above say to Vii.

Vii's voice moved away from the door. "I don't have the right body for a dancer. I'm all tits and hips. This sheath is supposed to support, you see this band? It rubs me right under my breasts. I have this red mark every single day."

"You're insupportable," the Guard said. Vii giggled.

"Don't make me laugh. It hurts, see."

"I, errr. I don't see it."

"It's not for lack of looking." Vii laughed from her new spot on the wall. "Here, I'll show you. By the light there, you can see, a solid red band. Follow me."

"Infiltrate," Shatha said.

They passed through the Guard common room. Ileth had glimpsed it briefly upon first entering the Serpentine. The troupe helped themselves to cooking implements and pots at the little stove. Ileth took a bucket of water.

"This is the tricky bit," Shatha said to them at the next wall. All was dark beyond, though they could make out vague shapes in beds lining either side of the interior wall.

They went single file between the flanking bunks in the nearly lightless room, the dancers barefoot and the next thing to silent. Shatha was stepping carefully at the front, feeling with her toes as she stepped for anything that might trip them or be knocked over.

"Gods, do they do nothing but fart?" Fyth said through her over-dress collar held to her nose.

"Shhhh!" That was from Shatha at the front, still feeling her way.

"Their insides must be solid cabbage and onions," Preen whis-pered.

Having run the gaseous gauntlet, the troupe arrived at the wingmen's rooms, oddly like the Dancers' Quarter in that there were partitions with the benefit of curtains. The dancers knew how to open curtains quietly, and found the cells for Dun Klaff, Heem Beck, and Vor Rapp, the ring-leaders of Ileth's ceremony. They did their best to avoid bothering with the other wingmen. Though still an apprentice, Sifler was in one of the officers' rooms, reading by the light of a candle. Ileth put her finger to her lips and slid his curtain shut.

Shatha took Dun Klaff, who was sleeping facedown. Fyth put a cooking pot over Heem Beck's prominent nose. Ileth readied her bucket, standing at the foot of Vor Rapp's bed.

Shatha raised the cane, then checked her fellow dancers. "Chastise!"

She brought the cane down hard on Dun Klaff's buttocks. Ileth heard a satisfying *thwack* as she sent a wave of water rolling across Vor Rapp from crotch to face. Fyth banged the soup pot with a metal ladle, ringing it like an alarm bell. Perhaps the biggest shock of all was cour-tesy of Preen, who let loose with a terrifying shriek right in Dun Klaff's ear. As he startled awake, she tried to empty his bedside snuffbox on his head, but she couldn't work the latch in the dark so she settled for jamming it deep into his boot.

The barrack roused itself at the alarm.

"Retreat!" Shatha cried, her wig now askew from the blow to Dun Klaff's buttocks. Everyone hurled their cooking implements at the walls, intent on making as much noisy confusion as metal and fortifi-cation could create, and ran for the light of the entry room. The fleeing dancers inspired hoots, yells, and whistles from the Guards turned out of their beds at the alarm.

"Oh no you don't," a pair of shirtless apprentices said, moving to block their escape through the doorway.

Santeel's leg shot out from the portal. She managed to trip one and held the other back, using a toilet sponge-stick like a stabbing sword to keep the exit clear.

"On me, troupe! Rally to me!" Santeel shouted. "Stay back, if you know what's good for you."

They piled out into the entry room. Preen was already laughing.

Ileth brought up the rear. She stood for a moment next to Santeel, as more and more young guardsmen gathered. Some stood on their beds for a better view of events. Ileth thought the moment called for a gesture. She remembered something she'd seen in Galantine lands, when a Tribal had been haggling with a villager over some trinket and failed to agree on a price. The villager had called her a vile name, and she responded with a gesture.

Ileth did her best to imitate it. She raised her dress hem above a buttock, slapped herself lightly, and then used that hand to make an aristocratic "be off with you" gesture while showing her teeth to the Guard. The Galantine villager had certainly seemed insulted by it.

With that, she and Santeel ran, a rearguard for the others. Vii executed a fine leap from the stairway landing and joined them.

"What happened to Vor Claymass?" Ileth asked.

"You know Rapoto, if he thinks a girl's in distress, he'll lever up the Beehive itself to help," Santeel said. "I told him to fetch me a hot swirl."

"There's no swirl in the Serpentine," Vii sighed. "Would that there were."

Santeel dodged a flung apple core from behind. She hurled the toilet sponge-stick at the cluster of Guards framed by the light of the doors to the guardroom. For all her skill with fencing, she wasn't much with missiles. It fell rather wide and very short. "Well, he'll be busy looking for a while then, won't he?"

"That was over quick," Vii said, wiping her smeared lips. "Too bad, it was just getting interesting up there."

"What did yours do?" Ileth asked.

Vii rearranged herself in her dancing sheath as she retreated; the

jump had jostled things loose. "It started off with a lot of failure to attend to duty. I sort of rushed him through lewd acts once I saw you all were inside. We didn't get as far as flagrant consortion, but maybe I'll be luckier next time."

Full of military thoughts from the well-planned raid the previous night, Ileth spent a laborious morning working on her commission in the writing room of the Masters' Hall with her only company a dragoneer composing a letter. Or she decided it was a letter, as he smiled as he wrote. The dragoneer set his pen to rest, gently dried his lines, then favored her with a nod as he rose and left her to finish. Ileth's smudged report was two pages of close-written paper with a great deal of crossing out and marginalia and only a hint of a solution. She rolled up her paper and visited the gate but didn't see Sifler. After last night's raid she didn't brave the section of the wall with the Guard barracks to ask after him, so she returned to the Dancers' Quarter.

No one was there. It was rare for everyone to be out, so that meant there was only one place for them to be: the Rotunda. She went up and found the troupe arrayed before Falberrwrath, formally apologizing to the dancers for losing his temper. He made no attempt to shift blame to anxiety over his about-to-hatch eggs, and when he saw that Vii wasn't among them, he asked Ottavia to take down a written note.

Ileth thought it a handsome gesture.

Ottavia, in turn, to show there were no hard feelings, sent Ileth to keep Falberrwrath company that evening. He hadn't even touched his wine. Perhaps he smelled the sleeping-draught. She brought one of Ottavia's music boxes that played a cheery tune, but the great old red didn't ask her to dance. He spoke of his own hatching—a two-egg clutch, just himself and his sister, born during the Scattering after the Fall of the Lavadome Tyrs. There'd been great rejoicing at their birth, the first dragons born to their dragon-clan after the terrible losses in the Age of Fire, whatever that was.

Ileth, who'd been going over her commission in her mind, was

working on the idea of a solution. She'd heard odds and ends of stories about the fighting over the Scab, how bad it was, the fact that they'd been taken utterly by surprise by a couple of second-rate Galantine dragons no less, but never the complete story. While her idea had nothing to do with the Scab, some of her problem was the same in principle.

Falberrwrath seemed in a mood to talk, so she asked him. He liked telling his war stories. Ileth was a natural listener. Though you more or less had to listen when a living hill of muscle and armor spoke.

"The Galantine War was a disaster from the first dragons-up. We were played right from the start. Ever hear of the Three Barons?"

"No. Tell me," Ileth managed to say in Drakine.

"That's not bad for a human, and a little one at that. Well, there were these three Borderland Barons from the Galantine king's protectorates—those old bits of the Vales that stayed loyal to the king when the Republic was proclaimed—who sent out feelers claiming they wanted to join the Republic, since they were doing better business with us than the rest of the Baronies and they were sick of all the tariffs and duties and taxes. We believed them, or the commercial lines did. The Galantines were clever bastards for humans, I'll give them that, it was a scheme worthy of old Tighlia of the Rock. There were a lot of powerful merchants, town folk, and such who were planning a revolt, figured they'd be better off with us than they'd be with the Baronies. These Barons used their fake revolt to flush their political enemies out into the open and cut us off at the wing joint besides. They revolted, we sent our forces over, including dragons, the Galantine king screamed invasion, but well, it's an invasion they wanted us to make because they were layin' for us.

"That's just the first part of the big trap we blundered into. Part two was the Scab. Now the Scab, you know, big fortress island at the end of the Tonnage Lake. Always two or three dragons there as it was the southeast end of the Republic and next to the Galantines to boot, and just a little farther down the Blue Ocean and our trade routes south and round east to the Hypatians, the Old Coast, Cold Coast, and so

on. Important post. Had some of our best dragons there: Fespanarax, Agrath, and Mnasmanus. Pure gold in the mouth, those three. Should have had more, but, you know, every joint of mutton and swallow of ore costs."

It made Ileth's heart hurt to hear those names. Fespanarax, because he'd been secretly working for the Galantines and she'd been too blind to even suspect it and suggest he be watched on his return. Agrath, because he'd been Annis Heem Strath's dragon, and they'd died together in the war, the dragon falling atop her, protecting her with his armored body. She'd heard the story from the lips of the man who'd commanded the dragon-killing company himself.

"Well, those dragons got shifted quietly for the big surprise we thought we were pulling on the Galantines. More the fools us. There's not much space at the south end of the fortress where the river narrows and flows quick, tricky part for boats, it's almost like a waterfall the current is so fierce, craft get pulled upstream by oxen on tow paths. Well, what the clever Galantines did was rather than have their dragons up in the air fighting ours, they had them hidden just off the lake. They wore this sort of apparatus on their backs, turning them into something like a walking bridge. Into the water they went, hung on to each other while their men looped the two halves together with rope, and their storming column was across the water before you could say 'For Egg and Tyr.'

"Of course once they had the Scab, they had a plan to keep it. Meteor men, those damn Fencibles, highpoons, harpoons, bombards for launching snaggy chain, they had the lot. We tried to burn them out, but the Scab's built bottom-to-top not to burn. I could show you all the bad patches of scale on me I caught trying, but you'd be here until morning. There's enough Galantine iron in me still to start a smithy.

"So that's how we lost the Scab and with it the war, plus good markets in the Baronies and south and east into the Inland Ocean and across. Of course it took some months for it to even register that we'd lost good and proper with the Assembly. They're down on dragons now. 'What good are they if they don't win us wars,' like it's the

dragons' fault that the Galantines outnumber us on the ground six or eight to one and have figured out how to disperse their camps and columns to make them safer from dragon attack. They've learned to go dark at night. See, unless you get lucky with weather and terrain, their scouts sound the dragon alarm, giving them some minutes to prepare, and they do a lot of training about what to do when the dragon alarm sounds. We'll have to adjust our tactics. They said the days of dragons were over when they started shooting meteors at us, but we adjusted for that, right? We need the brainy types, human and dragon, to figure out new ways to use us, is all. See, that's where we'll beat 'em in the end. Humans and dragons really working together.

"But they don't listen to me. I'm a big fighting dragon, not a thinker. That was the argument: Assembly's out of money, banks failing, Sammerdam Exchange lower than the Black Shaft bottom. Now's the time to take a gamble."

All the talking made Falberrwrath thirsty, and he drank his draught of wine and soon fell asleep. Ileth returned to her commission, begging scrap paper and old envelopes from Ottavia and using her Charge's desk, lamp, quills, and ink. She knew she should be tired, but she wasn't, and she couldn't account for it. Something was sparking in her mind; Falberrwrath's flinty talk had struck old steel in her imagination. She still didn't have any idea how to phrase things; a good deal of military terminology was opaque to her. She turned over the idea of hunting up that Vor Rapp as Quith had praised his mind, but decided that evening was no time to poke around the Guard barracks after last night.

She rose early, gathered her notes, and used them to assemble a report fulfilling her commission. Her solution presented endless difficulty. She didn't know how to phrase any of it so that it wouldn't sound like a hope tossed to the breeze, with no more design to it than some farmer's son balancing on a fence post and imagining himself a king of all the lands in his view.

But such plans had to exist. She could model her report on one, just as she used to model her correspondence to the Dun Troot servant

Falth on a book of letters. She read over the first part of her commission, hardly touching breakfast, as her mind worked. She wanted to be a dragoneer, so shouldn't she write it as a dragoneer? And where could a dragoneer's battle plan be found?

The archives. She'd just finished dressing—Fates, there was the problem of the sash again—and went out when Ottavia started waking the others to see Vii depart. She was leaving to assist Joai in her little kitchen.

"Joai's been trying to get someone younger to help her, why not me?" Vii spoke of her plans to add swirl to Joai's more routine menu. "Served midmorning and midafternoon, just like a Sammerdam swirl room."

Ileth would miss her. Vii had been her first real friend in the Dancers' Quarter.

Dun Klaff and two other wingmen, Heem Beck and Vor Rapp with his big ring, had volunteered to carry Vii's things by way of a peace settlement between the dancers and the Guards. Perhaps there was a secret romance; they'd all been novices in the same draft as Vii and she'd heard Santeel speaking to Vii, saying something about getting Dun Klaff to leave her alone. Speaking of whom, Santeel had helped Vii pack an old trunk of hers and warned the men to return it.

"We'll be prompt about it," Dun Klaff told Santeel. "Best be quick when a favor is owed."

Ileth chuckled to herself and waited for Santeel to put him in his place. She liked to cut men off at the knees and was good at it, but the Dun Troot spirit was elsewhere today. Santeel just looked at her feet.

Come to think of it, there was something odd about Santeel. Her overdress wasn't its usual immaculate self, and it showed signs of wear. Her stocking had a hole. The double duty of being an apprentice and dancer both must have been wearing her down.

Quite a contrast next to the trio of wingmen, also of Santeel's class if not quite so illustriously named, similar physically, identical in their shiny military dragonriding boots, each sporting odd haircuts that

made it look like a contest to see who could give the other the choppiest and most uneven cut with a razor. They had the newer, simpler style of riding rig favored by the men of their generation with money—shorter coats cut at the waist with a tight girdle built into the back for the safety tether and slightly puffed shoulders for insulation. It gave them an exaggerated triangle of a silhouette. Ileth thought longer coats looked more gentlemanly, but that was just what she was used to seeing on "her" trio of dragoneers.

If these three ended up replacing Dun Huss, Amrits, and the Borderlander, the Serpentine would be worse off for the switch.

"It's Ih-Ih-Ih-Ileth," Heem Beck said.

"Be quiet," Vor Rapp said, glancing at Ileth's scar.

"Traskeer's been riding a lot of the apprentices. Looking to shorten the roster and make things look good for the ledgermen," Vor Rapp said, turning his ring to his palm so it wouldn't get scratched as he carried Vii's trunk. "One of the boys in the Guard fell asleep on watch and says Traskeer's marked him in his index for elimination in the cut."

He'd obviously heard the same rumors traveling around the Serpentine.

Dun Klaff struck a pose, one leg straight out, his sword-hand elbow out resting behind his body while his left gestured at Ileth. "Should I make dragoneer, I believe I want a dancer as one of my wingmen. I want three wingmen, if they'll let me have three: a right good cook, someone with a physiker bent to keep a dragon sound, and a dancer. You might do, Ileth."

Ileth was tempted to ask who the other two would be, just to see if a fight would break out if he didn't name both Heem Beck and Vor Rapp.

"I am flattered, sir." He seemed to be counting unhatched chickens. Behind him, Vor Rapp rolled his eyes and edged away.

Vii made the rounds, saying her good-byes. She had rearranged her hairstyle to cover the small injury to her scalp.

"I look forward to trying your swirl," Vor Rapp said to Vii, as he and Heem Beck each took a handle of her trunk. "I've only had it once

in Sammerdam. The way things are going for me here, I may ask you for a job washing dishes."

"You're much improved since our swearing-in," Vii said, squeezing his hand. "Just one girl's opinion, but there it is."

"Can we get this over with, Rapp?" Heem Beck asked.

Dun Klaff, who seemed to be annoying Santeel by paying attention to Ileth, bowed. "Duty calls. Consult me with any difficulties in your apprenticeship, Ileth. I'd be happy to help."

Ileth bobbed mechanically in return.

Vii had a bundle over her shoulder. A scarf slipped out as Vii turned up the passage. Ileth picked it up and caught up to return it.

She overheard Vii talking to Dun Klaff: "You don't have to lay it on so thick with her. No money, and you're not her type. She has a stutter, she's not stupid." Ileth decided to return the scarf later. Instead, she took a tight, quick passage up to the Long Bridge and trotted to the archives.

Gowan told her Kess was sleeping. Something about his tone told her not to ask questions about why his Master was sleeping, so she asked him if there were such things as written records of battle plans, orders, things like that.

"Yes, hundreds; every time formal orders are written they end up here, if someone thought to preserve them, which isn't often enough," the apprentice said. "I must say, you look better with the pins out of your head. You're still pretty."

She smiled.

"You wouldn't have anything about . . . about f-fighting pirates in the North . . . in the North Bay? They told me it used to happen, before I was born."

It turned out the archive had its own smaller archive, in a series of catalogs. It was cleverly fashioned, a sort of book held together by bolts of steel like screws. You could open the screws and place a new sheet anywhere you liked. Gowan consulted one.

"We index things by year, subject, and location. Names of dragons and their dragoneers come up a lot, but we don't have that properly

indexed, just a rough one for the most famous ones because every now and then we get a biographer in here or a descendant who wishes to know more about a famous ancestor. Ah, here are the pages for campaigns in the north. Not much."

He showed Ileth the page. It had a few old pre-Republic entries about a war against the Wurm, a great empire in the north, now decrepit and somnolent. There were only three entries after the founding of the Vale Republic. A name caught her eye.

"Annis Heem Strath!" Ileth said.

The apprentice looked at the notation. "Yes, looks like she was up there. About nine years ago."

"I m-met her and her—and her dragon as a girl of seven." *Met* was not a big enough word for it. Annis Heem Strath was the dragoneer who had issued an invitation to her to join the Serpentine. How sincerely the invitation had been issued she wasn't equipped to know and now would never know.

"Would you like to see it? There's a notation that the report is confidential, but that just means none outside the Serpentine may view it without permission from one of the Masters."

Ileth felt a small thrill, knowing she could see "confidential" documents. She nodded.

Gowan found it quickly—he was apprenticed here for a reason—and she took it over to the well-lit, chairless reading table. Gowan was talking about the difficulties in maintaining and organizing documents, saying something about dust and mold. All Ileth had eyes for was the linen envelope and the document in Annis Heem Strath's own hand. She had lovely regular writing, and Ileth felt a new urgency in improving her own hand.

"Looks like a reconnaissance report," Gowan said, paging through it. "Seems she was sent up to see how feasible it would be to destroy those pirates. There's a rough plan and some estimates."

Ileth felt a chill run through her body. "Fates fates fates fates fates," she whispered. She remembered Agrath had a damaged wing from whatever they were doing up there. She'd met them in the early

morning, which probably meant they'd been flying all night. Ileth forced her brain through some of the math of flying speeds and what she knew about the size of the bay. Yes, it was possible.

"What was that?"

"N-nothing."

There were some aerial sketches of the coast of the bay and the straits leading out to the Inland Ocean, principal harbors, fortifications. She didn't know the Rari had fortifications.

Ileth read through it. She tripped over some military terminology and descriptions of defenses. She knew what a highpoon was, and a bombard, and she was pretty sure she'd heard Falberrwrath speak of the dangers of "wingchain." There was also some talk of the sorts of ships the pirates used, designed to be quick, handy, and easily filled and emptied of the men for boarding their prizes. There wasn't much talk of the prisoners taken, but Ileth knew from growing up in the Freesand the ransoms and losses of men if they were not paid. The men were made slaves and the ship either added to their own fleet, torn apart for salvage value, or sailed off to a port where buyers weren't too officious about a ship's history.

Annis Heem Strath noted that the Rari had no dragons, but they were sometimes visited by dragons affiliated with the Wurm. Gargoyles were mentioned, something Ileth had thought were mostly stories to frighten children into being home before dark. The report finished with an incident where Agrath had his wing pierced by a projectile fired from a fortress guarding the Rari harbor while on night reconnaissance.

"I've heard of gargoyles but thought they were just stories. They really exist?" she asked Gowan.

"We have an illuminated book in the natural science section with quite a few drawings of them. Torturing humans and even a dragon, if you can believe that. They were bleeding the dragon into great jeweled cups. They're tangled up with the history of the dragons somehow. I'm no expert, but I know our dragons despise them."

The Captain told stories about them, but she always assumed they

were tall tales like the hundred-limbed sea monsters that pulled apart ships or that island full of nothing but women who would sometimes take sailors to keep their race alive. When enough were impregnated, they'd kill the sailors. The Captain had an odd sensibility when it came to the sorts of bedtime stories to tell nine-year-old girls.

There was a suggested plan to destroy the Rari. According to Heem Strath, it would take between nine to eighteen dragons, with the attacks coming in waves, one to smash the fortress and scatter the aerial defenses, and following waves to destroy the pirate craft and finally their boatyards and docks. The aid of the Republic's warships would be helpful, but the Republic's fleet, such as it was, was harbored in Sammerdam and would have to be brought all the way around to the Inland Ocean, a difficult prospect that would require a diplomatic effort and heroics of navigation and supply. Heem Strath mentioned that the Governor was difficult where dragoneers were concerned, citing the expense.

Tight old Governor Raal. What a shining example—losing a silver to save a few figs.

"So this plan was just filed away. Never used?" Ileth asked.

Gowan shrugged.

Ileth kicked herself for asking such a stupid question. It obviously hadn't. There'd certainly been no campaign against the Rari in Ileth's lifetime; had there been you couldn't have stepped out of the Lodge without tripping over celebrants. She covered by asking for a definition of "darklighting," which Heem Strath mentioned as the most vital task of the first wave.

"Have to look that up myself," Gowan said, moving to the reference book wall.

This document solved Ileth's greatest problem in her commission, the suggestion of a solution. She could simply reference the Annis Heem Strath plan to suppress the pirates found in the archives and suggest a new reconnaissance to see if alterations needed to be taken. Perhaps the Rari had reinforced their steadings. But she doubted it. If anything, the pirates had grown more insolent in the intervening

years; they sometimes brought their overrigged vessels into sight of the shore of the Freesand, sending the fishermen hurrying back into port. They seemed very sure of themselves.

Gowan returned, saying he needed more time with the index to find out about darklighting.

"May I ask you a, well, a strange question, Ileth?"

Ileth thought it would be nice to go an hour entire with one of her fellow apprentices without odd requests. She looked up at him and nodded. He was at least a decade her senior. Having a friend in the archives had proved helpful already.

"The cut on your eye—looks much better with the pins out, hope that didn't hurt too much—I heard a curious story from that girl Quith saying someone is after you."

"Quith?"

"Well, she told it to me in confidence, but I think she meant confidence as in other people. As you were the subject of the discourse, I don't feel a need for secrecy. She has this idea that the Galantines want to eliminate you. She thinks there's a Galantine agent among the apprentices and one of them was supposed to cut your throat and make it look like an accident."

"Quith said this?"

"I know. Supposedly you uncovered something there and they have to eliminate you now."

Ileth laughed at that. "The-the only thing I learned in Galantine lands was cooking farina and nannying and how to attach a beer barrel to a dragon. Women there don't do much other than—other than have babies and sew clothing for them."

Quith read too many novels. Had Ileth inadvertently learned some great secret, they could have murdered her easily enough at the Baron's estate and made up a story about a pox. Though she wondered if the kindly, animal-fancying Baron would actually do it. It would have taken a direct order from the Galantine king himself, probably.

"Quith and her . . . dramatics. I've been back and forth across the Long Bridge by myself in the dark any number of times this week.

Now I'll be looking at the shadows, making sure there's no one lurking there to chuck me off."

"Oh, didn't mean to frighten you." Gowan gulped. "I was just . . . concerned for you. Forget it."

He started to make noises about needing to get back to his sorting and cataloging or Kess would be angry.

"One more thing, Ileth. Don't think I credit what Quith says, but what my Master said about a will is important. I don't mean to give the game away, but it's one of the little checks they have on apprentices here. It's a sign that you take your role seriously, that you are organized about those who will come after you."

"Like a test?"

"Well, it's not a survival or a physical exam or a jury defense or anything like that, more something that gives the Masters a sense of you."

She blew on her fingers again, and Gowan smiled. "No money for law."

"You don't need it. Just write down who you leave your property to, seal it, and mail it to yourself here at the Serpentine with *IN THE EVENT OF MY DEATH* written big and bold on the envelope near your name somewhere. It'll hold up as a will in any court you can name, our mails being under Republic law. There's a whole stack of them at the post-cage. Give it to the Post Commissioner, he's here twice a week or more."

Another silent, unannounced test of some unwritten rule. She wondered how many she'd passed, how many she'd failed, and what they counted for. Oh, to be a bird at the windowsill when the Masters met to discuss the apprentices!

Still, the mail idea would not be difficult. She had tax-paid letters, envelope, and paper all in one, from Falth; it would be easy to re-address one to herself and add the legend. Sealing it was easy; stubs of wax could even be found in the Dancers' Quarter, and her knuckles did for a family design. Ileth knew Vyenn's mail commissioner, from

writing letters updating Santeel Dun Troot's family about her progress. Which was a thought: perhaps good old Falth, Santeel's tutor or whatever he was, would allow her to draw enough coin from Santeel's account to pay for a sash. So far the "friendship of the Dun Troots" hadn't amounted to much; perhaps she could get a sash out of it.

She resolved to write a letter that day. "Who should I leave my music box to?" Ileth asked, as it was her only valuable possession, unless you counted the dragon's old books on mining and forestry and so on cataloged in the archives.

"If you don't have a relative, the Serpentine is the usual place. Your possessions will go to whoever needs it, income to the legacy account. The legacy account is vital. They use it to make up for shortfalls from the Republic. I know, I archive the counting-house records four times a year; they come like clockwork."

"I don't have an income."

"Oh, of course, well, maybe someday. Generous pension, huh?" He smiled at her, a little unsurely. Something about the Serpentine made all the boys awkward. Maybe it was the smell of dragons. Or the punishments Sifler told her about.

Gowan gathered up the report. "I need to put this back in the archive."

"I can refer to it again, if I need to?"

"Of course." He took a thin slip of paper and wrote down a number, then handed it to her. "This is a reference number, saves looking it up. Even Kess will fetch it for you if you've saved him looking up a reference. Just in case that grave opens for me that requires my own testament being read."

Ileth laughed with him at that. Judging from the thickness of the roof and the narrow, turned entrance, even if the Galantine dragons attacked and laid down fire, Gowan and the archive would survive.

Back outside, the height of the sun shocked her. Time was running out on her. She'd used up all of her morning.

She hurried to the gate and found Sifler coming on duty for one of

his four-hour shifts. He asked her how her commission was proceeding, which was decent of him.

"Well, I've made excellent progress, so I thought I'd engage in a bit of spycraft for you. You say it's a stationery store and bookshop, right?"

"Yes."

"Well, I'd like to go in and buy a book. I'm sure they'd talk a good deal to me, if I were a paying customer."

"That's a sound strategy."

"There's a weakness to the . . . to the strategy. I've no m-money."

"Master Caribet doesn't know that," Sifler said.

"Master?"

"Oh, he ran a school in town for a while. It failed."

"What is the young lady's n-name?"

"Eswit Caribet."

Ileth committed the details to memory. "Any advice f-from your military academy on running a . . . running a reconnaissance?"

"It has to be carried out by such elements that can move quickly and easily, and escape at need, because what they learn about isn't much good if it never makes it back. Unless you're carrying out a reconnaissance in force, then you need to—"

"I'm more the escape-quickly type," Ileth said, which was true enough. She'd crawled out of the attic vent at the Lodge, quitting the only home she'd ever known in the time it took to draw ten breaths.

Sifler gave her directions to the shop, in his usual precise style. Ileth was eager to meet this Eswit, just to see what sort of girl this odd little monkey fancied.

She jogged down to Vyenn. She needed the exercise as there hadn't been any dancing lately, and after the morning in the archives, time was running short. Using his directions, she found the shop on one of the side streets. It had a sign mounted above its big white-painted doors, though they had heavy ironwork, making the white paint look like someone's attempt to brighten up a prison.

Caribet's didn't look any more like a shop than a school. It was next

to an impressive-looking house and seemed like the sort of place a family might store a carriage or stable their horses. Some rooms above, with a flower box just over the bolted-on sign, probably served as the family residence.

Ileth peeked inside. There was a nice arrangement of writing paraphernalia up front, and a long counter with paper and so on displayed atop it. Books lined the wall. In the back there were a few desks piled with more books, save one that was cleared off that had an unhappy-looking boy clinking his heels together as they swung from his chair. The boy was reading aloud.

A man of considerable girth listened to the boy. He wore the black plainclothes of a schoolmaster, not as shabby as some of the teachers desperate enough to accept the Captain's wages and meals up in the Lodge, but his neckcloth was stained and yellowed.

He muttered to the boy and beckoned her in with a welcoming smile.

"May I be of service, young lady?"

"P-p-perhaps. Your shop was . . . was recommended to me."

He smiled, pleased at the news. She suspected the pleasure would last until he sniffed out that she was penniless.

Ileth realized one of the bookshelves in back by the student was an upended horse trough. It was actually a clever reuse of the thing; they'd installed wooden shelves. She heard a *creek-thump!* and a girl rose from behind the counter like an apparition. She had a delicate chin and expressive eyes, and was a little on the small side, like Ileth.

"Father, do you need me?" The girl looked at Ileth closely.

Ileth leaned and saw that she'd come up from the cellar through a trapdoor.

"Listen to Ger recite, please, Eswit." He turned back to Ileth and started asking questions about what sort of book she was looking for. Ileth cleared her throat and stammered out that she was trying to learn about strategy and tactics.

He stepped lightly for such a broad man to the first shelf in the store, behind the paper counter his daughter had just vacated. "Have

a brand-new one on that very subject, *Commentary on the Late Galantine War* by Heem Vollosh. It has a very good appendix with all the latest military terminology most lucidly explained. Six maps. Printed this very year, young lady, so it is absolutely up to date."

He showed her a rather plain-looking book. The title and author were handwritten on a plate pasted to the cover.

"How much is it?"

"It's selling in Sammerdam for seventy guildmarks, but happily this copy was a printer's proof, so I can let you have it for forty. It's the cover, you see; the seventy-guildmark one has leather and titling."

Ileth blanched. A hand on a fishing boat up in Freesand might see forty guildmarks over a summer if he had a good captain and the fish were findable.

"I haven't—haven't nearly so large a s-sum, sir." It was the truth.

Master Caribet sighed. "We can all sympathize. These are difficult times. I can let you read it here under my supervision, cost is two figs a book. Of course if you wish to borrow it to do so, I need a security the same as the purchase price, for obvious reasons . . ."

"Ah. W-well, I haven't time today. Perhaps another time."

The smile reduced a little. "Perhaps. I must warn you, if it sells I can do nothing for you."

Ileth thanked him, complimented him on his shop, and backed out the way she came in.

She'd made it to Broad Street and turned back up toward the Serpentine, walking at a hurried pace so she'd still have part of her afternoon in the Serpentine to work on her commission before Ottavia returned. She stepped around a cobbler who had taken some re-soling work outside, tapping away at shoes, and who reminded her that her Galantine boots needed attention, when she heard a call from behind.

"Miss, oh, miss!" a girl's voice called.

It was that Eswit. Ileth stopped and let her catch up, even moved toward her so the cobbler wouldn't overhear, not that he seemed interested in the doings of young ladies. She had a delicate handkerchief tightly clenched in her left fist.

Eswit was out of condition; the short run had her breathing heavily. The Captain would have put her to work carrying water while he timed her with a sandglass, had one of his girls gasped so after a short run.

"You are returning to the Serpentine Academy, yes?" Her face was almost as red as Sifler's.

"Of course," Ileth said.

"Would you deliver a note for me?"

"Possibly," Ileth said. "I cannot say for certain until you tell me more."

"There's a young man," Eswit said. "He comes into our shop. I've talked with him twice and I'd very much like to get a note to him without the bother of the mail, or me being seen walking up to the fortress. Any of the girls in town who do that, well, there is speculation. Vyenn is full of peeping eyes and ready tongues."

She leaned over to examine the cobbler behind Ileth. Ileth warmed to her. Sifler would be delighted.

"We can do each other a favor," she continued. "There's two figs in it for you, if you still want to look at that book." She showed what she'd been concealing in her palm, wrapped up by the lace. It was a fig, all right.

"Settled," Ileth said.

"On your oath you'll deliver it to him and no other?"

"Y-yes." Another commission. She accepted a note, extracted from the hidden recesses of Eswit's simple overdress. It was closed by a wax seal the size of a small plate; the girl had really let herself go with the sealing candle and ribbon, and the precious fig rode atop it like a dragoneer.

Eswit straightened up, as though a burden had been lifted from her shoulders.

"Whom shall I take it to?" Ileth asked, though she knew the answer.

"His name is Rapoto Vor Claymass, from Jotun. I don't suppose you know him?"

"A...a little," Ileth managed to say, through the sudden roar of surf in her ears. "How old are you, Eswit?"

"How do you know my name?"

Ileth thought fast. The surf in her ears faded. "Didn't your father call you that?"

"Oh. Yes. Well, I'm fifteen. So I'm old enough to be in society, and understand my heart when it guides me."

"What if I'm secretly in love with him t-too, Eswit? I wouldn't be the only girl in the Serpentine who has her eye on him."

"You are at the Academy. Courtship is forbidden. Beyond that, you've given me your word you'll deliver it and taken the fig."

"Thank you for the compliment, Eswit. Of course I will deliver your note."

Ileth stopped in the Kingfisher's, with its three white sashes in their different grades of quality, and found that her fig couldn't purchase any of them. Even good wool socks were more. She tried to buy on credit, but the man in the wig who worked the front clucked his tongue. "I can tell a girl on an allowance from one without. The laces on your boots are tied where they're broken and don't even match. If times were good I'd risk it, but there's a new batch of novices in and one's bound to make apprentice by winter."

There was nothing to do but return to the Serpentine. She rolled the fig in her sock for safekeeping.

She hurried up the long slope to the Serpentine, feeling weighted down by failure, and gave her password at the gate.

As it turned out, she didn't have to search for Vor Claymass at all. He was walking up and down before a line of male novices drawn up in the center of the plaza, a whistle dangling from his neck on a lanyard. They all wore heavy, wood-braced packs and were saying something about keeping close enough to touch during a night hike. Ileth recognized shelters and bracing poles, water bottles and camp cooking gear. Another apprentice, one from her group but not much known to her other than that she'd been told he was a soldier's son who grew up in the Scab, checked their packs from behind.

She had no idea of Vor Claymass's duties as a wingman these days.

She'd lost track of him while in Galantine lands, had never asked about him in the infrequent letters she sent.

Ileth wondered if she could call him away from his group for a moment.

More than one novice watched her approach with interest.

Rapoto smiled a genuine enough smile. "Good to see you, Ileth. You're looking well. Sorry about that fall with your eye. It looks much better."

"Thank you, Vor Claymass. May we s-speak privately, sir?"

He stiffened a little at the formality of his well-known Name.

"Take a break, cadets," he told the novices. "Don't take your packs off, I don't want to waste what's left of the day getting them straight again."

They sat down, a little wobbly under the burden of their load. The other apprentice took his place in front of them.

Ileth walked a small distance away.

"I have . . . I have a n-note for you." She held it out.

"I look forward to reading it, Ileth. Beautiful linen quality. I didn't know I was this grade of paper in your esteem." He smiled that diffident smile that used to make her innards do somersaults. He was a little taller, better looking if anything. He wore an air of command, and wore it well.

"It's not from m-me."

"Santeel knows good and well that tormenting me in this way—"

"Not S . . . not Santeel either."

"Now I'm really curious. Do they have you running messages?"

"Don't you recognize the hand? It's that girl from the bookstore in town, Eswit."

He looked as shocked as if she'd just slapped him. "How on earth . . . why didn't she just bring it to the gate?"

"She said Vyenn had too many peeping eyes and ready tongues."

The apprentice from the Scab, who must have had sharp ears, gave a loud chuckle.

"Enough of that," Vor Claymass said over his shoulder.

"It's not what you think. It's not the other thing you would think, either. Go down about four thinks and you'll be about right. In any case, I thank you, Ileth. I should get back to my duties, but if I may bother you a moment more: I'd like to hear of your experiences in Galantine lands when you have time. Perhaps when we are both off duty I can stand you a summer punch in Vyenn. Sharing a bowl would be a pleasant way to spend an off afternoon."

"It would feature in my . . . in my m-memoirs," Ileth said, and instantly regretted it. One of the curses of a stutter was even when you tried to say something in jest, it never arrived quickly enough to make it seem like your wits were in order.

Vor Claymass stiffened and put on that hard wingman-officer face. "If you'll excuse me, apprentice."

"Rapoto, I'm sorry. It's been a wing-over-and-tail-first of a day. I would like that punch, if it wouldn't break that little Eswit's heart. I did learn something of the Fencibles you might find useful if you ever fight them on dragonback. But I'm one servant with two masters these days, and neither's happy with me."

For some reason, quoting Traskeer made her angry at herself.

He turned up the corner of his mouth. "That's the Ileth I used to know. Well, the offer stands."

She fled, note delivered, fig earned, commission fulfilled. She managed to chop this mythic head while still new, before it could grow any more. Or so she hoped.

If she returned to the Dancers' Quarter Ottavia would either give her an assignment or set them to drills and fatigues. Dinner was being set up in the Great Hall and the first diners were going in, including Sifler in his Guard uniform.

She hurried to the archive, retrieved her commission report, and managed to get him as he filled a plate. Even though there were mutton chops, a favorite of the apprentices, Sifler had a simple meal of fish and piles of vegetables.

Ileth didn't want to wait in line, though her stomach growled in hunger as she smelled the food.

She intercepted him. "Spare a moment?" she asked.

"More than that, I don't go on duty again until the eighth hour after noon."

She led him away from the noisier tables to a smaller one on the other side of the fireplace and speaking pulpit, where they sat together.

"Aren't you hungry?"

"Not just yet. I wanted to talk to you. Eat up, don't m-m-mind me."

"Summer vegetables," Sifler said, raising a forkful and sniffing in appreciation. "Have to enjoy them while we can. It'll be pickled cabbage and musty potatoes soon enough."

"No mutton?"

"Too greasy. They say fish sharpens the mind anyway, and it looks like you've brought me some mind work."

Ileth nodded.

"We could do it at midnight, here. I'm relieved then."

"You'd lose s-sleep."

"So would you. You want your commission finished, I want to hear your reconnaissance."

The situation was almost funny. Each jealously guarding the little scraps of knowledge and ability, afraid that if they yielded first the other would cheat.

She offered him what she reckoned was her prettiest smile. "Could you look at what I have so far?"

He yielded. "Of course." He began to read. "Do you have a fair copy?"

"That is . . . that is the fair copy."

"We may need to spend more time on your hand than I thought." He dug into his fish, chewing thoughtfully as he read.

Ileth glanced around. A few of the other diners were stealing looks at them. Generally, the women grouped together; mixed tables usually had a dozen or more. It was odd to see two apprentices of the opposite sex, close together at one of the little wall tables the wingmen and dragoneers used. There was bound to be comment.

"Interesting problem you decided to examine. It's not exactly news; everyone's complaining about the decline in trade to the south and the Inland Ocean."

He read further. His eyebrows shot up; he stopped chewing and set down the paper. He took a deep breath and picked it up again, went back to eating and reading. Finally he set it down. His mouth worked, but he didn't say anything. Ileth found it amusing that for once her conversation partner had trouble finding words.

"You know, Ileth, when I praised your strategy yesterday, I think you took it a bit far. How old are you?"

"Sixteen, seventeen next spring."

"Sixteen. And you're suggesting a war. A war?"

"These are . . . these are pirates. D-do you declare war on p-pirates? I thought . . . I thought you just hunted them."

"The term I've heard is 'suppression,'" Sifler said. "Well, I suppose it's all theoretical anyway. Master Traskeer put you on a commission; let's give him one that'll set fire to his cursed index. Eighteen dragons up and victory in days. What a joke."

"It's what . . . it's Heem Strath's recommendation."

"The tactics have to support the strategy. At least she got that right; too often it gets reversed in the heat of things."

"I'm not sure of . . . of the di-difference."

"Had it pounded into my head that tactics are easy enough; tactics are what you do when the enemy is in front of you. You destroy them with whatever means you have. Strategy is the real art. Strategy is what you do when there's nothing obvious to do that will hurt the enemy, your overall plan."

"You should be a lecturer."

"And you're a quick student. Even with the aid of this Heem Strath's report, it's a remarkable document, Ileth. I like the lack of fancy language, the calls to republican politics, the history of the Vales. It's just short, clear sentences with verbs right out of the *Litanies*."

Ileth smiled. "That's how I learned to w-write. Copybooks with . . . copybooks with quotes from the *Litanies*."

"Others have done much worse with much more."

The praise warmed her. She patted his hand in gratitude, saw the thoughtful look in his eye, felt a sudden urge to ensure that he disliked her.

"S-Sifler, about that bookshop girl—"

"Yes?"

"She has—she has her heart elsewhere."

Sifler looked alarmed. "Who?"

Ileth didn't feel any need to keep it a secret; all she'd promised was that no one would know she sent Rapoto the note.

"Vor Claymass."

Sifler's face went blank. His lips twitched. For a moment she thought he might cry, but she decided he was just working his mouth as he thought.

"Our good lieutenant. All I did was mention her to him." He went silent for a moment. "Well, even better for me." He collected his utensils, put them on his plate.

"Better?"

"Rapoto will dally with her, if he hasn't already, her heart will be broken, and she'll need to pretend, publicly, that it's not. Most likely she'll be highly desirous of appearing in public with his equal. Why not me? We're both Names."

Ileth almost giggled at the idea that Sifler was in any way an equal to Rapoto Vor Claymass. "Good. I was worried you'd get into a duel or something with him."

"A duel? That's your game, Ileth, not mine."

"I don't know that it's my g-game." Sifler was nice to talk to. She hardly stuttered.

"It's what the Serpentine Guard talks of when your name comes up. You fought a duel with a man three times your size."

"I lost. Very nearly died—"

"You're certainly considered spirited. Heem Beck claims that your spirit is why he's so sure . . . never mind."

"Never mind what?"

"You don't want to know."

"I'm sure I don't," Ileth said, though she did want to hear how she was viewed in the Guard quarters. No doubt being caught kissing Rapoto in an unlit stable came up, with plenty of salacious embellishment to make the story fun to tell.

They arranged for him to make a fair copy of her commission after he was relieved at the gate. Ileth, with another head practically chopped off the beast, bolted her only food of the day, then went over to the Masters' Hall for paper, ink, and a fresh quill before the clerks went off duty, her heart in her throat the whole time, worried that Traskeer would see her still without a sash.

In her hurry to gather up the paper she dropped a sheet. It fluttered as it sailed off behind her, reminding her of something . . .

Inspired, she hurried to the Beehive. There she kept an eye out for dancers, lest she hear that Falberrwrath demanded her attention, and went to the flight cave. She peeked into it; it would be just her luck for a dragon to be about, tired and deciding that a dancer would be just the thing to relax him and settle him for sleep after a long flight. No dragons were there, just the humans who served them. The flight cave was shutting down for the evening; the apprentices there were hanging up equipment, lugging saddles to trees for storage, inspecting buckles and bracing lines and girths for signs of a sharp bit of scale cutting through, putting out some of the lamps and refilling oil in others. A dragoneer lounged at the mouth of the cave, his feet dangling into the summer air and the long drop to the Skylake below, smoking. He was shadowed but she thought it might be Dun Huss.

For once, she didn't want to speak to him. She found one of the older apprentices carrying an armful of tack. He looked familiar.

"Excuse me. Some time back I flew . . . I flew with some dragons into Galantine lands. You might have been working here then, I remember you."

"You're Ileth. You flew Vithleen on a mail run your first flight. There was a mix-up that day."

"Yes," she said.

"Here." He handed her an armful of leather traces. "It was oiling day. Help me."

They went to an anteroom filled with lines of leather hung from wooden pegs sticking out of the wall. He began checking their length and hanging them up according to some scheme, shorter ones at the bottom, longer at the top.

Ileth helped him finish his sorting and hanging, then spoke: "We had white streamers tied to the dragon wings, I remember."

"Yes. We do that for most Galantine trips. Even now that there's peace. If the diplomats have some great need of getting a message through quickly, it's still best to send the dragons with truce streamers."

"Exactly. Could I have one?"

"A truce streamer? May I ask why?"

"No."

"I like you, Ileth, so I'll give you one for exactly that answer. They're just scrap cloth anyway." He led her to a much darker chamber, where everything was cast about and not so neatly organized, but much of it was up on shelves, or in barrels or cases. He hunted around a trunk that reeked of camphor, extracted a long piece of cloth, another, a third. Finally a white one appeared. "This one's too new." He dug around a bit more and found a ragged, stained one. "Yeah, this is scrap; it would fall apart or get caught on scale and shred as soon as the dragon folded his wings. Not even long enough for a streamer, really. Yor'n now."

He passed it to her. Ileth stretched it out in her arms, admiring it like a wedding gown. "Ah! Perfect!"

"Perfect? Length of old, torn sailcloth?"

"But it's white."

"Not fit for much these days. I doubt it's even one from yor'n trip, if you were wanting a souvenir."

Ileth thanked him profusely, folded it, and wound it about her waist.

"Ahhh," the apprentice said. "That's the worst-looking sash I've ever seen in me life."

"But it . . . is a sash." He was right. It was ragged. She could fix it, somewhat, when she had time. Just not right now.

She made her long, careful trip across the bridge, wishing she had a glass so she could see how her sash looked with every step. There were all the mirrors in the Well, but she couldn't go there; Ottavia probably had the troupe doing drills and fatigues right now and she didn't want to be diverted. She intercepted one of the night grooms she knew, on his way to the Beehive, and begged him to pass word to Ottavia that she was on a commission from Traskeer and would return very late.

She worked with quill and ink in the Great Hall, hardly heard the midnight bell, and waited. She began to wonder if she'd been forgotten. She put her head down, just to rest for a moment, and the next thing she knew she was being shaken awake.

There were clattering sounds from the kitchen. "Fates, what time is it?"

"Not yet four. My relief was late," Sifler said. "I'm glad you're still here, but Ileth, I'm exhausted and I have the midmorning watch. I'll make a mess of it. Give it to me."

She passed him her version and some blank paper.

"I can pay you two figs."

"Keep it. When you have a bit of money to your name you can always give it to me. I'll do this just because. We'll work on your handwriting together another time."

She yawned in front of him. Terrible manners, the Matron over at the Manor would have a fit; you might as well have gas in public as yawn when a man spoke to you, but she couldn't help it. Sifler didn't seem to mind. "Thank you, sir," she said, by making amends.

"You shouldn't 'sir' me. Well, you should if I'm at my post with my hat on. But otherwise you're quite the sister I never had, Ileth."

"When . . . when might I expect the . . . expect the fair copy, brother?" She meant it to come out as a joke, it was a word strange to her tongue, given the Captain's Lodge, but it felt nice to say. *Brother.* She had to stop herself from saying it again.

"I come off watch at noon. I'll do it then."

They made arrangements to meet when he'd done up her fair copy.

She thanked him again and fled to the Beehive. As she looked at the clouds and the halo about the lighthouse atop the Beehive, a trick of the architecture projected a ring when the clouds were low and thick; she guessed that rain or a thick fog was on the way. The air felt heavy and her footsteps echoed oddly. In fact, she turned a few times on the Bridge Lane, certain that she heard someone following her. Her own joke about an assassin throwing her off the Long Bridge felt suddenly real.

There was some light, thanks to the lighthouse and the reflection from the clouds, about as much as a bright full moon. There was nothing about on the road, and now that she was almost to the gardens and the amphitheater there were no corners to duck around or alleys to dodge behind. And no assailants appeared. It could have been birds.

The only people she met on the road were a couple of novices up early and out the door of the Manor, hurrying to clean the Great Hall before breakfast. They bobbed at her sash and she nodded at them. They wore gloves to save their skin, but it looked to Ileth like the tattered gloves would soon give way and they'd have calluses like everyone else in the Serpentine.

A thought popped into her head like a struck match. She remembered something she'd been told. Was it by Galia, when asked about getting promoted? She thought so but couldn't be quite sure.

"Novices," she called after the girls.

They turned, probably expecting a dressing down from a tired apprentice who wanted to take it out on someone.

"It's your . . . it's your lucky day." She put the figs on her thumb, sent them spinning in their direction. Her aim was true, but her distance was bad, they sailed high. One of them had quick hands and snatched one out of the air; the other found the second coin after it fell. The girls examined their offering. Too bad it wouldn't buy them new gloves.

"You were my first," she said, giving a little bob, meaning the first formal recognition of her apprenticeship.

One of the girls made a face. Probably wealthy. What was a fig to her? Something your father gave you at the sweet shop after you wrote your name for the first time.

Still, your first obeisance was supposed to be lucky. She got two out of it. Did that negate it or bring her extra luck? She hoped the latter.

The Dancers' Quarter was quiet. Ileth passed through the curtain. She heard soft snores from behind the heavy decorative hanging rugs that sectioned off Ottavia's bedchamber. She dodged down the little triangular alley to the dancers' dormitory and fell into her rope bed clothed.

Shatha shook her awake. She heard the clatter of tea.

"Ottavia wants early drills," Shatha groaned. Ileth sympathized.

"You. Found a sash," Santeel said, yawning. She stressed the word *found*.

"I found a sash," Ileth agreed. "It'll be better once I've worked on it."

"You can't possibly make it worse. That must be a comfort." Santeel looked a fright. Ileth wondered if she'd slept at all. Maybe one of the dragons had kept her dancing until dawn.

They drank their tea quickly and went off to the great chamber, each carrying a small music box issued by Ottavia as they had no musician this morning. One of the female dragons stood in front of the mirrors with her dragoneer, that Garamoff whom Ileth had seen in Vyenn, pointing out where the grooms hadn't properly attended to her scale behind her legs, and the dragoneers apologized.

"It'll be taken care of today, Nephalia," Garamoff said, with the tone of a man reassuring a wife of many years.

Ottavia knew better than to interrupt a dragon inspecting the work of her groomers. After a few more minutes of complaints about the state of her teeth and claws, Nephalia jumped back up to the chamber above. Garamoff moved off to find the master groomer, muttering about his missed breakfast.

"The life of a Serpentine Dragoneer," Ottavia said, looking point-

edly at Garamoff's back as he moved off. "No one writes ballads about scraping droppings off their scales." Her stare switched to the end of the line that held Ileth and Santeel. "I would rather dance." She lifted a knee and gave an elegant little flutter-kick for emphasis.

The troupe lined up in their usual spots where they could see themselves in the mirrors and check their alignment, Ileth out on one wing next to Santeel. They left a gap where Vii usually stood. Ottavia put Fyth in Vii's old spot.

They alternated drills, where they rehearsed individual gestures and combinations, and fatigues, exercises that strengthened and gave endurance to the muscles. When Ileth first joined the dancers, she'd been told the drills were fatiguing and the fatigues made your muscles feel like they'd been drilled and drained, and it was as true today as it ever had been. She felt like a first-dayer again when they finally stretched their hot muscles and dabbed sweat out of their hair.

Santeel excused herself when they took a break for water at one of the trickles, running hard now as it was no doubt raining outside. "It's repair and maintenance, still," she said, when Shatha asked her what was on for today. "The next rotation can't come soon enough. I heard I was being passed up to the physiker, but who knows."

Ottavia didn't look any more bothered by Santeel's departure than she did Nephalia forcing a late start. She just ate a handful of nuts from the pouch she carried around and massaged her feet.

They talked a little afterward about routines. What dances they performed only mattered to a couple of the more artistically minded dragons; as long as they worked up a good sweat for the others, their duty was fulfilled. Ottavia's ideas of developing dragon dancing until it was considered just as respectable an art as painting or music mattered to them, not the dragons.

The drill-and-fatigue pattern continued through the morning. Finally, they stretched and broke for lunch.

Midday meals weren't a part of the culture of the Serpentine, but the dancers often took them because of the enormous energies expended in their drills. Ileth thought of that young physiker, Gift, and

his talk about the body just being a system to keep the muscles going. What would Santeel make of him, if she was rotated to the physikers?

"Ileth, your eye looks better," Ottavia said as they broke away. "Eating plenty of eggs? Eggs are the best thing to have if you don't want a scar."

Ileth nodded.

"I've been meaning to talk to you about your position with the dancers. I've given it some thought. Despite our being short with Vii gone, I think we will be all right. Caseen has submitted the names of no less than eight novices who want to be placed with the dancers—I'll actually have to choose! So if flying is your dream, I don't want to deny you that. I'll make the same sort of allowances for you that I do for Santeel."

Ileth was stunned quiet for a moment. "This means . . . means so much to me. Thank you, sira."

Ottavia patted her arm. "I hope you have the same energy as Santeel. Honestly, I don't know how she does it."

"I'll work as hard as I can for you and the troupe, whenever I'm not in the apprenticeship rotations."

"Of course. I'll also give you the same warning I gave her: if our duties to the dragons suffer in any way, you'll have to leave the troupe. The dragons must be attended."

Anything Santeel could do, she could. She put the thought of failure out of her mind. "Thank you for being fair with me."

"What may seem fair now may turn cruel. Suppose you fail in your duties to the dragons and the troupe and I give your bed to another girl? Where will you make your bed? Santeel, her Name and money give her options. She could even take lodgings in town and walk to the Serpentine each day, like some of our wealthy dragoneers."

Ileth hadn't considered that. She couldn't go back to the Manor. She supposed she could throw herself on the Matron's mercy and play the part of the contrite wayward girl. But to go back to the Manor with its sermons and chore wall and being elbow-to-elbow with dozens of other girls every moment, after the freedom of the Quarter . . .

"What I've taken too many words to say is that you'll be dancing on the proverbial knife edge, Ileth."

After lunch, Falberrwrath called for a dancer. Ileth volunteered. She found him listless and distracted. He said the eggs were about to hatch and it had all the dragons tense but he especially felt it, them being of his line. She set to work, but after two dances, the big red veteran dismissed her. "It's not helping and I've resolved to be more considerate to you humans. Go and give Ottavia my thanks," he rumbled, turning on his side and sighing. He rumbled something in Drakine, but the only word Ileth understood was *war*.

Back in the Dancers' Quarter, they had a visitor. She found Sifler with three of the troupe waiting on him as he sipped tea, precariously perched on two pillows.

For someone who confessed absolutely no experience with women, he seemed to be making himself agreeable. Fyth was tut-tutting over his officer's cap, brushing the fur felt and bemoaning the state of the liner, and Preen was pouring him tea. "A friend of my mother's had that kind of double-wall tureen, so convenient for parties, but there wasn't a heating element. The tea stays warm all day with nothing but a little charcoal, you say?"

Ileth thought of breaking it to him that any man Ottavia admitted to the Dancers' Quarter would get this sort of fete, but decided his confidence would benefit from the attention as much as his hat.

Sifler set down his tea and rose. "Ah, Ileth, they were trying to dissuade me from hunting you down while you were dancing."

"We didn't have to try that hard," Fyth said.

She explained that Falberrwrath was in a mood and had dismissed her.

"Still sorry I missed it. I think the last time I saw you dance was the Feast of Follies. The night of the fire."

She must have looked pained. He changed the subject. "I have your fair copy," he said, turning and sending his teacup to the floor. Preen managed to deftly save the cup but not the tea. Sifler apologized and dabbed at the spill with the end of his sash.

The dancers exchanged amused looks. "Do you want to read it over? I could make a quick correction if necessary; I see there is ink and quills on your esteemed Charge's desk."

Ileth took him off to one end of the common room. Though no one had expressly told her so, she had a feeling men were not allowed into the alley where the dancers slept.

He couldn't resist a glance down the short alley with the tiled washroom at the end. "So these used to be some kind of monastic chambers? I'm sure the monks weren't as fond of pillows, tapestries, and hung veils. All the music boxes are fascinating."

"We couldn't get by without them. There aren't enough musicians with free time."

He handed her the sheets.

The handwriting was beautiful, line after line filling the page as evenly as well-laid bricks. He'd changed a word here and there, and, embarrassingly, fixed a good deal of spelling. Ileth knew more words than she knew how to spell.

She must have winced as she read.

"Something wrong?"

"No. I'm such a terrible speller."

"It's not universal. There's a tradition to how things look in matters pertaining to the Republic. I used that. The Philosophical Commission keeps trying to raise money to do an authoritative reference, the Basis, they call it, but it doesn't have enough subscribers yet."

He fell silent as Ileth continued reading. She didn't know what the Philosophical Commission was and finishing the document was a good way to cover that up, though why she wanted to hide further examples of her ignorance from an ungainly boy she didn't want to think about at the moment.

"It's lovely. I can't . . . I can't thank you enough."

"They'll be serving dinner soon. Shall I walk you over? To give it to Traskeer, I mean, not eat together again."

"I need a moment to change. I don't want to go outside in a damp sheath."

Sifler turned that endearing shade of red. "The rain will do that for you. It's still coming down."

She wanted a fresh sheath in any case, so she changed while he put the paper back in his map case so it wouldn't be wetted. She admired it when she returned.

"Are you s-supposed to be using S-Serpentine G-Guard equipment for your copy-copywork?" she asked, once they were safely out of the Dancers' Quarter and the troupe had thanked him for his visit.

"You're on a commission, given by a Master. I'm obliged to aid you if I can. You know that. I see you found a sash."

"Do you think he'll hate it?"

"It looks a bit desperate. I don't know him well enough to say. Selgernon was more easygoing, but even he would probably ask, *Do you think your attire is a credit to the Serpentine?*"

"I'm going to fix it up."

"The knot is beautiful. What is that?"

"It's called a . . . called a good-luck loop. Sometimes you add one to your lobster trap or your netting if you've had a bad season."

They hurried out of the Beehive and into the rain.

He parted with her in the Masters' Hall, entering so he could give her the papers from the map case, once they verified that Traskeer was in.

"Meeting of Masters, in the old Dragoneers' Hall. You may be here a bit," the page said. Ileth watched a novice, this one obviously one of the Matron's girls new to physical labor, straighten from where she polished the floor to rub her back. Ileth gave her an encouraging smile.

Sifler wished her luck and departed to his dinner.

She waited in the small, well-lit writing room, studying the fair copy. She'd hate to be caught not knowing a term Sifler had inserted in the interest of clarity, but if anything he'd trimmed out a few of the military phrases she'd copied from the Heem Strath report she'd named and referenced repeatedly as being a plan for the proposed campaign. She'd added her own ideas for returning the men of the

Freesand. The only words that she couldn't say were hers came at the end, when he added an additional reference to the Heem Strath report in sort of a brief summation. Maybe you were supposed to say the same thing two or three times according to whatever style and rules of an official commission report existed.

The door to the writing room opened. "They're back," the page said.

Since the inevitable was going to happen, best not worry about it. Ileth tested her hands to make sure they weren't trembling and went up.

The Masters Traskeer and Caseen walked the hallway at baby-crawl speed, heads together in conversation, faces and shoes still wet from the rain, but they must have taken the precaution of putting on their oilskins. Ileth retreated to the shadows in the hallway by Traskeer's office and let them talk.

"Cuts will be endured. It'll roll down, as always. The poor apprentices and novices," Caseen said. "Handed-down clothes and old shoes and one less meal of meat."

"Will the dragons stand for it, is what I want to know. We may lose some," Traskeer said. "Perhaps that's the plan."

"If it is a plan, it's the work of a cretin."

Ileth was trying to hear more when a throat-clearing interrupted her.

Another apprentice, the shaggy-haired boy she'd seen cleaning the plaza, waited on the bench. He must be from the draft that came in while she was in Galantine lands.

"I'm Ileth," she said. She saw he too had a sheet of paper. He kept folding and refolding it.

"Bellerin," he replied. "Sixty-seven draft."

"Si-sixty-six," she said.

"He's making me write up on the Big Ti—on the Beehive. Find if something needed fixing."

"Same. Vyenn."

They could go no further on the conversation, as Traskeer squelched down the hall in his wet shoes.

"Just a moment," he said to them as they rose to acknowledge the Master's arrival. Ileth bobbed, and Bellerin gave a short bow.

He called them in. His office was cool and stuffy and still just as bare as the last time. He sat in his chair and it creaked.

"Well?"

Bellerin and Ileth looked at each other, then placed their commissions on his desk.

Ileth, being senior, said, "Our com-commissions."

"At last, Bellerin," he said, taking the boy's sheet. He glanced at the paper. "Improve your hand, apprentice. This won't do for a formal report. I'll have Kess at the archives saying he can't read it to categorize. And do something about your hair. You look like a shepherd boy. Dismissed."

Bellerin ducked out. The Master looked at Ileth's paper, turning up the pages.

"That was quick work, Ileth."

"I'm trying to catch up with the rest of my draft."

"Creditable."

He set her commission aside without another glance and rubbed at the bridge of his nose, eyes closed. He opened them again, and his gaze fell on her waistline. "Dooms, what happened to your sash?"

"I'm s-sorry, sir, I realize it's in a . . . in a state. I only just found the cloth. I shall improve it."

"If you're not resourceful enough to come up with a decent sash, I'm not sure what to do about you."

"As I said, I can . . . I can im-improve it."

"What is it? Bandages?"

"A s-s-signal s-streamer from a dragon's wing."

"Remove it. Let me examine it."

Ileth stood still, too shocked to move.

"I'm not asking you to disrobe. Your sash, please."

Ileth fumbled with the knot, then handed it to him.

"It's a rag. Is that all the pride you have in your position as an apprentice to the Serpentine Academy? Walk around in a rag?"

In an instant she was eight again, in the Captain's Lodge, getting another one of his dressing downs. Though in some ways this was better; her sash was a genuine disgrace. The Captain just turned ferocious on his charges the way some men would kick a dog. If you looked at your shoes, he cursed you and told you to look at him when he was speaking. Another time, if you were looking at him as he spoke, he cursed you and ordered you to keep your eyes averted. Whatever you did he could find fault.

He touched it to his lamp and squelched over to the stove, where he discovered that the wet sash had failed to properly ignite. He went back to the lamp, found a dry length, saw that it was lit, and tossed it into the stove.

"Sir!" Ileth managed. "I could have m-made something of that."

"Be quiet. You're out of uniform, Ileth. I'll make a note in your index file. You're off to a poor start as an apprentice. I was perhaps swayed too much by the good accounts of others when we first met. Now that I've observed you, I'm surprised they trusted you with a trip to the Baronies." He searched her face. Did he expect tears? He wouldn't get them; girls from the Captain's Lodge did their crying in private. She took a hot little pleasure in denying them to him.

"Dumb insolence, eh?"

"May I retrieve my—"

"No. You're dismissed."

"May I . . . may I ask about where I'm to start apprenticing, sir?"

"Once you present yourself to me properly dressed, I'll assign you to a lot. Not until then."

She slipped out as quietly as possible. Well, her commission was done.

Maybe she should stay with the dancers. Ottavia was demanding but not cruel. She could have made something of the sash. So much for the luck knot.

The walk back in the rain gave her time to think.

It was full dark by the time she returned to the Beehive. The rain had tapered off into puddles and dripping sounds. She walked down

to the Dancers' Quarter, took a little hand lamp such as the dancers used to accompany themselves through the darker stretches of the narrow human tunnels in the Beehive, made sure it was out of oil, and went to the mirror well in the Rotunda. From there it was a short trip to the flight cave.

No dragons were being readied; only a couple of apprentices were cleaning saddles and securing harnesses.

"I need lamp oil. May I draw some?" she asked.

One of the cleaners stood, went to the offices for the keys to the storeroom, and handed them to her. They were used to supplying needs for the dancers, as they practiced nearby. The flight cave always had plenty of lamp oil; you wanted to be able to see what you were doing when rigging a saddle to a dragon.

Ileth took the key and opened the lock of the storeroom. She went in, filled her lamp, checked the passage again, and lit it, and then explored further into the recesses where she'd been that morning. Nothing had been altered, and she found another white streamer right away. It was new from the loom, wound tight on a roll.

Might as well be hanged for gold, she thought, taking the best one she could find. She wrapped it around her waist several times—it was plenty long—feeling the new material pass through her fingers, already planning how she'd fold it thrice before sewing it.

Well, no going back now. She glanced out in the passage, then jangled the keys as she returned them. One of the apprentices waved.

She'd pilfered from the Serpentine. She'd done that. Well, she'd stolen before.

Back in the Dancers' Quarter, she sat at Ottavia's worktable with needle and thread, which was always kept handy given the stress the dancers put on their clothing. She trimmed the sash neatly, carefully trimmed the ends to an ideal length, then folded the sash so it was about the width of a man's palm. It took her until well past midnight, she guessed; the bells didn't penetrate this deep into the Beehive.

She tried it on, knotted it, and used Ottavia's small hand mirror to examine herself top to bottom. She found a comb, tucked it in her

overdress, and walked back to the up end of the Serpentine. The rain was coming down heavier. Fall had arrived early, it seemed.

The Masters' Hall was all but lightless. A single night attendant paced the lower floor and startled as she banged through the door, dripping.

"Ileth reporting to Master Traskeer," she said, not bothering to wait for a reply.

Upstairs, she stood in front of her reflection in one of the dark hallway windows to tame her wet hair. She judged herself presentable.

She pounded on his door as though to wake him to escape a fire. "Master Traskeer!" She gave it a moment, then pounded again.

The door was flung open. Traskeer was in nightclothes, holding a night-candle. "Ileth!"

"R-reporting for my assignment, sir." Water dripped off everything drippable. Traskeer stepped away from her, perhaps fearful of the snarl she suspected she displayed.

"At this hour?" He didn't invite her into his office.

"Properly dressed. As you . . . as you s-see."

"You made me dream of gravestones toppling with your pounding, Ileth."

Ileth couldn't see how she needed to apologize for dream-gravestones.

"My assignment?"

"You want an assignment at this hour? Very well. Go out and run the walls until you fall and break your neck. That's your assignment."

"You'll notice I have my sash, sir."

He blinked the sleep out of his eyes and brought the candle forward. "So you do. So you do indeed. Simple, I see you went with something to go under a sword-belt rather than the wide ones currently in fashion with some of the young ladies. Quick work, considering you only left my office this evening. Where did you get it?"

"I stole it out of the flight-caves stores, sir."

"You *stole* material that might be needed to identify our dragons? For your own use?" But he said it quietly.

"Yes, sir."

He snorted.

"Well, that is a terrible mark against you. I shall have you in front of an honor court."

Ileth was wondering how else she could provoke him, short of violence, when Traskeer yawned in an exaggerated fashion.

"And yet sometimes, Ileth, just sometimes, when I'm woken at night and go right back to sleep again, I forget everything that transpired, except for sort of vague impressions. Like gravestones toppling. Can't remember what was written on them now. Hope it wasn't my name. That's supposed to be a bad omen. I want to get back into my bed before it goes cold. Hopefully all I'll remember in the morning is that you finally showed up with a proper sash. Dismissed."

"Thank you, sir."

He half closed the door, then turned a baleful eye toward her.

"Enjoy your run. I'll send someone to retrieve your body."

PART TWO

PREPARATION

"The spider designs for the fly, but must be
prepared for the broom."

—A VALE PROVERB

5

It was often said that the looms of the Serpentine Academy work slowly but produce the finest material in the Vales. Ileth had heard the expression a few times and had always taken it literally, assuming there was a little workshop somewhere that wove material for the dragoneer dress uniforms.

It turned out to be a metaphor, patiently explained to her by Santeel Dun Troot as Ileth waited for her formal apprenticeship to start.

What it really meant was that the Serpentine's traditions worked in their own way, making sure no novice rose to apprentice without showing some quality, and that the apprentices were worked, warp and woof, until they became wingmen practically unrecognizable to anyone who'd known them as sheepish novices coming through the door.

They had to learn how to maintain themselves and their equipment, how to cooperate with each other and pass information up and orders down the hierarchy of command, and most importantly of all, the art of keeping a dragon in fighting trim.

Ileth and nearly three hundred other junior apprentices found themselves grouped into drafts according to the year they entered. These were then broken down into manageable "lots" of about thirty for general training and "crews" of up to a dozen for more specialized duty. (Ileth, as the draft of '66 had been already rotated through much

of their first-year training, found herself in a "lot" with the draft of '67 novices who'd already been promoted to apprentice along with a few others of her class who'd been late to be appointed apprentice for one reason or another.)

Her "cross lot," as these mixes were referred to, had twenty-two members, fifteen from the draft of '67.

One of the first things they did with a new lot of apprentices was get them on a dragon and in the air. Ileth found herself in the unaccustomed position of being the most flight-experienced apprentice, and did what she could to help the others along. They always gave a very easy first flight (which had any number of crude names attached) on a placid dragon in the mood for a few leisurely turns above the Skylake at a modest altitude. Any overconfidence brought on by the first easy flight was tested quickly with more demanding trips to the limit of human and dragon altitude and aggressive maneuvers designed to shake up the unfit. A few had unsound teeth, or fainted whenever they were in the air, or had constant dizzy spells and nausea from the motion, or grew so panicked that they were useless to themselves and the dragon. They were found other duties. Joai, who ran a little kitchen and nursed the slight injuries that happened throughout a typical day, was one of these. Ileth took a few more "introduction flights" while their lot was filled up by bright new novices from the draft of '67. Nobody in her lot decided to become a groundling for failure of nerve or physical soundness, though about half returned from one of their test flights with their breakfasts splattered across their flight coats and cloaks.

Their "introductory" flights were on an energetic young dragon Ileth knew named Aurue. He'd been born scaleless, giving him a dull gray color and making his lighter underside look sickly as there was no bright scale to contrast against it. But because of his youth he was easy to mount, he could fly longer without much tiring, and she believed him the fastest and most nimble of wing in the Serpentine complement. He was capable of speeds, both on the flat and in turns, that no other dragon of the Serpentine could match. If you could survive Aurue, you could handle anything.

Aurue took particular pleasure in swoops at terrifying speed beneath the Long Bridge. He built up enough speed so that at the peak of the rise, the feeling of weightlessness ended with the splatters and stains Ileth had seen. Ileth's stomach didn't so much as gurgle. She loved the sensation of clinging to a dragon's neck as it spun and swooped and dived and rose.

"Does nothing frighten you?" Aurue asked as they landed lightly back in the flight cave. Landing there instead of on open ground was considered something of a stunt, but Ileth was game for anything Aurue threw at her.

"Not when I'm in the air," she said. When she was little, the Captain had sometimes liked to take his charges out on the bay in a one-mast sailboat. It could be a very lively ride in rough seas, and Ileth had delighted in clinging to the masthead. Dragoneering was even better; sometimes you were upside down.

It was fascinating to watch a dragon's head in these evolutions. It stayed as fixed as a star on the horizon. Aurue's body would gyrate out of an inversion while his head remained dead level, a fixed point in a whirl of earth, horizon, and cloud.

Later, as she unsaddled him—she was the last flight of the day, the flight cave was emptying—he grumbled about pressure being brought on him to choose a dragoneer. "I can hardly tell one human from another. I'm always grateful when one of you is unusually dark or pale or tall or short; I have a chance of remembering their name. How am I supposed to choose one out of the lot of you?"

"I thought the Masters presented one," Ileth said.

"They give names. What can I do with names? If I like a groom, they tell me: No! Not suitable. Frustrating."

"I'm sorry," Ileth said. "I thought you'd have wingmen lining up to get to know you."

"They come. They talk. And talk. And talk. I do not like it. Either the listening or the speaking."

Ileth could appreciate that.

She took off his harness and saddle and hung them up. "I sympathize

with you on listening all the time. Your Montangyan is excellent. It flows."

"Perhaps. I—to speak honest, humans frighten me."

"You don't seem frightened of me."

"I like your smell. The others are right, you are one of those humans who love dragons. Never tense with the prey-smell, unless you have blood flowing."

Ileth ignored that by wiping off the saddle. Dragons didn't sweat, as far as she could tell, but their riders did.

Aurue decided to change the subject. "Vithleen's eggs are tapping now. Did you hear?"

"No!"

"Heard for myself this morning."

Ileth nodded. Dragons didn't always appreciate a smile. "They say once they hatch there will be a special feast."

Aurue's tongue flicked out, testing the air. "The dragon shelf-chat passed the same news, so it must be true."

Ileth had seen a herd of cattle penned up near the gardens. She thought it might be for the Feast of Follies, which held unhappy memories for her. She'd volunteered to miss it and be on duty to dance or assist the grooms and feeders should they need it, giving others a chance to dress up and celebrate.

Aurue continued: "As you are a human who can be trusted to help, I wanted to ask your advice."

"My advice?"

"To choose a dragoneer. I'm not a judge of humans. I don't know a good one from a bad one. I trust you to make a sensible choice. Taresscon will not let me have peace until I name one."

It made Ileth oddly pleased to know that sometimes the dragons had difficulties with their superiors too.

"I'll do . . . do my best," Ileth said. "But you'd be . . . you'd be b-better off a-asking one of the Masters, or Hael Dun Huss. He's who I'd go to."

"I don't know him well. I must have a dragoneer. Taresscon wants good politics with the humans."

Ileth had decided to play politics herself lately. She'd spent time doing everyone's washing and volunteering to dance as often as possible, as her apprentice lot was still idling, getting a little more experience in the air as they waited for a Master to be named.

Vithleen's eggs hatched the very day Ileth spoke to Aurue, two males and one female, a red and a gold, with the female the usual green. Unfortunately one of the handlers working with Vithleen failed to get the hatched male away from the other as he came out of his egg and the red was injured. Newly hatched males would fight until there was only one survivor, but among certain dragon societies, the Serpentine being one of them, the males were separated at birth until they could be trusted not to tear each other to bits.

Everyone talked of a celebratory feast, paid for and put on by the dragons and in dragon style—great troughs of food outdoors, in other words—and there was general curiosity, as the dragons hadn't sponsored a feast since before the late Galantine War.

Ottavia was anxious that the dancers might be expected to do something above and beyond in honor of the occasion and asked Ileth, who was handing out favors and running errands, to go to the Charge's tower and ask. Ileth thought it would be a good opportunity to seek help on the matter of Aurue's odd request about helping select a dragoneer.

She'd been to the Charge's tower before. The Old Tower dated to the earliest days of humans in the Vales—and looked it; it was one of the barest and least comfortable constructs in the Serpentine. The Charge had been restoring its condition in his rare gaps of free time.

Unlike the other Masters, Charge Roguss Heem Deklamp didn't have an apprentice to help him with his duties; he had two full wingmen, one male, one female, both of long service, not that different in age from the Charge himself.

"He's engaged, Ileth. A storm that's been long on our horizon is

here at last," Wingman Dogloss said in the outer sitting room. She'd been formally introduced to him, but they'd never spoken privately. He'd joined the dragoneers unusually late in life, after a disappointment or something, she'd heard from Quith. He had dashing good looks accentuated by a beard with two white streaks going down from the corners of his mouth (Santeel told her that there was some art to it; the style was popular in Sammerdam at the moment with men who wished to appear distinguished) and a commanding presence. She'd heard stories that when Roguss Heem Deklamp was announced at assemblies in Sammerdam or Asposis, Dogloss was frequently taken to be the Master in Charge, as the actual figure was short, dark, owlish, and potbellied, and while he certainly possessed a certain amount of appeal when speaking, he wasn't the sort of commanding, broad-shouldered dragoneer you met in novels.

"Shall I—shall I come back?"

Dogloss thought it over. "Under other circumstances, I'd say yes," he said, quietly. "But Commissioner-General Navarr has the wind and altitude on us. I'd like to show him that the whole Serpentine doesn't freeze up just because he strides through the gate in all his majesty. Maybe you coming out of the sun would do just that."

Ileth knew the name and title. He'd overseen and served as star juror in the jury that had examined the poisoning of Vithleen and the theft of the eggs. She remembered the frustrated looks of the other jurors, but Commissioner-General Navarr had urged her to take all the time she needed to properly form her answers to the jury's questions. She didn't know much of him, though Dun Huss's wingman, Preece, who'd accompanied her to her questioning, said he was part of a faction that thought the dragons an expense that didn't merit the enormous costs that went into their upkeep and support.

Ileth wished she'd visited at a different hour. She'd rather dance until her toes bled than have to stand in her patched overdress and broken-laced boots in front of great men. Up in the Freesand, a commissioner of the Republic poking around was considered a bad

omen; she could only imagine the power a Commissioner-General wielded.

Aurue had asked her if anything frightened her earlier that day, and great Names frightened her more than barking gate-hounds. "I think . . . I think I'll c-come back later."

"No, now is best," Dogloss said. He rapped hard on the door to Heem Deklamp's office. Ileth hurriedly checked her novice pin and her apprentice sash. She'd done both just before arriving at the tower but couldn't help repeating the examination.

"Sir, I have an apprentice here, it's urgent," Dogloss said in answer to a query from within.

"Enter."

She followed him and froze two steps in.

Ileth, in her shepherd days in the hills above the Freesand, had once sought shelter from a sudden cold wind and rain in a half-ruined barn. The part under the still-intact roof was filled with crows. She could still remember all the black backs as they rose.

It was much the same in Heem Deklamp's office. This time she didn't shriek, as she had with the crows.

A throng of officials, all in the plain black attire of the Republic, stood, sat, or leaned about the office, with Heem Deklamp sitting casually at the edge of his desk with his other wingman behind. Ileth had heard of her but never met her, as she was almost always visiting posts for Heem Deklamp. She was a tiny woman, one of nature's alterations to the usual human pattern. At the moment she was seated in Deklamp's chair with paper and fountain pen in front of her, making notes.

Ileth bobbed, slowly and deeply—as she would have if she'd been invited in to Heem Deklamp's office, never mind the rest of the officials, and the Republic's commissioners, all seven of them plus Commissioner-General Navarr.

He was as she remembered. Taller than most, with a flat, stern face that had only a sharp nose breaking the plane, and the fullest head of

white hair she'd ever seen, of a uniform color and length swept back and neatly cut off at the collar like a tailored cape. He wore a polished silver gorget on a heavy chain below the white collar of his shirt. It caught the eye, set against the plain republican black.

Deklamp checked his marvelous pocket timepiece. "It is opportune, perhaps, that we now suspend the discussion for a meal. They should have dinner available at the Visitors' House by the time you return."

The assembled commissioners looked to their leader. "Yes, perhaps we can return to the outstanding questions tomorrow with renewed spirits," Navarr said. His was a pleasing voice. It carried as though he was used to speaking to audiences.

He glanced at Ileth, then gave her a second look, sort of an appraising air.

"Apprentice, I believe we've met," Navarr said. He stepped, or rather loomed, before her. She found herself staring at the silver gorget: it had a sort of curved lip that went up as if to catch crumbs fallen from his chin. Lettering and scrollwork had been beautifully engraved on it, but most of it was too tiny for her to make out, though it did have the year 2902 in the center, the year of the Republic's founding.

She bobbed again, more quickly. "Yes, Com-Commissioner-General."

"You went after the eggs, recovered them from the Skylake. I remember your testimony."

One of the Commissioner-General's associates gave a wry smile at another.

"Yes, sir."

"Your experiences in Galantine lands were useful. I am happy to know you are still here." Navarr turned to Deklamp. "Charge Deklamp, we will talk more when we've restored our tempers with food."

Dogloss hurried to get the door and the assembly formed up to follow the Commissioner-General out. There appeared to be some protocol about it, though as far as she could tell from their clothes, nothing much distinguished them except varying heights. Even their

faces were identically shaven clean and without sideburns. The first one after the Commissioner-General did have a silver chain about his neck for his half cloak, but no gorget.

"Excellent point about the purchase of cattle," one of the retinue at the back end of the file said to another. The man in front of them turned and hushed them.

Deklamp looked at the smaller of his two wingmen. "Make sure they are properly attended." The wingman's eyes narrowed just a trifle. "Oh, Serena, have you been introduced to Ileth? Ileth went with Galia to Galantine lands to care for Fespanarax, forgotten be his name. Only Ileth came back, sadly."

"I'm somewhat acquainted with the matter," Serena said. She stared at Ileth, nodded. "Good to meet you at last, Ileth. Excuse me."

She left, stepping quick, with a slight rolling gait.

The Master in Charge surveyed the room and locked his face on Ileth in that owlish fashion of his. Maybe Serena stared so in imitation of him. "Don't mind her, Ileth, it's been a tiring morning. You've never come to my office without being summoned. It must be important. How may I help?"

When he spoke thus, Ileth felt the devotion many others had admitted.

Ileth asked about the feast first, that being the easier subject. "I doubt the dancers will be called on. The exact words from the Beehive were 'Let every human rejoice and eat with us, and spare everyone from their duties you possibly can.'"

Ottavia would be relieved.

"There's one more matter. I'm not sure of the rights and wrongs and procedures for the whole thing, but it's the . . . it's the dragon Aurue. We are f-friends. He has asked . . ."

It took a little time for it all to come out. The dragon's unusual request, her wanting to find the best possible match for him.

Deklamp and Dogloss exchanged looks. "So he is staying. Good news."

"The better news is he wants a dragoneer," Deklamp said. "Ileth, you're my star's daughter* today."

"Then you . . . then you will advise me? Or him?"

"Gladly. Aurue won't ever be a famous battle dragon with *laudii* all over his wings, but he has gifts that compensate his lack of scale. Storms and thunder, we need him, scale or no. This comes at a good time for us."

"I am . . . I am happy to hear s-so," Ileth said. "May I a-a-ask h-how?"

"Oh, it's politics and favors being offered and paid. Affairs of the Assembly. Nothing for you to worry about. I'll consult with the Masters about your matter once I've concluded this business with the Commissioner-General. Odd way to go about it. Usually the dragon has someone in mind."

"He's an odd dragon," Dogloss said. "Very quick in the air. Hesitant on everything else."

Charge Deklamp dismissed her, telling her that he hoped he'd see her at the feast. Dogloss showed her out.

In the outer chamber, she asked Dogloss about Serena. Any woman who made dragoneer was of supreme interest to Ileth. Ileth had heard of her a few times but had never met her, or anyone like her. Ileth, who'd never had much learning except by example, was always interested in what sort of woman rose to prominence in the Serpentine.

"She flies the Charge's dragon, Telemiron. Telemiron is slim for a male. Have you met him? Perhaps not, he's hardly ever here. He's quite as unique as she is. They're a good match. Our best navigator. My Master has too many cares here to fly much, so Serena is about making the rounds to the posts, his eyes and ears and tongue in the world outside the Serpentine. I don't think she spends twenty days a year at the Serpentine if you total all the hours. If you have a special interest in

---

* In mythology derived from old Hypatian legends, your fate-star will sometimes send a young girl as a vision who points the way to some manner of boon or treasure or guides you along a path when you are lost.

getting to know her, she's good company. I'm sure she would offer dinner in Vyenn."

"I'd like that," Ileth said. "If she is loose of her duties some night."

"Speaking of duties, I have to go over some figures with our Charge. Enjoy your evening, Ileth, knowing that you flew to his rescue when he was outnumbered and heavily pressed. You're the hero of the Old Tower today."

It seemed to her that the Serpentine was on edge. Ileth guessed it had something to do with the Commissioner-General and his party. Everyone was tense, fussing with this or that when they weren't doing actual work, making sure every dropped scale was accounted for and dragon-meal properly weighed and recorded.

Ileth couldn't quite cite anything specific that made her feel tension. Apprentices and novices hurried about; did it seem they stepped faster? She decided that as she was at the up end of the Serpentine she'd take dinner in the Great Hall. Did the dinner crowd at the Great Hall seem hushed, with conversations being carried out in low tones, heads and bodies leaned closer together than usual over the table? It seemed so, to her.

She ate alone, at one end of a long table crowded with exhausted novices, who gave her fresh scar curious looks but didn't speak to her. She didn't dine often enough in the Great Hall to have any regular companions, and Sifler wasn't about.

Finishing her plain meal of fish on a bed of leeks and fat summer carrots, she was about to take her plate and fork to the washtub when Velleker ascended the pulpit. He'd put on his green pauldron, a sword, and a short cape for the occasion. He rang the bell and the diners quieted. His thin, handsome face broke into an easy smile.

"We have glad tidings from the Beehive: the clutch of Vithleen and Falberrwrath has hatched, two males and one female. Taresscon, speaking for the dragons, would like to remind everyone that the Cellars are off-limits to all but the grooms and feeders already on special duty. A feast day has been declared for the day after tomorrow, hosted

by the dragons in the Rotunda. Falberrwrath will be there to accept any offerings of coin or metals for Vithleen. There will be alterations to usual routines. The cooks especially will need extra assistance, so those of you who are released from other duties would be welcome to lend a hand for part of the feast. The dragons are paying a labor bounty to everyone who works the feast. I know this is not usual Serpentine practice, but we do bend the rules when the dragons wish to celebrate. Oh, Charge, I didn't see you there, do you have anything to add?"

Charge Deklamp ascended the pulpit. From the top and her angle looking up at him, nothing visible to her but his hunched shoulders and intent stare, he looked even more like an owl in a tree. The assembly quieted. "Dragoneers of the Serpentine," he said, and the last voice or two in the audience quieted. "We have a commission from the Assembly visiting. Offer them every courtesy. Answer every question. Bar no door, withhold no record. They may ask some of you about your experiences in the late Galantine War. Consider yourselves free to speak as though to a fellow dragoneer. We have nothing to hide from the Assembly or its assigns. The more helpful we are to them, the sooner they will depart and fulfill their commission. That is all, except that I hope all of you enjoy the feast day the day after tomorrow. In order to accomplish that I am releasing, from my own family stores, one valoon* of wine or one flask of brandy to anyone who works the feast in preparation, service, or entertainment. The usual standards of drunkenness while on duty will be enforced, as always, so you may have it registered to your account and have it meted out at any time. That is all."

Wine (or a smaller amount of brandy) being given out inspired a faint buzz of hushed talk. Ileth had never been in the Serpentine when the Charge issued wine.

---

* About two and a half liters. By the very generous pouring standards among the dragoneers, this is a traditional serving for a team of seven attending a dragon on campaign in the field, a dragoneer, his two wingmen, and four apprentices or novices. Those who wish to set an example of moderation or stretch out a bottle ask that their wine be issued at the "cut ration" of about half that serving.

"That's the first wine he's handed out since they took down that black-and-gold monster over the Scab," someone at the next table said. "That was a death-toast in his honor."

"No, it was for Agrath, the silver," a wingman corrected. "The death-toast was for him. Reconnaissance never found the black-and-gold's body."

"Who was his dragoneer again?"

"Annis Heem Strath," Ileth supplied, feeling much of the pleasure of the announcement leave.

That night Ottavia, as a special treat for her dancers, managed to get permission from Taresscon and the Charge to go down and see the hatchlings. Ottavia made them all promise to retreat at the first sign of irritability from Vithleen. Mothers of hatchlings fresh out of the egg could be dangerous.

Ileth was familiar with the chamber in the Beehive Cellars; her first duty as a dancer had been to keep a failing old dragon known as "the Lodger" company.

Vithleen lay like a great green wall between the two male hatchlings. She'd lost a lot of flesh since Ileth had ridden her when a mix-up in the flight cave put her atop Vithleen for a courier run. The female hatchling, perhaps already sensing her job as a neutral go-between, scuttled around her mother's forelimbs to sneak stew from first one male's trough and then the other's. Ileth smelled liver. The slaughter of the cattle brought in for the feast had already begun. Dragons adore liver, but Vithleen was content to leave it for her offspring and just nibble at a platter of scorched cubed beef.

The males, bellies already swollen from their feast, ignored their sister and snoozed, twitching.

The mother dragon waved her head back and forth, up and down, making a trilling sound. Ileth, after matching the noises to the movement, decided she must be using her head and the breathing passages in it like a musical instrument, changing the sounds by altering the angle they came up out of her voice box, if the dragons had the same

sort of humming strings the natural philosophers and physikers said humans possessed.

"We're lucky," Ottavia whispered. "I think that's singing."

"You don't know?" Santeel asked, and the others shushed her.

"The last time there were eggs here I was just out of novice year," Shatha whispered. "I never heard Yarienne sing. I did hold a bit of the shell and saw the hatchlings."

Santeel Dun Troot, fidgety with curiosity, kept jumping up to see over the front rank.

Ottavia stepped forward. "Congratulations, Vithleen."

"Thank you, uhhh. Oh, I know you, I'm just tired."

"Ottavia."

"Yes, the dancer. Falberrwrath is always going on about you all. Oh, is that . . . errr . . . the one who went after my eggs, back there. Hullo, Ileth, that's it."

Ileth stepped up and bobbed. "Con-congrat—"

"Thank you, dear."

"You should rest," Ottavia said. Ileth silently agreed, Vithleen looked terrible. She was used to seeing Vithleen thick with muscle capable of defying even the winds of a blizzard. She'd had a long vigil over her eggs and survived a poisoning. Ileth hoped she wasn't ill with parasites on top of everything. Were the grooms combing through her waste?

"That's the sixth time I've been told that today, dear. When the males start minding me when I tell them to keep away from each other, that's when I'll rest. I don't hold with barbaric notions about instinct, and I'm not losing a hatchling while I have strength to lift my head or push them around with my tail."

"Perhaps Falberrwrath could—" Ottavia said.

"Perhaps not. I won't have any throats torn out because he decides his daughter needs to hear about the Battle of Broken Bridge. I have him getting me charred cattle skins. Fried good and crisp. I'm so hungry for charred cattle skins right now it's hard to put into words."

The dancers congratulated her once again, bobbed obeisance one by one, and departed.

"Be a dear and ask where my fried skins are!" Vithleen called after them.

The feast went off. The commission circulated but did not join; they ate at their lodgings in Vyenn but frowned at the flood of beef and pies and brandy atop groaning tables. Ileth hoped someone told them that this dragon-sponsored feast was extraordinary; she'd never had this much food in her years since enrolling in the Serpentine and could count on her fingers the number of times she'd seen beef served.

In the days following the feast as the leftovers were consumed down to the last joint, the Serpentine was poked and prodded by the visiting commissioners. If anyone knew the truth of their investigation, they weren't speaking. There were plenty of guesses, though.

Some said they were looking for spies, others that they were the agents of some big wheel at the Exchange in Sammerdam looking to put the dragons to more commercial use now that peace had been restored with the Galantine Baronies. Others said that they were looking for waste and excess to further cut funding given by the Assembly. After one more long meeting with the Master in Charge, rumor had it that they were about to depart.

That night Ileth was taking an extra hour using some cast-off paper from Ottavia's correspondence to improve her lettering while Shatha read aloud when a page called to them from outside the heavy curtains to their rooms.

"Stranger in the Dancers' Quarter," a page called, rustling the curtain that closed off the Quarter so that the curtain rings clattered. You couldn't make much noise with your knuckles on the stone of the Beehive.

Shatha wrapped a towel around her head and went to check. "I'll call for her, sir."

"It's one of the commissioners, for you," Shatha said, glaring at Ileth as though it were her fault. She motioned for Ileth to remain where she was and hurried toward Ottavia's sleeping enclosure.

Ileth spent the moment it took Ottavia to rise fixing her appearance and putting on her apprentice sash and novice pin, the closest

thing someone of her station could come to full uniform of the Serpentine. This sounded official.

Shatha hurried out of Ottavia's room and returned to the curtains where the visitors waited outside. Finally, Ottavia appeared, looking much as she always did, cane in hand, save for her hair, bound tightly up with a purple scarf. She shot an accusing look at Ileth, as if she were responsible for Ottavia's interrupted sleep rather than the commissioner outside.

She crossed the Dancers' Quarter and passed to the other side of the curtain. Ileth couldn't hear much of the words exchanged, other than an "Oh, did he?" from Ottavia.

The curtain rings made their clattering warning again and Ottavia pointed her cane at Ileth. "You've been summoned to an interview with the commissioners. I shall allow it despite the hour, but I'm coming with you. Put on your shoes."

Ileth, not knowing what would be asked of her or how far they were going, put on her walking boots. She did it quickly. Commissioners of the Republic wouldn't like being kept waiting.

Ottavia surveyed her appearance before they passed out through the curtain. "Good enough."

"You need—you needn't come, sira," Ileth said.

"Oh, yes I do. Seems once a year I have to squash this sort of thing, and firmly."

Ileth had an inkling of what she meant by *this sort of thing* but followed in silence out to the passage, where a page and a man in plain black waited. She recognized him as one of the group from Deklamp's office.

"My orders were to just bring the girl Ileth," the commissioner said.

"My duty to my dancers supersedes any orders," Ottavia said evenly. "Commissioner-General Vor Navarr will understand if I have to speak to him about this unusual request."

"He doesn't care to have the *Vor* added to his name," the commissioner corrected. "And he is the one who asked for her."

"That is surprising, considering the Commissioner-General's reputation, but while I will permit her to go out at this unusual hour in the spirit of cooperating with your work, I must again insist on accompanying my dancer. I can't imagine what one of the Republic's commissioners wants with a dancer. Is he curious about how her up-work is progressing?"

Ileth hardly heard the byplay. In her head, she was reexamining the brief encounter with the Commissioner-General, wondering what had brought on a summons. She knew the kinds of powers an ordinary commissioner held when it came to criminals and other threats to the security of the Republic. What could a Commissioner-General order?

"I will not waste everyone's time arguing the matter," the commissioner said. "May we depart, so the hour does not grow even later?"

The page and the commissioner led them up through the East Stair to the Upper Ring and out. There were faster ways to get to the Long Bridge, but visitors to the Serpentine weren't insulted by being asked to slip down little alleys and passages or pass through dark galleries. There were many secrets to life among the dragons that were reserved only for those who were oathed in to their service.

Though the commissioner kept a pace that even the page had to puff to match (he was new and had been well fed at home in his early years, it seemed to Ileth), Ottavia kept up easily. Her cane was more an affectation than a necessity. She stayed silent until they reached the up end, where they stopped at the little red side door where Ileth had spent a hungry, lonely week waiting on fate to see if she would be admitted as a novice.

The page called down for one of the Guards to open the door.

"The Commissioner-General isn't staying in the Visitors' House?" Ottavia asked.

"The Commissioner-General often works late. The Gables in Vyenn is more convenient for us; we can all share the upstairs, and our work can be carried on in privacy." He leaned over and gave the Guard a quiet password and the Guard opened the bolt. Of course the

commissioner could have done this himself, but he obeyed the Serpentine's procedures like any other citizen.

"I'm surprised he could find so many rooms at the Gables," Ottavia said. "The summer weather being pleasant."

"The innkeeper complained that his bookings are not a third of their usual. He was happy to have a large party."

Out on the path, where they had to walk single file along the wall, Ottavia gripped Ileth's hand and probed the ground with her cane as she walked behind the commissioner. They fell far enough behind that they could speak.

"This old trick. An apprentice's password is only good during the day. You'd be stuck out here all night, the old dog. You spoke to him before, I believe?"

"About . . . about Fespanarax and the Galantines," Ileth said.

"You must have made an impression."

They couldn't talk further, as once they rounded the corner of the Serpentine by the gate, the commissioner waited on them so that they might walk down the road together.

"It's a fine night for a walk," Ottavia said, stepping out with her cane.

"They say night air is wholesome," the commissioner agreed.

Vyenn wasn't quite so pretty at night. The colorful flower boxes were in shadow, and the few lit windows did little to add cheer to the empty streets. If anything, it made the emptiness lonelier. There was laughter and singing down by the wharf; poor trade wasn't going to destroy a fine evening for the bargemen.

The Gables had a light on either side of the door. The commissioner took them in and the innkeeper roused himself from a chair before the fire to greet them. The commissioner nodded, Ottavia called him by name and took his hand, and the innkeeper informed them that the Commissioner-General awaited them in a downstairs dining room.

Their escort went in to announce them.

Ottavia threw a look at Ileth. She stood close. "The Commissioner-

General is either bold in his vices or had enough manners to offer you dinner first."

"I don't . . . don't think it's *that*," Ileth said.

They were brought in. Commissioner-General Navarr sat at one end of a well-lit table with several opened letters in front of him, writing on a portable blotter. His commissioner broke precedent slightly in introducing Ileth before Ottavia. Ileth thought it was to put Ottavia in her place and silently looked forward to Ottavia's retort.

Her thoughts were interrupted when she saw the sideboard to the dining table. It was piled with little baked goods, bowls of elderberries and cloudberries, and honey-glazed sweets, some of which she didn't even know the names for, all on neat little saucers that seemed to have been manufactured just to hold the treat. There was a bowl of fine sugar just in case the berries weren't sweet enough.

"My correspondence has caught up to me," Navarr said, smiling at them, leaving the letter half-finished and putting his pen back in the ink. He stood and walked around the dining table. He was still dressed for his visit, though the silver gorget had been removed. "From the description you must be the dancer-in-charge. Ottavia, is it?"

In this setting, without a crowd of younger men about, he didn't seem quite so old. Ileth wondered if the white hair was natural. His eyes and teeth were both bright and his hair only a little thinned. He didn't walk or stand like a man weighed down by age.

"Sir," she said with a nod.

"I asked for an interview with Ileth, alone."

Ottavia planted her cane and leaned forward. "You are free to interview her all you like, Commissioner-General. I'm here to ensure nothing else happens to her. Perhaps you are not aware that apprentices aren't allowed outside the Serpentine at night unless they are on a specific commission. She'll need me to get back in."

"Why would she need to get back in if she's to spend the night in my bedchamber?"

"Sir!" Ottavia said.

"It is not what you were thinking. I prefer when people speak their minds plain, in good simple Montangyan words."

"Your joking is in poor taste."

"I do not joke. I will speak plainly: I wish to speak to Ileth alone. With her age, her common upbringing, and the fact that she is a dancer I can understand why you assume a carnal motive, but I have no interest in her other than as an instrument of the Republic. You may wait for her beside the fire in the main room if you wish. You can escort her back and save my associate's legs."

"The Commissioner-General must understand my alarm at a summons for a girl her age at this hour," Ottavia said.

"If you don't want people thinking your dancers a troupe of jades, then have them be decent and cover their legs and arms."

If Ottavia had been possessed of hackles they would have been up. "Ours is an ancient art. There are reasons for the attire. You cannot blame me for Heem Tyr's prurient paintings."

"If only I had the time to devote to discussions of art that you have at your disposal, madam. The longer you remain in this room, the later it shall be when you do return. I only expect to keep her some minutes; you may reprimand me if the midnight bell sounds and you are not on the road back to the Serpentine. Though I have taken all the rooms in this inn save for that pensioner's to save complaint. One is not occupied, and you and young Ileth here may have it if you wish to walk back in the morning light."

"I think it best that we return tonight." Ottavia looked at Ileth. Ileth felt confident enough to give a quick nod.

"Very good, Commissioner-General. I'll retire to the hearth and await Ileth or the midnight bell."

Ottavia went out, as did the commissioner, who shut the door behind him. She sensed that he was standing just on the other side of it.

"Sit down, Ileth," Navarr said, pulling out the chair at the head of the table. He went over to the side table and its many platters and dishes. "May I get you something? I am a simple man, but I will

indulge my sweet tooth and I found a good bakery on this very street. Almost the equal of Sammerdam, if not Asposis, in the delicacy of its flaking."

"I . . . I've never had any of these. Which one is the best?" To his credit, the Commissioner-General waited for her to finish speaking without the irritation most displayed about this point.

"May I select for you? These are very good, it's called a cinnamon crisp." He put something before her that looked a little like a rolled-up piece of canvas, brown and dusted with something reddish-brown.

He took a similar one and sat down at the corner next to her. His letters were far off at the other end. He picked it up with his fingers, took a bite, and smiled at her expectantly until she ate.

Her mouth came alive. It was delicious. She'd had cinnamon before, at the Baron's, but that was sprinkled on apples rather than with a sugary treat.

The Commissioner-General regarded her as she ate. He seemed to take pleasure watching her enjoy the crisp.

"You present as a girl who needs more friends," Navarr said. "So many of your compatriots at the Academy come from powerful families who smooth their path. Your path was a rough one. Out of a lodge, living on wit alone, yet you have attentive manners. You waited for me to take a bite to make sure it was to be eaten as finger food."

"My . . . my stay in-in-in Galantine lands improved my manners," Ileth said. Which was true enough. The Baron's daughter had planted and cultivated manners in her, and Ileth had found it an interesting diversion from the tedium. Even useful, with men like the Commissioner-General.

"Ah, yes. Your observations there impressed me. Our Republic has need of such talent."

Ileth finished her cinnamon crisp with a pang of regret of a pleasure come and gone. While the other delicacies tempted her, she had the sense that the conversation with Navarr would reach a crisis soon, and she didn't want to meet it with a mouth full of custard.

"How so, sir?" she asked when it was safe to speak without crumbs flying from her mouth.

"I have had inquiries made about you, as you have probably guessed. I've had a report that letters pass back and forth between you and the Dun Troot household. Now, it so happens I'm familiar with that family; they have royalist inclinations and keep an aristocratic attitude and lifestyle. That is in their right. I know they dote on Santeel, as she is their only daughter. I imagine the correspondence relates to her."

"You've read the letters?"

"Never! Mail in the Republic by those not in a prison or institution is not opened except on the order of a jury. But who mails to whom is not secret. There has been correspondence between you and a man named Falth in the service of the Dun Troots; the only logical conclusion is that you are either reporting on that Dun Troot girl or, despite Serpentine Academy traditions against servants, quietly acting as her servant and sending requests and requirements to the family."

"Maybe I'm earning a fig here and there running her mail to the Post Commissioner. The gate office is a long way from the Beehive."

The Commissioner-General frowned but accepted that answer.

"Tell me why you left your home and risked so much to join the Dragoneers."

Ileth fumbled through her explanation that ever since meeting a dragoneer as a seven-year-old, she had a dream of spending her life around them. She hadn't even known she could grow up to do such things. Annis Heem Strath had expanded the dreams of what her life could be.

"The rote answer is to serve and defend your people and the Republic."

"I-I appreciate the Re-Republic more, after seeing life in the Baronies. At the Lodge growing up, we were more enthusiastic about a full stewpot than politics."

"So when you see our own good red-and-white banner, how do you feel?"

"Like I am . . . like I am home. I m-m-missed it in Galantine lands."

He questioned her more about what she saw there, what made her more appreciative of the Republic. She talked about the Baron and his haphazard standards of justice. He could punish, exile, even hang people with very little to moderate him other than his own gentle nature. Yet when the Baron and his friends trampled crops or knocked down fences on hunts and races and whatnot, the people of his barony were just supposed to accept it as a price to be paid, like taxes.

Navarr liked that answer. "You are a thoughtful young lady, even if you have difficulty communicating some of the unexpected depths. I suspected some precision of mind when I heard your report on your experiences in the Baronies. This interview confirms it."

Flattery, in Ileth's experience, presaged a request. Ileth waited for it.

"Would you like another sweet before you go, Ileth? Tea? Or perhaps a good milky swirl, it's quite the sensation with young ladies in Sammerdam these days, and just the thing before a nighttime walk to your own bed."

Ileth shook her head. He rose to his feet and she followed his example.

"You . . . you just had me brought for-for-for c-conversation, sir?"

"Yes. Was I not clear? You interested me on my last visit. As I had to come again, I wanted to learn more about you in less intimidating surroundings than a jury chamber. I have."

He went over to his desk, picked up a pen, and scratched something on a little rectangle of paper. "Please take my card." He walked over to Ileth and handed her a small, hardened piece of linen paper. It had his name, title, and *Posy Court, Sammerdam* in neat press printing. "Just in case you are ever in Sammerdam and find yourself loose from other attachments. I'm afraid I indulge my weakness for the bakery there, too, so you are always welcome for tea and cake."

Ileth traced her finger over the printed letters. They were raised up on the paper. Most distinctive.

"They're the latest thing in Sammerdam. Some of the young ladies

like to collect them from their favorites. But don't think of starting a fashion of them with mine; I am not anyone's favorite within the walls of the Serpentine. Know that if matters here do not proceed as you expect, I have need of sharp minds and quick reflexes in the red-and-whites."

She'd never heard of the red-and-whites. Quith would probably know, or Santeel. She looked at the reverse side of the card. He'd written his initials and scratched an *X* with an overlong leg and a dot opposite the long leg, like the hilt of a . . .

"Is th-this a sword?"

"I'm flattered you can distinguish it. I'm no artist. Yes." He lowered his voice. "If you ever feel that our Republic is in danger, from any source or corner, without or within, present this card at any post or to any commissioner. As you've visited me, I shall return the favor and visit you. If there is a threat to your person or great need of haste, simply include the word *sword* in your note or message, in an innocuous fashion if you fear a more plain message being read. I am able to call on the most skilled swords and meteormen in the Republic, at need."

Ileth thought it a strange offer and disliked the idea of screaming for help—at least to these crows. He had a point about the sword business, though. She was almost as defenseless as when she'd come in as a novice. "As a dragoneer I . . . I hope to be one that others call on . . . call in if they're in danger, sir."

"Of course. But some dangers can't be destroyed by a blast of dragonfire. Now, I'll exercise age's prerogative and announce that I wish nothing else of the evening but my bed. Good night, Ileth."

"Good night, Commissioner-General," she replied, going out into the common room of the inn.

Ottavia excused herself from conversation with the innkeeper. He looked sleepy.

"Well?" Ottavia said.

"He asked me some questions about the . . . about the-the Baronies. Not what I expected."

"Not what I expected either. I should have taken his age into account."

They decided to walk back to the Serpentine. Ottavia enjoyed the honorary rank of a Master and could come and go at will. The only curious thing in their return was her question about Santeel. But she held it until they were safe within the Serpentine again.

"As we have this moment alone, Ileth—I know you and Santeel are friends, of a sort. Is she well? The quality of her dancing is falling off. I thought a reduction in her drills to make allowance for her apprentice duties would make sure that she's better rested, but to me she dances like a girl who hasn't slept for a week. Is there something wrong?"

It was understandable that Ottavia would think them confidants. They'd both been sworn in together, and even taken their first flights on the same day. Ileth had helped Santeel's father ease into the idea of his daughter dancing in public, even if the "public" was dragons.

"She hasn't said anything to me," Ileth said, honestly enough.

"Maybe it is that she's starting to apprentice under the physikers," Ottavia said. "Not many do, and fewer still have much success at it. I understand it's mentally and physically quite demanding. I must make sure she sits down and eats. That's probably all it is."

As she readied herself for bed, Ileth looked at the sleeping Santeel. She did look like she'd been running ragged; the skin in her face looked pinched, and even asleep her eyes looked tired. And there was a strange rasp to her breathing.

T he next day Santeel was up early for drills and bright as ever. Ileth received a note from one of the clerks in the Masters' Hall. A dragoneer had been posted to her lot and she was to report for the beginning of her formal apprentice training.

"At last!" Santeel said, her eyes merry. "I should hate if you fell too far behind me. I always try harder when I have a rival. Who is to be your dragoneer?"

"It doesn't say," Ileth said.

The note informed her that she was to report to the hippodrome groaningly early, at the fourth-hour bell, which meant Ileth had to be up in the Dancers' Quarter at the third. So fearful was she of sleeping through that unaccustomed hour that she didn't sleep in the Dancers' Quarter. She spent the night in the flight cave—which always had both Guards and a clerk on watch no matter what the hour—on a pile of cargo netting, having asked to be wakened when the bell sounded. Ileth begged the Guard and the clerk to pass her request on at the end of their shift and have someone wake her at the third bell.

Were she a full dragoneer, she could just order a page to do it and ruin someone's day if she wasn't wakened on time.

They kept their word. The clerk shook her awake as the third bell sounded.

He had a badly pocked face. "Good whatever-you-want-to-call-this-unholy-hour, Ileth," he said. He seemed amused.

"Many thanks," Ileth said. She realized he was the overnight clerk who'd let her rummage about for oil when she stole the streamer that was now her apprentice sash. She wondered if he recognized it.

He shrugged. "Glad for something to do. Next time have them settle you in behind the office. That's a warm corner, vent from the kitchens runs up through it, and we see you when we pass in and out so we don't forget. The dragoneers sometimes catch a quick nap there." He used a rag to wipe off the chalked block letters saying WAKE HER AT 3 above the netting. Someone else had scrawled something obscene about how to wake her in smaller letters below. Ileth brought up an eyebrow. At least whoever had added to the instructions had phrased it cleverly.

"Sorry about that. No one in the office wrote it, I'm sure of that. I know their hands." He had a green apprentice sash. Today began her journey to one just like it!

"Dath Amrits had an early flight on Etiennersea?"

"No, a late return. How did—oh. Yes, that is his sense of humor."

Ileth, too excited to find out who her first dragoneer would be,

wouldn't let adolescent jokes spoil her day. She just smiled and stuck her fists together, knuckles toward the flight cave clerk. "Keep the Troth, sir," she said. She'd seen the encouraging gesture now and then in her novice year at a few important moments, but this was the first time she'd used it on someone else.

He mirrored it reflexively but smiled as he did so. "Anytime, *uhh* Ileth. I don't know the rest, my apologies."

"There is no rest. It's just 'Ileth,'" she said. "Everything aligned and proper, sir?"

"Run a comb through your hair. It's Sef, by the way."

She thanked him again and did her best to sort out her hair.

She'd gone to bed gripping a heel of bread and a bit of cheese saved from the feast, wrapped up in old paper. She found it in the netting, ate it, and refreshed herself at the cistern the dancers used, then struck out at a good walking pace for the hippodrome.

Arriving in plenty of time, she reviewed the other faces in the arena, where they sat on benches in the half that didn't open up against the stables. She looked across at the stalls. The last time Ileth had been here, Rapoto Vor Claymass had pulled her into a stall and kissed her, and she'd been kicked out of the Manor. She ignored the past and thought about what was about to start in her life. She'd heard a lot of stories about what an apprentice's first dragoneer had them do as they started off on the "circus." Usually it was some form of physical toughening. She felt equal to that; there couldn't be anything worse than the drills Ottavia put them through. She was happy to see that Quith was in her group. Quith, a bit of a scatterbrain unless the subject was social connections and affiliations, hadn't much impressed the Masters but had finally made it. She knew another, Zante, Zan to his friends, of which Ileth was most certainly not one. He'd been thrown out his novice year for filching scale under a renegade named Griff who'd gone over to the Galantines when Ileth had discovered his scheme.

She surveyed the boys, none particularly well known to Ileth, though there was a groom who'd been there the wild night of the egg

theft. The only other girl was obviously young, a novice who had made apprentice early. She wore lenses on her eyes. She must come from money.

The group stirred. A wide-shouldered, narrow-waisted man in a porthole-necked work tunic and wide girdle walked out into the center of the hippodrome. His attire was simple and sleeveless, and ended at midthigh. Ileth had a hard time guessing his age. There was no gray in the dark curly hair cut tight against his scalp. She'd seen him riding about now and then—you noticed a man built like that on a horse—but hadn't known he was a dragoneer. She thought he was a specialist as he always seemed to be involved in herds and wains being driven into the Serpentine, unloaded, then passed out again.

A few quiet groans broke out.

"Oh gods, it's the Horse," one of the lot said.

"I knew it. When they said 'hippodrome' I just knew it."

"Well, I'm off," another said, rising. "I don't care if they make me work the chicken coops until the next lot's organized."

Ileth, next to Quith, looked at her. Quith had a scared expression on her face. "What?" Ileth whispered.

"From the trials. Remember? They call him the Horse." Quith must have been referring to the physical tests the other applicants had undergone while she'd been starving on the doorstep.

He had two wingmen, dressed similarly. She'd seen one at that pile-in with Rapoto.

He stepped up to the low wall of the hippodrome set before their seats. He had put on a genial smile for the occasion, showing immaculate teeth.

"Congratulations, apprentices. I am the Master of Horse, dragoneer in charge of your lot. A few of you know me. The rest of you are in for a surprise."

He let that sink in.

"The first thing you should know about me is that I'm no dragonrider. I hold the title as a courtesy. Horses are my love and my duty. If you can ride well, you will find a dragon an easier job."

Ileth wasn't the sort who pointed out irony, but she could appreciate it. She'd rarely seen a man who looked more draconic. With his close-cropped hair and angular features, he seemed designed to cut through air easily, and he oiled his skin so it gleamed like polished scale. He also took very good care of his teeth.

The Horse brought up and introduced his wingmen. Ileth liked the way he moved: gently, gracefully. She hadn't met many men who'd make good dragon-dancers, but she believed he could do it. "What do you think, lads, should I give them the good news, the bad news, or the worse news?"

"The bad," an apprentice near Ileth said.

The Horse inclined his head. "I didn't speak to you. Wingman Surrim, take this apprentice over to the Beehive and run him from the Catch Basin to the lighthouse. Encourage him if he falters."

"Yes, sir!" the wingman said, pulling a short, flexible speed-whip from his belt. He cracked it, loudly enough to startle the whole lot. The apprentice who had spoken up rose to his feet and was trotted out of the hippodrome with the wingman running lightly at his heels, whip dangling. "Here's your bad news, apprentice. You're running all the way there," he said on his way out.

"Can they whip us?" the girl with the spectacles whispered. "The Matron said they couldn't whip us."

"Give them the good news, sir," the remaining wingman said.

"The good news," the Horse said, turning back to his new lot with an easygoing smile. "The good news is my lots of apprentices have the best record of being promoted to wingman once they have earned, and you will earn it, their green sash. Look up the rolls in the archives at your leisure. The bad news is I lose about half of them before they get their green sash. Some leave, some request other duties, I even had one die on me. Unsoundness of the heart or blood vessels, the physikers said. But that's what I do, I sniff out weaknesses. The gods didn't give me these nostrils for show."

Ileth, considering him, decided that his nostrils were bigger than most, or maybe it was just the angle they were set at in his nose.

The Horse stepped over to the end where Quith, Ileth, and the '67 girl with the lenses sat. "Girls in Horse Lot. One-two-three! You'll find my nose doesn't make special allowances."

He lost interest in them and paced back to the center of the hippodrome.

"Do you all mark my attire? This is a fatigue tunic. They're simple to make. I have some material and thread in the stable workshop. You'll spend the rest of your morning making them for yourselves."

He led them over to the workshop where Ileth had been for the pile-in. Folded towers of felt were arranged on a tack table, along with sewing instruments, razors, shears, measuring tapes, and so on.

They set to work. Ileth and the girl with the lenses both copied Quith's actions. She was clearly the handiest at the sewing table, after they watched the way she arrayed her instruments and fabric.

One of the apprentices said that he was willing to measure and cut, but sewing a hem was women's work, he'd never picked up a needle in his life. The Horse told him that he would do the sewing for the three girls, even if he had to stay up all night to do so.

Ileth gladly handed over her measured-and-cut cloth. She'd had enough mending in the Lodge to last her until her gray years.

The simple sewing was mostly finished by breakfast. He brought them as a group—save for the apprentice who had to sew the three extra tunics, who missed his meal—to the Great Hall for breakfast, lined them up by height, and then had them sit down to eat in that order. Some of the wingmen elbowed each other as the Horse led them in and put them in line for their food.

They sat in the same height order. Ileth would have rather been next to Quith; the boy she had on her left ate with his elbows wide out, and the one on her right looked shocked when she didn't give him her toast to have with his porridge, as he wanted extra. She was jealous of the girl with spectacles. She was smallish and had a seat on the end where she could shift down a little and give herself space.

The apprentice they'd left to finish the extra tunics had disappeared, the unfinished sewing thrown on the floor with a dirty and

distinct footprint stamped on it. "You'll have to finish on your own, it appears another apprentice has left us," the Horse said. He assigned a wingman to supervise and had the rest get into their new tunics, hanging their clothing in unused stalls. Then he passed out leather girdles such as workmen and some soldiers wore. He instructed the girls on how to wrap scrap leather around their waists and secure it with horse lead-lines, as there weren't any work girdles sized for them.

"Any former cobbler's apprentice here who can fashion a girdle?" one of the wingmen asked. No one responded.

Ileth looked over her half-done tunic. What sewing had been done was started badly, but by putting the girl with spectacles—Finila—on pulling out the bad they finished and were dressed in the work clothes by the time the Serpentine changed the gate-watch at midmorning. Their wingman took them out the gate.

"I'm sure to get red," Quith said, eyeing the sun, alone in the sky without even a wisp of cloud for company.

"Rub some m-mud on your face and shoulders," Ileth suggested. Finila looked horrified.

The wingman led them around the bay, going steadily up until they reached something Ileth had heard about but never visited—the quarry. It was a limestone cut, partially washed by artesian springs that fed down into the Skylake. At the bottom of the quarry lay a pile of limestone cut into bricks. The Horse and his wingmen had arranged the lot into a chain designed to pass stone up out of the cut to a growing pile on the trail they'd just ascended.

"Do we have to use picks and things?" Quith asked, looking at her hands.

"No," the wingman said. "Cutting limestone—it's a skill. You need experience and judgment. Some cutters from Vyenn do that. We'll just be hauling it down to the Serpentine."

The Horse trotted up the limestone chain, surveyed the mass of more or less brick-shaped stones, and looked at the attire of his three girls. "Good. You're here just in time to start the mid-meal. We'll need to eat. Go back to the Serpentine and get bread, milk, and honey for

thirty. Pickled eggs, too, if they have some. We have cups and such here for water."

There was nothing to do but obey. They hiked back, asked the chief of the Great Hall for baskets with the mid-meal, and returned loaded with food. Ileth carried a great jug of milk in front, balanced by a wicker basket with bread strapped on her back. Quith carried the pickled eggs, and Finila the honey and some cheese the cooks thoughtfully included when they heard the Horse had his lot at quarry work. Quith complained the whole way of the weight of the glass jug. Ileth switched with her, but Quith only carried the milk twenty paces or so before groaning and demanding the eggs back. Ileth enjoyed the new respect in Quith's eyes as they hauled the meal up the mountainside.

At the quarry, the pile of limestone had grown, the human chain had been rearranged, they were facing different directions, and new boys stood at the turns. It was like at dance drills: when your muscles were so fatigued you found it impossible to raise your leg again to the front, you switched to the rear.

They broke for lunch. Water wasn't a difficulty; there was plenty flowing down the mountain and out of the rock walls to the stream down to the Skylake. Some of the apprentices washed themselves before eating. They lined up for Ileth, Quith, and Finila to pass out food. Ileth had to do some quick figuring to work out how to portion the loaves, but Finila was ahead of her. "Half a loaf each, including us and the wingmen—and we'll have two loaves to spare that way in case of accidents."

Her calculations proved dead correct.

After the break, the girls had little to do other than run water to the workers. When they weren't answering calls for water, their dragoneer put them to work pulling out pieces that had interesting coloration and setting those aside, telling them they'd be used at doorway posts and corners. By now the boys were faltering, sprawling on the ground or sitting with head drooped between their knees. Ileth volunteered to take a turn at the passing line and Finila followed her example. The

pair wrapped sweat-rags around their palms to save their hands as best as they could.

It was tiring work that made her shoulders ache and her hands burn.

Their dragoneer passed one boy, sitting on a stump next to the creek groaning and massaging his back. It reminded Ileth of Traskeer's phrase about crying on a stump. The Horse tapped the side of his nose as he pointed at the relay chain. The boy groaned as he got to his feet and rejoined the lot.

The attenuated brick chain could no longer pass from hand to hand. Those remaining walked the short distance to their mates. The Horse, sensing his lot were near the end of their energy, called frequent halts to let people catch their breath and some of those who had fallen out rejoin and others take a break. Several of the boys retied their tunics as loincloths to allow the sweat to flow more freely off their backs, where it traced patterns in the limestone dust. They looked like statues come to life, like in some fable about a sorcerer who could animate stone.

The sun finally touched the western mountains and brought relief. The Horse blew his dragon-whistle and the wingmen yelled at everyone to stop. They sorted out their clothing and picked up the lunch baskets and jugs for the trip back. Some of the boys gallantly offered to carry the girls' burdens, but Ileth was content to put the empty milk can in the bread basket backpack and shoulder it home. Quith and Finila were only too happy to hand their burdens over and chatted with the boys on the way back. That is, until they approached the gate.

The Horse started a song and his odd lot wearily joined in. His wingmen closed up the back of the file, prodding with their stiff whip-handles rather than cracking them. They passed under the Dragon Gate singing "Our Scarlet Star," a popular rowing song that most everyone in the Vales had heard from a canal or harbor at one time or another, about a landlord's beautiful daughter named for the trumpet-shaped national flower. The version the Horse led them in was

different from the one Ileth was used to up on the Freesand Coast, though Finila still blushed at even its milder lyrics.

"Horse Lot: eat a good dinner and early bed," the Horse said with a smile, both naming and dismissing them before the Great Hall. He smiled like a cat in an attic full of mice. "We start again, same time tomorrow." Groans broke out. Ileth was tired, very tired, but many of the newly named Horse Lot looked shattered.

In the Great Hall, Quith ate her fish and harvest squash mechanically in near silence. "Can't keep this up. I'll be the first tossed out."

"There's already one out," Ileth said tiredly. "The boy who wouldn't sew."

"Two," Finila said. "You forget the one who left before he even introduced himself."

"We're H-Horse Lot now. Eat like it," Ileth suggested. Ottavia was always urging her tired dancers to eat more. The girl nodded and showed her shy smile.

Quith had just finished her meal when the wingman Pasfa Sleng walked by. He was in a new flying rig, a short coat cross-stitched and padded in an attractive diamond pattern so it could both be warm and keep with the simpler lines of the uniform tunics coming into fashion.

"Not your fa-favorite these days?" Ileth asked.

"Very much still my favorite," Quith said, watching him with more appetite than she'd shown for her dinner. "But he's never noticed me. I've tried. All the sad old tricks. Dropping things near him, pretending I can't make out something in a book, I even cut myself once when he was on kitchen and I was washing up."

"You didn't." Ileth had heard a few tricks for attracting attention, but cutting yourself was dipping your toe in a pool of madness.

"I did. He helped me bandage it and then had me sit and fold towels. Didn't even ask me about it when we were done for the day."

"Don't—hurt yourself again."

"I've learned a worthwhile lesson from it, as the Matron would say. Maybe I'm fooling myself, being here. I'm from a canaler's family.

Barges pulled by horses, you know. There were two when I was little, and one of the two wasn't worth talking about, running about Sammerdam and above. Now there's eight, which is the same number of brothers I have. And three sisters, me the middle. Father used to joke with his brother, who handled the horses back then, that kids were cheaper than crew. Now I'm not so sure he was joking. My sisters are pretty enough, Giath, the older, she's already married with a baby, and Loith will be married soon as she's sixteen or she gets her family started pleasure-before-rites, as they say on the barges."

Dinner must have restored Quith somewhat, as she went on:

"I wanted all that, but I'm too plain."

"Quith!"

"Oh, Ileth, you don't have to pretend, we've known each other long enough to laugh at polite lies."

"We've had a hard day. We shouldn't be thinking about anything but where to soak our feet."

Quith ignored her advice. "I used to cut out the wedding announcements from *Accounts and Notices* and pin them up next to my bed. Quite a few Names first met here, you know. I came here because I'd read that there were ten boys for every girl. I suppose it's true, but I'm cooped up all the time with our minority and the Matron prowling around to make sure no one is slipping in through the windows. It's a strange set of boys. Half of them don't deign to notice you and the other half run like rabbits when you say 'good morning.' My mother told me the odds would be good, but she forgot to warn me the goods would act so odd."

"Isn't it better to be the aunt who flies around on a dragon? Your nieces and nephews won't give you a mo-moment's peace when you visit."

Quith smiled. "C'mon, they don't make our kind dragoneers."

Ileth didn't want to argue with Quith. Quith would probably mention a dozen names of girls of "their kind" who whiled out their apprenticeships, never having done anything of importance, and ended up cleaning in some inn or sewing overdresses.

Ileth walked with Quith back to the Manor. "Please let there not be a lecture tonight," Quith asked the fall stars as she said good night.

"You have to wash that tunic we made today. Nap in the laundry. I used to do it."

"Ugh. I'm already dreading tomorrow," Quith said. "I'd put my purse on us losing at least one tomorrow morning, unable to rise."

"I'm not counting on-on-on anything other than you b-being there. It's easier with a friend."

Quith's mouth flicked up. They hugged and parted.

The Dancers' Quarter and bed had never seemed so far away. When Ileth finally arrived, sore-legged and with an aching back, Ottavia rose from a cushion where she'd been reading with relief that made Ileth think her bed was even farther away.

"Ileth, I was beginning to worry. You've had a long day."

She just nodded in reply.

"Could you do me a very great favor and see to Cunescious? He's had a bad landing by the up end and tore up a foot on a bottle some fool left by the roadside. He wants someone to take his mind off the pain. Santeel danced while he was being stitched up, and she's worn out."

Ileth nodded dumbly and moved off to wash up in their little room at the end of their alley and rinse out her new work tunic. Quith had her worried; usually when she talked, she was lively, discussing connections forming and withering among the little collections of friends in the Serpentine. She never talked of herself, not deeply. Cutting herself to get Wingman Sleng's attention . . .

She checked Preen's tea-warmer, desperately needing tea, and just her luck, it was empty. Preen must have had a busy day as well. She could build it up again with a little charcoal and started to do so.

Santeel met her coming out of their tap-room. Santeel was drying her hair, looking bright and alert.

"Ileth, you're filthy as a canal dredger. What have they been doing with you?"

"Limestone quarry. The Master of Horse is a great believer in fatigues."

"I've heard the Master of Horse cultivated physical culture to an extreme," Santeel said, testing the dust on Ileth's overdress and looking at her fingers with a frown. "Overdoing it on the first day to shake out the weaklings, no doubt. He did the same thing at the trials while you were outside on the step. Do you want me to boil you a couple of eggs to have before you turn in?"

Santeel's spirits lifted Ileth's.

"I'm to dance for Cunescious." She tried to match Santeel's cheery tone and make it sound like she was looking forward to it.

"I was just with him. A cool rinse did me wonders. You're right about cold water being salubrious."

Ileth smiled wanly. Santeel was in one of her cheery moods. "Tell you what, Ileth, let me go in your place so you can soak your clothes and sleep."

"No, Ottavia was specific—"

"I'll speak to our Charge. I sat all day listening to the physiker talk about how to cut open muscle to extract barbs, or trying to make wing from tail out of that old dragon anatomy book I've come to hate, so I'm fresh as the wind off the White Spine. You can do me a favor in return. Write Falth one of your snoop-letters and explain that I've been much in society both in the Serpentine and Vyenn and feeling the shortcomings of my wardrobe. I need at least two new dresses for the winter and a dress uniform. My parents must send me more money!"

True enough, Santeel had been looking shabby of late. Ileth knew that Santeel kept a close eye on the calendar for when her quarterly allowance would be available to draw against, but had always been under the impression she had enough money for whatever the shops in Vyenn could provide. She used to complain about the poor selection and laugh off the prices; Vyenn wasn't Sammerdam or Asposis, after all.

"I thought you . . . thought you hated me for writing—"

Santeel touched her playfully on the nose. "Nonsense! After I thought a bit I realized it was just the sort of device my parents would employ. Falth was probably told to keep a lookout for a girl my age.

How are they paying you for it? I never see your name over at the accounts."

"They're not. They just . . . just send me postage-paid paper I can fold into an envelope."

"I thought you northern types drove harder bargains than that. Well, cut-rate or no, I'd still appreciate a letter appealing on behalf of their daughter who looks a shambles in her old clothes. I'm sixteen now, practically a wingman, they should have given me a whopping great increase in allowance, don't you think?"

The intensity crackled off her. Ileth gave in, after a halfhearted request that she might need Santeel to fill in again until the Horse left off trying to kill them to shake out the weaklings.

"Eat pumpkin seeds, dear," Santeel said, having quickly climbed back into a dance sheath and covering towel, as she hurried off to explain that she'd cover Ileth with Cunescious. "Best thing for sore muscles and they're easy to find this time of year. Ottavia often has them squirreled about in those jars where she keeps her nuts. I won't tell."

Both parties of the compact were true to their word. Santeel and her boundless reserves of energy danced for Ileth those first few evenings while she rested her tortured body, and Ileth wrote a long letter to Falth about the shortcomings in Santeel's wardrobe.

Everything in Ileth's history made her want to dislike Santeel: nobly named birth, pampered upbringing, all the rough spots smoothed and polished, and anything she wanted given at the snap of her perfectly filed fingers. But she was generous with lending or giving away clothing—not just worn castoffs, either; Ileth's best dancing sheath was from Santeel. And she was so artful about it: *Ileth, I'm about to put this in the rag basket, unless you could use it . . .*

She never held her Name over the other dancers, even though she was one of the best; her technique in all respects was better than Ileth's and her knowledge of music added emotion to her performance that even the dragons were able to appreciate. When she was doing her

washing, she always went about to ask if anyone had anything that needed to go into the tub.

But if you irritated her, she could be terrifying. Even Shatha obliged her by taking care to examine the floor for her dropped wig pins morning and night. Preen used extra tea leaves when Santeel joined them so it was just as she liked it. Woe to the dancer who wanted to make porridge on their little stove when Santeel had an appetite for eggs, onions, and potatoes. And she never let Ileth forget that her hair could pass for a boy's.

Ileth's days, on the other callused hand, grew only a little easier as her muscles adapted to the toil. Her legs were fine, but how her shoulders and arms hurt! The Horse put his lot to carrying the mountain of quarried stones down to the Serpentine (Ileth now knew why so many of the buildings had such fine limestone exteriors). He insisted on having meal breaks all the way up at the quarry, so Ileth, Quith, and Finila had to haul food and milk up the mountain twice a day so they could be fed midmorning and again at midday. They jogged about with canteens, bringing water to the boys taking the rocks down to the Serpentine.

There were fewer boys falling out in the afternoon, but the pace still slowed and Ileth joined in carrying stones so they could finish and get back to the Serpentine to be first for dinner. It caused agony to her fingers and forearms.

Quith and Finila had it worse, as they hadn't been at Ottavia's drills and fatigues. Sorting stone gave them horrors about the state of their hands. Every time Quith or Finila sat down, determined to quit and ask for a job sweeping in the halls or pushing a feeding cart for the dragons, Ileth got them up again:

Don't give him the satisfaction.

The boys are just as tired as you.

It's just another test. You know how they like to test us.

It occurred to Ileth that she might be prolonging the torture by keeping Quith and Finila in the lot. Perhaps the Horse drove them

relentlessly until he lost a third or a half or whatever his goal might be in sniffing out weakness with those dragonish nostrils of his.

At last, after six days and a morning's work, their allotment of limestone was safely in the Serpentine and ready for the dairy's walls. Strangely, the Horse brought them back up the mountain and had them sit in the flat circle of dust where the piles had been. His wingmen were mysteriously absent.

"You've worked well this week," the Horse said, his usual cheery smile a bit wider now. "I saw some gutting out and filling in—thank you, girls, you went above and beyond in carrying rock—and you did what was on paper eight days' work in six. I work my lot hard. Hard work can't always be rewarded, but my lots are fairer than most."

He led the lot farther up the mountain on a little trail on the other side of the cut, with Ileth just behind him. She was able to observe his wide calf muscles at work as they climbed, sometimes on all fours, up above the cut to the source of the water trickling into the quarry. Nobody complained about the difficult path. They weren't carrying rocks.

They arrived at a sheltered notch in the mountainside with more limestone falls all about three mountain pools, surrounded by ferns happy in the moisture. The air felt wet and misty here thanks to the splash. The wingmen met them there. They'd been busy filling their tin cups from a tapped cask of beer stuck in the crotch of a tree.

"Real Tyrenna grain beer, not Vyenn ale," the Horse said, showing off the cask and baskets. "Fresh bread knots lye-boiled from Vyenn, heavily salted, and figs. You've been hauling rock, you should have figs."

Everyone knew the story that the first trade in the Vales was in dried figs brought up to the miners in the mountains, who missed the sweet treats from their homeland. The fig tree was emblazoned on the Republic's small coin.

The Horse bent and swirled his hand in the water. "Sadly, it's not a hot spring. But comfortable."

Ileth experimentally touched the water. He was right, it couldn't be called hot, but it wasn't cold either. A tepid spring. The water had the

same vaguely metallic taste as the stream flowing out of the cut whose taste Ileth had come to know so well during the work.

"So this is the cut pool," Quith said.

"Tourists from Vyenn sometimes find it worth the climb," the Horse said. His wingmen busied themselves pouring.

The Horse lifted a rope with a length of tenting and divided off the smallest of the three pools from the other two. "So my young ladies can enjoy themselves in privacy, keeping modesty—and other virtues— intact."

They retrieved beer, food, and figs. The wingmen had neglected to bring plates, but there was plenty of well-splashed rock about. Ileth set hers down near the pool, glanced around, undressed, and slipped into the water. While it wasn't the bracing cold of the Freesand or the Sky-lake, it felt fine on her muscles. She'd heard Santeel speak of her mother taking mineral-water baths.

The other two joined her, keeping their clothes nearby for a quick grab. Ileth decided to eat her bread first as it seemed likely to be wetted by all the mist floating around. It was interesting: salty and chewy on the outside, tender inside.

"So that's why he's called 'the Horse,'" Quith said, lifting the divider and peeping through the gap.

"What?" Finila said.

"Too late, he's in," Quith said, lowering the divider again. "So this is the limestone-cut pools. Gossip says more than one Serpentine girl has climbed up into these pools virgin and come down a woman. Tiss from our draft, the one who the Matron used to have read aloud: she had a fine old time up here with that apprentice from the flight cave. The one who's always logging stuff."

Ileth, herself the subject of salacious gossip that had thankfully gone stale, didn't ask for details. Instead she popped a fig in her mouth, leaned back, and shut her eyes, savoring the sweet fruit as she tried to ignore the hooting and splashing from the other side of the tenting. "This would be fine if it were just us."

"But a lot less fun," Quith said, peering under the tenting again.

One of the boys made a hooting sound and she gave a shocked gasp and giggled.

Singing broke out on the other side of the tent wall. A ribald song started, sputtered, and died off. The beer was taking effect.

They switched to a new tactic. "Come over, come over, won't Ileth come over . . ." they sang.

"Not on your life," Ileth called up at the clouds.

"Come over, come over, won't Finila come over . . ." Finila, who had water all over her glasses, shook her head, looking terrified.

Ileth spoke for her. "Why? Nothing worth seeing over there."

Quith yelled, "You've had too much beer!" They took it as a challenge and Ileth heard a good deal of splashing and clinking.

"Come over, come over, won't Quith come over . . ."

"Well, I'm going to do it," Quith said, standing up.

"Quith!" Ileth said. Finila sank even deeper into the water so just her eyes peeped out.

"You have about six scandalous stories around your name. I don't have any," Quith said, pushing aside the curtain and jumping in to general male acclaim.

"Ha!" Ileth heard Quith say. "You were right, Ileth. Nothing much worth seeing. No, not even that."

Quith broke out laughing and Ileth risked a peek. She was in the water, hunkering down so it came up to chin height. She'd herded the boys in her pool to the other side like a particularly wolfish sheepdog.

"No more of this nonsense," the Horse said. "Quith, jump back to your side of the curtain, before you bring the Committee down on me with half the Assembly behind."

"Blame it on the beer," one of his wingmen said. "It's good beer."

"The Committee wouldn't like girls drinking beer any better," the Horse said. "I'd be sent up before a jury as a corrupter of youth and shipped off to the Azures."

"It would make a good painting," one of the boys said. "Bare breasts always sell. Three women enjoying beer in a hot spring."

"Lukewarm spring," someone corrected.

"I've always wanted to model," Quith said, getting out of the boys' pool and returning to her side of the curtain.

"O nymph, be mine—" someone started to recite, but was abruptly cut off when a fig hit him in the face. Quith closed the curtain.

On the way back, Ileth was once again put in line just behind the Horse. She took a few quick steps to get next to him.

"Thank you for this," Ileth said. "We enjoyed it."

"Should have known it would get out of hand. I should have sent you and Quith and Finila into Vyenn with a few figs for a respectable tea. I'll hear about it from the Matron now and be lucky if she doesn't write the Committee."

Ileth had never heard of "the Committee." "That's the second time you've mentioned a committee. Some group of Masters at the Serpentine?"

"You never heard of the Committee of Public Health, Ileth?"

"I . . . I don't think so."

"They're not the terror they once were. Back in the first years of the Republic—no, it goes back further than that. You know the Vales were originally settled by miners."

"Yes, everyone knows that. Miners and trappers, in the north."

"It was just men. The only women they ever saw were in trips to brothels or establishments that ran a brothel as a sideline. Even as the Vales grew, in the days of the king and his court, the Vales has had a reputation as a strange area, full of oddities. Like the dragons. Yes, the dragons were here before us, but that's a history I'm not fit to tell. But the Vales always had a disreputable air, and every town with more than one street having a jade or two didn't help. The king wasn't doing anything about it. Some say it was one of the causes of the declaration of the Republic. A roused dragon has nothing on the wealthy shipping line owners who find their only son erupting with pox. Everywhere you looked people were disfigured. Masks and false noses. In the early days of the Republic, the Committee of Public Health was an attempt to fight the disease."

"Where I grew up, when the lodge-keeper had his friends over, I used to pick up their tankards with a hook and use it to drop them in a boiling pot out of fear of it."

The Horse chuckled. "When the Republic was declared, the Committee of Public Health cleaned up the brothels, shut them down. That wasn't their only goal; clean water for everyone was another, functioning sewers. Treated those they could. But the Committee got highhanded, asking for more emergency powers. They started shipping off people deemed incurable to the Azure islands. Penal colonies, you might call them. 'Pits of despair,' I'm sure you've heard that phrase."

"It's from a book, right?"

"Yes. It's about a young man who falls in love with a prostitute and she gets shipped off and he goes in search of her. *Arana Denn*, it's called, named after the girl he's searching for. It's a famous novel, because much of it is just the author's observations of what he saw on these islands."

"So people who read the book stopped them?"

"There were other reasons. The Committee started going around pressing people for donations. If you donated, you were a good citizen in their eyes, if not, they put you on the next ship out. Eventually they picked on the wrong bunch, the Canalmen's Syndicate, I think it was, and they had the money and political backing to put together a commission of investigators and lawyers and brought them before a jury. They were financially and socially ruined."

"Then why are you afraid of it?"

"The Committee still exists. Dragonfire, a few of their pits on the Azure, have people in them even today. They even do good work, here and there, checking that garbage is burned and buried and every province has a physiker-general with the authority to order quarantine. Mostly they're wielding power through their influence at the Assembly these days. They don't like the fact that boys and girls are both admitted to the Serpentine. They're always sniffing for weakness, too."

Ileth wondered if she should stop bathing in the Skylake. She always thought she'd just been giving the bored sentries a moment or

two of harmless diversion while she cooled off after dancing, not risking a moral inquisition.

"If they get evidence that the Serpentine is the den of libertines they believe it to be, it'll go into their *Record*—that's a journal they print, the *Record of the Accounts of the Committee of Public Health*—and then we'll be hearing about it for years."

Ileth smiled. The Matron had a whole bookshelf of annuals of the *Record*. She'd sometimes had her girls read aloud from its "Devotion Page" in the quiet after dinner. Interesting to know its history.

After the week-over, the Horse put them to work digging a drainage trench from the dairy. Ileth, Quith, and Finila found themselves keeping track of tools and feeding everyone at mealtimes. Proper work for young ladies.

Ileth watched the Guard on the other side of the Bridge Lane drilling with pikes, knocking hay bales off a swinging wood beam that she supposed represented a horseman. It looked like fun.

Ileth found herself looking forward to her talks with Quith on the way back to the Manor. It took her mind off how tired she felt and the soreness in her feet and legs. It was almost like her first days in the Serpentine, when she and Quith were crammed up together at the top of the attic stairs.

Like the night Ileth was talking about another dragon meeting being called, and the dancers needing to attend. "I sometimes think the girls are here . . . well, to kind of be like you dragon-dancers. Only for the boys. Something to divert them."

Odd thing for Quith to say. Quith usually dealt in the here and now and what happened to whom.

"That's interesting. How so?" Ileth asked.

"Sometimes you say you soothe them, and other times you divert them. It makes me think of my mother with my father when he has a hard day."

"I suppose."

"I think we do the same thing with the boys. Having a few girls

around keeps them all tense and energetic, like a thunderstorm boiling up to release lightning. Life on the boil."

"Life on the . . . boil?"

"It's one of Mum's expressions, you know, boiling water giving off steam. The urge to reproduce. Like beasts in rutting season, there's all this extra energy to accomplish things and distinguish yourself. Each sex is trying to show off. If it were just boys here, they'd be like a pot of water without any flame under it."

"None of them even bring me to a simmer," Ileth said.

Quith narrowed her eyes. "Nobody? Not even Rapoto Vor Claymass?"

"Especially not Rapoto Vor Claymass. That Blacktower trio . . . I wouldn't mind dancing with that Dun Klaff, if you want me to admit to something, but nobody's making me swoon. Certainly not enough to-to risk my apprenticeship. Did that once, thanks to a gripe pot and relief that I was still alive. Never again."

"Oh, so that's why I saw you taking the air on the Long Bridge this summer out of the top of your overdress in just your sheath. To impress the dragons," Quith said. "And anyways, 'never has to go a long way and always falls apart on the trip.' That's another expression of my mother's."

"I was probably letting the sweat dry off. You have sharp eyes, if you saw that all the way from the Manor."

"I heard about it at dinner."

"Who noticed?"

Quith shook her head, smiling mischievously. "Wouldn't you like to know. He was impressed."

"I'm not as modest as the Matron would like. Or even Ottavia, I suppose."

"What's she like?"

"She's not the Matron. There are still rules. She'd bring the roof down on one of us if we smuggled a boy into the Quarter, which is impossible because we're packed in there like fish in a salt tray."

"Yes, I often feel like the Matron's beliefs aren't entirely consistent. We have the finest young men of the Vales here, but if they see an

exposed shoulder they'll throw you down and plow you like a spring field with rain on the way."

"Quith!"

"Sorry. I've been distracted ever since that trip to the pools. It was fun to be looked at for once."

"There are much better ways to be looked at. Think of a . . . a victory parade in Sammerdam."

"I don't think we'll be winning victories any time we're apprentices. Caution and retrenchment."

"What's that?"

"Oh, just something I heard from one of the wingmen who were giving those commissioners a tour. He said they were talking caution and retrenchment ever since the Galantine fiasco."

Ileth went silent after that.

Ileth followed Santeel's example in learning how to split her duties between the dancers and Horse Lot. She and Santeel rose early, with Shatha, and put in time in the predawn at drills and fatigues. They'd then eat a quick breakfast in either the dragon kitchens or the Great Hall depending on Santeel's training and where Horse Lot was expected to assemble, and then spent the day with their fellow apprentices training. Then they'd help with the dancing at night.

The trick was getting enough sleep.

In good weather Horse Lot engaged in outdoor labor of some kind maintaining the Serpentine, labor seemingly designed to drain every last iota of energy out of their young bodies until they barely had strength for dinner. Fixing, washing, mucking out, gardening, pulling creepers off the walls. There were training drills too, putting out mock fires by forming bucket chains and keeping the water flowing for an hour wherever the gutters and sluices most needed a good flushing out. Some of the boys ended up with rat bites from the vermin deluge flushed out, and the girls were sometimes set to work washing out wounds with vinegar before dressing them. Ileth would have liked to prove that she could kill rats with the best of them—she used to be

able to pick a rat off a barrel of flour with her sling—but the Horse and his wingmen wouldn't let her go into the gutters and sluices. Perhaps it was just as well; the odors would have been hard to remove and the dragons might have objected to her aroma.

Fall closed in with rain and wind. Master Traskeer was called away again on some unfinished business at the Assembly and he departed with an unusually large escort of dragoneers. Ileth wondered if it was some attempt to awe the Assembly with a display of the Republic's aerial power. Her lot didn't notice his absence. They started working with the horses a little, just going around in circles with them, the Horse correcting their seat, or heels, or elbows each time they passed him.

Ileth began to understand the Horse's method. You figured out jobs by doing them. The wingmen were always ready to step in to answer questions, but you mostly worked things out with each other, learning who was best at what. Finila, she learned, had excellent hearing, listening like a terrier for rats in the sluices and telling the boys where to look. Quith was the lot's directory; she always seemed to know who was where and what they were doing. Ileth became the lot's handywoman, fixing everything from flapping bootheels to dull knives and improvising breathing masks for the rat-killers with rags, camphor, and rosemary. She drew on her years of experience in the Captain's Lodge, running it on nothing but breeze and spit, as the Freesand expression had it.

With the last gasps of warm weather, the Serpentine opened its gates for the Feast of Follies. She skipped the feast; bad memories wouldn't allow her to participate, though she did help with such gathering and sewing for the costumes as were within her abilities. Instead she somewhat redeemed herself with Ottavia by being on duty, dancing by music box for bored dragons who weren't interested in watching their human allies celebrate.

It wasn't much of a celebration. The food, more like ordinary Serpentine fare with punch and molasses snaps, disappointed. The wind was bad so only protected lights on the Long Bridge could be up, and

there weren't many parties up from Vyenn. The town was in the throes of hard times and there wasn't money for frivolity. Just a few merchants who did business with the Serpentine and of course the fishermen came with their families. Ottavia said the dragon-dancing exhibition drew a good crowd and there was some talk of building a theater in town where they could exhibit.

After the Feast, the weather turned cold. The Horse moved his lot to training indoors in what was left of the hippodrome.

Ileth soon learned that whatever her skills as a dancer, she was awful atop a horse, easily the worst in her lot. Most of her lot were experienced pleasure riders, having visited friends and played games on horseback since their youth. Even Quith looked more comfortable up there, riding easily with her hips swaying with the horse while her posture stayed up. Ileth found herself lurching about, elbows out and toes pointed in, hunched over as the trotting horse's back pounded at her buttocks.

"You have some work to do," the Horse said. "I thought you dragon-dancers were supposed to be graceful."

"When I'm on m-my own legs," Ileth said, looking at the ruin all the riding was making of her wool winter stockings. They looked like a badly constructed ladder.

They heard their first lectures on fighting atop dragons and used quite good clay models someone had made years ago to learn about warlike formations the dragons took on foot and in the air, alone, with a partner, or a trio. Rocks represented dragoneers, straw shafts enemy lines. The Horse surprised them by saying dragons often preferred to fight on foot. They could hug the ground, protecting their vulnerable undersides, and keep their wings tucked tight behind their great muscular shoulders. As part of a battle line or array they could have their sides guarded by allied humans. Their scales were at their toughest when deflecting arrows, crossbow bolts, and meteor shot from directly ahead.

"*Dragon on the ground, dragon safe and sound,*" the Horse quoted.

They practiced basic military evolutions, using horses from Vyenn and more prosperous farms that had a horse or two exclusively for riding. The visiting horses didn't care for the dragon-odor and were skittish and hard to control. Ileth felt particularly bad for one mare whose owner said he'd have to send her to be slaughtered as he couldn't afford her anymore. The Horse tasked her with acclimating the mare to dragons, since she proved such a hopeless horsewoman.

Ileth convinced Aurue to visit the horse in a sheltered corner of the Serpentine wall with the horse well tied down. After its initial screaming terror (Ileth had never heard a horse give its terrified, piercing scream, and it took days for the sound to get out of her head) with Aurue just standing placidly and making what seemed to Ileth humming noises, the horse settled down a little, but its eyes were still freakishly white as it stared at the dragon, and its back hooves shifted about nervously as though they had a mind of their own.

"I talked to her," Aurue finally said. "She's not much for conversation, but she no longer thinks I'm going to eat her. She's still fearful of my smell."

"Horses talk?" Ileth asked.

"Most animals do. Social ones. Cats, cats and dragons really get on. Eagles, most of the great hunting birds will talk to a dragon. Vultures like us especially. But with these herbivores it's not much better than grunting and pointing, though I've been told you can get sense out of a pig."

"Why don't humans understand them?"

"You humans are in-between. Not animals, not dragons. Any progress with my dragoneer?" He didn't sound enthused about the matter. Nor was the Serpentine. Any rumors about a full dragoneer position opening up set tongues wagging, but Ileth hadn't even heard Quith mention it.

"I just had a note from the Charge this morning. He wants to speak to me after dinner. If convenient. As if a first-year apprentice will turn down the Charge of the Serpentine. I suspect it's about you." Ileth was proud of getting a speech like that out so easily. Strange how her

stutter faded with dragons, as long as the dragon was a companionable sort like Aurue.

"Good that he's polite. Taresscon growls at the younger dragons. Says she's too old for niceties. *If you can't fly the weight, go eat the fish somewhere else.*" His *griff* twitched. "I'm not her favorite."

Ileth found it amusing that the younger dragons had their own difficulties with the elders.

They went back to the horse. After an hour's work, Ileth managed to ride her all the way around the dragon. Awkwardly, but she managed to keep her elbows at her sides and chin up. Most of the time.

Meetings at Charge Roguss Heem Deklamp's tower had never led to anything but difficulty for Ileth (a sentiment shared by most of the Serpentine, though Ileth was in no position to know it at that moment). She approached the door at the invited time, interested for Aurue's sake. He had become her favorite dragon. Yet she never danced for him.

Ileth looked at the darkening sky and wondered. Charge Deklamp had once told her something about saving dark business for the sun being down, and with winter coming on and the air already frosty he might consider it an ideal night for skullduggery.

Dogloss let her in and she was astonished to see the three men she considered "her" dragoneers: Dun Huss, Amrits, and the Borderlander. Serena, wingman to the Charge himself, was also there, standing quietly behind the Charge at his desk. A large-scale map had been hung up on the wall behind the Charge's desk. Ileth instantly recognized the outline of Pine Bay—labeled on the map as *The Great North Bay*—and the Freesand, and all the lands of the North Province. West it extended to the beginnings of the Borderlands, and east to the straits that led out to the Inland Ocean, Daphia south of them, and the Rari coast all along the peninsula that turned the straits into a key shape or a hairpin.

So. The meeting wasn't to be about a rider for Aurue, then. She wondered if it could have something to do with her report.

"Good, Ileth is here," the Charge said, owlish eyes droopy and staring. "We've been at this too long. Let's take a break for something warm and restoring. Ileth, you look chilled. Dogloss can fill a tray with mugs of something warm, would you?"

Ileth, as the junior of the assembly, helped Dogloss with the refreshments. Dogloss told her it was milk with old tea leaves and some spices; the Charge liked to have it in the winter before retiring. She carried in the steaming pot and ladle, with Dogloss following behind, and put it on a little serving table that had been cleared of books by Serena. Ileth poured everyone cups. There was some talk about the new dairy. The first few cows were not producing much milk, but everyone believed they were just upset by the dragon-smell and would do better in the spring.

"None for me, spiced milk gives me wind enough to empty the flight cave," Amrits said. "Wouldn't have any of that sluice-clearer your family has the nerve to put their Name on, would you, Deklamp?"

"Of course. Dogloss knows where it is."

Once they had their warm milk, with Amrits taking wine, the Charge looked around the room. "Good company, dragoneers," he said.

The Borderlander snorted and muttered something about a *milk toast*. She supposed it was a personal joke. They drank. The milk had that spice she'd had with the Commissioner-General, cinnamon, in it. It was warming, and she felt infinitely more at ease than the last time she'd tasted it. Even more warming was the idea of sharing a toast with those she considered the Serpentine's best dragoneers. She'd even helped build the dairy that supplied the milk.

"Now, Ileth, no doubt you recognize the coastline behind my desk," the Charge said, after they'd emptied their glasses. Everyone took seats, except for Serena, who stood near the Charge. Ileth sat on the little couch she'd shared with Galia as a fourteen-year-old novice.

"The Headlands, Freesand, and Pine Bay."

"We in the south call it North Bay, but yes. We're planning to pay a call on your own Governor Raal and we thought the mission might be

helped by one or two northerners. Speaking in familiar accents, knowing the local names of things." He smiled at the last.

Ileth nodded.

Deklamp continued: "Governor Raal is a powerful man. The representatives in the Assembly from the North Province take their cues from him, and it's the biggest province after Jotun. We need his cooperation for a project we have in mind among your people, and this trip is hoped to help secure it."

Ileth didn't much feel as though they were "her" people, but she was intrigued. She wondered if the project concerned the Rari. Odd that Deklamp didn't mention the commission. Perhaps it was just a coincidence. She couldn't be the only one wondering how the Vales could trade with the rest of the world with the Galantines blocking the river south.

"I will help if I can, but don't think me an expert on the north. I-I've never even been to Stavanzer."

"You may be the small weight that tips the balance in our favor," Dun Huss said.

Ileth felt wary. Caseen, the Master of Novices, had said something about Governor Raal making an effort to return her to the Captain's Lodge. The farther she stayed from him the better off she'd be. "I just started with my lot."

"This is not another absence such as you suffered in Galantine lands," Charge Deklamp said. "We could order you to go, but I'd rather explain my reasons. First, these dragoneers asked for you. Second, I believe you are aware that Governor Raal is interested in you on behalf of the gentleman who ran the Lodge you . . . quit to enter the Academy. Perhaps if he can see you, hale and thriving in your new life, he'll stop sending letters to us about returning a runaway. He seems to believe that there was some sort of conspiracy to send you off to the Galantine Baronies rather than return you to your lodge's doorstep in the Freesand. Third, it would be valuable experience for an apprentice. Fourth and lastly, an extra set of hands are welcome with a party of dragons this size."

Ileth was persuaded. From the neck up, at least. Her stomach had gone sour at the thought.

"You're less quick to agree this time," the Charge said, owlish stare fixed on her. It occurred to her that in her previous meeting when the request to go to the Galantine Baronies was considered, all the faces were different. Dun Huss had been in the Baronies, Galia was lost to the Galantines, the Master of Apprentices was absent, and Caseen, the Master of Novices, had a new group to watch over.

"May I . . . may I know more about the purpose of the visit?"

The dragoneers exchanged looks with the Charge. "For now it must remain a secret. Have no fear, this is not some ruse to return you to the Freesand. You are signed on as an apprentice here. We have our end of the contract to keep up as well, you know."

"I will do my best."

"No doubt of that," Dun Huss said.

"Am I the only apprentice going?" Ileth asked.

"Why do you ask?" the Charge said.

"Four—that's a lot of dragons to attend."

"Contrary to the belief of our wingmen and the apprentices, dragoneers do take care of their own mounts," Amrits said.

"When shall we leave, sir?" Dun Huss asked.

"If the weather holds, tomorrow. Go scrounge up a few leftovers from dinner and have them by your bed, just in case, Ileth."

Ileth realized she'd be so busy she'd scarcely have time to draw breath. "I am to ride—"

"You ride behind me," Serena said. She had a dry, crackling voice. "Telemiron is a fine dragon, fast and smooth. The others will have a job keeping up."

The Charge and Serena covered the map again. "One more thing, Ileth. Don't say anything about the flight, even where you are going, to anyone but those in this room. May I have your word on that?"

The Charge of the Serpentine had never asked for her word on anything. Ileth felt something that washed back and forth between fear and excitement. "You have my word, sir."

As predicted, the evening was breathtakingly busy. On her way to the Great Hall to scavenge, she stopped by the hippodrome and found the Horse riding the mare she'd been adjusting to dragon-smell.

"This isn't a bad horse at all, Ileth. I think I'll buy her. I expect I'd get a good price."

She had to wait for him to complete another circuit to speak again.

"I shall be leaving on dragonback in the morning."

"Yes, they told me you might be away through the next week-over, possibly more." He stopped the horse, then urged the mare into an evolution where she spun about in a circle with her back legs as the center. "This horse had a good trainer. And he was going to send her to slaughter? Times must be very hard in Vyenn if he couldn't sell."

"I didn't want you to think . . . to think I had left the lot."

"Oh, I can tell when someone's getting ready to quit. Horses, humans, dragons, the body signals intentions before the mouth produces anything. Not you. You'll quit when you're stretched out dead in the mud." He smiled so she wouldn't take the suggestion too seriously.

"May I ask you something?"

He shifted the horse's hindquarters around and started riding it crossways through the hippodrome. Ileth had never seen a horse go forward and sideways at the same time, crossing its legs much as the dancers did when they did a move called a travel shift.

"That's what I'm here for."

"How long have you been at the Serpentine?"

"I was draft of forty-nine." That was seventeen years before her draft.

"All that time, and you still don't have a dragon?"

"It's not like that. I like the dragons. Forget the flying, I would like to spend whole evenings sitting and talking to some of them, but . . . well, it's this nose of mine. I could just never get used to the smell. Couldn't get the smell out of my clothes. Lost my appetite, and I like to eat. Horses are better. When I have my ale in Vyenn, the barmaids don't hand it to me with their arm extended like this . . ."

He stuck out his arm and turned his face away, wrinkling his nose. Ileth started laughing so hard she had to sit down.

"See, I'm not such a terrible fellow. I always make allowance for duty. Good luck on your commission, Ileth."

Word came early to the Dancers' Quarter the next morning that they would depart at midday, as the grooms would be taking extra time to grease four sets of dragon wings for winter travel, as it was likely to be cold north of the Cleft. Ileth rolled up her modest possessions and climbed into her flying rig. There was mild interest that she'd be gone for a few days on dragonback. Preen asked her about shopping opportunities and Ileth explained she was told she couldn't discuss the commission in any way.

She was nervous. More nervous than she'd been on her flight into Galantine lands her first year, and she couldn't account for it beyond an odd forboding poking about at her. The trip felt like an unopened envelope that you know contains bad news. She had a premonition of doom, that some wheel in the clockwork of her fate was turning and she didn't much care for it. She needed to be alone to think.

If you wanted privacy, one of the best places in the Beehive was the central shaft around the lift. It was partly a ventilation chimney, partly a passage so the dragons could move quickly, and partly a mechanism for moving heavier loads between levels. The lifting mechanism was a marvel of ingenuity. Some special pride of the tinkers. Ileth didn't know any tinkers; they kept very much to themselves and were even more cloistered from the everyday routines of the Serpentine than the dancers, but she'd seen them going about with their tools and notebooks and plans. Ileth would have been hard put to even prove they existed as she didn't know a single name among them. Their conversation on the rare occasions when she passed them in the halls was as esoteric as two priests speaking in Old Hypatian.

There were a pair of tinkers working on the cables of the lift-mechanism track while she took her air. She noticed Santeel Dun Troot in an overdress burning something in an old metal trough at the bottom

of the shaft where it led off to the Cellars. Each party ignored the other. She was interested enough that she made the climb down to join her.

"Not off yet?" she asked as Ileth hopped down.

"Santeel, what's this?"

"Burning bandages. Vithleen was wounded this morning."

"Wounded?" The news startled her out of her gloomy thoughts.

"She's fine. Bled worse than it was, as Threadneedle likes to say. The baby dragons were worrying at Vithleen; I guess dragons cut teeth just like human babies, or 'they grow and sharpen as they use them like cat claws' might be more accurate. One tore too deep."

Santeel was in one of her manic moods, thrusting bloody bandages into the flames and then raking everything about with a poker to make sure they were thoroughly burned. She never did anything halfway. If she made you scrambled eggs, there wouldn't be a hint of egg white anywhere in them because her arm had spun like a whirlwind mixing them.

"They'd burn more easily if the blood was dry."

"Threadneedle demands that the dressings be burned immediately," Santeel said. "He used to come and watch me do it himself, then he had his principal apprentice watch, and eventually they decided burning rubbish wasn't too much for me. Or did he ask you to come check on me and make sure I wasn't stealing bloody dressings?"

"Why would you steal bandages?"

"Because there's dragon blood on them. The witchcraft-and-alchemy set go wild for the stuff."

Ileth had been warned often enough against trying to get dragon blood and sell it outside the Serpentine. *You'd be put before a jury with the Masters themselves presenting charges*, she'd been told.

Ileth wanted to find out about Vithleen, but Santeel was grumbling about Threadneedle keeping her up late making her sketch pressure points for dragons if you needed to stop bleeding in a limb, wing, or tail and she'd have to miss dancing with the troupe. Her Master liked to follow up on a practical lesson like the one she'd had with Vithleen this morning with reinforcement of the theories she'd learned.

"Applying a tourniquet is a useful blockage. To hear Threadneedle tell it, anything that goes wrong with your health is a blockage. You stutter because you have a blockage somewhere in the nerves running to your tongue. Flow and blockage, blockage and flow."

The last of the bandages were in now; Santeel stirred the mass with a metal rod and left the rod in the trough to cook off any incidental blood.

"You know, I can go along with a lot of it; obviously blood has to flow through your body and we all know food comes in one end and goes out the other and if your lungs are all filled with mucus, the air can't move about properly, but then they get to some maladies and it sounds like a wild story by a bad liar who's been cornered. *Your mother's womb was never pushed back into place by the Divine Goddess of the Running Rose Salmon. Go to a temple hot room and burn some priest-blessed moss and lie on the floor with the soles of the feet together, that often brings her.*"

"Are they really like that?" The Captain had never had much use for physikers. Said they were a waste of money. He treated sick children with either ardent spirits or great spoonfuls of fish oil, depending on mood. He made a horrible drink of raw eggs and hot peppers that had them feigning full health so they wouldn't have to drink the foul stuff.

"Some of them. We saw a lot when our mother was terribly low. I understand it happened after I was born. I think one of those physikers they called in asked a great deal of questions about what sort of offerings she'd made to get her womb restored. It went on for years. Never did any good.

"Then finally this Boils showed up. I know that's a terrible name for a physiker, but apparently he was brought all the way over from the Old Coast to treat the Executor of the Exchange's boils and there was some confusion when he was entered into the Sammerdam city rolls because nobody understood his language and his travel guide wasn't much better. Physiker Boils came and started talking about the imbalance of the Four Elements and had Mother in baths at an icehouse and crawling through mud and then finally jumping to get more air under

her, and she started to get better. My father has sworn by the Boils Practice ever since. I'm glad it worked, because I love my mother, but the Boils Practice struck me as being as phony as a horsehair wig. There's a family rumor that Mother did act on the stage a couple times in her youth in Zland. Maybe she pretended to be better so Boils didn't have her run up the observatory stairs and jump off to get enough air around her."

Perhaps the Captain's health-through-freezing-seawater-and-fish-oil system wasn't so outrageous after all.

Ileth warmed her hands in the dying fire of the bandages. "I should see if I can make myself useful in the flight cave."

"Don't forget your manners up there," Santeel said. "I've only just got you to quit drinking your soup."

"I'll miss stepping on your toenail cuttings all over the washroom."

Santeel made a face, but there was no displeasure in it. "Fair skies, Ileth."

"Favorable wind, Santeel."

Ileth was a seasoned enough dragoneer to pack everything for the trip the night before into a single big canvas roll of the kind used by sailors. At the heart of it, protected like a seed in a piece of fruit, was her music box. A change of clothes, comb and brush, tooth-scrubber, and such were wrapped up in a roll held closed by some old costume cording. Luckily there'd been enough from the batch Ottavia gave her to relace her boots for the trip. It made her look like a soldier on campaign, but it didn't seem likely to break.

Santeel had offered her a jar of skin salve that she'd used on her training flights to fight wind and frost. With her exhausting schedule of dancing and training, she wasn't flying and suspected the oils would go rancid soon, so she pressed it on Ileth and insisted that she use whatever remained, as her anatomy studies didn't seem likely to end anytime soon. Santeel looked tired and ill. Ileth had too much to do at the moment to think about Santeel's health, but she did accept the salve with heartfelt thanks.

wounds. His wings were more sewn-up-and-healed rents than they were skin. She'd never met a dragon who so looked as though he'd been torn up and put back together. Yet this was their Charge's dragon, ridden in most cases by his wingman.

He had a small saddle on him, built for Serena's proportions. She showed Ileth the seat she'd arranged behind, sort of a leather saddle blanket looped around the dragon and a thick pad that fitted to the back of Serena's saddle. She also had a safety tether she could hook to her bracing vest.

"There are folds in the leather cover; they're dragon-sized saddle-bags, but they'll fit your legs just fine."

Ileth tied her bundle between herself and Serena. She knew her knots; it would stay put and not fly up and hit her in the face in case Telemiron had to dive.

"We'd better get up and saddled," Serena said. "I want to make sure you're set."

Ileth climbed up, slipped her legs into the holsters, and put on her tether. Serena examined the tether and her seat. "Good. Gauntlets on."

Serena swung herself up into her saddle with the aid of a mounting-hook. It was a wicked-looking tool, probably useful as a weapon in an emergency. A flight cave attendant stood by to help but wasn't needed. Serena and Ileth both then checked Serena's safety tether, and she pulled down her cap and put on her gloves. She nodded three times in a Commonist prayer and patted Telemiron on the neck.

"It'll be a good flight," Telemiron said. "Fine weather. Easy distance."

Ileth appreciated the reassuring tone, but as far as she could tell the speech was directed at Serena.

"Weather doesn't matter to Old Coin here," Serena said over her shoulder. "Finds his way through anything. You just watch—if the weather turns bad, Etiennersea will call Telemiron to the front and have the rest form off him."

Ileth watched the front of the line of dragons. The light outside turned the lead dragons and dragoneers into silhouettes. Etiennersea

shifted her long neck this way and that as she looked outside the flight cave and then back in at the line of dragons, then lowered her head to Dun Huss. Dun Huss took a careful look at Ileth, then put his hand on Mnasmanus.

"Up in your saddles," Dun Huss called. His voice carried like a trumpet.

The three dragoneers mounted.

A flight cave attendant made one final run up the line, getting a nod from each dragoneer. Amrits made a chopping gesture with his arm to the mouth of the flight cave, and Etiennersea opened her wings and jumped. Her wings and Dath Amrits's yellow scarf caught the air and they plunged out of view.

"Brace, now," Serena said.

Soon Etiennersea appeared again, rising, wings beating hard, and Mnasmanus jumped. He was so strong his tail had hardly disappeared when he was up and rising, and then it was Telemiron's turn. He didn't step forward to the lip but preferred a run out of the flight cave, and Ileth had to experience being shaken back and forth by his snakeback gait before he was in the air. He hardly dropped at all and smoothly gained altitude toward the others, swiftly climbing above the lighthouse. When the Borderlander atop Catherix joined them, they formed into a diamond shape and turned west as though heading for Sammerdam.

Etiennersea took the lead, with Mnasmanus on her right and Telemiron to the left. Catherix rode to the back and a few dragon-lengths higher, though whether this was a standard variation on the diamond formation or Catherix just liked riding above her companions Ileth didn't know. That wild night of the egg theft the Border-lander had said something about Catherix diving on enemies like a hawk.

Telemiron's judgment was correct; it was good weather for flying. The mountaintops were hidden by clouds, but there was excellent visibility below the cloudline. Ileth had no trouble picking up the road she'd taken to the Serpentine all those years ago.

The dragons, except for Catherix, kept a close formation. She'd

been told it was easier for them to move through the air formed up like an arrowhead if they bunched up to where their wingtips were almost brushing.

Once they were among the mountains of the Spine they turned north, weaving among the mountaintops, going this way and that like a ship tacking into the wind, taking advantage of updrafts.

Ileth charted their progress on the map in her head. She'd spent countless hours of her youth studying the Spine, planning her escape from the Lodge, choosing the surest route to the Serpentine.

When they could just make out the Cleft Pass, separating the North Province from the rest of the districts, the dragons turned back east, wheeling at a distance that would make them invisible to the Republic's officials in the pass. Again, more secrecy. They soared up through the Blue Range and entered her home province.

She saw Dath Amrits gesture to Dun Huss and tried to follow the pointing arm. She knew enough about dragon-signals to know that gesturing with his hand formed in a blade rather than a fist or pointed fingers meant he'd spotted a landmark and no danger was involved. Ileth's mental map failed her at this point; she knew they were still at least a horizon or two from Stavanzer. If they were headed for the principal city of the north and the Governor's House, they should be headed northeast.

"Where are we going?" she asked Serena.

"Doesn't hurt for you to know now," Serena called back. "Stesside."

Ileth knew the Stess, it was a river that flowed out of the mountains and joined the Whitewater at Stavanzer. "What's 'Stesside'?"

"I thought you were from the north? Governor Raal's family estate."

The Captain had never talked politics with his roustabouts. She didn't know anything more about Governor Raal's life than she did the man in the moon, beyond that he was to blame for the rapaciousness of tax collectors and incompetent dredging in the Freesand channels.

They passed over the northern foothills of the Blue Range. She

made out a stout, squat five-corner tower. It couldn't be called a ruin, but the roof was more hole than roof and it showed no sign of occupation. A more comfortable-looking great house was below, on a more sheltered slope beneath. It had a vast barn, paddocks, and sheds in good meadowlands where the thick forest of the mountainside ended. The great house wasn't the only habitation. She traced the jagged line of what must have been the Stess with some manner of working building with a tall chimney and a few little houses scattered around it, though you could scarcely call it a village. As they circled lower, she saw barrels on carts and scattered about outside near doors and loading platforms. She remembered a dinner during her Galantine captivity when one of the Baron's brothers remarked idly that all the old families in the Vales made their money in either mining or brewing and distilling. Ileth guessed Governor Raal came from a distilling family, since nobody bothered putting water in barrels unless it was in preparation for a long sea voyage, and Pine Bay was leagues off to the north.

They landed on the grounds of the estate near a big barn, coming in for a landing in a frozen paddock. The dragons, breathing hard from their flight, gave off great clouds of vapor as they exhaled. They'd brought the clouds down with them, Ileth thought. She watched them stretch and settle their wings, each a little different. Mnasmanus shook himself like a wet dog and his scale rattled like a thousand coins being shaken in a cauldron.

Ileth forgot the cold in her limbs, watching with the same awe she'd felt at seven. Nothing was better than being around dragons. Nothing. They'd have to cart her out of the Serpentine cold and dead.

Finally she looked around Stesside from the ground. The air felt familiar to Ileth, a wet cold that passed effortlessly through everything but the thickest layers. She tried to sink into her flying coat.

"It'll snow and we will be miserable," Catherix said to the Borderlander in her thick Montangyan, sniffing at the barn.

"Plenty of room to squeeze in. Or you can tent up under your wings," the Borderlander told her.

Dun Huss strode up through the draconic fog bank to Ileth and Serena. "If anyone asks, we were on our way to the Notch, had a sprained wing on Mnasmanus, saw Stesside, and set down."

"My last meeting with Raal ended on an unpleasant note," Serena said. "You should start things off, sir. Ileth, you can help me with the dragons. No talking required."

"Ileth, you hear that?" Amrits said. "Try and keep your howler shut for once."

She nodded, smiling at him.

"See what I mean?" Amrits said to Serena. "Gab gab gab. It never stops with this one. Drives a man mad."

Dun Huss took his elbow and pulled him toward the Borderlander. The three clomped off toward the house.

Serena had them remove the saddles and they hung them in the driest corner of the barn. Ileth wiped them down, and by the time they were done with that, there were some gardeners or shepherds, judging from their long coats, signaling them from the edge of the paddock. They had a barrow and a tall washing basket.

Serena beckoned Ileth to follow.

The men politely removed their hats. "We've orders to bring food for them dragons."

The barrow was full of joints of meat, rather stringy. The washing basket had a great pile of rabbits. It would take both her and Serena to carry the rabbits. They weren't even skinned.

Serena pulled open the gate. "They're quite safe, if you wish to approach and say hello."

"Bad luck to even get near one, missy."

Ileth took the barrow and let them retreat. Between the two of them, they managed to get the rabbits over to the dragons.

The dragons were not impressed with the Governor's fare.

"That's mostly tripe," Mnasmanus said, poking with his snout in the barrow.

"We're eating rustic, I see," Etiennersea said. "They didn't even skin the rabbits."

Ileth had skinned plenty of rabbits to feed sheepdogs. "W-would you like me—"

The dragon rattled a *griff*, a friendly form of chiding. "No, apprentice, if we're going to eat rough, let's eat rough. My dear old dam always told me to eat more hair. Keeps your scale from dropping."

The Borderlander soon returned from the great house. He'd left his sword inside and carried a great curved bow and a quiver of arrows.

"Introductions are done. I said my piece, since I'm the most recent dragoneer to poke around up here. It's all argument now and I'll just make things worse. I'm going hunting."

"With a bow? Doesn't he have a meteor you can borrow?" Serena asked.

"I had one of those damn things blow up in my face one time," the Borderlander said. "Besides, if you can creep close and quiet on a stag, taking a man unaware's easy. I like to keep in practice." He turned to his dragon. "Catherix, if you can spot some herds for me and make them go into deep timber, I'll have a better chance. Ileth, there's to be dinner tonight, at the Governor's table, with his wife. Fine lady. You're specifically invited. He said don't worry about dressing, he understands."

Ileth felt the blood leave her face. The Governor. He'd been writing letters about her, demanding her return. Now she had to face him over a dinner table.

Serena pursed her lips. "Men understanding and women understanding are two different things. What the Governor's wife thinks of us might influence him."

Catherix brightened at the mention of hunting, swallowed her mouthful of rabbits, and walked out into the paddock, her tail flicking about like a cat following scratching in the walls.

The Borderlander nodded at Ileth, which was as good as a reassuring arm around the shoulder from other men, and he and Catherix moved off uphill. Catherix found a little hummock of land and

launched herself into the air. Ileth liked watching dragons at any time, but taking off was her favorite. She loved that first *crack!* of wings catching air. She watched Catherix spin up into the air, dragon's head intently studying the landscape as her body pitched about it.

With the dragons settled as comfortably as they could be in and about the barn, Serena opened her own rolled kit. It was interesting that she packed like Ileth, rather than employing baggage like the other dragoneers. Ileth wondered if she came from a nautical family.

"Let's see you in your best," Serena said.

"You've seen it. It's the same dress all the novices and apprentices wear."

"Then what's all that?"

"It's my music box, spare sheaths and such for dance."

"Oh dear, well, we'll have to do something."

Serena went to work rooting around in her own collection. She found a collar and neckplate with fancy lace that Ileth could wear over her shirt. "I put this under my formal tunic for a feminine touch," she said. "It will hide that man's shirt-top. Try not to spill wine on it."

"Don't you wish to wear it?"

"I can get by with about anything . . ."

Ileth wondered if that made her a better envoy from the Charge of the Serpentine. She had this way of making you comfortable around her and throwing you a little off-balance that Ileth was beginning to appreciate.

"I'll avoid wine."

"Do you object to powders and such?" She extracted a little case, like a flatter jewelry case, that opened to reveal a rather poor mirror, but it served.

Ileth had learned a little from the Baron's daughters at Chapalaine about how to apply such things.

"Only a little. Never had money for that sort of kit."

Serena chuckled. "Oh, you can still powder up even if you're nothing but purse-bottom. Many's the night I've had in Sammerdam or Tyrenna with just some soot smeared around my eyes."

Ileth watched her work. The transformation was startling. Her eyes looked larger, more emotive; they drew you. "In the north painting yourself is . . . is—"

"I know. We'll just do a little at your eyes. You'd be surprised how intimidating it is to some men. That's my great vice, men. Can't stay off them."

"You?"

"You know, like they say of the captains, girl in every port? I knew a man or two in most of the big cities. I'm a dragoneer, why not? There are some who are drawn to me because I'm an oddity. I don't let that happen so often as I have to be more respectable representing the Charge; I've had my fun with that and it's done. Now there's just my consort in Sammerdam—"

"You have a consort?" Ileth didn't know such things existed for women.

"He's not expensive. It's freeing. I get a presentable, attentive, and mannered man out of the deal. I never feel like he's trying to get a dragon to show up to entertain the neighbors."

As they worked and chatted, the men returned and changed for dinner, using a horse-trough pump to wash up. After a few words about the cold, they took turns working each other's faces with razors.

"I can't bear a cold-water shave," Amrits said, as Dun Huss wetted him with the towel Dun Huss had had his razor and soap rolled up within.

"Good for the skin," Dun Huss said.

Ileth found watching the men shave each other fascinating. Intimate, even a little affectionate, but without eroticism, like a couple of little boys peeing on a snowball together.

After they were done, Amrits rubbed his chin. "Blasted unfair. You've the better shave thanks to my hard work; the honorable up there will think I'm the slapdash."

"Who are you trying to impress? The wife? I've only seen one old woman about in the kitchen."

Amrits rubbed under his chin and gave Dun Huss a disgusted look.

"He knew I was coming so he hid all the good ones. Reester all over again."

With the delicate lace collar installed hiding the fact that she was wearing a men's work shirt, and a sweat-stained and worn one at that, and her thick overdress with its not-at-all-delicate straps, Ileth worked her hair as best as she could in the poor little mirror of Serena's case. She did like what Serena had done with her eyes. In better clothes she would have felt the equal of even Santeel.

The party departed for the house, avoiding the dragon footprints that had punched through the frost and found mud. They circled to the front so they might make a proper entrance.

"They've no children and you're not to bring them up," Dun Huss quietly warned. Ileth nodded. Not having children underfoot would be a pleasant change from Galantine lands.

Dun Huss wore the same dress uniform she'd seen when she was sworn in as a novice. The only decoration on it tonight was his old novice pin. Dath Amrits was gorgeous in new velvets and the latest in trousers. The men hung up their swords in the hall as soon as they entered; a family servant helped them with their cloaks and discreetly checked to make sure no one had mud or horse leavings on their boots.

"The Governor hopes you don't mind being received in the dining room. His wife prefers to sit."

"Of course."

The Governor's great house felt very old and crowded, compared to all the light and air she'd known at the elegant house in the Galantine Baronies during her internment with the dragon Fespanarax. The only room of a size worth mentioning downstairs was the dining room, long and spacious and opening on the upstairs where an empty gallery looked down. It was the hub the house had been built around. Ileth liked the look of the sitting room at the front. She'd glanced in as they passed; it felt warm and had upholstered chairs with a good window looking out on the lane up to the house.

In the dining room Ileth smelled wood oil and flowers. It featured a long, broad table that could easily sit twenty if the diners didn't mind

crowding. Then there was a largish gap between the table and fireplace where you could gather, standing, or arrange chairs about the fire for talk.

The Governor, his wife, and two servants in plain black awaited them by the fire. The chairs had been shifted from their usual spots—Ileth could see impressions on the rug—so the visitors could warm themselves by standing by it. The Governor's wife was seated.

Ileth, though she'd lived much of her life in the North Province, had never even seen the Governor or his carriage or however he went about. She knew he rarely left his working residence at Stavanzer. Business went to Governor Raal; he did not go to find it. He had an exaggerated, bony face with a prominent nose and ears that made Ileth think of a puppet, though his eyes were gentle and friendly, and the wiry frame of a man who was physically active. He stood next to his wife's chair with both hands on it, as if caught in the act of helping her into it and pushing it comfortably close.

Lady Raal (as Ileth soon learned she was called) was beautiful, but delicate. Ileth thought her an indoor flower of a person. Her shoulders—bare shoulders at dinner were in style at the moment, so both Ileth and Serena were decidedly out of fashion—and hands didn't suggest much activity.

Ileth noticed that the Governor's wife sat in a chair with an elegantly knitted shawl draped casually over her legs. The dining room chairs all had high, arching backs and wide arms; even in Galantine lands she thought they would be impressive. But there were extra pillows propping the Governor's wife up.

"Fresh faces in Stesside," Governor Raal said. "You've made us very happy."

"We don't often entertain at the country residence," Lady Raal added. "We hope this exception is as pleasant for you as it is for us."

Ileth warmed to them. Some of the unaccountable anxiety at this meeting disappeared up the chimney, vanishing with the chill. It was good to hear the familiar tones of the north again, though they were softened a bit by good education.

Dun Huss took over the job of introducing Telemiron's riders. "Charge Deklamp's wingman Serena you've met before, and to complete our party is one of our promising apprentices, Ileth. She was lately on a commission in Galantine lands and had some memorable experiences there."

Governor Raal nodded at Ileth, but his wife leaned so that she could see around Dun Huss. The movement made Ileth realize she was hiding, which wouldn't do for a Dragoneer of the Serpentine. She stepped out, realizing she was blushing and wishing her hair weren't such a fright. She performed her best obeisance.

"See, the object of your kind interest is healthy and thriving," Dun Huss said.

"We were relieved to learn the Rari hadn't snatched her. That was the fear of the lodge-keeper, a retired naval captain who devotes himself to charity now."

Charity! Ileth could spoil the dinner with stories of the Captain's charity.

"Please, sit," Lady Raal said. "The soup is ready to be served."

The dining room was pleasant enough, not at all stuffy thanks to the opening above and doors at either end, but dark, lit by the fire and a few candles. The wooden floor was old and creaky, but perfectly clean. The walls were simple wood panels, unadorned, which was strange as most houses in the Vales arranged as many paintings as they could on every wall, but these were bare unless you counted the carefully stained burls-and-knots decoration. The plates were equally simple, but Ileth noted they had a fine golden rim about them.

The Governor pushed his wife's chair close to the table and the men sat as soon as all the ladies were settled. The Governor himself poured everyone wine, starting with his wife and then moving down to Ileth and Serena. When his own glass was full he sat down.

"Find favor," he said, raising his glass. His wife murmured the same.

Ileth thought that was a good sign. It was the homey sort of a toast given up north at the start of a new venture, or before a trip or voyage.

Dun Huss glanced at her and Ileth tried to put encouragement in her eyes.

"Fi . . . find favor," she repeated. She just touched her lips to the rim but didn't drink, not wanting to risk the borrowed collar.

Her stutter cued the men and Serena to repeat the Governor's words. They drank. Except for Serena, who just raised her glass. The man who'd met them in the hall appeared with a tray of soup. The Governor and his wife looked at their guests expectantly. "Please, go ahead."

Amrits tried the soup. "Excellent. Not just saying that because I have an appetite from flying, either. Excellent! May I ask?"

The Governor sampled his. "Fall vegetables, squash, some chicken broth, creamed. Our cook is a wonder with creams and sauces. Galantine, originally."

"She fled the—the late unpleasantness, decades back," his wife added.

"We've tried to get her to train a younger girl, but she seems to think once she gives up all her tricks and secrets we're going to send her off."

Dun Huss was almost finished with his soup. "This is very good. So you never finished the story of this lodge-keeper. Usually a lodge-keeper getting a ward out the door and into a position is considered a success. Ileth occupies an enviable position. I would think he'd count her as one of his greatest achievements."

"I understand he'd arranged a position for her," the Governor said.

Ileth suppressed a snort. *Arranged.* Meaning he'd found Ileth a job, pocketed whatever money had been handed over to secure her employment and travel expenses, and having drunk it didn't have the ability to offer restitution to whatever great house she was to go into as a cook or a maid.

"We have so many orphans," the Governor continued. "Hard times. Rari raids. A husband and father is taken, the wife seeks work elsewhere and lodges the children until she can send for them. The expected letter never comes."

"Tragic," Dun Huss said. "But there is a solution."

"Yes, well, it feels like—it feels like pushing all my coin into one pot at the gaming table. My father was a great one at the gaming table, and the family is poorer for it."

Ileth's suspicion that this visit was to plan an operation against the Rari—strange that it was being done so soon after her interest in Annis Heem Strath's old plan—resolved into certainty. Had she put a bug in Dun Huss's ear about it with her queries? It didn't seem likely that Traskeer would have brought it to anyone's attention, given his opinion of her. But then he had disappeared to his old haunts at the Assembly.

"When you gamble," Ileth said, speaking slowly and carefully to leave her brain and tongue no room to betray her, "there's no way to change the odds."

Governor Raal looked at her as if she'd suddenly sprouted horns. Dun Huss made a small settling motion with his hand. "We encourage our younger dragoneers to contribute," Dun Huss said. "Sometimes we in the older generation benefit from the courage and enthusiasm of youth."

"I like my table free of political matters," Lady Raal said. "Perhaps we can move on to the meat."

The dinner proceeded through roast lamb shank and a turkey pie and finished with a baked cherry dish with a crust on top. Amrits tasted politely and gave his slice of cherry pastry to Ileth. Ileth was happy to eat her fill. The only thing she didn't touch was the wine. Serena did not have wine either but drank two glasses of water, complimenting their hosts on the water.

"Then our tastes are alike," Governor Raal said. "I believe the Stess's source is the best spring in the north."

The men stood to excuse themselves, and the Governor's wife, when solicited by her husband as to how she felt, insisted she wasn't a bit tired and would like a little peppermint tea to settle her dinner and hoped the men wouldn't abandon them too abruptly to continue their discussions. They could have music.

"If there's music, perhaps Ileth could dance for us," Dun Huss suggested. "Nothing overly expressive, please, Ileth, you've just had a large dinner and we don't want to upset your digestion."

"Yes, I would like to know about dragon dancing," Lady Raal said. "My cousin in Zland mentioned it in a letter. I believe she saw an exhibition that was a sensation."

While Ileth removed her boots and lamented the state of her stockings, the all-purpose servant opened one of the wood panels revealing a sort of deep closet and pulled out a keyboard-chest. The Governor himself sat on a bench produced by the servant and tested a few keys.

"Will a parade step do?" Governor Raal asked.

Ileth nodded.

"She does this alone, without a partner?" their hostess asked as Ileth bounced lightly, flexing her knees and warming up.

"Yes. The dragons find the movements and the music relaxing."

Ileth felt everyone's eyes on her.

"No need to be so nervous, dear," Lady Raal said.

Governor Raal started in on a parade step. He faltered a little at first but soon warmed to the instrument. Ileth, mindful of Dun Huss's instruction, hardly lifted her knees more than was needed to bring her toes to ankles and do little kicks and side steps. She did go up on the balls of her feet and rotated, kicking to the points of the compass to help her in each quarter turn.

The Governor stopped playing for a moment to applaud. "Oh, that was precisely done! Truly! Why, you seem to float as though the air is water!"

"This is rather sedate," Amrits said, drinking Ileth's untouched wine. "In front of a dragon there's more spinning and leaping about."

Ileth's dancing had an effect on the Governor's wife. Her eyes were wet. "How lovely. How accomplished! But what sort of torture chamber are you running on the Skylake, sirs? She has a scar as wide as a knitting needle on her eyebrow and her nose has been broken! Do you send girls into battle?"

"Accidents," Ileth said. Her nose had been broken long before she

passed through that red side door into the Serpentine. The Captain's wards had a lot of accidents.

The men stood, saying they would adjourn to the drawing room, but only after Governor Raal turned his wife's chair and pushed it closer to the fire. Ileth noted that the chair legs each wore little socks to make it easier to move about on the wood floor. He settled the blanket on her lap again and they clasped hands.

"I think the answer must be yes," she told her husband.

Ileth could just see the legs and shoes of the dragoneers in the next room through the big shared fireplace as the men sat down, attended by that all-in-one butler who'd met them at the door.

An old woman with her hair tied up in a scarf Galantine fashion brought in tea, and Ileth and Serena moved a pair of more comfortable upholstered chairs close to the fire. Ileth tried to lean close to the fire so she could hear what was being said in the next room, but they were burning pine logs that snapped and cracked over the low voices of the men.

Fortunately, Serena did the talking, as instructed. Ileth restricted her conversation to one-word appreciative remarks about the tea.

"You needn't be reserved, Ileth," Lady Raal said. "We're as warmly republican as any family."

Ileth smiled in response, vexed because she thought she caught Dun Huss saying something about the interval a dragon needed to replenish the fire-bladder. She'd much rather be in with the men.

"As hostess, I shouldn't mention such things, but the cost of sugar has become terrible, quite terrible. The Governor tells me it is because of the Galantine duties on river trade up from the coast. My dear sweet tea used to be such an affordable indulgence."

"Too bad we can't drink dyes and gems and copper out of the Azures," Serena said.

"When I was a little girl it all used to go out through the north. I remember the warehouses. I used to play in my father's warehouse before the fever. Like a rabbit warren, so many tunnels between the crates where only I could fit."

The old woman clearing the table groaned at the weight, and Ileth excused herself to help her.

The Governor's wife looked distressed. "You shouldn't carry so much, Ignata; Severan will attend to the table."

"I was idle in the kitchen, thought I should start washing up. Thank you, miss." She wasn't northern. She must be the Galantine cook. Ileth wondered if her speech was a Galantine accent long accustomed to Montangyan.

Ileth, carrying empty wine bottles, followed the cook through a short serving pantry to the kitchen. It was cramped and old-fashioned—even the Lodge had a newer cooking hearth—but there were a great many more copper baking pans and vessels, in good order and arranged along the walls and hung from the ceiling, and someone had installed a small pump and sink.

"This is nice," Ileth said.

"You are Ileth? From the Freesand Lodge?" Ignata asked, looking at Ileth sharply.

"Y-yes."

"Knew it as soon as I looked at your eyes and chin." She touched Ileth on the cheek, leaned close, and hugged her. "You even smell like your mother."

"You knew her?" Ileth asked.

"Girl, follow me down here. We can talk."

She lit a stub of a candle off a twig drawn from the quiescent fire. The stub went into a little carrier and she led Ileth through the kitchens and to a narrow stairway down.

"We can talk in the root cellar. Wine cellar would be better, and nicer, but I don't have the key for that."

She took Ileth to a narrow portal that was more panel than door and led to a stairway that Ignata had to turn sideways to get down. It was crowded, as the fall store of onions and potatoes and squash was in, along with jarred tomatoes and great stores of dried peas and fruit. "All set for winter. The Governor doesn't do much entertaining at this

house, but his secretary and clerks and counting-book come and stay sometimes when he's visiting, so we need plenty in store."

Ileth didn't care if the whole of the Iron Company of the Borderlands came for dinner, she needed answers.

"You . . . did you know my mother?"

"Know your mother? I cut the cord the night you were born. Not quite under this roof, but you're Stesside-born. I heard her name you."

"How did she—how did you end up here?"

"Oh, I was your mother's nurse when she was a girl. When she had to flee the purge I went with her. I was Directist, same as your family; most of the servants were. Horrible business. Your grandfather stayed to help the new owners with the estate after the Strictures; why he thought he had to given the price they got it for, he should have set fire to the place—well, there I go, bringing up the bad old business when I have herself's daughter here to look at. You've a bit of a stutter, I hear, but then so did one of your uncles, and your own grandfather used to take great pauses when he spoke, because when he was a boy— there I go again."

Ileth heard the door above open and startled, every nerve on edge.

"Ileth," Amrits called. "Our good Governor wants to see you dancing *for* the dragons."

"I'm—I'm helping . . ."

"Ignata," the old woman supplied.

"Leave her, our host is wondering what happened to you."

"You better go," Ignata whispered. "There could be trouble, me talking to you."

Ileth hesitated.

"Go on. I won't croak on you. We'll talk another time."

Ileth followed Dath Amrits out to the barn, stiff with frustration. It looked like snow; she smelled the possibility in the north air and felt the weight of the clouds. Well, if they were snowed in, so much the better. She could find an hour to escape and talk to Ignata.

Still no sign of the Borderlander and Catherix. She hoped they weren't lost in the darkness; Stesside didn't offer much in the way of

light. The dragons wouldn't all fit in the barn, so they'd arranged themselves where they could look into it, where she'd perform with the barn doors around her as though on a formal stage.

"Ah, here she is. I wanted to see you dance for the dragons, Ileth."

Serena, it appeared, had remained behind with the Governor's wife.

Ileth changed in a corner behind bales of fodder. She would be dancing for men. Again. But then the only stranger to her was Governor Raal.

Skin pimpled in the cold, she set out her music box on a bale of hay, the barn as her backdrop, the area around the door as her stage. Mnasmanus, who might have been signaled by Dun Huss, Ileth couldn't be sure, gave an appreciative rumble that was somewhere between throat-clearing and *go on*. Telemiron showed an active interest too. Etiennersea made room for the humans, shielding them from the wind with her bulk and raising a wing to keep the north wind from coursing directly into the barn, and just peeked into the barn around the edge of the door.

Well, if she was to be a dragoneer, she'd have to get used to doing her best no matter the circumstances. She'd dance in the long men's work shirt as though she were hot and sweaty in some dragon-warmed corner of the Beehive.

Dun Huss put his fists together discreetly, knuckles toward her.

Dath Amrits opened the music box with a flourish. He looked vaguely disappointed that there wasn't a sculpture of a reclining nude inside. The music started and Governor Raal gave an appreciative "ahhh."

It wasn't her greatest performance. Her muscles were cold for the first routine, she slipped on what she hoped was a mat of straw for the second, and only on the third did she feel like she'd done anything close to what Ottavia would expect (not just in terms of the cascades of sweat running down her back).

The Governor applauded and the dragons rattled their *griff*. It sounded like an army of tinkers mending pots, but then Ileth had a feeling that they'd been told to be demonstrative.

After, Dath Amrits himself brought her a drink of water and a towel from the house while Dun Huss talked to their host.

Ileth retreated to her hay racks again to put her overdress back on—why she could perform in just her sheath but not either strip down to it or climb into her clothes again in front of an audience, she would have had more difficulty than usual putting into words, but it was so nevertheless—and she heard the Governor speak to the dragons.

"How was your dinner, now? Enjoy it?"

Mnasmanus shifted on his feet like a nervous horse. "Get a lot of rabbits up here, do you, sir?"

"A hundred-sixty-weight* in meat a day is what your dragoneers say you live on."

"That's a minimum *average* ration, on campaign," Dun Huss said, puzzled at this declaration. "Our dragons often go a few days on next to nothing, then return to a post and eat hearty. Like most hunters, they are used to not eating, then eating a great deal."

Raal bristled at being corrected and drew himself up. Ileth swore his ears stuck out even more, like a dragon's *griff* being opened in battle. "And fatted flesh, greased meats, and oily fish if they use their fire, yes, I know."

"Do you have some concern?" Amrits asked, suddenly serious.

"I fear you dragoneers are like the builders who promise a bridge, accept a price, and deliver a ford, as building a bridge is an impossibility at the agreed price. Of course if I produce more money, I will get my bridge."

"I thought we'd decided to let the matter rest overnight," Dun Huss said.

Serena appeared, as though sensing a fight and coming to a fellow dragoneer's aid. She marked Ileth's music box. "I missed more dancing, I see."

---

* About sixteen pounds.

"I'm sure my wife was glad of female companionship," Governor Raal said. "Stesside is beautiful, but remote."

In the midst of the conversation the dragons all looked up. The humans followed them and a few moments passed before they could see what had produced the sound that had drawn them. A pale white shape descended, just a little unsteadily in the wind.

At first Ileth feared that Catherix was hurt, but as soon as she came to perhaps a man's height above the ground, gliding over the paddock and further terrifying the horses, she dropped her burdens with a series of thumps and came in for a landing.

The Borderlander descended, a little tiredly, with a bony old goat slung over his shoulder.

"Got a nice deer and two wild hogs. You have a lot of these hogs in your foothills, Governor. Do they give your farmers trouble?"

"There aren't many farms in the headwaters of the Stess. The men in the lower country get them, if they venture out of the hills."

Ileth and Serena inspected the game. One of the hogs and the deer had been killed by arrows. The other looked like it had had its neck snapped, and there were dragon-tooth marks in its back. Catherix had hunted too.

"Snapped some of your arrows, Governor," the Borderlander said.

"Oh, you made good use of that old bow. That's worth a few arrows," Raal said. "I don't hunt myself."

"Venison!" Telemiron said. He didn't speak much, at least around strangers, so Ileth was surprised at his enthusiasm. "We're always about cities, so I rarely get game."

"Can't they just breathe fire on the meat?" Governor Raal asked. He was staring at the dragons.

"If we do, it'll have a horribly charred taste," Mnasmanus said. "That doesn't taste any better to us than it would to you, sir. But I'd be happy to burn a hog if you are curious."

Etiennersea expressed herself in Drakine. They felt more than heard the low-register sound. Mnasmanus said something back.

The Governor was taken aback. It was fun, seeing him on his heels

after his high-handedness with Dun Huss. "What in the world was that?"

"Dragon speech," Dun Huss said, in his usual friendly way. He was too good a diplomat to mock Governor Raal's alarm.

The party broke up once the dragons settled in with their second, superior dinner.

Ileth slept, or rather didn't so much sleep as she lay there pretending to sleep and fighting her thoughts, in a hammock. She'd always liked hammocks, and the barn had dozens as they were a good way to store things up off the ground clear of vermin and could serve as emergency beds. She volunteered to remain with the dragons, as at least one member of the Serpentine should, through the night. She slept cocooned in blankets hugging her blanket-covered music box. Its presence comforted her.

The next morning Dun Huss breakfasted early with Raal and then they took a walk down the lane of the estate together—publicly to admire one of the views of the Stress valley below, but Ileth suspected that a decision was at hand. The other dragoneers breakfasted with Lady Raal. The Borderlander skipped the meeting and helped Ileth feed the dragons and put salve on their wings where the winter wind had chapped. The dragons ate and drank sparingly, as they expected to fly again this morning.

"But will it be north or south?" the Borderlander mused.

Ileth guessed that south meant the visit had failed and they'd be returning to the Serpentine to announce that the Governor had not given his approval to the plan. What would north bring? A scouting expedition?

"I say north," Ileth said, basing it on an encouraging nod Dun Huss had given her as he stepped out the door with the Governor.

Ileth was willing to let the day bring its fate. As she poured salve onto a rag and wiped Mnasmanus's wing joint she looked about the grounds, lost in thought. This morning she viewed Stesside with new eyes, knowing she'd been born here. She wondered where. One of the bedrooms? This barn? In some attic of the distillery downstream?

She tried to keep her mind off the old woman who'd cut her cord, Governor Raal, and his wife and attend to what the Borderlander was saying about spitting meat next to the fire rather than over it so the fats and juices could be collected into a pan and how that could be achieved at a campsite with even minimal cookware and vessels: "It's why I never go anywhere without a cast-iron frying pan and plenty of salt."

"I shepherded as a girl. That's all I had in the hills."

"You know, girl, I can just tolerate you—" the Borderlander started to say when Dun Huss led his party out of the old great house.

Ileth stood up. Dun Huss walked fast and hard, with a face like an approaching thunderstorm. Serena and Dath Amrits were having a hard time keeping up.

"South, I'm guessing, by his face," the Borderlander said.

"No, north," Dun Huss said. "Everyone eaten?"

The Borderlander reported: "Dragons are fed. We're just finishing up, Ileth and I."

"Let's get them saddled."

"Ileth," Amrits said. "Be a dear and saddle up my dragon. I want to inspect—"

"Saddle her yourself," Dun Huss said. "Ileth, you can fill everyone's water reservoirs from that spring they make so much of. You can find it by following that path with the white stones." He pointed out a path leading off the grounds, easily identifiable thanks to the whitewashed stones on either side of it. It went off in the direction of the old fort they'd overflown. Ileth nodded.

Serena kept her face carefully blank, but then Ileth had learned she didn't give much away through expression, which was probably why the Charge had her as a wingman flying where he couldn't.

Ileth collected their canteens and bottles and distributed the weight—everything dragoneers carried always came with plenty of straps and hinged hooks for securing it—and clomped off to the path, trying to come up with an excuse to visit the house for a last good-bye when she returned.

The path was longer than she expected; the trip took a good half

hour. Part of it branched off toward the ruined castle, but the stone-flanked path turned toward the sound of fast-running water. Dun Huss had probably given her this job so they could talk strategy without her hearing. Or perhaps he needed to put matters to the dragons. Ileth had been in the Serpentine long enough to know that they were consulted on matters great and small.

The path was a good one and had been improved at the steepest climbs by thick timbers arranged into stairs at the worst bit. When Ileth finally reached the source of the spring, she found a little pool, improved somewhat with stony banks and joined stones ringing it so it made more of a pool than a pond, with a bench against a huge boulder. A brass plaque bolted on the boulder informed the visitor that this source was discovered in 2724 Old Hypatian by two names she didn't recognize and one "Raal."

Ileth filled her bottles from the agitated water, which fell out of the pool and down a waterfall forming the beginnings of the Stess below. The water was chill and after doing a quick survey of the surrounds and the path, she washed up, thinking she'd been washed with these same waters after being born.

She decided she could drop by the house in order to thank their hosts and see if she could catch Ignata in the kitchen, but all the dragons and their mounted riders were waiting at the bottom of the path. The dragons had trooped all the way across the field for favorable wind, leaving muddy prints. Well, the soil would be the better for it and the worms would be happy, even if Ileth wasn't. With a last, regretful glance at the great house holding stories from someone who knew her mother, she joined the dragons and dragoneers.

"I made sure to secure your music box," Serena said, patting Ileth's tightly rolled bundle.

The Borderlander handed Ileth her coat. "I admire what you did with this old thing," he said. Was this a departure or an escape? Why were they hurrying her so?

"That dancer, Vii, she helped me with it," Ileth said.

"Vii?" Amrits asked, always ready to talk about dragon-dancers.

"Oh yes. She came around with an old jug asking for coin to start a swirl fountain. I threw all I had handy in it. Blessings on her soul for it, it's good to have someone improving the old stones rather than looking for ways to save a few figs."

Dun Huss himself checked her seat once she was behind Serena—and Serena's tether and such, as a courtesy. "Girth good, Telemiron?" he asked.

"I like it a little tighter when I'm carrying two," the dragon said. "I'll trade the pinch of the straps for knowing the load won't shift about."

Dun Huss set his boot against the saddle girth and pulled it tighter by a notch. Telemiron flicked a *griff*. Dun Huss returned to Mnasmanus and climbed into his own saddle and attached his safety tether. "Dragoneers set? Yes? Whenever you are ready."

Ileth found it curious that none of the household had come out to say farewell, save for the man who'd brought the food in the big barrow the previous day, who was inspecting the brushy area where the dragons had done their elimination, probably in the hope they'd dropped a few scale. But there were windows they could watch from.

Ileth had done ground takeoffs before and braced herself. Dragons could cover short distances at tremendous speed—the famous dragon dash that has to be witnessed to be believed—but for anyone atop one it was a ride to remember, even though dragons did their best to hold the base of their neck as still as working muscles would allow.

Etiennersea checked the wind and the sky once more. A good cold wind blew in from the distant bay. She muttered something to Amrits and opened her wings halfway, holding them high.

When she rushed off, throwing up mud, and jumped into the air, the rest followed in a ragged line. Ileth hung on to the dragon with her legs and Serena with her arms until she felt the legs quit and the wings take over with steady, air-cutting beats. Ileth glanced back at the field, now thoroughly torn up by the comings and goings of the dragons. Already the wintering birds were flying in to check the divots for exposed worms.

Ileth regretted leaving Stesside. But if they were going north they'd

have to come south again on the return trip. Perhaps they'd return with more messages.

They stayed low, just at the edge of the cloud cover, so the dragons could drop down and navigate with their eyes. Ileth wondered if even that would be possible for much longer. A veil of snow looked to be coming in from the north.

Ileth just made out Stavanzer off to the west, so her homeland, the Freesand, would be north of that, not that she had any great desire to see its hilly coastline and muddy, sandbank-choked estuaries.

For someone brought along for her expertise on the North Province, she had only a rough idea of what their destination might be, given their direction. East of the Freesand was a plateau that ended in cliffs overlooking Pine Bay. She didn't know much about it, other than it was good country for sheep and shaggy goats and not much else, flanked by the waters of the Freesand on one side and the straits on the other. It was called the Headlands. North and east of that, across the bay and the straits, that was the Rari coast.

They were in the air just long enough to get cold when the snow closed in. The dragons flew lower and still lower, until they were just above the treetops.

As Serena predicted, Etiennersea called Telemiron to the front. He beat his wings hard and took the lead, and the other dragons formed up off his wings with Etiennersea just behind. Even Catherix clung tight at the rear, her nose in some danger of getting hit by Mnasmanus's tailtip.

Ileth was grateful for Serena in front of her, even if she wasn't bulky enough for a proper windbreak. She clung to Serena's back like a mating toad. Telemiron might have adjusted their course, it was hard to say, and they broke out over grazing country. Ileth caught glimpses of barn rooftops and hay shelters as they fought the wind and snow. They came to sort of a low channel of a wide, shallow valley with a wandering stream that wasn't quite a river, and Telemiron turned up it, following it roughly northeast. They passed over a town and the dragons circled it twice ("two bell towers," Etiennersea called to Telemiron) to

make sure of it, and then they turned north again, this time following some hedging that probably marked a road, currently hidden by the falling snow.

Telemiron made another turn at a shelter-shrine, and they flew until they saw flat rooftops of a long, rectangular wooden building whose uneven outline reminded Ileth of a big ship with a forecastle and high quarterdeck in back. It had a flat roof, unusual in the north. Serena made the landing chop with her arm and watched for acknowledgment waves.

The dragons circled the building. It was another great house, of a distinctive design, built of thick, horizontally laid timbers built up off a platform of stone very much like the big limestone blocks of the Serpentine's walls. The windows were little wider than arrow slits. One could call it a fortification. She wondered if the Rari ever came up the cliffs and raided inland, that there would need to be a post like this. The roof was covered in what looked like smoothed river stones and gravel such as might be used in a decorative garden, with flower boxes arranged on it, with canvas covers to protect the soil inside from the winter winds.

Ileth heard a signal bell ringing below. She followed the sound to a watch platform on the roof, where a figure in a dress with a red-and-white scarf fluttering in the wind pulled at a bell rope that worked a bell in a sheltered enclosure like a birdhouse. After pulling, she waved at the dragons. They must have been expected.

As the line of dragons turned around the house, Ileth's nose caught a hint of the sea on the hard north wind, but just a hint, if not welcome (because it reminded her of the Captain's Lodge), at least familiar. The house must be near the shore. The ground was uneven, broken by cuts with exposed rock, with bare grassy hummocks interspersed with low runs full of small trees and bushes, now taking on snow. The dragons settled for landing in a line on the road. They alighted gently, aided by the brisk wind and uncertainty about the footing.

"There's ice underfoot," Telemiron said over his shoulder. "Be careful climbing down."

The steaming dragons, each with a dragoneer walking next to its head, made for an impressive parade on the approaches to the house. Despite the weather, the dragons moved at a deliberate pace, giving the house plenty of time to arrange themselves for whatever this meeting was to be.

The house matched the weather—hard-edged and cold-looking, thanks to the accumulating snow. They were met out front by three or possibly four generations, it looked to Ileth. There was a very old man, held up by a cane on his left and a middle-aged woman on his right, both in heavy ship-coats. Two more women stood close together, thick shawls thrown over their shoulders, younger than the woman the elderly man relied on for support, with widow's pleats in their well-made dresses. The latest generation was represented by a young man and a young woman, around her own age or a few years older. The young woman was the one who'd been ringing the bell; Ileth recognized her patriotic red-and-white scarf. Ileth guessed from her size and face that she was younger than her companion, a tallish young man trying to grow sideburns without much luck who'd put his boots on the wrong feet in his hurry to get out the door.

"Good to see dragoneers about again," the old man said with a weak and trembling voice. He had difficulty keeping his chin steady.

Two more figures exited the great house, a man in the uniform of the Auxiliaries and a fleshy, hulky man in a bearskin coat who was perhaps the most sizable man Ileth had ever met, other than the dreaded Gorgantern of her novice year. They were content to wait behind the rest. Ileth recognized the bearskin man from the Freesand, as the Captain had called out to him on occasions when they met in the Freesand streets. He had something to do with shipping, or perhaps shipyards. Master Jut-something-or-other. Jutting? He hadn't been a particularly close friend of the Captain as he'd never visited the Lodge, which was a good mark for him in Ileth's personal blue book.

"Let me do the introductions, Grandfather," the woman he leaned on said.

The old man patted his support's hand. "I'll leave everything else to you, Comity. Not this, dear. Not this."

He took a step forward, shaking her off, and probed the ground with his cane before settling on it with both hands. His thin hair blew in his eyes but he ignored it.

"Welcome to Sag House, dragoneers, and double welcome to your dragons. It's been too long since the Old Post held their kind. Indeed, too long."

The house didn't look like it was sagging. Ileth surveyed the surrounding landscape. The house was set in a bowl feature, mostly surrounded by rounded, grassy hills, sheltered from the cold winds blowing in off Pine Bay. From above, it had looked like a sag in the ground, come to think of it.

"Thank you, sir," Dun Huss said, blinking at the snow flying into his eyes by the fluky wind, and commenced his introductions. He started with the dragons and the accompanying dragoneers, and finished with Ileth, who was introduced as "one of our young female apprentices who spent her childhood in the Freesand."

The old man looked from Ileth to Serena and back again as if he'd already forgotten which young female he spoke of, but the others gave Ileth encouraging nods, one northerner to another.

In return, the old man introduced himself as the head of the Aftorn family. Ileth had heard that name; it was known in the Freesand in shipping, mines, and lumber. Gadikan Aftorn was the elder, supported by his granddaughter Comity. The two ladies in shawls Ileth always thought of as "the widows" afterward—they'd married into the Aftorn family and lost their husbands; one died fighting a fire on his ship and the other had been taken by the Rari. The bell-ringer was Gandy, daughter to one of the widows; the young man, her cousin Astler, was linked to the old man through his mother, Comity. Ileth thought she must have married young to have such a grown child.

"I'm sorry you had such bad weather for flying. Was it very difficult not to become lost?" Comity asked.

"The dragons have a good sense of direction," Amrits said. "If we'd struck the shoreline we would have tossed a coin to try east or west. Would have made it eventually."

"That's the Sag for you, the only thing consistent about the weather is that it's bad," Gandy said. She was a lanky young woman and gestured and twitched about as she talked like she was being worked by an inexperienced puppeteer who hadn't quite gotten the hang of her strings yet. Perhaps the dragons made her nervous. "I should like to go up on a dragon and get above the clouds. It's been weeks since I've seen the sun."

"You're exaggerating again," her cousin said. "The sun was shining just yesterday."

There was some talk about taking the dragons to the Old Post. Everyone involved in the conversation except Ileth seemed to take it for granted that there was plenty of shelter for the dragons nearby, but Ileth couldn't see where. Amrits and the man in the Auxiliary uniform talked about fresh meat for the dragons. Ileth didn't know uniforms well enough to guess his rank, but he had silver buttons, and gold gleamed as much as gold could gleam in the weather on the hilt of his short-bladed sword, so she guessed he was someone of importance. The Auxiliary officer offered to go with the dragons to their lodgings, under a mile away but by a treacherous path.

"I don't mind the walk, Dath," the Borderlander said.

"No, Etiennersea is my responsibility, and the other dragons are hers. I'll go and no doubt return with an appetite. Try not to bore the ladies."

"May I c-come?" Ileth asked. "I'd like to see the Old Post." So much for her "experience" with the north; they kept taking her to places she'd never seen. If only they'd wanted to know who bought empty brandy bottles in the Freesand—she had plenty of expertise in that.

Amrits nodded and the Auxiliary officer stepped up.

"I'm not part of the family, but if you need a guide to the Old Post, I'll take you. Taskmaster Henn," the Auxiliary said. Amrits gave a bow and Ileth bobbed. "It's not far to the entrance."

They crunched through the snow among the dragons. The humans slipped and slid as they walked the path.

"I'm fearful one of you will fall and I'll step on you. Why don't you ride?" Mnasmanus said.

The Auxiliary hardly startled when the dragon spoke. Usually people new to dragons took some time getting used to the idea that it wasn't some trick. "I've never ridden a dragon. We have a couple in the Auxiliaries, old and very touchy. They don't let humans on their backs."

"Easier than a horse," Dath Amrits said. He hurried up to Etiennersea and climbed into his saddle.

Henn unlatched a leather strap on his sword sheath, and it dropped to an easier distance for riding. Ileth put Henn into Serena's saddle— a little awkwardly; she took a bootheel to the eye as he swung up into it. He was concentrating on the dragon and didn't notice he'd struck her, so she said nothing. He couldn't use the stirrups, so his feet just dangled. Ileth climbed up and sat behind, careful not to touch his uniform lest she catch something on one of those expensive buttons.

The snow slackened; the wind ceased to blow it about quite so hard, and Ileth could look around with interest. She could see a sharp horizon around a lighthouse to the east; these must be the cliffs she'd been told that marked the northeast extremity of the Vales and the Republic.

They negotiated a steep slope where the path effectively disappeared among the rocks thanks to the snow, but the dragons simply climbed over the obstacles. Ileth, once up the slope, had a better view of the lighthouse. It was short and stumpy and let what was probably tall cliffs under it do much of the work. Ileth saw a gap in the ground ahead, some sort of notch, or perhaps a canyon.

"The top entrance is—oh, the dragon found it."

The green dragon turned and used her tail to fling up some dead creeper. The dragon disappeared into a break in the ground. Mnasmanus reared up and looked about.

"We're about four dragon-lengths above the sea," Mnasmanus said.

Henn shifted uncomfortably in the saddle, unused to the dragon's size. "It's an old river, part underground. I worked here, years ago.

There was talk of making it into a local headquarters and warehouse for the Auxiliaries, like your Serpentine, as the interior is easy to expand, can be reached by sea, and has plenty of fresh water, but they decided the location was impractical. The Rari coast is just across. On a clear day you can see it."

Telemiron climbed down a broad path and into the shelter of a roofed area. It was easy enough to turn the river canyon into a cave tunnel; all you had to do was add a roof. In some ways it was better than a cave; there were glassed skylights to admit light, though they were cracked and dirty and in some cases missing entirely, but they still served to light the gorge.

"Best get off here," Telemiron said. "The footing's good, and I may have to crouch. Mashing you would be a poor start to this."

It was fun to explore the shallow "caves." There was a steep, wide slope down to the river. The sound of water filled the interior. Bats and barn owls and sea birds had taken up residence. At the bottom she saw that the path opened up into a sea cave where the river flowed out and joined the waters at the northeastern edge of the Vales. It smelled of salt water and droppings. The cave was larger than the flight cave mouth, but not as useful as it was mostly water. Ileth, from her study of maps and nautical charts, knew this as the Cope Channel, where the sea waters leading to Pine Bay were narrowest. Tricky waters; you had to negotiate a hairpin channel before reaching another bay that widened into the Inland Ocean, with unreliable winds making matters worse.

The sea cave had been improved. The river that formed the cut had a dam built into it with a channeled fall, and the dragons were drinking from it—she guessed below the fall the water was too tainted by salt, which dragons couldn't consume in quantity without provoking diarrhea any more than humans could.

Mnasmanus probed at the dark corners and a family of raccoons fled.

"I thought so," Mnasmanus grumbled.

"Used to be a jolly post," Telemiron said. "I liked to swim out of this cave. Salt water and sunshine on the rocks, best scale cleanser there is. Too bad they didn't keep it up."

"Shame to leave it to the raccoons and birds," Henn said.

Ileth felt rather than heard Etiennersea say something to the others.

Henn plucked at Amrits's sleeve. "What was that?"

"Drakine. Sometimes they like to talk among themselves without us understanding."

"She and Catherix are going to rest in one of the upper shelves, out of the wind," Mnasmanus said. He was right; at the moment the wind blew out of the cave mouth, no doubt channeled by the river cut. A good dragon-smell coming out of the cave would keep the raccoons away.

Henn walked to the edge of the wharf and looked out the cave mouth. "We have some barrels of salted pork and mutton for the dragons. Sorry there's nothing fresh, but for now this campaign's marching on breeze and spit. We didn't think it wise to try to run more than a single boat in. Didn't want the Rari marking new traffic."

"Less said about that the better," Amrits said. "I'm surprised you know."

"I've been tasked with the staff work, and figuring what it will take to put this place in order," Henn said. "So far it's just me and the people at Sag House; Comity was the one who I worked through. I don't think anyone's even told the old man anything, other than that some dragoneers were coming to inspect the Old Post. Same with the others."

Amrits craned his neck about, staring into the water at the edge of the wharf.

"Ileth, you should come see this," Amrits said.

She trotted over to the masonry forming a wharf. It was in superb shape for not having been used in years, through the freezes and thaws of the north. Of course the weather would be moderated in this cave, with the seawater cushioning the changes of temperature. Still, whoever had built it had done a good job.

"Look at that starfish," Amrits said.

It would have been harder not to look at it. The creature was huge, clinging to the shallow bottom of the cave, easily the size of a wagon wheel. It was a bright red like hot coals with little white lines forming

a tiled pattern all over the body. While the coloring was remarkable, its size was what shocked her.

"I've n-never seen one so big. I didn't know they could get like this."

Amrits smiled. "My guess is when he was a young starfish he sat there at the bottom eating dragon waste, just as his ancestors did. Maybe we had an unhealthy dragon here and there was blood in the stool, who knows. It's the jars in practice out in the wild."

"Jars?" Ileth asked.

"Oh, you haven't had your physiker lectures yet, I suppose. You'll see. I don't want to spoil the fun."

Henn joined them. "If I dared, I'd pull him out and toast him. A decoration like that would be worth some money in Stavanzer."

"Oh, leave it be," Amrits said. "They say seeing a bright star at the outset of a campaign is a good omen. Maybe that includes starfish."

Amrits seemed to think so. He turned jaunty at the prospect of a campaign, and his eyes lit up like a dragon's. Or maybe it was just the thought of the lonely widows back at Sag House. "Now I have an appetite. Let's open up some of those brine barrels and get back to the house in time for a hot meal with the others."

After a hearty, and salty, meal, the dragons were content to nap out of the weather, getting their first comfortable rest since the trip began, as dragons felt as tucked in and safe in a cave with walls all around as humans did in a familiar bed. Amrits, serious for once, explained to Ileth that dragons were only truly happy in an underground nook with plenty of echo so they could hear anything creeping up on them.

Back at the Sag—they clomped through the mud of the trail left by the dragons—there was the classic midday welcoming food spread out for them, still-warm bread and sausages swimming in a sea of brown-sauced beans, with plenty of strong tea. The wealthy didn't eat that differently from the ordinary in the north, though the bread at Sag House was much better than it had been at the Lodge. Everyone else

had already eaten and Ileth grazed on what was left after Amrits and Henn filled their plates.

Ileth liked the house. The ceiling beams and riblike staves made her think of childhood stories of boatmen inside a whale. The small windows, set high to admit a little light rather than a view, reminded her of belowdecks on a ship. She overheard the eldest of the family speaking to the Borderlander about its double-walled construction. Sand filled the space between the layers of heavily tarred timbers. It wouldn't burn or batter easily.

There was a single iron chandelier, and oil lamps hung about with plenty of little shelves and sconces to set more candles at need. It looked like the family was accustomed to spending their time together in the hall, in little groups or alone as whatever their duties and habits needed. Musical instruments were hung up or sat behind glass in cases.

The widows were together on a sofa sewing, ignoring the talk between the dragoneers, Comity, and the men. From what Ileth could see, Comity was the axle that spun the rest of the household. When some men came in to ask about the meat in the smokehouse, Comity told them where to put the finished joints. When Gandy said she was interested in seeing the dragon saddles and fittings for equipment more closely, she went through Comity, who asked Dun Huss. He told Ileth to show her Telemiron's that evening. Eventually Dun Huss, Amrits, Serena, Comity, and the two other men disappeared into the study, supposedly to look at a new survey map of the Headlands that they had, more recent than anything at the Serpentine.

The Borderlander had pulled the patriarch's chair close to the fire and stood next to it, listening to his discourse. Every now and then he would bring a plate or a drink for the man, carefully setting it on a little stool that served as a table next to his comfortable armchair, as tender as Governor Raal had been with his wife. Ileth smiled at this side of the Borderlander; usually he spoke short when he didn't just ignore you. Ileth wondered if the senior Aftorn was an old acquaintance.

Ileth gathered a plate full of the leavings of lunch and sat down to eat at a long table. There was tart cider to go with the tea, or water. Ileth chose the cider.

Amrits exited the study within a few minutes and was soundly thumped by the younger Aftorn, hurrying down the stairs by the study in the main foyer. They exchanged a few rounds of after-yous and entered the great hall, and Amrits went to fill another plate.

Astler approached Ileth and shifted his feet, which were now in shoes on the proper feet. He had sandy hair that was more or less a thatch of cowlicks that looked like they resisted attempts to shape it.

"Excuse me, uhh . . ." he began.

"Ileth," she supplied.

"Yes, Ileth. I have to apologize to you. I was told we had four dragons and their dragoneers coming, and to set up rooms for you. The house already has guests, you see, and while it's big, there are only so many bedrooms. I didn't anticipate a fifth dragoneer."

"I'm just . . . just an apprentice," Ileth said. "I can sleep in a chair."

"No. No, you are our guest. Please sleep in my room." He smiled as he said it, as though nothing could make him happier than being turned out of his own bed.

"Tremendous idea, Ileth," Amrits said, passing close with perhaps his third helping of sausages and beans. "I wonder if one of the ladies has space for me?"

"No, I don't mean that, of course," Astler said. "I can drop anywhere. I want you to have a proper bed after your exertions."

Amrits looked as though he might bait the boy further, but she shot him a pleading look. It was a kind gesture, and she didn't want to see him tormented. Beyond that, it was enjoyable to have the attention of a boy near her age who wasn't a potential rival for a wingman posting. "Thank you," she said, relieved that her stutter let her get out that formality despite her nerves.

"Great sausages in this house," Amrits told the boy as he walked back toward the study with another helping.

"Thin for a man who eats like that," Astler said, watching him go.

Ileth didn't know much about Amrits's habits. She'd rarely seen him with a plate in the dining hall. "He's an-an acquired taste. Jokes a good deal, but isn't false. He really likes those sausages."

"Oh, you needn't be nervous around me, Ileth. Aftorn name or no. I'm everyone's dogsbody. Let me get you some more cider."

"I'm n-not nervous. Just a stutter."

Astler looked horrified that he'd embarrassed her. Ileth smiled warmly and excused herself.

Ileth went over to the fire, where Astler's great-grandfather was in animated conversation with the Borderlander.

"Piracy was a small problem in those days," the ancient said. "A ship, two, a year. Sometimes the crews and ships were bought back, sometimes not. The dragon in the post by the old lighthouse, the Channel Cave, would go across and if they found the ship . . . reprisal! For a while, all was well again; the pirates did not dare send wooden ships against dragons. We lost fewer ships to dragons than we did to storm. But the people here, they grumbled at the expense, at the special taxes. Because you dragoneers solved the problem.

"Then one day emissaries arrived, offering a treaty. The Wurm king, who they were liege to, would curb the pirates for a price in order to 'command the waters,' a price much less than dragons. At first they said no, but then there was a falling-out between the shipowners and the Governor, some feud, and they went back to the Wurm king and said yes. That was the fatal mistake."

Ileth knew nothing about the Wurm, other than that they were beyond the Borderlands, and that people in the Freesand spat when they said the name. Not a tiny *phttt!*, either, more of a retch. And then only rarely, probably because of the effort required to keep custom.

"But once the dragons left the Old Post, then the tricks began." The senior Aftorn looked into the fire. "The false lights to fool ships into steering into the rocks—wrecks belonged to the Rari and their Wurm lieges, you see. They would wait for a storm and take a ship, saying that it was wrecked by the winds, and then the demands came for an increase in the channel fees.

"It grew worse. The knaves were doing so well, others came to get in on the bounty. Weaponsmiths, shipwrights, some were from Daphia or faraway lands, but a few—yes, even people of the Vales crossed the water. Some in those crews chose a life helping sail the ships of those who took them hostage. Soon the piracy was quite open; they stopped even pretending that they didn't have a channel warrant or some other bit of paperwork and the ship had been seized until the matter could be resolved."

The old man had a fair amount of wind when angered. Ileth gave him that. He still had a good mind; Ileth knew bits and pieces of this story but she'd never heard it collected this well.

"Always came the ambassadors from the Rari or the Wurm asking for this or that bit of money to redeem prisoners or get a ship back. The sums were not outrageous, for if they made them outrageous, the ship-owners might fight. There were efforts made to arm the ships, travel in convoy, but the Rari always had more men to put in boats and more fast ships crammed with men looking for plunder. Now no ships get through unless special ambassadors and pilots are on board, and so great is the cost that the ship might as well fly the Rari flag, for there is little enough left over after their fees to even pay off the crew."

"Terrible," the Borderlander said.

"So that is where we are. Hardly a ship passes through these days. This family used to sail fourteen under the family flag. Fourteen! Now they're laid up or sold for scrap."

Dinner came, with the conversation devoted to innocuous matters. Serena and the Taskmaster and the big man in the bearskin missed it, cooped up over their maps and work. One of the widows brought out a framed painting of the Serpentine, Beehive, and lighthouse above and passed it around, asked the dragoneers if it was accurate and what this or that building or feature on the Beehive signified. The elder Aftorn had seemed to forget that they were dragoneers and was startled at the news that the dragons might be returning. "Yes! That's just what we need," he said, as if just hearing the news.

"If only that Raal were a man of fortitude and hazard, like Lake. Now *he* was a governor."

"Grandfather! No politics during dinner," Comity said.

After the dinner broke up, the dragoneers asked the youngest generation of Aftorns if they wished to meet the dragons. They took a walk together toward the cliffs to let their dinner settle. Amrits gave Etiennersea a massage by walking carefully up and down her back barefoot, pushing with his heel at the heavy musculature or even rocking about on one leg for the biggest, toughest muscles. Gandy found this fascinating and perched on a barrel, watching the comparatively small man atop the reclining green mountain, with Etiennersea giving encouraging little noises as he worked. The Borderlander cleaned out Catherix's teeth, nostrils, and ears, then worked the leading edge of her wing over with kitchen grease, oiling the skin against the cold weather.

As he did so, he gave Ileth pointers about what to look for on the dragon's tongue, nostrils, eyes, and ears. Young Astler observed, asking permission whenever he approached the dragon.

The Borderlander lectured in his short, gruff manner. Coatings on the tongue, mucus in the nostrils healthy and unhealthy, discolorations of the eye, where parasites liked to hide in the ears, and the best kitchen implements to remove waxy buildup if proper grooming tools—the best ear-reamers were made of flexible whalebone—weren't available.

"First and last, do the teeth," the Borderlander said as he worked on his dragon's mouth. "Don't be afraid to have them hold their mouth open, rest with their head on its side or even upside down—you have to be careful with that, though; some dragons get very sensitive in that position and will accidentally snap, so don't be afraid to jam a piece of thick line right in on that pink bulge there. That's the hinge. Ask them to hold their mouth open by holding on to the rope—but clean those teeth out, especially around the gumline. A nail or a fishhook will do fine to dig out bits of food and bone if you've nothing else. If you can only do one thing for your dragon, clean the teeth."

Ileth nodded. He passed her a sort of a curved probe that was a cross between a filleting knife and a sickle, though the edge wasn't honed like a knife's, and let her scrape away at the gumline on Catherix. Astler hung over her shoulder showing a deep interest, but Gandy kept covering her nose and scurrying out to the cavern mouth for air.

Ileth had polished dragon-teeth before with a little ash and a rag; it was sort of like cleaning silver, but the Borderlander took his dragon's dental care to an extent she hadn't seen before. It was smelly—she was extracting bits of the dragon's preflight breakfast from two days ago as well as yesterday's game at the Governor's—but interesting.

"An infected tooth will take a dragon out of action as effectively as a wound. Even be lethal, if the sepsis spreads. Keep your own clean while you're at it."

The Borderlander did have a set of excellent teeth; they were the only part of him that didn't look worn and weathered.

Gandy helped Amrits put his boots back on. He'd been assigned night duty with the dragons at the Old Post and would remain while the rest retired to the house for bed. "Your attire's not what I expected at all. More like for cold-weather travel than war. I always imagined your carrying dragon-fang daggers and dragon-scale armor and helmets with their horns."

"Be a bit rude, wouldn't it?" Amrits said. "How would you like it if our dragons landed in your yard with necklaces of human skulls and human scalps used as earmuffs and nose-shields?"

"Oh. Of course. I—I suppose I still think of them as sort of big, dangerous horses." Astler seemed about to say something, but Gandy cut him off with a look.

"Takes a while to get over their size, and of course you must take great care not to be squashed by accident. Ileth can tell you about a friend of hers who was bowled over and torn up a bit by scale. Most seem miles above us. That's just because they sail through the centuries after we're dust. They've seen it all before so they all come off like a conclave of philosophers. I've learned not to bring my little heart-

breaks around to Tinny; she'll just sigh and tell me I'll be dead in no time, so don't bother her about it."

Ileth couldn't imagine Amrits heartbroken about anything, but then it was hard to get through the fence of jokes. She didn't really know him.

The dragons settled in to sleep. None required dancing to soothe them; they were all too tired from flying in a snowstorm.

Gandy walked Ileth back to Sag House. Astler stayed to make sure Amrits was comfortable. She told Ileth that she'd show her to her cousin's room. "You're lucky, he's clean for a boy. Aunt Comity is exacting."

This led to a chat about what sort of young men she'd met at the Serpentine. Gandy'd been reading novels and imagined constant romances, rivalries, and elopements on dragonback. Ileth disappointed her with a few terse words giving her the truth of the matter.

Sag House was quiet by the time they returned. Lights were still burning in the smaller room where the men and Serena had been meeting.

Ileth took a lit candle in a holder and followed Gandy up the stairs.

Astler's bedchamber didn't quite deserve the word *room*—it was more of a berth or a cabin, tucked away at the end of the hall, right down to a single circular window. It did have the innovation of a closet behind a sliding panel to save space, and it was a high bed with a desk built beneath. The big open wall opposite the bed-desk had hooks for hanging outerwear and hats and so on. There was a little cabinet with a stonework top that had a pitcher and basin on it. There was water inside. The cabinet contained a clean chamber pot with aromatic wood chips and charcoal inside, probably as a gesture to the guest, as it struck her as expensive to fill fresh each night.

But rather than cloaks and so on hanging from the walls there were drawings, sketch after sketch, mostly nature studies in pencil. Some were quite rough, some deep, detailed studies that looked to have been the work of days. Ileth had barely set down her little bundle with her music box when she started examining them. He appeared to like

birds best, but there were a lot of plants as well, grains and grasses rather than flowers. The sea oats he did reminded her of being a little girl on the Freesand's bars. She paused over one bird's portrait. It was a woodpecker's head that was particularly detailed; she wondered how he'd gotten close enough to get the detailing on the eye and beak and feathers so precise. It was lifelike enough that she kept expecting the eye to turn.

A few books stood on the desk on a clever sliding bookend. They seemed to be well cared for and were educational reference books. The most distinctive was a plant reference for horticulturalists; the binding had reinforcing ridges and the gilt-edged pages were extra thick with plentiful artwork. She flipped through the illustrations and it seemed Astler copied the style of the reference studies.

It struck her that if she took her inspection any further it might seem that she'd searched his desk. She didn't want to be thought a snoop. She put the horticulture volume back, not trying to place it exactly as it had been. Then she reprimanded herself for letting what a boy might think channel her actions. She decided to turn in. A few moments of curiosity examining an interesting-looking book and then sleep. Just what a busy dragoneer would do.

Still full from dinner and tired, she filled the washbasin with water and washed for the night, combed out her hair, and took an extra few minutes with her teeth with the Borderlander's lecture still fresh in her ears.

At first the bed defeated her; there was no obvious way to get into it. She tried from the back and had no luck, and then nearer the door she discovered a projection on the support perfectly sized for a foot. She climbed into the bed.

The linens were fresh but smelled like moth sachets. A featherbed, soft and cozy, enveloped her. The head pillow was sagging but serviceable.

She turned her nose into Astler's pillow. There was a faint smell to it, not lavender or anything like it, a fresher and sharper aroma. He didn't seem the type to use scent. Maybe his shaving soap? Whatever

it was, it was nice, even relaxing. She was used to the soaps and smells of women in the Quarter, that or dragons, and it was something different and warmly comforting in its way. She drifted off wondering about the tantalizing aroma.

She was asleep for a time, she couldn't say for how long, when she startled awake. It took her a moment to place herself, and what disturbed her. Someone was beneath her, at the desk.

"Yes, sir?" she said, half awake and old reactions from the Lodge putting words in her mouth. The Captain would want his boots taken off after a night's drinking.

"Sorry," came a half whisper. "Getting my pencil box. Remembered my notebook but forgot my pencils." It was Astler. "Your breathing made me think you were asleep. Sorry to intrude."

"It's your room." Ileth was awake now, waiting for her heart to quit pounding in alarm.

"Not tonight, it isn't. Here it is, sorry to trouble you." Something rattled in his hand.

"Forgive me if it's . . . if it's too personal, but what is that smell, like oranges or something, on your pillow?"

He stepped close; she could just make out his outline in the dim light coming in under the door. He thought for a moment. "Probably my father's toilet soap. I've sort of adopted it since I started using a razor. It's from Zland, lemons and oranges, I think. It's all I remember of him. Smell stays with you for some reason."

"I'm sorry."

"You grew up in a Lodge in the Freesand, so I expect you had it worse."

"How do you . . . do you know that?"

"I asked that Serena about you. I wondered what kind of girl becomes a dragoneer."

"The kind that show up for a draft."

"Do ordinary girls get admitted?"

So whatever ordinary is, I'm not it? Ileth thought. That was interesting.

"Any-anyone who can pass the tests. Are you asking for your cousin?"

"My cousin? I can't see her cleaning a dragon's teeth. She might join to get at some dragoneers. We're too far from Stavanzer. She's at the age where she wants men courting her."

Poor Gandy. The Headlands were even more remote than the Freesand. "We have a few like that at the Serpentine."

"I think to really become expert at something, well, you have to take on kind of a monastic life about it, exclude everything but your study. Are your classrooms mixed? I've never heard of that outside the smallest country schools."

Classrooms! "No, it's more like an apprenticeship. Workshops, kitchens. You learn by doing."

"Apprenticeship? With all those Duns and Vors?"

"That's why they call it the Serpentine Academy. So the elder Duns and Vors don't have to say their son's off apprenticed to a *mlumm-scoop*."

"*Mlumm?*"

"Dragon-scat."

It was strange to converse with a young man like this, a face the faintest of shadows, like their bodies had fallen away and just their inner selves were talking. Ileth found she liked it, at least with this boy. She propped her head up on her arm, glad that he'd forgotten his pencil box.

Astler widened the door a bit on its track. "Still, not sure it's a good idea. I've never heard of an academy where they put boys and girls together. Romantic impulses would overthrow attention and concentration and learning."

Ileth stifled a guffaw. "My lodge was mixed, so maybe it wasn't so strange to me. It works. Everyone's too busy for that sort of thing. And there's no privacy. Either no boys about or twenty."

"I suppose that explains why you're so at ease with me, just the two of us in a bedroom."

"With someone else I might not be."

"You're at a military academy. You'd run me through if I tried anything."

Ileth held up her hands. "No. Completely defenseless."

Astler cleared his throat. "I have my pencils now, so I'm out of excuses to be here. I wanted to sketch out some of those shapes of dragon scale while it's still fresh in my head, and I find myself more interested in talking to you."

"I . . . I don't think I've ever been c-complimented on my conversation," Ileth said.

"Truly? I could be here all night. You're quite—" He cut himself off. "I should let you sleep," he said, nipping out the door and shutting it before she could object.

She had difficulty sleeping after that, wondering just what direction his *quite* opinion led.

T he next morning, hearing the silence in the house, she thought she was the first up as she dressed. She went down the hall and downstairs with boots in hand to stop from clomping.

The door to the study was open for a change. Judging from the guttered candles inside, the work had gone very late. There was a map case on the table, everything put away and closed, and it would have been the easiest thing in the world for her to open it and examine whatever was inside. She took a cautious step into the room.

She sensed a presence to her left and turned to face it. Dath Amrits had finished his watch at the Old Post, evidently, and sat in an armchair pushed close to the ashes and charred remains of the fire. She would have liked to take his cameo in that profile; it would make a lovely memory someday. Head tipped back, nose like a mountain peak, mouth open, and that enormous pipe-bowl lump at the front of his throat shifting ever so slightly up and down as he breathed.

She backed out of the room, still holding her boots.

A call followed her out.

"Ileth, make us a cup of tea, would you? That's a dear," Amrits asked sleepily.

Was everything on the man a ruse and playacting? Had he pretended to be asleep just to see if she'd peek inside the map case?

Tea sounded fine in the chill of the fireless house. As she approached the kitchen she heard, and smelled, cooking.

Ileth followed the smell of sausages, where she found Comity and a male cook—or whatever he was, he wore a butcher's leather apron over a winter-wear work jacket—already up. The man was reading off a written list to Comity. She nodded and sent him back outside.

"Is there . . . is there tea, sira?" Ileth asked.

"Sira! Oh, call me Comity, dear. You are . . . you are Ileth. Do I have it right?"

"Yes."

"Easy to remember, you're the only one sounds like us, except for the tall one in the sheepskins."

She started filling a tray, then put a kettle back on the hot stove.

"Now, breakfast. We have a sheep each for the dragons today. I was told that should be enough to content them. The smokehouse has been very busy. Do you think that will be enough for today? I should have liked young cattle but they're expensive this year. Prices always go up when there's doubt and difficulty in the Sammerdam Exchanges or some bank fails."

"They'd love that. I think they were expecting fish, so close to the sea."

"We don't have fishermen brave enough to go out this close to— well, you know. Them. So it's sheep. Astler can help distribute them. I'm sure he wants to bring his paper and lead and do some sketches. He went on a bit about their scale and wings last night. You saw his drawings in his room?"

"Yes. He has a gift."

"I think so too. He's my world now," Comity said.

Ileth put tea on a tray and anticipated a demand for some toasted bread and brought it out to Amrits.

He waved vaguely at the table. She set down the tray and gave him his tea.

"That's better," he said, after a test sip. "Tosh, is it always this cold and damp up here, Ileth? It passes right through to your bones. Give me good icy mountain cold any day, you can keep that out with thick hose."

"You . . . get used to it."

"How did you sleep, Ileth? That Astler boy didn't pull the old *I've misplaced my pants* dodge, did he?"

"I slept well, thank you. Nobody kept me up, I'm sure." Well, she'd kept herself up. Something about being in a great house brought back her Galantine manners. "May I ask you something?"

"As long as it doesn't require me getting out of this chair until the tea has warmed me."

"Why am . . . why am I being kept out of these conferences?"

He took another sip of tea. "Ileth, you're just an apprentice. Nothing for you to do." The words might just as well have been a tired sigh.

"I still would like an opportunity to learn. You don't think I'm a spy or something?"

Amrits shot her the sort of look you might see down the sights of a crossbow aimed at you. "Certainly not. The Galantines wouldn't use someone like you. Don't be huffy with me, now. You know what I mean. Every agent I've ever heard of was a smooth talker with social connections from Sammerdam to the Scab. You're—you're quite the opposite of that."

"I can see that this has something to do with the Rari."

"Proving you are no fool, but we already knew that or we wouldn't have brought you. Keep out of it."

She heard boots coming down the stairs and he went quiet. Dun Huss entered, with his face a little red from being shaved and his neckcloth clean and fresh.

Dun Huss ordered her to check the dragons, so she passed the news about mutton for them, excused herself, and ended up running into Astler by the door, where he was tying a sort of winter work coat about his waist. They exchanged oddly awkward *good mornings*.

"My mother tells me I am to be of assistance to you," he said, putting a little notebook into a pocket of the coat.

Outside, Astler found a two-wheeled cart that he said used to be used for milk deliveries. As he wasn't sure the cart horses would stand the smell of dragons, he offered to haul it himself, if Ileth would just help push on the inclines. Together they loaded the sheep from the smokehouse and set off on the snowy track. Astler threw an improvised rope harness around his shoulders and picked up the stays and they set off, Astler pacing with effort.

"My great-grandfather is always telling me to get more exercise," he said, pulling hard and shifting his feet about for better purchase.

Ileth took a stay and hauled as well. After hauling limestone, the cart wasn't so bad; the wheels had most of the weight.

"You are a fresh breeze, Ileth. My cousin would be worried about her hands," Astler said.

She was wearing knit gloves! Although most of the fingers were worn through. She held up a hand to show him. "Mine were ruined long ago."

"They look nice enough. Wouldn't want to draw them, though. Hands are hard to get right."

"Is that why women are always holding flowers in their lap in portraits?"

"That's it exactly."

She watched the tendons in his arms strain to keep the grip with those long fingers of his. She liked his hands too. It was easy to imagine them on her. Why did she allow her mind to wander there? Maybe it was being away from the Serpentine and its strict routines. She was like a sailor, fresh off a ship.

Astler broke in on her imaginings. "Forgive me for asking, but did you get hurt in training?"

It was obvious where he was looking. Ileth wondered if she'd be asked about the scar over her eye for the rest of her life. "No. An accident."

"It gives you character. I'm sorry, I'm always saying the wrong thing. Or the right thing, badly. I shouldn't have mentioned it."

"I never dreamed of being an artist's model anyway, so no great loss. There are plenty of other dancers for . . . for Heem Tyr to paint."

"You're wrong there." She thought a young artist would leap at a chance to talk about Risso Heem Tyr, and Ileth could add personal anecdotes about the dancers she knew he'd painted. Ileth, wrong about boys again.

"I didn't see any people on your wall. Do you draw them?"

"If I draw them from the back, wearing gloves. My faces always come out flat, too. I've given up on people; I think I just don't have the knack for expression, for all that I wish to. I wonder if I could properly capture a dragon? You know, there's not much dragon art in the Vales. I've seen dozens of paintings of horses, cows, sheep. Pigs even. I've never seen a portrait of a dragon. Just tavern signs and road markers."

"Not long ago, in Vyenn, I saw a very bad depiction of a dragon on a tobacconist's sign. I'm sure you could do better. Your birds are lovely, and detailing scale would be a lot like feathers."

"Do they let ordinary artists in the Serpentine, or just the Heem Tyrs of the world?"

"Oh, yes. You only have to write and get permission."

He adjusted the rope over his shoulder, placing it more comfortably, then spoke again: "Perhaps I can write you and you can bring a request to your superiors. Of course I'd have to get permission from my mother. She only let me go to Stavanzer but once."

Ileth was much, much more interested in talking about him writing her letters. Bugger Comity.

"I'd like that."

"I'm being presumptuous. I just don't meet that many . . . personages of my age. My mother even pulled me out of the youth militia after young Harban slid down a hill and broke his leg. You'll leave soon and I will miss your company." He lunged to get the cart over a rock. "I will write you."

How soon, she wondered. They were nearly there, the lighthouse loomed near. "Don't they keep that lighthouse going?"

"It's in disrepair, like everything else at the Old Post. I was, oh, seven or eight when it last worked. But my great-grandfather did have someone in a little while back to inspect it."

"We have a lighthouse at the Serpentine."

"Yes, I've seen it on bookplates."

"They don't do the real thing justice. You should see it in person." Ileth could have bit her tongue. It was working more or less properly for once, and was running wild. Astler would think her desperate.

He didn't seem to notice. "The lighthouse keeper and his wife would tell me stories about dragons, back then. They said any place where dragons lived, their magic can remain a long time."

"Magic?"

"You're a dragoneer. You haven't heard those stories?"

"No."

"Well, it's not a magic story, really, not like the one about the traveling showman who put his dying son into a wooden puppet or the town where people disappear for a hundred years at a time. I mean the idea that dragons are vehicles of magic on the earth. More dragons, more magic; the farther they recede, the more the magic fades. Elves disappear, dwarves turn into stone, nobody can turn lead into gold anymore, all the stuff you read in the Fairy Tome, gone."

"We didn't have a Fairy Tome in my lodge. I was educated with Directist copybooks."

"That's grim stuff, isn't it? Liars having their tongues burned and all that?"

"It terrified me at first, but later the drawings were sort of fascinating. Whoever made the woodcuts had some strange ideas. I mean, no one could actually still be alive, walking around holding their liver in their hands, right?"

"I wouldn't think so."

"You couldn't accuse those faces of being flat."

Astler laughed. "Not if you're to do justice to a man walking around holding his own liver."

Ileth felt herself warm. She imagined if she descended into the

dragon caves below the lighthouse, she'd glow like a firefly. Astler was so easy to talk to! The words just came out. Both of them from shattered families, both raised up by cracked walnuts. Imagine being pulled out of the youth militia! She'd seen the boys hiking about in files, fixing fences, doing archery in fields. It was hardly putting to sea on a ship bound for the Hypatian coast.

"Speaking of liver, that's usually a dragon's favorite bit of an animal. Better get these down."

The Old Post was already smelling of dragons again. The only one of the four who was awake was Etiennersea. She was stretched out on the wharf where the river emptied out into the straits.

"Breakfast, Etiennersea," Ileth said, announcing herself.

"I heard you both since you started down from the entrance. Mutton?"

"Yes."

"I thought so. Hard to tell sometimes when it's smoked. Oh, I am looking forward to a good fat northern sheep. I get tired of the Serpentine's fish. Especially lately, with the fillers and bones. Everyone's complaining of blockages."

Astler stood dumbstruck as she spoke. Well, it took everyone time to get used to it. Etiennersea had excellent Montangyan. It allowed her to complain with precision.

Speaking of blockages, there was no dragon waste around for her to clear up. Ileth was grateful for that. Astler's bright impression of her might be dimmed after seeing her shovel up dragon *mlumm*. They must have let the river carry it out into the bay.

Ileth went around the dragon's head and drank in the fresh sea air. "Are you keeping a watch?"

"Of course. If the Rari came poking around, I'd have to kill them. We can't let them know dragons are here."

It startled Ileth to hear of men being hunted and killed the way you'd destroy vermin infesting a granary. Though she could see the brutal logic of it. Etiennersea was a dragon and had a dragon's sensibilities.

Astler couldn't help glancing out at the sea. He looked nervous, but being around a dragon often did that. He seemed an imaginative young man, perhaps picturing how easily the dragon might end his life, like a terrier snapping a rat.

Ileth tried to keep her face neutral, as if fighting and death were part of her experience. She'd grown up hating the Rari for the death and loss and poverty they caused; better than half the siblings in her lodge had been orphaned by Rari knives and shafts and chains, but she still wasn't sure if she could kill one, even in battle. She'd wanted to bleed Gorgantern, wound and humble him for insults and injuries—she still fancied the hearing in one of her ears was a bit off because of his cuffing her—but to watch the life leave his body? It was a test of being a dragoneer she hoped she'd never be called to pass.

Ileth dropped her burden and Etiennersea shifted into an eating position, turning so she was farther back in the shadows of the cave.

She heard the other dragons stirring. Ileth checked Astler by taking his hand before he went off to look. One of the first warnings she'd had in the Serpentine was not to wake a dragon if it appeared to be active in a dream. You were to go some distance off and blow a whistle or a horn if it was necessary. They stood there, neither dropping the other's hand, while the dragons woke and the low humming of their calls to each other started.

"Sparks, what is that?" Astler said.

"Dragons speaking to each other in their own tongue."

"Feels like on a ship when the crew is dragging anchor chains about."

"They speak in such a way we can't hear it. Or can hardly hear it."

"So this is why the philosophers thought they were speaking to each other with their minds?"

"Something like that," Ileth said, hoping he wouldn't probe her natural philosophy any further. He probably knew more about such things.

"You have an interesting life, Ileth."

She didn't know what to say to that. "I've been lucky." Which was true enough.

"I was born lucky. You made your luck."

She was silent for a moment, trying out different replies. "They say no dragoneer survives all his chances. The man who oversaw us our first year there, the Master of Novices. He dragged a leg and had burns all over his face. It could happen to me."

Astler looked at her sidelong, head tilted, giving her a good view of the thatch of cowlicks. "Did he say he wished he'd never been a dragoneer?"

"No. I wouldn't... I wouldn't s-say he was proud of his injuries, but he thought it important that we all knew about them. Accept such possibilities."

He thought for a moment. "You think it's more courageous if you accept risks like that without thinking of those injuries, or is the truly courageous one the man who imagines all those horrors happening to him, but he carries on despite them?"

"You want my opinion?" She'd never had a boy ask her such a philosophical question.

"It's why I asked. I'd like to know which one you are."

"I haven't thought about it. I'd say there's really no difference. Do you get the job done? That's the test."

"Still, it's so desperate to have to make your women fight. I mean, how did they ever allow it at the Assembly?"

"No one *made* me do anything. What seems desperate to you was a chance to live a dream."

"I wish I had more possibilities to my future. Astler Aftorn is expected to be the patriarch of a new blossoming of the family tree. Most families are shaped like a pyramid, you know, that last surviving elder at the peak and a heap of great-great-grandbabies at the bottom. Ours is more shaped like a diamond, with a bunch of childless widows and cousins in the middle and me and Gandy at the bottom. I'm to find some girl with roomy hips and get to work."

Ileth blushed. "You make it sound like cattle or something."

"Oh, I don't mean the amorous arts themselves, I—it's just I have this one role I absolutely *must* fill. Everyone gets a worried look whenever I climb on a horse, like I'm going to break my neck or fall onto a fence and tear off something that won't grow back."

"There's Gandy."

"Oh, she's silly. She'll marry whoever calls her beautiful and sends her flowers after a dance. Some fortune-hunter will get her, and then I'll be headbutting with him for the rest of my life over inheritances."

"Run away and join the dragoneers."

"I couldn't do that. A lot of people in the Headlands depend on our family. I'd be letting them down too. Gods and Fates, it's like some wretched drama. The one girl—"

"Excuse me," a deep draconic voice said as a dragon approached, like a ship clearing a fog bank.

They made room as Mnasmanus trundled down to drink after his breakfast. Ileth should have offered to clean his teeth, but she wanted to keep talking to Astler. Maybe he was right about having the other sex around breaking your concentration.

"The one girl what?" she asked.

He put on that shy smile again, the shy smile that was occupying an increasing amount of her thoughts when she wasn't busy. "Oh, you know those sorts of stories. He falls recklessly and irrevocably for the one girl who it's impossible to be with, but it all works out all right in the end. My aunt reads them, and I think Gandy skims them looking for the shocking bits about pregnancies."

"We didn't have those sorts of books at the Lodge either," Ileth said.

"Just as well. Life isn't like that."

"It's routine, yes, but I bet a week ago you weren't . . . you weren't thinking you'd be in a cave full of dragons talking to a girl about pregnancies. You'll have to excuse me now. I need to see if Mnasmanus there needs me to clean his teeth."

They spent one more day at the Sag, living quietly, keeping the dragons as much out of sight as possible. She grew to know Gandy better, as the girl suddenly took an immense interest in her and practically moved in with her in Astler's room. She was tiresome company at first, but once Ileth learned to filter the chatter, it was more like having a songbird as a companion. Ileth had to say *yes* or *no* or *thank you* a few times an hour, but other than that Gandy's discourse unspooled like thread fed into a loom.

Thoughts of Astler disturbed her and she felt in danger of becoming one of those characters he mentioned who set her heart on an impossibility. Equally disturbing were the looks of Dun Huss, or rather the lack of them. While no charmer or conversationalist, he was affable and she'd always found that just standing near him offered a sense of safety and order that had been lacking from Ileth's life since—well, since ever, so she enjoyed his presence. But every time she came near him in the Sag, he suddenly found he had another duty to attend to and excused himself. She grew increasingly certain he was keeping something from her. Something important.

With another man, she would wait until he'd had his dinner and wine, refill his glass, and as he drank judge his mood and see if she could draw him out. Even the Captain had a free, kindly tongue with a good dinner in him and just enough brandy to make him easy, before he grew mean again at the fourth pour. But Dun Huss would drain half his glass at dinner and then refuse more while he still had that much to finish, then scuttle off with the Taskmaster or Serena, Amrits and the Borderlander to the study. Then she and Astler would start to chatting and her concerns would fade away in the glow of his conversation.

On their final night, they reopened a wood-floored storeroom at the Old Post, set a fire under an ancient cauldron that had been too large to relocate, and made both humans and dragons a meaty stew. Winter peas and potatoes, dried herbs and some stewed-and-jarred

tomatoes, plus the local beer, made a decent enough braise fit for the palates and digestive systems of humans and dragons. The group's mood struck Ileth as content, as though matters were now in motion to the satisfaction of the dragoneers and the Taskmaster from the Auxiliaries and the shipping gentleman. They all walked about the Old Post like the new owners of a house who had great plans for its expansion.

Something was in the offing, and Ileth resisted the impulse to let the dragoneers know just how many details she knew. After all, she'd consulted Annis Heem Strath's plan often enough to recognize its outlines being roughed in.

The morning of their departure, Ileth noticed that Astler seemed to be smelling rather strongly of his father's shaving soap. He'd washed his hair with it and not all of the flakes had come out. She wondered if it was because she'd mentioned she liked it.

Dun Huss broke the news that their flying party had to separate.

"Three are going on to Stavanzer. Ileth, we're commissioning you to fly to the Serpentine bearing messages and get back to your apprenticeship."

Ileth startled, awkwardly thrilled that they'd used the word *commission* in the presence of the family, as she was now beginning to think of them. She'd almost called Gandy *cousin* while pouring tea last night. "By myself?"

"Yes. My advice is a good running start and a headwind," Dath Amrits said. "All it takes is belief in oneself and arm strength."

Both the widows laughed politely and murmured compliments.

The Borderlander clapped her on the shoulder. "Catherix is taking you. She's tired of meetings. She knows the way home, and you should start learning how to return to the Serpentine from any point on the compass. Just keep going south. Once you're over the Blues you can practically see the lighthouse. When she's back on her shelf, you'll attend her until I return." The Borderlander was famous for not wanting wingmen, to the dismay of all the wingmen-at-large hoping for a position.

That was news. Being charged with a dragon's care in the place of her dragoneer! Better than the word *commission*, though perhaps to the Sag House family the significance wasn't so obvious.

"Don't sign for anything extravagant," Serena advised. "Catherix may try to take advantage of your inexperience."

Ileth would have liked to go to Stavanzer. She'd never even been in the north's largest city. But whining about orders wouldn't impress any of the dragoneers or Serena. Ileth suspected Serena's opinion might count for more with Charge Deklamp than that of the dragoneers.

The Borderlander shuffled nervously. "If the dancers have need of you, you can leave it to the grooms and feeders, but check on her dawn and dusk. She'll run you ragged. Don't always let her have her way."

"As a good wingman should," Dun Huss said.

Ileth quietly choked on her food. *Wingman!* She reached for water, washed it down.

"Don't measure yourself for a sword-belt yet," the Borderlander said, frowning at Dun Huss. "I don't take wingmen."

"I was merely repeating the old axiom that if you wish for a position, show that you can perform as the position demands."

"Now, about my crossbow," the Borderlander said.

"Why are you bothering her with the crossbow?" Amrits said.

The Borderlander shrugged. "Heard something big in the air about the lighthouse before dawn. Could have been gargoyles."

"Gargoyles! You should have told us." Comity and one of the widows squeaked.

"I think I know what that was," Astler said. "It's the canvas over the garden boxes. Sometimes the wind works one loose and it flaps."

"We haven't had gargoyles overhead in my lifetime," Comity said. "Didn't they die out?"

"You're making everyone nervous," Dun Huss said. "Ileth, test his crossbow and make sure you understand how to safely use it. Not because I believe there are gargoyles about, but because as a dragoneer flying on her own you should be confident with one."

After breakfast the Borderlander took her outside and showed her his crossbow. There was nothing distinctive about it; it looked to her exactly like the ones she'd seen hung up on the walls inside the Serpentine, a standard model built for the Guards. There were no frills or flourishes, badges, special sights, or notches in the stock.

But it turned out to be modified after all. The Borderlander turned it over and Ileth marked a larger-than-usual plate for the trigger and some small screws. "Don't let it fool you, it's not an ordinary crossbow. I like a light trigger. The tinkers rigged it up for me. You see this slide? It's easy, you can work it with your thumb. That's the trigger lock. Cocking it makes a racket, so I cock it somewhere close to the ground and quiet, then keep the safety on and no bolt in it. I only put the bolt in when I have a target. Then trigger lock off once I'm sighted and *only* once I'm sighted. I don't even touch the trigger until I'm a breath away from shooting. Then press the trigger, barely takes a twitch."

Ileth gulped, feeling a bit overwhelmed. She'd had exactly one morning of weapons training when she was first a novice, when they'd paraded the girls out into a field and let them examine a collection of weaponry, both from the Vales and captured in other lands, and learned the names of the various swords and pikes and clubs and bows and crossbows. They'd been allowed to pick them up but hadn't otherwise been trained. She'd used a sling as a child and been fair at it, good enough to kill rabbits for sheepdogs, anyway.

"Now I'll watch you," the Borderlander said.

"I really don't see her needing it," Amrits said. "Catherix is twice as fast as a gargoyle, unless she's taken unaware. As if. You're wasting your bolts, and I know how much you spend for them."

"Practice ain't waste."

He cast about outside the kitchens and found a partially rotted squash in the pig trough about the size of a squirrel. While the others checked over their saddles, he set the squash on a fence post for the Sag's empty horse paddock (the horses had been removed to somewhere closer to the village with the dragons visiting).

She was able to handle its weight without trembling. For as long as she needed to aim and shoot, she thought. He showed her how to open the handles to cock it, slipping your foot into a fitting in the front and then pulling with your back muscles. "It's not powerful as some, but I like something I can load quick and easy. I have a hook built into the saddle rig on her neck there so you don't need to use your foot, just lay the bow in the groove there and pull."

He had her try it, and with the crossbow cocked (the trigger lock engaged automatically when the string clicked across its little point). The bolts weren't like any she'd seen on the table that day; they were little three-bladed points that matched the three arrow feathers at the other end.

"The way the grooves on the quarrel heads are set, they spin a bit, goes into the flesh like a carpenter's drill," the Borderlander said. "You hit a gargoyle or a deer center-body, it'll do enough damage that it'll be down fast."

"Why do you keep bringing up gargoyles? You're scaring the girl," Amrits said. Maybe the Borderlander was doing it to get at him. Amrits kept glancing up into the sky every time they were mentioned.

"Just be careful and don't hit your dragon. They'll go for the wings anyway, slash at them. If you miss a gargoyle and hit wing you'll just punch a hole."

"This is too much. Ileth, don't let him worry you. You're not flying into battle."

"What are we training her for, then?" the Borderlander asked.

"You're not flying into battle *today*."

He showed her how to sight through the little metal V near the trigger mechanism, putting the top of the quarrel's tri-blade on the target and getting everything lined up.

"It's not true archery, since you're not playing around with distance and figuring how the arrow's gonna fall off. This kind of crossbow's not much good outside about the length of a big dragon, nose tip to tail, unless you got fifty of them lined up in a battle array, that is."

For her first shot, he had her stand only ten paces away.

She followed instructions, cocking the bow, double-checking that the safety locked all the way down (that was the one quirk in the weapon, it seemed, the trigger lock was not as reliable as the rest of the mechanism). She thumbed the point of the quarrel, noting the subtle, drill-like channels in the point. They must have been made by a superior craftsman. Maybe that was what the Borderlander spent his pay on, since it certainly wasn't clothes or personal comforts.

"Aim for the smallest thing you can see. Let's say a gargoyle is chewing on your dragon's wing. Aim for its armpit, or its ear, not the whole chest or head. On that gourd, pick out a wart or that bit of black rot."

She aimed.

"Now slide off the lock."

She pushed it with her thumb and she felt rather than heard a click.

"Breathe out and as you breathe out, touch the trigger."

The trigger didn't let go as soon as she pressed it, as she had feared it would. She re-aligned her sighting at the slight surprise and pressed. With about the effort it would take to press her finger into soft dough, the crossbow released with a *TWONK!*

She was concentrating so hard on the little flange of the arrowhead in the notch of the back sight, she didn't even see the gourd fly into pieces.

He sent her to retrieve the bolt. It was easy enough to find. The head and the feathers were notched and damaged, but the shaft seemed untroubled by the gourd's destruction.

"Try again with this chunk," the Borderlander said, setting a big piece on the post.

"Oh, now you're really wasting your bolts," Amrits said.

"I just want her confident with it if it's going to be in reach," the Borderlander said.

Ileth shot again, hit again. That trick about aiming at something small worked.

"You could have feasted all of us for a whole evening on what you're spending on those damned special bolts," Amrits said.

"Gargoyles," the Borderlander said, as a child might say *boo!* to scare a younger sibling. Amrits jumped a little and the Borderlander turned away from him to hang the crossbow on Catherix's saddle, chuckling softly to himself. Ileth decided there must be some history between them she didn't know.

The Borderlander inspected the string on the crossbow and secured it on its saddle, then latched a thong closed so it couldn't fall off or flop around even if the dragon turned upside down. "If you forget everything else, just get a good grip with the stock hard into your shoulder and put that top arrow blade on target."

Dun Huss was suddenly hovering, checking the saddle girth and securing straps and the safety tether. He triple-checked the dispatch case, lock, and fitting to the saddle. "I think you're worrying her needlessly. It won't come up."

"If it does, I want her to be able to take care of Catherix and herself." He patted the pale dragon, not quite white but not close enough to any other color for her to be called anything else. The dragon turned her back to him and licked him up the back of his head, like a mother dog licking a pup. Ileth had never seen a dragon do that to a human.

"Awww, get off," the Borderlander said.

"You've been to the smokehouse," Catherix said in her thick Montangyan. "A ham hangs. Tasty."

"Ileth, this is an important commission," Dun Huss said, so quietly even Catherix would have difficulty hearing his words in the wind. "The Republic's in more trouble than most know since the defeat in the Galantine War. Money's dried up. The Assembly is talking about fewer dragons in the Serpentine, and I don't dare tell you by how many apprentices and specialists let go. This has to go soon, and it has to go right. Go straight back to the Serpentine."

Was he worried she'd find an excuse to return to Stesside and speak to Ignata? The thought had crossed her mind, but she'd discarded it. They'd commissioned her to return to the Serpentine. She nodded.

With that, the dragoneers mounted. The Borderlander rode behind Serena. Every one of the family save the old man was there to see

them off. The widows kept close, holding hands. Gandy kept looking at her cousin and Ileth, as though watching the two principals in a staged drama. Comity and the two remaining gentlemen spoke about their own upcoming departures.

"We'll keep low until we're well away from the coast," Dun Huss said. "It's too light out for these supposed gargoyles, but there might be ships on the bay."

Ileth searched the horizon toward the Rari coast. Everything was shades of winter gray: gray land, water, the mountains of the far coast with perhaps a hint of blue.

"So much effort, and cliffs just over there," Catherix grumbled. Ileth wasn't about to argue with a dragon, but she fell into line with the others.

The dragons set themselves up to face the wind. Ileth felt cold air blowing in from the northwest. It would be a chilly flight.

Before she could get her thoughts properly in order, the dash began and they were aloft. They circled once, low, over Sag House.

Ileth marked Astler waving with great sweeping arm gestures and felt a pang. Gandy waved both ends of her red-and-white scarf. She watched the figures shrink. It was a new experience to leave someone behind.

She turned her nose to the dragon's course. If they'd flown on this course, they might have passed right over the Captain's Lodge, but the dragons turned inland and flew at treetop level to the west-southwest, toward Stavanzer. She only saw one person out, a man loading firewood onto a heavy cart. He dropped his armful when he saw dragons approaching and instinctively stepped behind his cart. Ileth waved but he didn't return it.

Once well clear of the coast and with the Blue Range going green with trees, they climbed. Catherix took her usual position above and behind the rest. It was more work for her, but the dragon would do things her own way, much like her rider. Ileth, with little to do but try to ignore the cold and not to impede the wind too much, glanced

above and behind them now and then, musing that the dragons resembled their riders. Mnasmanus, like Dun Huss, was very polished and attentive to duty, Telemiron, like Serena, was physically different but almost supernaturally talented in other areas. Etiennersea was happy to be forward, the center of attention. Catherix was a loner, even when flying with other dragons. Did the dragons somehow sniff out a kindred spirit when choosing a rider? If so, what sort of spirit did she have? Was there a stuttering dragon who liked music? Maybe she was wrong; Etiennersea wasn't like Dath Amrits at all. Quite the opposite really, she seemed a very serious and responsible dragon. Maybe he was the outlet for a silly side of herself she didn't dare show, like those stories of kings keeping fools and jesters about to keep from feeling the weight of responsibility all the time.

Catherix rocked, startling Ileth out of her thoughts. Dun Huss on Mnasmanus was pointing first at Catherix, then south.

"We break off," Catherix called back.

Ileth signaled with an exaggerated nod, indicating that she understood, and gave a dragoneer salute, not sure of the exact protocol but it felt right. Catherix put on speed and overtook the others. Ileth gloried in the honor of having the salute returned, dragoneer-to-dragoneer. How many people could claim such a moment? And gone again, only a memory already . . .

Ileth watched the dragoneers turn into silhouettes and then vanish into the clouds.

Catherix rocked in the fluky winds of the Blue Mountains, passing between the peaks south. She found some air to her liking and rose again. Ileth huddled deeper into her coat collar.

Ileth, always too ready to look under mental rocks for the dark side, considered Dun Huss's words on her commission. Cutting dragons would be a calamity for the Republic. Had everyone forgotten that it was the dragons who saved them—repeatedly!—against the Alliance of Kings? And as a mere trifle of a side effect, cutting dragons meant cutting the people who took care of the dragons. She wondered what

was in the cases. Something with Governor Raal's seal? Estimates by Taskmaster Henn and that big man from the shipping lines? Folded maps with close-written plans? Obviously something had been decided and the Serpentine needed to know right away.

Ileth returned her concentration to her dragon and the landmarks passing below.

The flight back, in fine cold weather with Catherix happy to be able to fly at her most comfortable pace rather than keeping to the speed set by Etiennersea, was the sort of travel that made the rest of the Serpentine's service worth it. She could watch the pattern of the clouds on the land below, pick out little farms and crossroad taverns, even count herds in winter pasture. She wondered if anyone was marking the dragon above, knew its name, nudged a friend—*That's the Borderlander's dragon, mate.*

They passed over the double wall of the Blue Range and the heavy forest between. She'd heard wingmen talk of their "survivals" in those woods, where you had to care for a downed dragon on your own with nothing but your wits. She marked the blue of the Skylake beyond.

Either the air was warmer here or she'd begun to go numb.

The Skylake was a blue deeper and darker than the horizon above. She admired the triple peak of the White Sisters opposite the Serpentine and then the fortress itself as she approached.

It felt good. A homecoming. It was like her spirit was drawing life from the landscape beneath; every smoking chimney and huddled herd of sheep and fallow field of oats fed some of its bounty to her.

"No dragons. Room for fun. You chance flight cave, yes?"

Ileth was game. She slapped the dragon's shoulder. Then she paused. Suppose a fluke of wind sent them crashing into the side of the Beehive? Suppose her cases of plans went into the Skylake?

The Borderlander had told her not to always give Catherix her way. Had that been a hint? Was this a test, something secretly arranged, to see if the joy of a fun stunt would make her forget her duty? "Another time," she shouted. "Land carefully, on the road." Catherix made a

stomach-churning tight turn and swooped in toward the Pillar Rocks and the road where dragons usually landed. Well, call it a compromise.

Despite the sudden descent, Catherix alighted as gently as a soap bubble blown from a child's hand. Ileth had never experienced such a gentle dragon-landing.

"Ileth on . . . on Catherix with d-dispatches," Ileth said to the apprentice who came dashing from the little landing office in the shelter of Mushroom Rock. Did she have to add "arriving" as if the dragon had just floated down like a blown dandelion seed?

The attendant checked the lock and added a note to the log. "Case and lock intact. For the office of the Charge only. You'd better wait with them. I'll send for Dogloss."

"Food. Plenty food, plenty, while we wait," Catherix said.

"I'll see to it," Ileth said, dismounting. She watched a messenger run for the Charge's tower. It occurred to her that the Old Tower was convenient for news from an incoming dragon. Perhaps that was why the Charge had reestablished the office there.

The landing shack was used to dragons coming in hungry and had a pot of warm fish stew ready. She dumped it in a feeding barrow, brought it to Catherix, and Ileth stood there with the cases, watching the dragon eat until Dogloss arrived.

The dispatches were duly handed over, and he double-checked the case-count and seals before accepting them. "Fine work, Ileth. See to your dragon." *Your dragon.* Ileth's heart skipped a beat.

She led Catherix across the Long Bridge like arriving with a locked case of secrets was an everyday event in her life. She feigned a bored expression as an apprentice said something in a novice's ear as they walked past, Catherix still running her tongue about her snout to get the last of the oily fish stew inside.

Back at Catherix's shelf on the Upper Ring she loosened her saddle girth and unhooked the reins from her ears, not that Ileth had made any use of them. Ileth removed the saddle—a few idle grooms followed in the wake of the newly arrived dragon and helped her.

"Where's the old scarecrow?" the groom asked.

"I'm not sure," Ileth said, honestly enough. "He s-s-sent me back with me-messages."

She patted the Borderlander's great trunk with its odd collection of buttons set into the lid. Now that she'd seen Galantine uniforms up close, she recognized a few. She wondered what they meant. Odd that none of them were partly melted or scorched, though; Ileth thought most of the dragoneers' enemies ended up burned to ash.

Ileth spent the next few days visiting Catherix three times a day, getting back into her Serpentine rhythm. Her lot had started riding the few Serpentine horses out the gate on longer endurance runs.

Horses seemed delicate and sensitive compared to the dragons. Cleaning them took no time at all, and they accepted their grooming without complaint. The dragons, on the other hand, were giving the humans an earful about everything. They complained about the quality of the food. Fish heads, tails, and other offal were being ground up and made into "meal" with oats and other fillers. The dragons were calling it chicken feed or worse. Some were refusing to eat it, Catherix among them.

Ileth, whose first job in the Serpentine had been gutting and filleting fish for the dragons, sympathized. Fish heads were fish heads, no matter how finely you ground them and what you added to mask the flavor. The feeders were unhappy because the dragons took it out on them, and the grooms had it even worse. Dragon excrement was foul, extremely foul, but compact and quick to clean up and dispose of. This filler diet tripled the size of their evacuations and added gas eruptions from both ends of the digestive tract. The Beehive's usual vaguely sulfurous oily smell now had sewage overtones and the sickening smell of rotting fish. Some of those working the rings where the dragons lived were tying kerchiefs over their faces and sprinkling them with cheap scent or pine oil.

Ottavia kept the smell at bay by spraying the curtain with cheap, colorless farmer spirits distilled from potatoes.

"Why are we feeding the dragons such rot?" Preen asked.

"Money's short," Santeel said.

"*Short*'s not the word for it," Ottavia said.

Ileth knew how much the dragons judged the quality of their life by the taste of their food. She'd heard from more than one dragon that service with the dragoneers meant not having to bother with hunting or diving for your food.

"Will they stand it long?" Ileth asked.

Ottavia frowned. "Shrentine told me there have been complaints. Any dragon who wishes to hunt this winter is being given leave, I understand." Secretly, Ileth wondered if this was part of the reduction in the number of dragons.

The dragoneers and Serena returned, and shortly after Ileth turned management of Catherix back over to the Borderlander, a note came to report to the Charge's tower.

She'd been at practice that morning and hadn't yet eaten, which was just as well, as she felt sick to her stomach as soon as Ottavia handed it to her, with its usual "at your convenience" formulation. But there was nothing to do but hurry to meet her fate. Delay would only make her guts go even more sour and brand her a coward. Whatever the news, it would be a relief, and afterward she could have breakfast. She put a rose knot, her favorite, in her apprentice sash and felt ready for whatever the meeting would bring.

Dogloss admitted her to the Charge's office.

Traskeer was in the office as well, drawing the warmth from the room like an open window. His face was its usual unreadable mask. Charge Deklamp stood next to his desk, impassive, and the always impressive Dogloss quietly rearranged letters on the blotter.

She saw the bottom of the map of the North Province and Pine Bay, but someone had thrown a tablecloth over it as a screen. Judging from the lumps in the cloth, there were pins or some other markers stuck in the map. There was a heavily notated roster of dragons on the Charge's desk.

"Ileth, sorry to call you in here. This is a conversation more

appropriate for Charge Traskeer's office, but he happened to be here, and I wished to be present. You're not in any trouble."

Ileth's heart eased off its pounding. Why did she feel doomed? She wasn't standing before a jury. Was Traskeer going to make an issue of her theft of the streamer?

"But it is a difficulty for us, and it has to do with you."

"Is this about my sash?"

"Nothing to do with your sash, Ileth. It looks fine," Traskeer said. "In truth—"

Deklamp held up his hand. "I told you I would handle this, sir. I sent Ileth north; it's my responsibility."

Responsibility and someone as important as the Charge having to pass on whatever this news was to her couldn't be good. Ileth felt the room sway.

"Please, sit down," Dogloss said. He moved to a chair, turned it so she might sit. She did, trying not to make it the collapse that it was.

"Sir, whatever it is, please—"

"Perhaps a small drink?"

"No, I'd—no, thank you, I'd rath-rather j-just hear it, sir."

"Well, it's like this. Delicate matter. I don't suppose you know that Governor Raal is claiming you are his natural daughter."

"Daughter!" Ileth said.

The Master in Charge held up a letter. "It bears no seal; personal correspondence with stationery marked as Stesside House. He puts it here, plainly enough, in the letter. Not quite the same as swearing to it in front of a jury, but in his own hand and signed."

"Daughter," Ileth repeated.

"We're as confused as you. You've never heard anything about your parentage? Even a hint?"

Ileth was grateful for a moment to pretend to think, to put her feet back on the ground and steady the swaying room. She sorted her words.

"Plenty of stories. Some noticed that the man who . . . who ran our lodge often kept me close to him when we went into town, so that

meant I was his natural daughter. There were also rumors that I was a Name's daughter being hidden away out of embarrassment. Hateful talk. I tried to forget those stories. As for my mother, the less said about those the better. Gossip is always worse when a woman's being carved and dished up."

"Too true," Deklamp said. "Did any of the stories feel right to you? Do you match any possibilities in looks or temperament?"

It took her a while to get the words out. Physically, she supposed she resembled the Captain more than Governor Raal, as he was from a Galantine family. It all seemed so very strange.

The group of men absorbed what she said.

"We can't do anything with village gossip," Traskeer said. "What do we do about Raal's claim?"

The Charge of the Serpentine took a deep breath. "Ileth, I may have to ask a great deal of you. You've always given us the impression that you were a proud and devoted young woman in our service. We have a few Names here who—well, they're marking time, making connections, getting the Serpentine associated with their family Name. You've shown yourself the kind of apprentice here for the best reasons. Tailer or no, I believe you one of the best of your draft."

The praise felt cold. Ileth knew something awful was hovering behind it, like the sugar that came with the medicine. Her voice cracked as the words came out: "You're sending me away. The Serpentine will no longer be my home."

My home. It felt so natural. Much more natural than *my father.*

Charge Heem Deklamp set his face as though she'd slapped him. "The dragoneers are a shield of the Vales, of our Republic. Our Republic is in a great deal of trouble. Our markets are reeling; such allies as we have think we're going under, that the Republic will collapse. Our trade with the east is being stifled. We have in mind opening the sea lanes in the north so our ships might get out that way—the shorter route, when all is said and done. As you are from the Freesand, you can probably guess what we are planning. I'm sure you can appreciate how

much better life could be if shipping could once again flow freely out of North Bay—Pine Bay, did you say you call it up there?—again. A military success would restore the spirit of our people, give confidence to our allies, stabilize the markets, get the banking cartels to believe in us again and reopen lending."

"Ileth is a good worker," Traskeer said. "But her interests don't extend to state finance. Why are you sharing all this?"

"I want her to have a sense of the weight and importance this campaign could have."

Ileth stiffened a little at the word *campaign*. She hadn't heard the word used to describe whatever was in the works yet. A campaign meant dragons fighting and arrows and burning ships. The Serpentine was an intricate machine whose ultimate purpose was war, and now it was on the table in front of her.

Ileth returned her attention to the Charge. "I understand the difficulty. I don't see how I could make a difference."

Traskeer spoke next, and she had to look at him: "The Governor has us over a barrel, you might say. It has to do with the political structure of the Republic. Key members of the Assembly, trusted with such matters, are discussing the campaign right now and their approval seems likely but not certain, which is why there is so much secrecy. War is expensive, for both the Assembly and the Governor."

Ileth's education had been as deficient in politics as it was in philosophy or the sciences. She knew that the people of the Vales voted for who would lead them in the Assembly, and the Assembly voted laws into action and authorized money to be spent, wars to be started, all the matters handled by kings and queens in other lands. She knew that governors were powerful, carrying out the Assembly's laws and acting much in the way a king would in directing their provinces with their own funds and finances. They also acted in a group in the Assembly in some manner, but she wasn't sure of the details.

Dogloss consulted the letter. "It's not just a claim about fatherhood. The Governor has set a demand that we return you to him. He

thinks we've acted in a high-handed manner on a trifling matter about the return of a runaway lodge-girl. He says if there is to be a fresh start between the dragoneers and the north, we have to pay off old accounts, so to speak."

It still seemed like madness to Ileth. "Why should he care? He never set eyes on me until we landed at Stesside."

Deklamp sighed. "I believe he wishes to assert his power over us in some form. You just happen to be it. Ileth, take heart. You are contracted as an apprentice here. You've done well. I've no reason to break that contract."

At this Traskeer shifted in his seat and began to speak, but Charge Deklamp shot a look at him and he closed his mouth.

Deklamp referred to something on his desk. Ileth wondered if it was a report in Serena's hand. "It is not as hopeless as it looks. You've met Governor Raal. He's a reasonable man. His position isn't quite as strong as he thinks."

"How can a man just state that he's my father and have people accept it?" Ileth asked.

"Lower your voice, girl. You're speaking to the Charge," Traskeer said.

Deklamp ignored him and the emotion in her words. "Dogloss, you're our legal expert. Perhaps you can give us the benefit of your opinion."

Dogloss took a breath as he gathered his thoughts and consulted a piece of paper with some notes and dates on it. "As far as we've been able to tell—and we're checking further—there is no claim of your paternity beyond this one. We do know that his name appears nowhere on your birth registry, just that of your mother. It was looked up and verified as a matter of routine shortly after you were sworn in as a novice. We're trying to ascertain if he's ever directly supported you—sent his own money to the Lodge you grew up in. If he hasn't done that, if nothing but local funds supported the Lodge along with the usual charities, he simply has no case at all and we can fight it out in

front of a jury. He can't present gossip as evidence. He might have a letter or some evidence from your mother, and if that's the case it becomes more difficult, but he hasn't mentioned any kind of proof in his letters to us.

"And speaking of gossip," Dogloss continued, shifting from foot to foot uncomfortably, "he and his wife never managed to produce children. Nor have they adopted. Perhaps as they are older now, they are feeling it."

"His wife . . . seemed lonely," Ileth said.

"She should get a cat," Traskeer said, and for the first time in the meeting Ileth felt that he might be on her side, just a little. Or it was his dislike of women showing itself again.

The Charge brought matters back to business. "Ileth, here is what we have decided. You will take a leave of absence, remaining under contract as an apprentice but with your apprenticeship suspended, and return to the north. You've proved a resourceful young woman. Perhaps the Governor can come to appreciate you and see that you belong with the Republic's dragons."

"Can't I just refuse to go?"

"You can, but the Governor is very close to the law of the land in his province. He can assemble a jury and make things much more difficult for us. Beyond that, we want this campaign against the Rari to move forward, for the Republic's sake. Giving way on this is the key that will unlock his cooperation."

They were always testing you. They hadn't invented this test, but now that she'd absorbed the blow of the news, she'd do her best to pass it. Sitting on a stump and crying about it wouldn't do. She summoned a brisk, upbeat tone: "If that's my duty as you see it, playing daughter and keeping Lady Raal company, I'll do my best, sir."

The Charge nodded. "That's the spirit, apprentice. You will go north again with my word that you will not be forgotten. There will be some excitement up there as the campaign gets under way, assuming the Assembly takes the final step and figures out a way to finance this last throw of the dice. Perhaps, as the Governor's daughter, you'll see

a little of it. When it is over, we'll contest the Governor's claim on you in court if we must. You are what, sixteen now?"

"Yes, sir. Seventeen in the spring."

"The Governor, even were he named as your father on your birth registry, will not be able to keep you anywhere you don't wish to be past eighteen, as you know. Are you paying taxes on—"

"She's quite poor," Traskeer said.

"Of course. I thought I saw something about an inheritance connected to her name. Or was that the girl with the lenses?"

Deklamp rose, came around his desk, and took her hand gently in his. "My advice to you, Ileth, is to make the most of this opportunity. He's offering his Name; take it. Going from Lodge-girl to the Governor's daughter . . . How many girls sharing a bench in a lodge dream of that sort of elevation? He probably keeps a carriage in the city. If he's anything like Governor Vor Gleiss he has more than one. Dresses made by seamstresses. Wigs, if your taste is to fanciful hair. You could look at it as a reward for years of patient poverty."

She smiled at him. It was easy to love this odd little man, even though a man whose family owned vineyards would hardly know that poverty *had* to be accepted with patience. You couldn't afford any other choice. "If these are your orders, I'll be the daughter the Fates didn't let them have. Perhaps we all may come out of this happy."

Ileth's dreams of elevation had mostly been vistas like she'd seen on her flight back to the Serpentine on Catherix. Being a governor's daughter was something for a person like Quith and her love of social connections.

"You've had a shock. It's a lot to absorb. Would you like a note that you be excused from duties for a day or two?"

"No, I should like to dance, I think, if they have need of me."

Traskeer cleared his throat. "That's the angle. If anything . . . distressing happens to you with the Governor, should his motives prove other than fatherly, get a message to me and do not omit details out of embarrassment. I dislike even mentioning the possibility, but we shall act as though his intentions are entirely honorable even as we

prepare for infamy. I will provide you with envelopes with Assembly postage. It's a hanging offense to interfere with those. The Governor may just find I have powerful friends, too. Dogloss, supply her with a few, would you? And draw some funds for her, just in case. Enough for a comfortable trip both ways. Out of my account, of course."

Dogloss nodded and Ileth thanked him. Perhaps he wasn't as heartless as one of his coup pieces after all.

Traskeer offered to walk her back to the Beehive. After taking the envelopes and her traveling purse, they started down the Serpentine's principal path toward the Pillar Rocks and the Long Bridge. Ileth marked five dragons flying practically wingtip-to-wingtip over the Skylake. That was an unusual sight. They tipped their wings and dived in a line, the second dragon's nose hardly separated from the tailtip of the first, with the others following in similar fashion. At the lake level, where Ileth thought she saw a cask floating with a little signal flag on it—it was hard to make out at this distance—the formation came back into the line abreast.

Five dragons training hard. That had to mean something. The Serpentine was preparing for war. Would the dragons be able to open the straits, or would this be the last gasp of a strangled nation? Her only part in it would be sipping tea with Lady Raal at Stesside. What a poor joke.

Even though she didn't much feel like dancing, Ileth forced her feet to proceed through the Upper Ring to Falberrwrath's shelf. She peeked into the spacious, prominently placed alcove where Falberrwrath slept (formerly it had been Fespanarax's) with its own almost musical trickle, but the big red dragon was gone. Perhaps he was in the Cellars looking over his hatchlings. Why had he called for a dancer, then?

She watched a novice, his fourteen-year-old shoulder muscles straining as he pushed a full feeding cart under the supervision of an apprentice. She was fairly sure she'd been oathed in with the

apprentice but she didn't know him beyond that. He nodded at her, face respectfully neutral. She envied him. Check the quality of the food—feed the dragons according to their taste. Rotate through different duties for the next four or so years.

She waited for Falberrwrath to return. A passing wingman told her he'd been called out to survey the opposite shore of the Skylake. She returned to the Quarter. The dancers were at afternoon drills, or tending to the dragons. She sank into her bed and wept. It was a game, like Traskeer's coup, and she was a very small piece. She'd been fed to Governor Raal to get him to make a move.

"Ileth, whatever's the matter?"

Santeel Dun Troot stood there. Her hair was a sweaty mess and she looked tired.

"Too much t-to tell."

Santeel squatted next to her bed and gave her a tentative pat. Physical gestures didn't come easy to a Dun Troot, Ileth had learned. "I thought you were in the north? You had to be happy to see the old streets of your home."

"That's the problem. This is my home. I'm losing it."

To her credit, Santeel looked grieved. "You're not being dismissed or discharged or whatever they call it?"

"Not exactly," Ileth sniffled. She did her best to explain. First it came as a trickle, then a torrent, like the bottom of a rusty bucket giving way.

Santeel took it all in and made no attempt to make her feel better. She just listened. For some reason, that struck Ileth more as an act of friendship than a *there, there, it's not so bad.*

"Can I get you anything?"

Ileth sighed. "What I want is brandy."

"I have something better. Have you taken Elletian snuff?"

"I've never taken ordinary snuff."

She disappeared into her sleeping nook, still talking: "I could use a little myself. I've been dancing for Shrentine. I think she just likes to

while away the time listening to musicians and as long as she has music on there might as well be a dancer to occupy her eye. I'm exhausted."

Ileth heard her move books about and then a distinct scratch-click. She returned with a polished lacquer snuffbox of Hypatian design. She opened it and took out a pinch of dusty tobacco.

"I like a sort of sweet flavor to it, reminds me of cake," Santeel said. She offered the box to Ileth. "Just a little, you're not used to it."

Santeel stuck her fingers up against her nostril and snorted. Ileth imitated her. Overlaying the familiar tobacco was a sweet scent, reminded her of some kind of pie, but the sweetness wasn't from any berry she knew. "You'll feel a new woman in a moment."

"The tobacco is scented with . . . with . . ."

"You ever had bananas?"

"No."

"It reminds me of bananas. Kind of sweet and soft and warm."

Ileth sat up, like a quick plunge into cold water without the cold water. She felt deliciously alive and aware.

"What kind of tobacco is this?"

"I'm not sure. It's expensive, I know that. It'll keep you dancing." Santeel took a little more.

"I need air and light," she said. "Let's get out of here. The lighthouse. Air and light both."

Ileth had never actually been up by the lighthouse. Santeel took her by the hand and pulled her up to the Rotunda gallery.

From there it was not an easy climb. Santeel lit a walking candle from a supply by a burning brazier, and they had to climb through rock again in a winding stairway that you had to bend to negotiate. You often had to lean to the right and support yourself with an arm.

They seemed to climb forever. "Do these stairs come to an end?" Ileth asked.

"It opens up on the mourning gallery. Bodies of our honored dead dragoneers are placed there, I'm told. Halfway between earth and sky."

"I wouldn't care to drag a bier up these stairs," Ileth said.

"Preen says dragons fly them up. Some call it 'the Last Ride,'" she said.

Finally, and happily, for even Ileth's trained legs were sore, they came to a cramped storage room full of rags and brushes and other items for cleaning, with wide, perfectly normal stairs leading up to a brightly lit room. They took the stairs up to a chamber about the size of a small cottage that, in a way, mirrored the architecture of the Rotunda below. An oval altar dominated the room, on its own raised dais in an inversion of the well off the Rotunda below.

Recessed crystals in the ceiling, some as small as a fingernail, others as big as a melon, sent shafts of dazzling sunlight directed to the altar. More light came in through a passage leading out to what looked like a balcony. They were near or at the very top of the Beehive, it seemed.

Columns set into the stone ringed the room, dividing time-faded frescoes of men in rather old-fashioned warrior attire or robes who looked solemnly at the ground.

"Wonder what those old beggars would think if they knew they were looking at a couple of girls who danced about half-naked," Santeel said.

Ileth stifled a laugh. "That's . . . that's disrespectful."

"It's just frescoes. It's not like there's a body being mourned."

Ileth wondered if Annis Heem Strath had been placed here. Or if, someday, she or Santeel might be bloodless and cold on the slab beneath the painted stone.

"You've gone gloomy," Santeel said. "Light and air."

Ileth stood and followed her out onto a flat. She wondered if it could be called a balcony or just a platform built into the side of the Beehive.

Whatever it was, it was an advantageous irregularity in the Beehive just big enough for a dragon to set down. Above, Ileth could see the pillars and glass pyramid top of the lighthouse, one of the most famous landmarks in the Republic. This was as close as she'd ever been to it,

even when flying. There was a Guard posted here, of course, keeping watch but mostly shooing birds away with a long pole with some rags tied on the end so they wouldn't foul the glass.

The platform she stood upon, at this dizzying height, had no rail or guard of any sort. She wouldn't care to stand on it on a stormy day, for even in the mild summer weather there was wind. Your life wouldn't be worth much in a winter snowstorm. The narrow steps—they could not be dignified with the name of *stairs*—leading up to the lighthouse did have a rope set in the side of the Beehive. She had the urge to sit down for some reason and stayed well away from the edge.

Santeel showed off by going right to the edge and gripping with her strong dancer's toes.

"Quite a view."

"Stop-stop that, you're ma-making me nervous," Ileth said. On the other hand, you could take in the Serpentine entire and probably a goodly chunk of the Vales from here. Only the southern end of the long Skylake was invisible; you could just see the tree-covered hills of the north shore from here.

She noticed a dark building with a flat roof among the growth atop Mushroom Rock. She didn't know there was anything up there.

"What's that?" she asked, pointing. It took Santeel a moment to figure out what she was talking about.

"On Mushroom Rock, you mean? That's the Wizard's Nest."

"We have—we have a wizard?"

"No, I think wizards are just in stories. The tinkers. You know, they specialize in equipment for the dragoneers, and the dragons. Like the armored eye-slits and neck guards, you ever see a dragon with one of those on? They came up with them."

"Oh, yes, the tinkers," Ileth said. "Do you know any? I don't think I've ever talked to one."

"They're not mixers. I don't even know how many there are. Surely not more than a handful. They're secretive, even the door up to their quarter is hidden. Still, they're part of the Serpentine. You can get apprenticed in with them. I think they choose you, not the other way around."

The cold winter air combined with the icy clarity of the sun cleared Ileth's mind. Whatever lay ahead—war, governor's retreat, dismal bed in a lodge, dragoneer's saddle—she felt capable of meeting it. She began to feel the chill.

"I see why you take snuff. I do feel much better," Ileth said. "But I'm getting cold."

"You get used to it, and it's not so intense. I'm a bit envious."

Ileth twitched her nose. She wanted to pick the tobacco flakes out of it; they were making her nostril itch. "It's making my nose run." She turned away and gave a discreet blow off the balcony.

"Well, was the view worth the climb?"

Ileth took in the Skylake. There were five dragons in the air again, exercising. "Worth a chill, too."

"You're luckier than I, Ileth."

"How's that?" Luckier! What had this snuff done to Santeel's reason?

"You came here. Same night as me. Same exact night. I often think of that coincidence. You had nowhere to go but up, really."

"No. Even at fourteen, I had opportunities to go down," Ileth said.

Santeel ignored the sad attempt at a joke. "You're from the gutter, but you're not of the gutter. Do you know what I mean? I never felt people who started out there were naturally bad. Couldn't improve their station. Even before I met you. The Republic's right about that, even with all my father's talk about people being either horses or donkeys or mules. I've met a few donkeys with fancy names. Still donkeys under the daycoats and fine dresses.

"Me, if I do well here, I hurt my family." Santeel waved vaguely at the buildings at the up end of the Serpentine. "I'm expected to be exactly like my mother and raise a daughter or two to be exactly like me. Like a workshop producing teacups for matched sets, and the sets better match or you'll be out on your backside. This was to be Santeel's little fling, like a tour of the Hypatian coast looking at statues and ruined temples, maybe a few weeks of experimental rutting with a similar well-bred boy from the Elletian coast and a great draught of

Mother's Red Purge at the end of it if need be, then back home and duty to the family right to the grave."

"Don't think there wasn't a plan for me," Ileth said. "Cook or maid, or if I was very lucky, wife to a fisherman with his own boat."

Santeel smiled. "Sad to picture you all red from the wind, pregnant, helping unload the catch. You're so pretty. You don't have that milk-fed Vale look, and you don't have the wild northern thing really either, maybe just a little of it. You're unique. You should have a portrait done. I bet the artist would sell copies, if he was good and you were in a decent gown. I could kiss you, you're so pretty, but then you open your mouth and I want to drown you."

Santeel wasn't one to use delicate phrases from behind fan-guarded lips. She squared off and unloaded, as the Captain used to say. "That's the second time you've told me you'd drown me."

"Is it? Oh. I suppose it's our family way to kill someone."

Ileth hadn't expected *that*.

"When I was six or seven, I had this little dog. I don't know if it had been bred to be small, smaller dog than any I've seen. Big, sweet eyes. But maybe it was the breeding, it was sickly. One day it just couldn't get to its feet. It could rise up on its front paws, but then it would flop over. It just panted. My mother told me that women were responsible for bringing life into the world. Sometimes it was our duty to take it back out again to spare suffering. So she filled a tub with warm water—"

Ileth wasn't sure she wanted to hear the rest of it. "Your mother is dark."

"You've no idea."

Santeel was silent for a moment, thinking, and then she spoke again.

"Before the puppy—oh, I don't even know how old I was. I was young. I was writing my name and reading a little, I remember. My mother's mother, my grandmother, lived with us. A very nice room. Family home, you know, more impressive than my father's. That was

my parents' marriage on a notecard. His family's money was the more impressive, but my mother's had the properties. Mums, that's what I called my grandmother, became ill. For a while she could still get around, then in a wheeled chair, and finally she ended up in bed. Couldn't leave it. I remember bringing her flowers to put next to the bed; Mother had moved it so she had the best view, and then my mother stayed in that room with her for . . . well, it seemed to me always but I suppose it was just a few days. I barely saw her. I listened at the door sometimes. I heard talk. Crying. Even laughing. Then one morning my mother was out of the room, looking very tired, and told me that Mums was gone. She hadn't seemed that sick."

"I'm sorry you saw all that," Ileth said.

Santeel helped herself to a little more snuff.

"Should you have that much?" Santeel was sweating despite the cold. The evening sun glimmered on the beads of sweat.

"I want to dance," Santeel said. "C'mon, Ileth, dance with me!"

Santeel moved out onto the balcony. Ileth lunged, pulled her back.

"In this wind? Santeel, you're mad!"

"But the sun feels sooo good! Winter sun is the best sun, don't you think?"

Ileth pulled more firmly and drew her inside.

Santeel seemed compliant, so Ileth took her toward the staircase. "We should return to the Quarter. I want to lie down."

She didn't really. What she wanted to do was see if she could make a sound on the Dragon Horn that ran up the wall of the Rotunda. She'd always wondered, and this might be the last chance. But what she really, really wanted was for Santeel not to go out dancing on that balcony with nothing between her and a plunge to her death but her sense of balance clouded by whatever was in this snuff.

They started down the awkward stairway running through the Rotunda dome, Ileth leaning, going slowly, supporting herself with her hand. Santeel tripped lightly down the stairs, bracing herself with both arms and swinging her legs down together.

"Ah-woop!" Santeel said, swinging, just as her hand slipped.

It didn't seem like a hard fall to Ileth, but she heard a horrible, distinctive snap. Santeel slid down two more steps with her leg folded under her, and not in a dance fold either.

"Was that my leg breaking?" Santeel asked, her eyes wide. "I can't move it."

Ileth did her best to stretch her out in the narrow, curving stairway. "I think so." There was no blood. That was good. Or she thought so anyway, her mind racing. If there was blood with a bone break you were as good as dead, she'd been told.

"I'll get help," Ileth said. "Stay here," she added.

Santeel thought that was funny. She started to laugh. "Ooooh, Ileth, laughing hurts. Don't make me laugh. Yes. You should hurry. Get help."

Ileth went down the stairs as quickly as she dared, found a novice checking candles in the Rotunda balcony, sent him for help, and hurried down to the main floor of the Rotunda and grabbed a wingman and sent him for a physiker.

"Not Threadneedle," Ileth said. "He's too slow. His assistant. Tell him to bring others. Someone strong."

She flew back up the stairs to Santeel.

"I can just feel my toes," Santeel said. "But it hurts when I try to wiggle them."

"Then don't do it."

"I think wiggling your toes is important. I can't remember why. The pain is getting worse. Would more sn—"

"More snuff is a bad idea."

"You're right. I'm keeping what's left. I've spent too much on it lately. Well, more than too much. Everything. Keep talking, won't you, Ileth? Until they come?"

Ileth tried to come up with a subject. "So that's why you had me write your family? All your money was going to snuff?"

"It kept me going, between the apprentice duties and my dancing.

It wasn't just snuff, they kept saying I owed more because I was late paying for it."

"You? A debtor?" It had always seemed like Santeel had money for any fancy.

"I owed for a while. They knew I was rich—well, my family was rich—he let me buy on credit. I paid them back, part of it. I had to sell some clothes and a bracelet and rings to do it, if I didn't want to end up like you."

"What do you mean, end up like me?"

"I don't—I—"

"Santeel."

"That cut on your eyebrow. They threatened to cut my face. It was a message. A warning."

"Over a debt?"

"Ileth, they never hinted that they'd cut someone else. I'm not even sure I have it right. If I were certain, I would have gone to the Masters. No matter what Vary said."

"Vareen Dun Klaff?"

"Yes, he's part of that Blacktower gang, with Heem Beck and Vor Rapp. Heem Beck is dreadful. He laughed when Dun Klaff threatened me. I could see him cutting a girl."

It took a moment for Ileth to absorb the shock. So Quith had sort of been right. Her wounding at the bridge ceremony was intentional. But it had nothing to do with her. She was just some nobody, the tailer, a thing they could use to frighten Santeel into getting more money out of her.

Up in the Freesand there'd been a village cur that didn't belong to anybody. It used to sleep on the painted wooden steps of the candle-maker's on sunny mornings. The candle-maker's wife would wake and prod it, gently, with her broom in the morning so she could sweep the steps and polish the door handle and the dog apologetically slunk away until she was done and returned inside, and then he'd resume his nap. One morning Ileth saw her husband kick the dog off the steps,

hard. The dog bit him, hard, on the fleshy inner part of the thigh just behind the knee before running off, leaving the candle-maker fallen on the steps clutching his leg with blood running between his fingers, calling for help.

Ileth felt ready to bite.

A groom arrived with bandages and a brace. Ileth had him wait, kept talking to Santeel, until the physiker Gift arrived. He didn't ask any questions but went straight to work bracing and making a sling that would allow him and the groom to carry Santeel the rest of the way down to the Rotunda gallery without too much movement to her leg. There she was lifted onto a proper litter.

"You want to work on her by the mirrors?" a groom asked. "Good light there."

"The physiker's office," Gift said. "I want to be sure it's set properly someplace where she won't have to be moved again for a few days."

Ileth walked next to Santeel's litter until they met Threadneedle on the road just past the Pillar Rocks. He was puffing and red-faced, as he should be upon hearing that a Dun Troot was badly injured. Gift spoke to him quickly and he glanced at the bracing on her leg. He picked up Santeel's hand and held it, walking beside her litter, fussing over her and prattling about what sorts of food she'd like brought for her dinner once they had her comfortably set up in a room.

Santeel chatted back, wincing through the greasy sweat of pain coating her face. Ileth considered for just a moment telling the physikers about the snuff, but after a doubtful moment she decided not to interfere. She had the little case right in the pocket of her overdress, after all. They'd find it when they undressed her to work on the leg. She bade Santeel farewell, promising to inform Ottavia of the accident. But instead of turning for the Long Bridge, she went to the Charge's tower.

She found Dogloss at his soup, working over papers in the outer office. They looked like rosters of dragoneers, but he shuffled them into a leather folio as she approached.

He must have read something in her face.

"Ileth, if you want to give the Charge a piece of your mind, I assure you, he's sympathetic. It can only hurt your case."

"No, it's not that."

"Well, when you swept up like thunder off the lake—"

"You said 'case.' I'm told you are an e-expert on the law?"

"Not an expert. I apprenticed as a clerk, for five years, learned a good bit of it. I didn't join the Serpentine until my nineteenth year."

"Why did you leave law?"

"At that age I had much stronger political sensibilities. The more I saw of the law, the less I liked it. Juries seemed to decide by the weight of the purse. Reprieves and pardons going to the wrong people, commissioners of the court evicting people from lands their families have held for generations . . . I said 'chuck it' and showed up at the gate, same as you. Felt odd, starting over. Felt odder when I was the only twenty-year-old novice. But right. A man should have one good blaze in his youth. My lung was pierced over the Scab. It's never been quite the same since but our good Charge took me on his staff. He even saw to it that I stood for law examinations and passed, though there's not a great deal of legal work in running something even so large as the Serpentine. Most of the arrangements with the locals predate the Republic. But if someone's called me the Serpentine's counsel, well, I suppose they're right."

"Is there any matter of law that prevents us from buying and selling things to each other? Wine, tobacco, weapons, medicines."

"No, none. You know the Republic, tradesmen and bankers and farmers who grew sick of *produced under royal warrant* and all the corruption that went with the king's warrants so you're free to charge any price you like on anything. There is a general prohibition in the Republic on trade in poisons and animals that are known to be diseased, a blighted crop, that applies to all of us as well. Here in the Serpentine we have strict rules about dragon blood, of course, or scale. Didn't you have something to do with discovering some scale thieves? I recall talk of it years back, before you went to the Baronies, when your name was discussed in that Fespanarax difficulty."

"What about collecting debts?"

"Are you in debt?"

"No ... a ... a friend."

"That's complicated. If the debt is guaranteed, well, that depends on if the property put up to secure the debt is stored in a bond warehouse or still in possession ..."

"Nothing like that. More an informal debt. What happens if you use violence to collect it?"

"I know that goes on in some low places, but no, absolutely not. Comes under the same laws as robbery, as a matter of fact. Someone who smashes a foot to collect a debt is treated by a jury exactly the same as a robber who knocks a man down to cut his purse. It's four years' labor unless the victim is permanently injured. This is getting dreadfully specific, what is this about?"

"It doesn't matter, yet," Ileth said. "I can't prove anything."

"My advice to you is to go to the Masters if you're in trouble with some shopkeeper. It may just be bluster, but I can write a letter that'll make them think a jury is ready to be sworn in."

Ileth thanked him for his advice and went off to tell Ottavia about the accident.

The next day the troupe visited Santeel. The chitchat in the Dancers' Quarter was divided on whether Santeel looked better than her injuries should have had her looking or worse for being wrapped up in an ill-fitting medical bed-dress with her hair a mess.

"The physikers say she's exhausted, utterly exhausted. Needs rest to heal," Shatha said.

Fyth sighed. "First Vii and now Santeel. The poor thing. She was using both ends of the candle for a long time."

Ileth didn't join in the discussions. She had the feeling they were wondering how much of Santeel's fall was mishap. Quith, who always made the rounds at dinner in the Great Hall when there was gossip fresh from the oven, quietly relayed a rumor that the lighthouse sentry had seen the two dancers struggling.

"Do you think she'll return to us?" Shatha asked Ottavia when they were back at the Quarter.

Ottavia sat at her desk, staring at the handle of her walking stick. "We must hope for the best and plan for the worst. Perhaps we can bring one of the new novices into the Quarter and make things easier for her by giving her Santeel's bed. With the understanding that she'll be returned to the Manor if Santeel is fortunate enough to return."

Ileth felt guilty she hadn't sat with Santeel more. While she was the last person Santeel would want to entertain her by reading, she could have helped her eat. She also wanted to hear the story about Dun Klaff and his threats again; perhaps with the snuff out of her system her memory might be clearer.

She'd been so busy with her dancing, making preparations to leave, and letting the Horse know of her need to leave the Serpentine for a year or more.

The Horse gave his gentle smile when he told her. "My nose couldn't have smelled that, Ileth. But I expect you'll find your way back to us sooner than that. Could be a shorter trip back."

"How could the distance between the north and the Serpentine change, sir?"

At that the Horse just tapped her on the arm. "Don't let them turn you soft. What's it like up there? I've never been. Forests? Chop and carry firewood."

On the way back to the Quarter she ran into a page who was on his way to the Beehive with a summons for her and made him happy by sparing him the walk there and back. She read yet another note to visit Charge Deklamp at her convenience. It wasn't "earliest convenience," which was a polite way of saying *at once,* so she waited until the next morning after her drills and fatigues. She wanted to be a dutiful dancer right up to her departure to make up to Ottavia the many indulgences her Charge had allowed.

Deklamp happened to be in the outer office with Dogloss, talking and sipping his milk-tea. Serena was off on Telemiron again, it seemed.

"You sent for me, Charge?" Ileth asked, after being bade to enter.

"I'll come right to the point, Ileth. There's this unfinished business of a dragoneer for Aurue. As you know, dragons select their drag-oneers, but Aurue seems set on you choosing his dragoneer. Claims not to understand men at all, and finds talking to them tiresome, but trusts your judgment in the matter. I've selected three candidates for you to interview. Halkeff is able enough, but for some reason he's never had a dragon take a liking to him. Then there's Gruss, who's the best topographic artist we have. Aurue would be an ideal dragon for recon-naissance. The third is Vor Rapp. It would be advantageous to the Ser-pentine to make him a dragoneer. Were I to choose, it would be Vor Rapp."

"Vor Rapp!"

"Yes, perhaps not the most intellectual company here, and I don't care for these little gangs and factions that inevitably form, and hap-pily he's taken the hint and shrugged off Dun Klaff. But his family is immensely powerful at Assembly. He's done creditable work here. His ability and diligence in carrying out his duties are exemplary. Strong sword hand. Navigates well. His only weak spot is leadership. I spoke to him recently about it: trying to associate with the best, and then making sure those coming up behind you have everything they need to keep the Troth."

Ileth didn't know how much he'd really had to do with the Santeel business. He certainly hadn't been nearby when she was cut; he'd been outside the files, running along and trying to keep up with Ileth as she ran the gauntlet.

"You know, this is a rather interesting way to offer a final test to these young gentlemen. The last thing they'd be expecting is for their promotion to hinge on the good opinion of a mere apprentice. Bit like *Ellefsa and the Three Suitors*." Ileth knew nothing of Ellefsa, whoever that was, or her trio of potential bridegrooms.

"I'll do my best, sir." He'd made it clear he wanted it to be Vor Rapp. So he wanted a secret test, did he? She had an ideal one in mind.

She spent a few minutes in the outer office figuring where best to find the wingmen in question.

Gruss was the easiest. He was in a well-lit attic in the Masters' Hall, drawing maps. He quickly covered his work when Ileth entered. She said she was looking for a map tube and they began to chat. He kept his body between his work and Ileth. He squinted as he looked at her.

She complimented him on the light, airy room, and he said he needed good light; his eyesight, never the best to begin with, had gotten worse of late.

"Do you wear lenses?" Ileth asked.

"Not for close work. Long vision is another story, but it wouldn't do to have the Masters see me with lenses. You're a girl; how would I look with a monocle?"

Bad eyes. That let him out. "Dashing," she said to the suggestion of a monocle, feeling like she owed him a compliment.

Halkeff was in the Guard detail, and she found him in the main Guard office deep within the thick Serpentine walls. He was tall, thin, and a bit stooped over, like a buzzard. She caught him lecturing Rapoto, and angrily. He held a short, sharp mounting-hook in his hand, and she wondered if any of the dragons let him dig the point into their scale. "I told you before: you can't be friends with them and command them. Who cares if they hate you? All that matters is they obey, and you find out who can gut fish and who can't." He had the raspy voice of someone who shouts a great deal, and slapped the mounting-hook into his palm as he spoke.

"Stranger in the Guard office," announced a young apprentice in a badly fitting uniform writing on a chart from a desk under a grille-window.

Ileth gave an excuse that she was looking for Sifler.

"Get out of my sight, Vor Claymass."

"My savior," Rapoto whispered, sliding past Ileth, flashing the charming smile of old.

"There's been some talk of Sifler being sweet on a mystery girl. You'd better not be it," Halkeff said.

"N-no, he's teaching me handwriting," Ileth said. She complimented

him on the elaborate knot in his sash, looking for something to engage him. "Does it represent something special?"

"It's a little tricky, it's called a no-concern-of-yours knot."

Ileth decided she didn't much care for Halkeff. She doubted scaleless Aurue would appreciate that mounting-hook, either.

Vor Rapp took some effort to find as he had a free afternoon. She had to do a good deal of asking.

She finally ran him to ground at the cobbler and leather workshop, wondering if that girl with three suitors from the play had to wear her boots out walking. It was an old building, and the narrow windows didn't offer much light to work. Vor Rapp was pulled up on a stool and portable bench, putting some new heels on a boot with short, wide-headed nails. His fingers were red from being struck, and he was swearing under his breath. As he leaned over his work she saw his signet ring hanging from a chain where it was safe from his awkward efforts.

"Got something for the workshop apprentice?" he said, just glancing at her. Then he took a second look.

"Ileth!"

"I'm glad you remember me, sir."

"Of course I remember you, you were . . ." He trailed off. "The tailer of your class."

"Interesting work?" she said, looking at his little collection of nails. They reminded her of the pins that had held her wound together.

He waited for a moment, as if wondering where she was taking the encounter. "I never apprenticed at anything useful my whole life. There's no great call for translators of Hypatian poetry. Thought I'd learn cobbling, just to see if I could."

His voice had a nervous catch to it and he made a great show of lining up another bootnail.

She'd heard the expression *smell the fear on him* and had always thought it meant a urine odor or something like that. Vor Rapp had greasy sweat on his forehead now. Was he scared of her?

"I have an important question to ask you."

Vor Rapp looked around as though frightened. "I had nothing to do with it."

Ileth sensed that he'd supposed his own reason for her visit. Well, if it had to do with her being cut, it meant he felt guilty about it. That was to his credit.

"Be calm," she said. "I just want to talk about it. As you see, I'm here alone."

"Such a stupid thing to do. If I'd known he was planning something like that, I'd have tossed him off the Long Bridge. You were entirely innocent."

"So why did he do it?"

"I can only guess."

Ileth brushed away some of the tacks and sat on the workbench. "Then guess."

He shook his head no but started talking. "Dun Klaff threatened Santeel but was afraid to hurt her. She'd go running to her father. I told him he was a fool and that he should just cut her off and let her sweat until she paid what she owed. Threaten her with scandal. I mean, you of all people. You turned out those scale thieves as a fourteen-year-old novice! 'She'll remember it every time she looks in a mirror and want to know,' I told him."

"Your conscience was troubling you. That's something. If only it had troubled you enough to act."

He had the good grace, or perhaps the experience, to look ashamed. "So what's my fate?"

"That's up to you. You know the truth about a crime."

"I told you I had nothing to do with that."

Ileth just stared at him, letting him sweat.

"Well, thank you for telling me, Vor Rapp. I'm content now. I just wanted to know."

"Suppose I take all the blame myself? Say I cut you to frighten Santeel."

Ileth wasn't expecting that. She had to think for a moment. "Still an injustice. Besides, you weren't anywhere near. Nobody would believe you."

"You're the injured party. You could demand an investigation."

"For a months-old wound I told everyone was an accident?"

"You've heard the story from my own lips."

"Vor Rapp—no one is ever going to know about this conversation."

"Even if I do nothing? Even if I tell Dun Klaff you know everything?"

"I'm making no promises about Dun Klaff."

"If I remember right, the last time you 'acted' there wasn't enough left of old Gorgantern to fill a bucket."

He meant that as a compliment, she supposed. He really wasn't good with people. But he was trying. Trying counted for a lot in her esteem.

"I'll let you get back to your boots," she said.

What happened that night Ileth only heard the next day, from Ottavia. Before morning drill Ottavia pulled her aside.

"Ileth, I have some shocking news. The accident you suffered at that bridge business, it was no accident. The person who wounded you was discovered. Two Guards fought a duel last night. Hael Dun Huss himself told me the particulars."

Well, if Ottavia expected her to be shocked, she did her best to look it. She reached up and touched the scar. "How . . . you mean it was not an accident?"

"It's a very ugly business, and it concerns the dancers. Our poor Santeel. It seems she's been taking snuff of a highly stimulating nature."

Ileth decided it was best to just nod.

"Yes, well, youth will try things for the novelty and experience. It appears this Dun Klaff character sold her a good deal of it on credit. I spoke to Santeel; she said he wanted to be paid off with, well, with intimacies Santeel was too well bred to relinquish as payment of a debt."

Ileth hadn't known that piece of the puzzle, but she wasn't surprised.

When Ileth first met Ottavia, she thought she combined maiden, mother, and crone all in one aging dancer. She was full mother as she spoke: "Dun Klaff threatened her with . . . I can't believe I'm saying this about a young man who went to Blacktower . . . threatened her with disfigurement. She defied him and told him to do his worst. Gods! Why don't you girls bring these troubles to me? I've been in the world. I've seen debauchery on rooftop gardens in Zland that few of you can imagine, and as a young dancer I was invited to certain private salons in Sammerdam—well, Ileth, there's very little I haven't seen or dealt with one way or another. *All of human radiance and misery,* as the poet said. Had Santeel only confided in me!"

"Santeel can be very private," Ileth said. "Her family Name."

"I must finish my story. It seems this Dun Klaff wounded you during that ritual at the bridge for being the last of your draft. He had a piece of sharpened dragon scale. As you probably know, dragon scale doesn't make a very good blade as it can't keep an edge, but in a pinch it can be sharpened. He had it concealed in his palm, and then when one of his confederates knocked Santeel and a few apprentices into you and you all fell with him just behind you, he took his chance in the confusion and slashed you. He tossed the piece of scale off the Long Bridge a moment later."

Ileth remembered Dun Klaff carrying the blanket over his hand, standing next to her at the rail of the bridge as he gave her back the blanket. From that height he could have jumped off himself and she wouldn't have heard the splash.

"Another of the Blacktower youth, one who hews closer to the ideals I thought they engraved into the boys there, found out about it. Confronted him. They quarreled, began fighting with swords, if you can believe. Their fellow Guards broke it up, but the Master in Charge himself went into the barracks and held an inquiry."

Ileth came close to confessing the whole thing but wanted to hear the rest.

"This is where it becomes difficult. Dun Klaff won't admit to anything, as there's just one witness against him and that Heem Beck, another Blacktower failure, it seems, is backing him up, probably because he was the one who shoved Santeel into you. All Dun Klaff has offered to do is resign from the Serpentine rather than face a jury. I've just spoken to the Master in Charge and he told me that, as you were the most injured in this, I was to ask if you would be satisfied with that, or would you rather put him before a jury of dragoneers."

"What do you think I should do?" Ileth asked.

"There was blood drawn with intent. I think he should face a jury. There may be other women he has ensnared and used who might be encouraged to come forward. As I recall, just discharging that big fellow from the Catch Basin almost cost you your life."

A jury would be a bad business for Santeel. Her father would certainly take her away.

Ileth thought of Santeel's words below the lighthouse. They'd arrived at the Serpentine the same day; they might both leave the same way, pulled out by their fathers. "It would probably be the subject of talk at the Assembly."

"I fear you're right. We need a victory they can praise at the Assembly, not another embarrassment to be passed about in salons and gardens."

Ileth wondered just how much Ottavia spoke to her friend Dun Huss. She sounded so like him at times.

"Let him leave. What's a scar? A colorful story from my apprenticeship at the Serpentine." She could have added that she'd seen a couple of young noblemen with scars on their faces in Galantine lands. There they'd considered it a mark of distinction, a proof of courage. It turned out she had Galantine blood in her from her mother; why not keep that tradition?

"I didn't want to mention this before so it wouldn't influence you, but the Charge said he'd be put out the gates in his ordinary clothes. As restitution for your injury, Charge Deklamp said his Serpentine clothing, uniform, sword, flying rig, all of that would go to you. You could probably sell it all in town for a good price."

"His Guard uniform, you say?"

"That would be with the rest, I suppose."

"I've always liked those hats."

"They don't let women serve as Guards, Ileth. You are coping with enough responsibility as is."

"Still, I want that hat."

Santeel was in good spirits when Ileth visited the next day. She had a clean, albeit tiny room with a window and a tile floor in the annex behind the physiker's. Ileth had no experience with hospitals, but they'd always been described to her as noisy, smelly halls where sick people staggered in and corpses were carried out. The apprentice who took her to Santeel told her that the current practice was to have seriously ill patients and the injured all separated, if possible, as it prevented the spread of pestilence.

"This is nice," Ileth said. "Is there any pain?"

"It feels more like a bad itch. The physiker says that is a good thing, it means the break is closing."

They circled round the food and whether Ileth should bring her anything on her next visit. Santeel said the book she wanted to read had already been delivered. Ileth finally told the story of Dun Klaff's dismissal.

"I should have exposed him as soon as he threatened me. But then my father would have found out and home I would go. He wouldn't stand for any woman in his family taking snuff. I can just hear him. *You know the kind of women who take snuff? Toothless old crones who sell tonics and silver polish to buy cat's meat for their dinner.* I can't leave now, not when I've come this far. I'd sooner throw myself off Heartbreak Cliff."

"Don't speak so."

Santeel reached for her and Ileth took her hand. "You know it's just dramatics, Ileth."

"That old dragon with the stripes told me that words are filtered thoughts and can become actions."

"You know, if I'd been sure, absolutely sure your injury was a warning to me, I would have gone straight to the Master in Charge. I figured he'd say something like *you'll be next* soon after it happened, but he never did. He seemed so tender to you there at the bridge, concerned. I'm sorry. Maybe the gods made me pay for my silence with a broken leg."

Ileth tried to cheer her. She didn't care for Santeel in despair; it was very unlike her. "You paid him back with that raid. It was a smashing success."

Santeel sighed. "Not a perfect success. I failed with Rapoto."

"You—you failed how?"

"Oh, I gave him a line about Dun Klaff pressuring me, which was true enough. I thought he might, well, not exactly fight a duel, but rattle him, anyway, because if he's doing it to me he's doing it to others. Turns out Rapoto suspected, maybe even knew more than he let on. He told me I'd walked into the fix, and it was up to me to get out again."

"Ottavia said something odd about him using the debt to try to extract . . . favors from you."

Santeel made a face. "That he did. I told him to go stick it in a stump."

"I thought it was go *cry on a stump*."

"He wouldn't get a foreskin full of splinters from crying."

Ileth laughed. "Santeel!"

Santeel relaxed into her pillow. "I've been among the dancers so long I've become obscene about everything. They're such an earthy bunch. I mean to say we're such an earthy bunch."

The verbal slip might mean Santeel was already reconciling herself to not being able to serve as a dragon-dancer.

"How's life in a hospital?"

"The first day I was very cranky. I missed my morning infusions. Or . . . you know."

Santeel could be free with her tongue, flicking it about like a lash, before she had her morning tea, but in the weeks since Ileth had come back from Galantine lands Santeel had been one giant raw nerve.

"The snuff," Ileth said.

"Yes. Done with that forever."

Ileth, not able to just sit beside a bed talking, felt the need for occupation. She offered to brush out Santeel's hair, and Santeel accepted with a smile. As Ileth worked they talked.

"Threadneedle says I have the makings of a great physiker. That Gift is interesting, much more expert on the subject. He doesn't flatter me like Threadneedle."

"Oh?"

"He says . . . how did he put it? He says you need a certain hardness to be a healer. You have to be able to pain someone briefly so they may heal properly. As I have very recent proof of when they set this leg."

"Bad?"

"They wanted to give me dragon blood, did you know that? Said otherwise I may have a limp for the rest of my life."

"Did you take it?"

"Of course not! I've seen the jars in the attic. Suppose I have children?"

Ileth had heard Amrits mention some jars. "The jars?"

"Oh, you haven't worked with the physikers yet. Ugh. Don't have breakfast on the day you get told about the uses and dangers of dragon blood."

All Ileth knew about dragon blood was that there were harsh penalties, including being put out the Serpentine's gates in your sheath, for anyone who tried to acquire or sell dragon blood. You could filch the odd scale to make a hairpin or belt hook and that was ignored, but dragon blood would bring a judgment out of her Directist copybooks.

"I've always been interested in what's going on inside bodies. When I was little, I used to look at this old illuminated text—hand-lettered, art panels, hinges on the cover, expensive I suppose. It was a cyclopedia, a little bit of all the sciences. It had this page that was a picture of a woman sitting in a chair and there was this windowlike opening to her belly; it had an oval frame with gold leaf and everything, and she had a little sort of tower with balconies and many doors inside her

where a baby grows and there were all these little people milling about, a hidden city of tiny people. It looked like a street festival. I think that's what I told my mother and she said a husband invites one of the little people out. It made me feel rather bad for the baby, actually, like he had to leave a nice party because he was called away."

Ileth laughed. "I was told there was a little garden inside me waiting for seeds."

"Let me guess—and once a month it rains!"

"Yes!"

"I heard that one too. One of my friends from the music circle in Sammerdam. She had a Galantine governess."

"Is there anything else I can do for you?"

"Yes. Write one of those letters to Falth. Tell him I've had a fall down some tricky stairs but it's nothing serious. The physiker is attending me and I'm up and about already."

"You don't look up and about."

Santeel smiled. She took a breath and swung her uninjured leg out of the bed and, showing the flexibility of the skilled dragon-dancer she was, touched the floor with her foot and lifted her buttocks off the bed by arching her back a little and straining with her leg.

"Up and out of bed, you see? No lies need be told."

"I'll tell Ottavia you're doing your fatigues even in the physiker's bed."

"Circa rain kisses on you, Ileth. Good luck in the north."

"Anything else?"

Santeel blinked a few tears out of her eyes. She held out her hand and Ileth took it. They exchanged a squeeze.

"We've had our times, haven't we?" Santeel said.

"Stop talking like a sick old woman. Our times have barely started."

Ileth promised to bring her a cup of tea the next morning and left. In her head, she was already choreographing a dance around the truth for a letter to Falth.

Like a ghost or demon summoned by his name, Ileth found a letter from Falth resting on her rope bed back at the Dancers' Quarter.

Ileth,

Forgive me for writing you about a subject that perhaps you had wished to keep private. I received an express from Santeel about your predicament. She wrote to claim whatever favor you had built up with the Name Dun Troot to be redeemed to allow you to stay at the Serpentine. Since no message asking for help has as yet arrived from you, I did not know how to react. While our family has a certain amount of influence at the Assembly, among the governors we have very little.

First, let me give you some advice as someone who has come to know you somewhat through our correspondence: to rise from a Lodge to the status of Governor Raal's daughter is no small thing. When I first met you I thought the brave leap you took into the Serpentine was a perfectly understandable move to better yourself and showed a wisdom beyond your years, for that is the best way to spend the abundant energy of youth. A position in a family like Raal's is better still, viewed through my social lens, but then I don't know your heart. Santeel has told me that any other future for you than service as a dragoneer is the Republic's loss, so I am set on doing what I can in the brief time Santeel gave me.

As to the legal issue of you being his daughter, of course you know that even if it is accepted, you have only to suffer a brief time before you may choose to quit his house and do with your life as you choose, barring a jury finding you in need of guardianship. I believe your future happiness would be best served by enduring the role as dutiful daughter for two more years and then returning to the Serpentine bearing an old and important Name, even if it isn't distinguished by so much as a Heem—though in these republican times, that may be to your advantage.

I cannot offer you much intelligence about Governor Raal and his wife as they haven't circulated in Sammerdam and I only have secondhand accounts from northern members of the Assembly, or rather their servants who are most often the most reliable source. The Governor himself is counted as a capable administrator of a province that has

fallen on hard times. He keeps a modest but comfortable house in Stavanzer and has a family home at the source of the Stess. He enjoys playing coup, cards, and pin-rolling. He attends the theater. As a younger man he enjoyed lively company. He is in good standing in the Republican Club, though I haven't heard he's been to the one in Sammerdam recently. He does attend the less distinguished one in Stavanzer.

The Governor's wife comes from a wealthy family but is infirm. She is a discerning lady, mostly resides at Stesside, and is frequently visited by her husband. I heard her described as his political brains but that was from someone with no love of the Governor, and I am not sure if that's meant as a compliment to Lady Raal or not.

I did have an odd reaction in one quarter to my inquiry into matters in the north. A secretary for the Assembly said that I shouldn't ask too many questions about Raal and the north just now or I might be thought of as engaging in spying! I didn't know what to say to that, other than that I was only interested in social matters for a young lady connected to the Name I serve. Governor Raal does not seem to be the sort of man to do anything precipitate, but you may find your stay up there more interesting than you think.

I shall understand if I do not hear from you for some time, but I desire to remain

Your friend, etc.
Falth

Time was growing short before she was to depart to Stavanzer. But she was spoiling for a fight, and had a hat to do it in thanks to her inheritance of Dun Klaff's uniform, sword, and flying rig. She sold the boots, which didn't fit her anyway, to Rapoto, who gave her a very generous price that allowed her to buy a used trunk in Vyenn and have it brought to the gates of the Serpentine. Rapoto, who'd advised her on the best place to obtain a trunk and what price was fair, said he hoped her absence from the Serpentine would be brief.

Ileth had to keep telling herself that it was less than two years, much less; she'd be seventeen in the spring and then she could count the days until she was eighteen and could return. Such a length of time didn't feel brief. Sifler and Santeel would probably both be wingmen by then, and she'd be like Dogloss, an aged first-year apprentice.

Such was her despair that she visited her old Master, Caseen, the battle-burned old veteran in charge of the novices. He was much the same. Perhaps he moved a little slower, his bad leg dragging a little more than when she'd first met him at fourteen. "Look at it as another part of your training. It wouldn't hurt for you to learn a little about how the Vales function, at least from a Governor's Office perspective. You always were weak on civics."

She thanked him and kissed his unburned cheek in gratitude. "You chose the right one. I wouldn't feel anything on the other," he said, showing that ghastly, twisted smile.

Ottavia had her own brand of encouragement:

"Try not to let your body go too slack," Ottavia said, echoing the Horse. "You're still not the dancer you were before you left for Galantine lands."

Ileth stuttered out promises about attending to her drills and fatigues. Then she started crying. In a way, Ottavia was the closest thing to a mother she'd ever known.

"It's hard to leave you, sira," she managed.

"Oh, Ileth, you're still so young. You're a tree still young enough to survive being uprooted. Your life still has so many branches to grow."

"Doesn't feel that way," she said. She felt snotty and wretched with emotion.

"It's a disappointment and delay, not a disaster. I thought, when you first came here, that you would be a fixture at the Quarter. One who'd become one of my older veterans, maybe one day take my place and teach a new generation, bring our art another step forward."

"And I disappointed you."

"No. It just wasn't to be. I'm an entire cemetery of buried dreams, girl. The only way you can disappoint me is by giving up on the dream

that brought you here and made you sit outside the door sucking live snails out of their shells. I've seen enough young dancers through the Quarter that I know the energies of youth can only be channeled to my liking so much. It's happened enough times that I accept it now."

There was one last happy duty: introducing Aurue to his dragoneer. They'd waited a few days for the business with Dun Klaff to settle before making a formal announcement.

She found Aurue on his shelf. Dragons liked to be raised up so they slept on a platform above a human's height. Aurue's chamber in the Lower Ring of the Serpentine was cramped, without good light, and a walk from water, making it one of the most difficult to clean. Fortunately, he was a cleanish dragon.

"I have news. I've found you a dragoneer," Ileth said.

"Good man?"

"How do you know it's a man?"

"I was told not to take a female. Taresscon, in her talks with your Charge, that short man with the staring eyes, discourages male dragons from being paired with female riders. I'm told it's a bad idea. Especially if you find her enchanting. Some say it's why Agrath fell, he was too attached to his dragoneer. It's why I didn't ask for you. Well, that and Taresscon said you were too new. Though I enjoy you, Ileth, you are quiet and soothing."

"I remember when you first came you hardly spoke Montangyan."

"I'm from the Dragon Isle. Nobody there mixes with men more than it can be helped. I wasn't sure I'd stay, so I didn't bother learning much more than the basics to order grooms and feeders about."

Ileth had heard legends surrounding that island in the north end of the Inland Ocean many times from the Captain's sailing friends. Humans were shunned there. Unless you were invited by the dragons that lived on the island, you were as good as burned setting foot on it.

"What difference does being from this island make?"

"There are, how to put this . . . there are three ways of thinking

about men in the dragon-mind. The oldest is that dragons are superior and must rule. That's been tried and it led to dragons coming within a scale's breadth of being extinguished. The second way is no good either, becoming like dogs or horses, fitting into man's world as his slave. That's been done too, briefly. I've heard it exists still, in a fashion, among the Galantines and the Wurm. Some argue that the Galantines control their dragons in some mysterious way. My grandsire, he believed dragons should be in the world as their own nation, guard their borders, just few trusted interactions through channels. Isolation. Maybe I'm of a philosophical bent like your friend you knew as the Lodger, but that seems like a route to stagnation. Humans are inventive. Who knows what they might come up with if they see us only as a foreign power and possible rival.

"I heard stories from some of my oldest relatives of a place called the Vales, where dragons and humans, well, they didn't live exactly together, I hadn't heard of this fortress or it came down in a garbled version, but it seemed to me they'd hit upon the only workable solution. We would be equal with humans. Protected by and answerable to the same law.

"I probably came here before I was ready. I had a falling-out with another dragon of the island. I was scaleless, and even though my grandsire was also a gray dragon, my prospects there were . . . limited. I planned and made an escape, clinging to one of the few ships allowed to visit, a Daphine ship, I later found out. I didn't even have my wings yet, but sometimes young wingless dragons are compelled to travel and I let the compulsion carry me here. It wasn't an easy journey. The Daphines spotted me but didn't make a fuss, pretended not to notice me. I was netted and sold to the Galantines, but at the Galantine border there was an argument because I didn't have scale; the Galantines thought the Daphines attempted some trick to get a dragon's bounty on some other creature and in the examination of my skin and body and arguments going on, during it I was able to get a claw on this head-harness muzzle they had me in. With the muzzle loose I proved myself

a dragon after all and escaped in the smoke and confusion and burning. They set dogs and riders after me but the pack of dogs was mixed; it was easy to pick off the leaders, and the others thought better of trying to tree me. I made it to water and the horsemen didn't dare follow me into it. Eventually a Galantine dragon appeared, searching for me, calling out in that odd Drakine accent they have, but after you've escaped a muzzle, dogs, and hunters, you think twice before giving yourself up."

Ileth stifled a laugh. Though he told it lightly, it seemed he'd had a terrifying trip to the Vales.

"I made it to the Serpentine not long before you did. It took me a while to even make up my mind about this place. I still don't care for the feel of a saddle and harness. Taresscon let me stay on approval, but it is time to choose."

Aurue dipped his snout. Ileth wasn't sure what it meant, but she held up her hand, and when he didn't flinch, she gave him a friendly pat. His skin was dry and pebbly and clean. She didn't want to insult him by scratching his ears like a dog, though she was tempted. She took her hand back.

"I suppose one human's much like another. What's he like?"

"He comes from an important family and a good school," Ileth said, still feeling the dragon's skin in her palm. "I know that. The dragoneers have a good opinion of him."

"Even if it is a poor match, it's temporary. I've been warned not to get attached to humans," Aurue said.

Ileth went to bed that night thoughtful. It took her a long time to drift off.

The pairing of dragon and dragoneer was a ceremony of great tradition, Ileth understood, from both her secret reading as a child and talk in the Serpentine's Great Hall. It always took place in the center of the Long Bridge. But this particular pairing, perhaps because of the winter weather and the simple tastes of the two personages involved,

felt more like a quick marriage where the bride is expected to retreat to childbed within days of the ceremony.

Charge Deklamp and Dogloss stood in good winter uniforms and best hats for it, representing the human side, along with Ileth, who had her flying rig coat over her overdress as it was a very cold morning. Sifler was also there, his used Guard uniform cleaned and pressed as best as could be done with the aged garment. Ileth wondered why; she hadn't mentioned anything about it to him. On the dragon side, Taresscon stood to one side of the Long Bridge along with young Cunescious, who was probably impressed into standing around on a cold morning because he was unoccupied, and Jizara, representing the females. They were the three youngest dragons of the Serpentine. Ileth didn't know if dragons formed close friendships. She imagined they did, but if so they didn't talk of it with humans.

It was the dragon's duty to step forward and request the services of the human.

"I ask you be dragoneer. To mine," Aurue said. His much-improved Montangyan seemed to have deserted him.

Vor Rapp smiled. He held out his hand with the signet ring, polished so that it gleamed, and touched Aurue on the *griff*. "I accept, sir."

Ileth had been told there was nothing more to it. No signing, no scarification, no exchange of totems. Dragons were long-lived; perhaps they kept it simple because a dragon could expect to have many dragoneers over his career and become closer to some than others.

"You do not wish a battle dragon?" Aurue asked. Ileth could tell from his tone that he was uncomfortable.

"If this is how I'm to become a winged dragoneer, I'll take it." Vor Rapp sounded as though he'd taken one of Traskeer's "accept any promotion" talks to heart.

"I'll be on my shelf, then. We will have ample time to . . . to get to know each other mores. More. I'm sure you wish to celebrate. I will leave you to it."

Vor Rapp thanked him in Drakine that Ileth wasn't skilled enough

to judge and turned away. The Charge and Dogloss congratulated him and departed, leaving him standing there with Sifler.

"You're calm," Ileth said to Vor Rapp, after waving good-bye to Aurue, who seemed eager to quit the ceremony as soon as possible. The other two dragons witnessing the ceremony didn't seem to speak to him after.

"I've expected it ever since they made me wingman-at-large. My father's probably been making the Charge's life miserable with demands for updates on my career." He held out his hand and glanced down at the big ring. "That reminds me. Sniffler, old son, how's the title of wingman sound to you?"

Sifler looked at Vor Rapp as if he were waiting for a practical joke to be revealed. "I wouldn't say no. But no one's sizing me up for a sword-belt."

"I just did. I want you to be my wingman. Why do you think I asked you to join me this morning?"

"What about Heem Beck?"

"Heem Beck is the sort of person I've outgrown. Choosing him would be 'impolitic,' as the Old Man would say. We used to call him the Brick back at Blacktower, if you recall, because he's thick as one. I want brains, old son."

"You shat in my bed."

"I am sorry."

"While I slept in it."

"It struck us as funny at the time. No, I shouldn't say that, it's still funny. But I feel bad about it now."

"You tried to get me to violate a chicken."

Vor Rapp held up a finger. "That wasn't all on me. That's an old Blacktower Shield Hall tradition. That's not just on me, I had to do it myself. Always admired the backbone of you telling us to release the chicken and go bugger each other, even if we did beat you bloody for it."

Sifler, after recalling a few more humiliations that made Ileth's first few weeks in the Manor welcoming by comparison, accepted the position.

Wingman! Ileth's prediction about Sifler had come true sooner than she thought. He seemed a little undersized for the role. She hoped he wouldn't trip over his sword the first time that girl from the bookshop saw him wearing it.

And with this final duty closed, it was time for her to go north and become a governor's daughter.

6

Ileth's first trip to Stavanzer was exciting, maddening, and above all brief.

All the excitement for her was in the first two days. The Borderlander flew her on Catherix to the Stavanzer mail office, which was on the town square big enough for a dragon's landing, and dropped her and her new trunk with the same sentimentality displayed when he turned over the mail to the Post Commissioner.

"This is good-bye. More mail to deliver, and I'm glad for it. Cities make me itch," he said. "Too much to keep track of."

The Borderlander made his farewell to Ileth by putting his arm stiffly out and grasping her left shoulder hard enough that she later checked for a bruise. He looked her in the eye and said, "Don't change a bit for him."

Ileth thanked Catherix for carrying her and her baggage.

"You should," she said, flicking a *griff*. "Tying trunk dragon. Audacity!"

"Don't take it so hard," the Borderlander said when Ileth shrank away from the reprimand. "You've given her something to grumble about until the week-over."

"Keep off!" he yelled at the city children, already gathering from every point in the compass to get a look at the dragon. Catherix escaped the children by using the public platform in the square—luckily

free of gallows, festival poles, or bonfire barrels—to make a quick leap into the air. Ileth admired her strength and the Borderlander's ability to keep his seat in such a dramatic takeoff.

With that he flew off to the north, just another mail carrier.

Except ordinary mail carriers didn't have a great case on their saddle with map tubes and sketching paper and a device shaped like a tiny crutch that she knew was used to determine distance. She'd peeked as Catherix was being watered in the Notch pass.

She had coin to hire a porter for the trunk and set off for the Governor's Residence. She was coming up in the world. There had been a time when all her worldly possessions would fit in a flour bag.

The porter knew her destination and she followed him. The great city house struck Ileth as uncomfortably like a prison. There were bars on all the lower windows.

She'd been preceded by letters so the butler admitted her and made arrangements for her trunk to be brought to her room.

Inside the Governor's Residence, she learned that her alleged father liked landscapes of farming and commerce in the north and plain furniture, which didn't make a very good match for the spacious rooms with elegantly carved wood moldings and parquetry floors.

Her room was on the third floor, but it was sunny and warm and had a view of the traffic in the square where before the house five streets joined.

The maddening part of her Stavanzer trip began that first night. Raal arrived late. He spoke to his bookkeeper, the butler, the housekeeper, and the cook in turn, and only then greeted Ileth.

He looked much the same to Ileth. "So good to have you here at last, Ileth. Business can wait. I will dine with Ileth at the Republican Club. It's chilly, do you object to the carriage?"

She didn't. She enjoyed her first trip in a carriage, though she was awkward in the polite business of being handed into it by her "father."

The Republican Club was one of those crowded city buildings, a little smaller than the two next to it, like the youngest sibling squashed on a small couch between two big brothers. It was a cheery-looking

place, though, with two lights on either side of the red entrance door with white panelwork and every window open-curtained and blazing brightly into the frosty night.

They were expecting the Governor. Two doormen took him and Ileth in and up to the second floor, where they had some odd-looking plants Ileth couldn't identify that seemed to be thriving indoors, tables with tablecloths of various sizes, and alcoves with more tables still.

Ileth realized she was in a restaurant.

They were seated in a room discreetly curtained off from the rest. Raal helped her understand how the menu worked, how you picked one thing from each list, and asked if she would like wine.

"Tea will be fine, uhh."

"You can keep calling me 'sir' if you wish, Ileth. 'Father' sounds equally strange to me. It will take time."

The dishes had names that struck Ileth as, well, equal parts fanciful and stupid, like "White Fish with Capers Liberty" and "Roast Chicken Assembly," and told you nothing about the contents of a "Man in the Mountain Pie." She accepted the Governor's recommendation of Winter Sprouts in Bacon, Market Stew, and Brandy-glazed Figs.

It was all delicious, arriving on the biggest carrying-tray Ileth had ever seen, with a dramatic opening of the curtain.

They drank tea after dinner. He asked her if she wanted a kneeler and quarter-table with candle for Directist prayer. Ileth thanked him and said she could make do with the edge of her bed and whatever light came in through the window.

"How do you like your room?"

"It's . . . very nice." It was clean, comfortable, and probably quiet, as long as you didn't mind the climb.

"I'm glad of that. Your mother stayed in it when she first came to the Vales. Sanctuary refugee."

At last, something other than polite chatter. "What was she like?"

"Young. Headstrong. Spoke five words of Montangyan but somehow always got her way about things. She was beautiful and st . . . unique."

"Tell-tell me m-more, please."

"You'll hear the story in full. Tonight should be happy. You begin a new life."

"I had n-no wi-wish to change the old one."

Raal frowned. "You should consider yourself fortunate. Dancers don't rise, socially. You're still of an age that it can be dismissed as youthful larking."

"Heem T-Tyr can't paint pictures of our youthful larking fast enough to satisfy his patrons."

"That is Zland. You're back in the north now."

They retreated to their cups of tea. Ileth reverted to her Galantine manners and made a few comments about the food and the quality of the tableware at the Republican Club.

Raal didn't accept the armistice: "That stutter of yours, I had no idea it was so bad. Has a specialist examined you? Is there any hope of improvement?"

"It's not such a problem when I'm relaxed. It's worse when I'm in difficulty. When I feel out of place."

"Then I hope you'll be comfortable with us."

"Us?"

"Lady Raal and me. I expect you'll soon become bored at the Residence. I am only there to sleep. You seem a vigorous, open-air sort of girl. I think you would be happiest at Stesside. You'll have the full attention of Lady Raal and when I visit we can be at ease with each other, I won't be pressed by duty."

As she digested that addition to the dinner, he confessed he should "make the rounds" of the Republican Club and packed her off back to the city residence with a club employee who showed considerable expertise in quickly, politely, and discreetly packing young ladies into a carriage behind the club and then driving them home. Ileth turned in and lay in the bed her mother had once used, wondering.

The Vales were famously accepting of those looking for an escape from one sort of trouble or another. There were special lodges for them that eased the friction while they acclimated, sometimes to the point

of an entirely new name and a skill. A sure mark of a recent immigrant was a new surname in Montangyan. Yet Ileth's mother, fleeing a religious purge in the Galantine Baronies, had been put up at the Governor's own residence.

He had her pack for Stesside the very next day.

Ileth couldn't understand this treatment of her. The weather even turned snowy overnight and he still insisted she make the journey to the country.

Snow meant she had to take a sleigh to Stesside, and that was the most fun she had since landing in Stavanzer. Even the Governor, who rode along to see her settled, grew more animated and named landmarks and other points of interest on their journey up the Stess and into the foothills. But the day's pleasure was ended abruptly when she arrived and, offering to help with dinner, found out Ignata was no longer part of the household.

Raal looked mournful. "She was too old to work this hard. She's in Stavanzer now, in a lodge. A very nice one, pensioned postmasters and customs officials, that sort of thing. Good people."

The new cook was a Galantine whose family had fled some sort of blight on their crops. There was some talk of Ileth learning from her in the kitchen and helping the manservant keep the family home tidy. Ileth recognized the irony; at fourteen she'd fled from a Lodge that promised no more of a future than domestic work, and after travel on dragonback across the Vales and to the Baronies and back, with a Galantine title no less, life had still arranged for her to care for a kitchen and bedlinens.

The Governor departed after week-over. He made an early start back, enjoying a leisurely private breakfast with Lady Raal while Ileth took the Horse's advice, found an axe, and attempted to reduce some quarters to kindling without maiming herself. The sound of it brought out Severan, the principal servant, who snatched the axe out of her hands and told her some men from the village downstream took care of their firewood needs. If she needed to occupy herself, there was ample dusting to do.

Within her first week, Ileth ran out of things to say to Lady Raal. Their conversation was limited to what sort of housekeeping she would do that day, improving Ileth's wardrobe, and how best to arrange her hair once it grew out to a proper length. Over dinner and for perhaps an hour after, Lady Raal turned into an expert conversationalist, gently probing Ileth about her life, the Serpentine, and what little travel she had done. Then Lady Raal would finish her wine and say "I must see to my letters," and Severan would help her to her bedchamber.

Ileth explored the grounds, climbed around in the ruin of the castle as much as she dared, and took a chill winter plunge in the improved source of the Stess just to give her body and spirit a challenge. She lasted long enough for the sun to completely traverse a winter branch.

With endless time to think, Ileth found herself comparing being a governor's daughter (who was never introduced to anyone or spoken of as his daughter) to her time in Galantine lands as an enforced guest of the Baron, and Stesside did not win out. Every time she turned it over in her mind, it became stranger. Why would the Governor, a busy man, exert himself pestering the Serpentine to bring her to him, only to banish her to what he must know was a dull routine?

The Governor had a small study at the house. She found a coup board and pieces as well as a book on the game nearby and set about learning. The Lodger had taught her that even a confinement could be turned to a chance at improvement. It had been proved in the Baronies, where she'd learned to care for a dragon, and a moody, cantankerous one at that, become fluent in Galantine, and improved her manners in elevated society.

If she applied herself, she might be able to do something similar with her time in Stesside. It was better than fretting and funking.

She asked Lady Raal about the coup set, whether she could bring it out into the front room with the good light to study it.

"Of course, dear. I will be happy to teach you what little I know. I learned it as it is one of my husband's passions, and while I don't share it, he might like to play you on one of his visits."

It turned out Lady Raal knew more about the game than that. She elaborated on the pieces in such a way that Ileth wondered if she was an expert on the game, or just naturally blessed with an excellent memory. She was a better reference than the book.

Ileth found herself admiring the woman, a fine mind that didn't let being trapped in a difficult body sour her spirit. Ileth practiced playing, switching from seat to seat and mimicking famous arrays and moves from the book. At last she convinced Severan to play, but he fidgeted and intentionally lost by bringing forth his captains unprotected.

Winter storms prevented the Governor from traveling to Stesside on the next week-over. There was little to do but read, keep up the fire, and bring tea to Lady Raal.

"It's so nice not to have to winter in the city," Lady Raal said, looking out the front windows at the blowing snow.

"Is it?" Ileth asked, putting down a book of plays that included one that Rapoto and Sifler had both quoted.

"Well, the prices of everything, the smoke, mud, and wet. Everything always drying and the smell of wet socks. People to entertain. I'm poorly suited to be a governor's wife."

"How does he manage?"

"Oh, he has plenty of invitations if he feels the need to get out. Any hostess is happy to tell a female guest that her dinner partner is the Governor. He doesn't favor any one table. There's his club if he wishes to sit comfortably over cards and lifewater or enjoy a game of coup."

"If you . . . if you wish to go to town, I could help you," Ileth said. One of the dresses Lady Raal had provided for her didn't fit, and Ileth had botched the alterations. Now it needed a skilled seamstress.

"No. I've tried that. I'm never happy there, and he's too distracted caring for me to properly attend his duties. Of course I wish he were here more. Selfish of me, I know. He enjoys lively society. I'm a sick, childless woman. He's still full of manhood, even with some gray showing."

She turned the subject to music. She could always talk about

music. Ileth didn't know enough about it. Lady Raal thought that strange for a dancer and tried to give her an education in the subject, but it was difficult without skilled players.

Ileth worried that her skills as a dragon-dancer were falling away. She kept herself exercised fetching and carrying, drawing water, and taking walks outside whenever the weather permitted. She found where Severan had hidden the axe he'd yanked out of her hand and took it into the mountainside where she could exercise with it in peace. Chopping could be heard a long way off.

Winter wore on, but Ileth, having her years of experience, sensed there would be one more fierce blast before spring. Then she would be seventeen and counting the days until she would be free to return to the Serpentine. The thought saw her through Lady Raal's routines of correspondence and craft.

She finally had a chance for a real game of coup when Governor Raal visited. Even Ileth, new to the game, figured out he was a mediocre player. Over the game she asked if her mother had enjoyed the game and from then on he was distracted. He didn't keep his artillery, the most powerful yet most vulnerable piece, behind a line of infantry, and he sent in his cavalry first before her formation had any holes in it at all and would expose them in unprofitable frontal assaults. Ileth decided that whoever his opponents were in his club in town must let him win for politics' sake.

She took his two captains and soon his fortress fell. He thanked Ileth but had no wish for a second game, and spent the rest of the week-over moody and avoiding her.

Lady Raal, who had previously professed no love for the game, suddenly took an interest and offered to "indulge my dear friend" and sat across the game table from her. She was a patient and frustrating opponent and Ileth never did succeed in beating her in the few games they had. She hardly moved from her opening formation until Ileth, out of boredom, would make an error in attacking and then she crept forward in a series of tiny moves, constantly shifting to meet whatever threat Ileth tried to develop. It was like playing a finger-duel with a

snapping turtle. Then, when what was left of Ileth's array was huddled out of range of the remorseless pounding of Lady Raal's artillery, the dragon came, leading the cavalry, and that was the end.

"I'm quite worn out," she'd say, smiling at Ileth after receiving the congratulations and an offer to get her tea. "I think I must lie down for a while. Is that the time? Oh dear, I should see how Cook is managing with dinner. Coup does absorb the better part of an afternoon, doesn't it?"

Lady Raal was an internal person, lost in her own thoughts, letters, books, and needlework. For all that she worked on her tapestries, there were only a handful hung around the house at Stesside in the upper rooms. Lady Raal explained that her husband was always asking for them; his social circle absorbed the few she produced every winter at charity auctions.

While searching, again, for the axe (she and Severan were in an increasingly creative duel over hiding it), she discovered a practice dueling sword of the Governor's from when he was a child, but other than a few experimental swings and lunges, she didn't know what to do with it. The bow and arrow the Borderlander had borrowed was a much better find. The bow was good quality, beautifully recurved and with a well-carved handle that was a good fit for her hand. But it was strung for a man. Severan reluctantly took it into town and some handyman there restrung it so it pulled easier for her so she could practice shooting arrows into hay bales.

Improving herself with the bow and arrow was enjoyable, sending arrows smacking into the side of the barn and startling the fat horses even more fun, but the arrows were equally old and her quiver of ten quickly turned to six and then two and then none as the fletching or heads broke off or the shafts splintered. Severan promised to get her more on his next trip to town but made it clear that he wouldn't make a special trip but would wait until they needed something.

"While you are looking, the barn could really use its own axe," Ileth told him. "I can never find the one in the gardening shed."

"The gardener frequently needs it in winter," Severan said, frown-

ing. "I'm sure Lady Raal would not want the expense of an unnecessary purchase."

A letter arrived on horseback, giving Severan an excuse to escape her. Ileth didn't even bother to see who it was from; the Governor frequently wrote his wife by express, postage being the only lavish expense in their lives. So she was surprised when Severan found her after delivering the letter, saying Lady Raal wanted her at once.

"My dear, you have a letter by express. I trust it is not ill news," Lady Raal said, handing her an envelope. Ileth recognized Santeel Dun Troot's hand.

She retreated across the front room to good light and read the letter, leaving Lady Raal to her needle and colored threads.

Ileth,

The Serpentine is in winter slumber and things are cold and dreary. First I shall tell you of the dragons, as I know how you miss them. The new hatchlings thrive, and attack Falberrwrath when he attends them. He returns to his shelf injured but in excellent humor, and as I often have to bandage him he tells me he misses you and hopes it will not be too many decades (!!) until you return.

There has been a great deal of training against an old stone ruin on the coast on the other side of the Skylake. Teams of dragons depart, assemble, and return exhausted and hungry at all hours. They have put on extra feeders from the new novices and are buying not just fish but all manner of geese and goats from all around and cooking them in bacon fat. The grooms tell me the greasy smoke from dragon-flame is hard to extract from scale. The spirits of the dragons are much improved by the improvements in the food and that passes down to all of us attending them. The Beehive certainly buzzes!

As for me, my leg is still healing, and I have been forbidden to fly so I know very little about the extra training. Something tells me you know more of this than I, for your favorite who I shall label ADH in the fashion of our mutual friend Quith has been here and there trailing

at the heels of that white-haired dragoneer with the hard face watching, and often flying out to observe, the sets of dragons in their training.

I think often of you, and especially of the months when we were both first novices under the Matron's roof. Maybe if we'd been closer then, we'd have both been spared difficulties.

In order to relieve the winter doldrums, I have permission to come visit you for a short holiday, from both my family and the Governor. Falth arranged the whole thing once I had the idea in my head, and as I write you I have in my hand a letter from Governor Raal inviting me. But I trust you to secure the permission of Lady Raal as well. I have never been to the north and look forward to passing a little time with you.

Your dragoneers miss you greatly. Well, the Sweet Dun Huss very politely asked that I cheer you, the tall grim one said he's been to the Governor's family retreat and would rather do another survival than return, and of course Dath Amrits wonders how a girl who managed to run away once can't do it again now that she knows the way.

If you are reading aloud, keep the next paragraph private. Say it is about my mother's health and read it to yourself: Amrits has been most helpful in tips on how to travel there and we have a plan to restore you to us. We were up until all hours discussing it and he even procured me some traveling clothes for my trip, making a special journey to Zland.

I will send a letter by air courier when I depart so you know help is on the way. I promise you a swift and furious campaign to retrieve you to the Serpentine Academy. Until then, I remain your most staunch and devoted friend, etc.

> Santeel of the Name Dun Troot
> writing from the Serpentine on the Skylake

Ileth didn't know quite what to make of the letter, but it was a welcome diversion for her brain. She wondered what Santeel had planned, or what Amrits had put in her head. She doubted it would be waking

Lady Raal up by banging soup pots together over her head, but the tone of the letter and the participation of Amrits suggested that anything was possible.

Lady Raal gave permission for the visit with alacrity as soon as she determined that Santeel was the one and only daughter of the Dun Troots and not some cousin or niece who was sneaking in an "of the family" between her first and household name.

"I understand they are an important Name in Sammerdam. I have heard something of their politics. Have you met the brothers? I believe there are two, one unmarried."

Ileth confessed that she hadn't had the pleasure and Lady Raal advised her to have the pleasure, quickly, before she became too much older or the unmarried one took a wife. "Could you not press your friend for a visit to her home?"

"That would be up to your husband." Ileth had learned that Lady Raal did not like it when she referred to the Governor as "my father."

She found herself looking forward to Santeel's visit, counting the days off until she was due.

They waited each day in the front room to watch the lane leading up to the house. Lady Raal had the cook do what she could at the little village market so that she could properly feed a Dun Troot.

At last, they saw a carriage moving carefully up the winter dirt of the road.

"Why, that's my husband's carriage. I wonder if he is visiting. Lucky coincidence, your friend should arrive any day."

Something flashed in the sun briefly as it flew from the opposite side of the carriage. It spun in the air as it dropped, so fast Ileth wasn't sure she'd seen it.

Lady Raal looked doubtful. "Was that the coachman's hat?"

"I'll go out and greet him," Ileth said, as a dutiful daughter should.

Ileth took the usual winter precautions—boots, a heavy hat, and a shawl—as she met the carriage. Severan followed her out. The carriage was much the worse from winter travel; the windows were very dirty.

The carriage didn't contain the Governor, just one sixteen-year-old society girl eager to be out of its confines.

Severan helped Santeel down from the carriage. Santeel was unusually red-faced and very merry looking. Severan leaned in slightly and sniffed at the atmosphere in the carriage.

Ileth could smell it too. A great wave of garish scent and ardent spirits rolled out of the carriage with her. Santeel didn't wear scent except at feasts, though she sometimes rubbed her crevices with a lemon if she didn't have an opportunity to change into a clean sheath.

"Ileth! My love! How I've missed you. An absent friend's kiss, dear!"

Santeel grabbed her by the ears and kissed her full on the lips. The combination of Santeel's enthusiasm, her physical presence, and the fumes rising from her made it the most overwhelming kiss Ileth had ever experienced. Had it come from, say, Astler Aftorn, her knees would have buckled and her toes curled. As it was, she was too shocked to do much but stand there like a statue. She could hardly have been more surprised at Santeel's unaccustomed loud behavior if she had pulled a short meteor and shot Severan down.

She glanced, embarrassed, at the window. Lady Raal was watching.

"Ooh, almost forgot my stick," Santeel said.

"Allow me, miss," Severan said. He reached into the coach and pulled out a walking stick of unmistakable design. It had a snarling brass ogre face at one end and a bright tip at the other and beautiful wood in between. Ileth had only rarely seen Dath Amrits without it, and it appeared he'd lent it to Santeel.

Santeel, limping with the aid of the walking stick, proceeded inside. Severan held the door for her.

"Oh, doors and everything. I was expecting to have to crawl in through a mud tunnel," Santeel said. She seemed to see the house for the first time. "Isn't this a lovely retreat."

"Please, come in," Ileth said. "How was your journey?"

"Your good Governor was kind enough to arrange for his carriage to meet me at the pass," Santeel said, loudly, as though she were addressing

the Serpentine from the Great Hall lectern instead of a friend in arm's reach in an entry hall. "I was happy to have an experienced driver on what passes for roads up here. But I was disappointed. In the novels about the north the young heroines aren't two leagues from their houses without some great shirtless northerner with a meteor in one hand and a whip in the other, reins between his great teeth, riding up to stop the carriage and ravish them. The only thing that stopped the Governor's carriage was sheep. I've arrived safely without so much as a stay torn, and the only outrage to my fundamentals is from the bumps in the road. Perhaps the coachman scared them all off."

Ileth showed her where to hang up her winter traveling cloak as Severan spoke to the driver about the disposition of the carriage, and the new cook, Eloana, came to take Santeel's baggage to her room.

Santeel shrugged off the cloak. Ileth gasped.

Her friend's choice of gown would be daring for, say, the Feast of Follies if she were trying to give up, well, modesty. In the north, which was a little more reserved about attire than the rest of the Vales, it constituted a scandal. Her overdress, while suitable enough from the waist down, didn't have much "over" to it above her waistline. The straps and bodice were minimal, at best, and designed to elevate and project Santeel in a provocative manner as obvious and functional as a clockmaker's shelf about displaying its wares. Santeel's blouse under what little overdress existed was thin where it wasn't left open entirely.

Eloana gaped for only a moment before hanging Santeel's cloak.

"Your w-walking stick is distinctive," Ileth said.

"A present from a gentleman admirer. Nothing like a good length of hickory in your hand, right, Ileth?"

"Hefty brass," Ileth said, but Santeel ignored her, tapping the stick hard enough on the wooden floor to create marks.

"Miss, please," Severan said, coming in behind.

"Oh, my wrap." Santeel extracted a light wrap from the cloak and settled it about her shoulders.

"Excellent, isn't it?" Santeel asked, turning. The back was conventional, except for exposed lacing, but then it had to be to support all

the lifting and cramming the front was doing. "Latest thing from Zland. I think the girls there are trying to tempt the Galantines out of the Scab so they can retake it. I wore it in expectation of the Governor coming to meet me in his carriage, but 'twas not to be."

"It's breathtaking," Ileth managed.

"That's it exactly. I haven't drawn more than half breaths since lacing it up. You don't have to ask about borrowing it, I've brought one for you. Just the shade for your eyes. I do hope we get to go to the Governor's Residence in Stavanzer together so you can wear yours."

"You're too much, Santeel."

"What are the men here like? Did some sorceress turn them all into sheep and geese? I've seen nothing else this whole trip."

Eloana bobbed. "Shall I tell Lady Raal your friend has arrived?"

"Yes, I'll introduce her directly."

"Not so directly I can't have a crap first, Ileth," Santeel said. "That carriage worked everything loose."

"It's . . . it's just out," Eloana managed to say, waving toward the rear of the house. Ileth was interested to hear someone else stutter for once.

"I'll show her," Ileth said. "Tell Lady Raal we'll be a moment."

After a comfort break for Santeel and a much-needed gulp of tea for Ileth, who feared Santeel had experimented with some even more exotic snuff that radically altered her personality, Ileth brought her into the front room. Lady Raal had set aside her loom and half-finished tapestry and Ileth wondered what the next humiliating act would be.

"Santeel Dun . . . Dun," Eloana said, bobbing as Santeel entered. She'd arranged her wrap so the panels crisscrossed, covering what the overdress did not.

"Dun Troot," Ileth supplied.

"You are welcome, Miss Dun Troot," Lady Raal said.

Santeel gave a genteel bob.

"Please join me. Would you like refreshment? There should be tea."

Through the window Ileth could see Severan hunting about beside the road. He bent and picked something up: a rectangular bottle of

green glass. He read the label and sniffed it suspiciously and made a face.

Lady Raal and Santeel spoke of the length and difficulties of her journey across the mountains in winter.

"The journey was a taxing one," Santeel said, swaying unsteadily and stifling a yawn. "Would you allow me to retire to my room for a short rest?"

"Of course, dear. Ileth, take Santeel up to your room."

"Oh, how jolly," Santeel said. "We have to share?"

"Stesside is small, and built as a summer retreat from town, not a winter one. There are several rooms upstairs, but they're chilly at this time of year. We want you to be comfortable, and Ileth told me you are used to having your beds next to each other."

"I don't mind. My trunk can go anywhere."

"Severan will see to your trunk. Rest, dear, and I look forward to getting to know you."

Upstairs and with the door shut, Santeel climbed out of the overdress—it seemed designed to be removed quickly, at need—and slipped into the prepared bed, shifting the little scented dry lavender sachet atop her pillow to the bedside candle-table.

"Santeel, what are you doing?" Ileth asked.

"I'm going to sleep, Ileth. Have you never traveled in winter? It's exhausting."

"You know what I mean. Since when have you started wearing scent?"

"Part One of the Plan. You're a slattern with slatternly friends. Part Two comes tonight."

Ileth groaned.

"Just let me lie a while. I drank just enough from that bottle to make me realistically pink, but I may have overdone it. I've never performed in the Ileth style before, at least to this extent, and I had to steady my nerves."

"Do you want something to be sick in?" Ileth said. She'd thoroughly

washed the chamber pot that morning, but not in expectation of a drunken Santeel Dun Troot.

"I'm not that bad."

"I'm relieved to hear it."

Ileth drew the curtains. "What have you and Amrits cooked up?"

"You'll see. It'll be fun. Tired now."

"I'll leave you."

"Ileth?" Santeel's voice said quietly from the dark.

"Yes?"

"You kiss like a wooden signpost. Firmament knows what Rapoto thought. Work on it."

Later, as they dressed for dinner, Santeel explained some of this "plan."

"Remember, Ileth, the slatterns-in-crime guise, we only do it here and there in front of the servants, never Lady Raal. Perfect young ladies with her, like the Matron herself was sitting there with her glass of vinegar water and a book of manners."

"How does being awful in front of the servants get me out of here?"

"You've never had servants, so you don't know. Especially when there are just a few, as here, they're more like family. They can be very proud. Anything that might discredit the Name goes right into the ear of the lady of the house so fast it's like someone's blown *dragons up* on the great horn. I don't know about the girl, but that Severan seems to me the one to work on. I could tell by that neckcloth. He'd like to chase me down the lane with dogs already. Are there dogs?"

"No. Not here, down at the distillery."

They came down to dinner and found Lady Raal looking nervous. Severan stayed in the room with her the entire dinner to help serve, rather than going back into the kitchen as he usually did for his own dinner. Ileth thought it might be to impress a Dun Troot, but after Lady Raal spent the first half of the dinner looking at them like they were highwaymen who'd barged in and sat down at her dinner table, she decided Severan had been talking.

Santeel's manners were perfect and Lady Raal eventually relaxed. After dinner, Santeel played on the keyboard and sang and became entrenched in a conversation with Lady Raal about musical forms and tempos and their possible effects on digestion and mood. Lady Raal became so animated in appreciation of Santeel's performances and conversation that it made Ileth feel like something that had just wandered in from a barnyard.

During the following days, Santeel only annoyed Lady Raal with her constant inquiries about when an invitation would come to visit the Governor in Stavanzer. Only then did Lady Raal's fearful attitude return and she made excuses about her having written her husband on the subject and she was looking forward to his reply.

Meanwhile, the secret war against the servants continued. They stole wine and liquor daily (emptying it out behind the barn rather than drinking it). They went into the village nearest Stesside, which supplied the workers to the distillery and the casual labor required of a house and grounds the size of Stesside, and made nuisances of themselves in the small public house and tobacconist's. Ileth thought Santeel overdid it when she started a screaming fight over Rapoto Vor Claymass, but it was still good fun.

Inspired by the scene in the village, Ileth finally managed to outslattern Santeel when they staged a similar fight in Ileth's room. As they stomped their feet and screamed into each other's faces, trying not to laugh, Santeel let loose with a string of profanity that impressed Ileth, who'd grown up around fishermen and sailors. Not to be outdone, Ileth volleyed back with such a collection of nouns, verbs, adjectives, and adverbs, all of them dreadful, that Santeel dropped the pillow she'd been beating on the floor and covered her eyes.

After they calmed things down, Santeel grew thoughtful. "You know, Ileth, you don't stutter when you swear."

Ileth told her it had always been that way. The only problem was, there weren't any jobs for women who could only communicate through profanity.

Ileth had never seen this side of Santeel. At the Manor, with the dancers, she'd come in and established herself and didn't have any need to be pleasant company. She tended her own affairs, certainly, gave her opinion perhaps too freely, but Ileth had never seen her try to be pleasing. She was very good at it, certainly a match for even the best of the Baroness's polished Galantine daughters Ileth had lived with for that year.

She paid closer attention to Lady Raal than any of the servants. When she appeared tired of working her loom, Santeel set up tea. A series of bad hands at cards made Santeel announce that she was tired and perhaps she could consult with Lady Raal on a good book from the small library at Stesside. She talked or was silent according to Lady Raal's inclination.

At night, when it was safe again to be open with each other, Ileth asked her about it, though posing the question was difficult because she had no skill at all in making people talk about what she wanted them to talk about with it seeming like her partner's idea.

"You're very good with Lady Raal. I've never seen her so happy and lively. She's like a flower box blossoming under your attention."

"Ileth, if we're ever in company, don't compare someone who's restricted to conveyance to a plant."

"Oh. Is it an insult?"

"It does belittle their capabilities in other manners."

Ileth thought about it. She'd been trying to compliment Santeel, but she could see her point.

"I never knew you could be so pleasing," Ileth said.

If Santeel objected to the double-edged compliment, she gave no sign of it. "Oh, my whole life's been one long preparation for this role."

"What role?"

"Ileth, are you being thick intentionally? A young woman in society trains to be married. Yes, you attend your husband but you're an absolute thrall to your mother-in-law."

"Not the children?"

"Not in my circle. You have an entire vanguard for the next

generation. Wet nurse. Night nurse. Then there are the nannies and later tutors."

"You had all those?" Ileth had few memories of her own early days. She remembered times when she had to be very quiet because the Captain was drinking.

"I got away from them whenever I could. In Sammerdam there are 'yards.' Sammerdam's like that, everything is fenced off from every-thing else. The best ones are owned by the families of my parents' so-cial circle, filled with toys and playhouses and such. When I was little there was one—this is one the more ordinary kids played at, children of guild artisans and boatwrights and glaziers and such, but Nanny took me because I loved it—it was nothing but this great pile of sand and a fountain pool. I'd build castles and dig trenches and make mud pies. If I'm ever married with children, I shall have my husband just fill up the grounds by the outdoor pump with sand and release them into it every day. Stuff the playhouses."

Ileth built up their nightly fire. Santeel had her depths. But getting her to open up was like convincing an oyster to show its pearl. "Aren't you afraid your mother's going to hear about these stunts?"

"My mother? Rumors from the north? She'll assume that whatever reaches her isn't a tenth of it anyway. If I were even partly as bad as my mother thought I was, I'd be on my second pregnancy or dead of ex-haustion. She thinks I'm like she was back in her day in Zland."

She finally saw a glimmer of purpose to Santeel's madness the day they received the bad news about the trip to the Governor's Res-idence in Stavanzer.

"I'm afraid my husband writes that his business is of such import that all his time is consumed with it. He cannot properly have you two visit. All the spare bedrooms are full of officers."

Ileth, who had learned to read between Lady Raal's lines, under-stood. The Governor wanted to quarantine whatever outrages Ileth and Santeel were planning to Stesside, where there'd be less talk. Ac-cording to Santeel, the next step in the campaign would be to make

them decide they might be better off dispensing with Ileth altogether and suggest more suitable company for Lady Raal, lest she bring scandal and disgrace to the Name Raal.

"I'm disappointed to miss all the opportunities for society in Stavanzer," Santeel said. "Do you ever wish for more company here?"

"Oh, I am so used to my difficulties now. There are doctor visits, and my husband is here much of the summer. But it was so nice to have you here to entertain me."

"Your situation reminds me of an aunt of mine. She is forced to keep to her home a great deal as well. She has a young lady, a Galantine, reside with her. She laughs and calls the girl her 'legs.'"

"She is lucky to have such a friend."

"Luck has nothing to do with it, ma'am. There is a service. I could have my mother forward a reference. I don't know if your health has ever permitted you to visit Sammerdam, but it sees all manner of good people arriving, seeking opportunities. Young women of family and accomplishment are paired up with households that need a trusted relative to help out in this way but for whatever reason don't have one."

"Is it expensive?"

"No more so than having a daughter about. Board, pocket money, perhaps some small comforts."

"I don't know if I could trust someone. It's one thing to keep servants for work, but . . ." She grew thoughtful. "I sometimes wonder if I haven't confined dear Ileth too much. A girl her age, with her . . . uhh, lively spirit doesn't want to spend month after month with a sick old woman. Well, I shall consider it."

Santeel concluded her visit with the same skill she showed organizing her arrival. The Governor's driver and carriage would bring him to Stesside, he'd enjoy one meal with Ileth and her friend, and she would depart the next morning for the Serpentine. Barring a disaster with the weather, she'd be met by a dragon and dragoneer at the Cleft Pass. It would undoubtedly be Amrits, aquiver to hear how the campaign he'd conceived with Santeel had played out.

Santeel's swift and furious campaign had been executed so brilliantly

that Ileth couldn't let her depart without some token of gratitude. She'd heard childhood stories about knights riding back to get a champion's cloak and a garland circlet placed on their head; wearing the "halo of victory" was an expression you heard now and then.

There were plenty of old blankets about the place, but Ileth couldn't drape an old blanket that smelled of insect-repelling herbs and oils about Santeel Dun Troot's shoulders as a cloak. Perhaps she could do the circlet. The problem was winter. There were a few plants that lived indoors in Stesside in pots, but she couldn't ravage them. In the end she trooped out into the hills above Stesside and explored the path up to the spring source and found an evergreen with suitably springy branches. At least it was green and fresh. She trimmed off an armful with a knife and went straight to work.

Just before Santeel closed her pack trunk, Ileth reached under her pillow and presented the wound ring of greenery to Santeel.

"What's this?" Santeel asked. She looked befuddled and a bit shocked, as though Ileth held a writhing snake in her hand.

"Your victory halo," Ileth said. "It was a brilliant campaign, in conception and execution."

The wheels in Santeel's head finally ceased spinning, and it appeared they'd settled on delight. "Oh, I see! Ileth, how—this is a lovely gesture. How classical! But the credit for the campaign belongs on another head." She picked up Dath Amrits's walking stick.

"No, it's you," Ileth said, putting the garland on her head and kissing her cheek. "I believe I shall be set free. I have a feeling Lady Raal is already scared to be in a house alone with me. Everyone has what they want."

Santeel smiled a bit of a bleak smile and blinked. The halo was askew. Ileth had sized it for her own overlarge brow. "So it would seem."

She rooted around in her clothing, found a wrap, and folded the greenery up in it. "I shall let Amrits wear it long enough for me to buy him a very large ale in Vyenn, and then hang it up in the Dancers' Quarter, if they haven't turned my bed over to the new girls. Maybe it will be the only halo I ever earn, so I shall do my best to preserve it."

"Oh, dear, what if Falth should hear that you stood a man a drink in a beer garden? We'd have your father back."

"See that he doesn't hear of it, then." Santeel chuckled.

"You can be cheery. You get to escape Stesside."

"I can, and I will. I think this visit did me good," Santeel said as she refilled her trunk. She had confessed to Ileth that she feared her dancing days were over. She'd gained a temporary limp. "What I most needed was a good challenge, to prove myself to . . . myself. Beyond that, I was able to aid a friend."

Ileth, eyes going wet, could only hug her.

Santeel squeezed her. "Let us make a pact. Neither ever forgets the other. If one is in need, the other comes. Always." She stared levelly at Ileth.

"Always," Ileth agreed.

Santeel stuck out her right fist, knuckles to Ileth, like half the gesture the Dragoneers of the Serpentine used to acknowledge each other when facing difficulty. Ileth mirrored the gesture, putting her fist up against Santeel's, her knuckles facing her friend. A special variation of the Troth only they would share.

Ileth did her best to look bright. "Tell Aurue and Falberrwrath and the rest I miss them. I will return."

"If some of the hints of that silly old gossip Threadneedle are true, Ileth, the dragons may be returning to you."

Governor Raal arrived on the promised date and brought good weather with him. He seemed delighted to make the acquaintance of a Dun Troot and passed good wishes to her parents. When they joined Lady Raal, the conversation turned to what delightful company Santeel had been and how accomplished and entertaining she was.

Talk moved on to Santeel's suggestion of a companion.

"What about Ileth?"

"Ileth will not remain here forever. She's a vital young girl; she doesn't want to spend her best years in the company of a sick old woman."

"Don't you like it here, Ileth?"

"It's-it's not that, sir. Lady Raal is right. A house, however comfortable, isn't my goal. I want to re-rejoin the Serpentine."

"We all miss her," Santeel said. "A trained dragoneer, idle at Stesside pouring tea when everyone is training so hard. It's not just our loss, it's the Republic's. I'm sure my father would agree."

The Governor winced. Ileth tried not to smile at Santeel's expert knife work.

"Who knows what the future holds," the Governor said. "She's helped me better understand dragons and their potential. Gave me a powerful lesson in their use on a coup board, too." He touched Ileth's cheek, very gently. The way he looked at her, Ileth wondered if he wasn't seeing someone else.

Ileth couldn't resist glancing at Lady Raal, but she showed no sign of disquiet.

Santeel departed with a present of a single bottle of Stesssource Lifewater from the Governor, and made a more dignified exit than she did an entrance. "Don't . . . ahh, use it sparingly, young lady."

"I have no head for spirits, sir," Santeel said. Severan straightened and frowned behind her. "I will pour a toast for the dragoneers on Republic Day and ask that all drink to your health as well, sir."

The Governor liked the sound of that. He helped her into the carriage himself.

They waved until she disappeared down the hill toward the Stess bridge.

"I am sorry you are left without a friend, Ileth," Raal said.

"You took me away from every friend I have."

Raal let his face go blank at the reprimand. "Yes, the fact has come home to me, in the contrast between you and Santeel and me and Lady Raal. You are both spirited young ladies. Lady Raal should have with her a woman closer to her own age and interests. It was a mistake, bringing you here thinking you could be a daughter to us."

"I am nobody's idea of a daughter."

"We will talk later, Ileth. I have some ideas about restoring you to

your friends, if you will be agreeable about certain conditions. I think as you have the trust of me and the dragoneers both, you would make an excellent representative."

"You—trust me?"

"Oh, you are a little wild, I understand, but that goes with being sixteen. That's the age to break a little crockery and sing on a rooftop. I know I did. Come, let's return inside. We will talk later."

The weather turned cold that night and a storm blew up. Santeel would be in the Cleft Pass overnight most likely, and stuck at the inn.

Ileth fretted a little, pacing back and forth in front of the window and watching the wind blow the first flakes of a new snow about. If the wind was this bad here, what would it be like in the Cleft Pass? Ileth had walked that road and it ran along a high lake for a very long way. Pictures of Santeel in an overturned carriage flooding with icy water haunted her.

"She has a bottle of lifewater to keep her warm." Governor Raal chuckled. But it seemed his carriage would be absent for some days.

One night, late, overcome by a cough and desiring water, she went down to the pump in the kitchen and found Governor Raal in the dining room, sitting by the remaining coals of the fire with his neckcloth draped across the back of his armchair and his waistcoat loose. He had his eyes closed, tapping the fingers of his right hand on the arm of the chair.

She tried to creep by him. His eyes opened.

"Sorry to disturb you, sir."

"You didn't disturb me. Sit down."

She avoided Lady Raal's chair and instead used one of the dining chairs, pulling it by the low winter fire.

"Ileth, I know you've probably heard rumors about me, about what happened with your mother. I want you to know I did love my wife. Always. But I was ... enchanted with your mother. I let a young man's passions get the better of me. You are living proof."

"I am?" Ileth asked. She still didn't see, or feel, any resemblance.

"This business of you being my daughter—well, it's time you heard the story. My part of it."

Ileth nodded. She clasped her hands in her lap to keep from fidgeting in her nervousness.

"Everyone thinks I married Lady Raal for her money. It's true. I did marry for money. I'm not even the Raal, she is. I took her Name. At the time she just seemed to me an excellent sort of girl with an unfortunate condition. It seemed she wouldn't live long. To my mind then, it reflected well on my character and career possibilities all the way down. I was in the Assembly and some suggested I should stand for governor. A famous Name would help. With the Name came money and connections, and she gave every indication she enjoyed my company and attention. She used to beat me at coup, back when she played.

"She . . . she understood a man's needs and didn't mind me enjoying social connections in her absence. Like your mother. There's always talk, but I didn't go parading them about. I wondered if I would remarry when she died, but then something wonderful happened, over the years. Two somethings wonderful. She didn't die and I came to love her. Now I'm terrified of where I'll be if she dies. I don't know what I'd do without her. Now it—the business with your mother, and others—all feels silly, and every time I'm tempted, I think of how easily the goaty older man becomes a figure of fun. I suppose you get timid when you're older, worried about your reputation. Timid about women. Timid about war."

"What was . . . what was my-my-my mother like?"

"You only need to look in a mirror to find out. Tireless as water, able to wear down stone in time."

"Why all the effort to bring me to you, when you've done nothing but push me away?"

"Your mother asked me to take care of it. It was—" His face writhed. "It was the last thing she asked of me. I agreed . . . and I botched it. Too afraid. Afraid of talk, of scandal. I shoved you off to that Lodge. I always have all these plans, you see. Even now. Oh, I can't

talk of this anymore. Let us change the subject for a while. Would you rather speak of returning to your dragons? Or I should say, them returning to you?"

Would no one in this drafty old house finish telling her about her mother? She fought to remain polite, weirdly vexed that he'd echoed Santeel. "Has anything developed with the campaign?"

"I've named you my daughter and you were a dragoneer, and the dragoneers trusted you with the earliest preparations so I believe I can tell you in safety. There was a final, secret Assembly vote, heads of committees only, granting the Speaker authority to use funds. Frighteningly limited funds; this is all such a gamble. As Governor I can put the province on a war footing, call up militia, and so on, but as of yet it's still planning and drafting orders. I had some of my connections in the business world and the Exchange set up three companies, one that is working on still-secret naval craft using old coasters—they're very nearly complete, I understand—one for road work and a new 'quarry' that will be a camp, and a third that is on paper a new meatpacking firm. Men have been hired. Of course right before the campaign we'll need a full vote in the Assembly, but the Speaker and the committee heads should be able to deliver. Unless there's a startling turn of politics. But the retrenchment faction is in disgrace ever since they found out Heem Stalleer was taking Galantine gold. And so little! What are men these days?"

Ileth thought it strange that the last implied that there was a correct amount of Galantine gold that made selling out your countrymen worth it.

They spent a few minutes talking about how she would get there, letters of introduction so that she could enter the camp, and he requested that she personally deliver a few notes of gratitude from him for families like the Aftorns who were turning over their property, fields, outbuildings, wells, and so on to the armed camps even now being planned out.

"My one great worry is the shipbuilding going on. But since these

are such unique vessels, unless they go under very close inspection, they may be taken for improvements to the docks near the border with Daphia."

As for the rest, the dragons would only be moved to the coast at the very last moment. The muster of the militia would be explained as a move needed to fight a plague in the swampy forests south of the Headlands. "It'll give everyone in Stavanzer something to grumble about: a governor who calls up the militia to do battle with bog fever."

"So that's it? I just return to the dragoneers when they come?"

"That's my plan. Ileth, why do you think I brought you here?"

"To keep your wife company?"

"I'd hoped life together and your own young heart would give you some amount of feeling for Lady Raal. That you two might grow close. Even see her as a mother."

It was impossible not to respond to the emotion in his eyes playing out in the firelight.

"I admire her."

"Just admire? No pity?"

"She is admirable about her condition. I see the effect it has on her. Can nothing be done? Maybe a trip to the south, I've heard it's easier on invalids?"

"Oh, we've been over and over that. It won't help. There's no surgery, no diet. But by the flash and the thunder, I'm going to give her some measure of health. Now that I'm almost through as Governor, one way or another, consummate strategist or bankrupt fool, I'll see her health restored. You're the key to it. I brought you here with every intention of sending you back. Once I extract a promise from you that you'll get me dragon blood."

Ileth froze. So she wasn't some chit in an old grudge against the dragoneers.

"I couldn't."

"They would not suspect you, Ileth. You're young, vital. You have a reputation for honesty. I was told you even uncovered some scale

thieves and recovered stolen dragon eggs by that Dun Huss dragoneer. You could have lived like a queen in the Baronies on what the Galantine court would have given you for those eggs."

"Why w-would that m-m-make you think I'd steal blood? A reasonable man, hearing those incidents, would come to the opposite conclusion."

"Hear me out. I've had physikers in; they tell me they can do nothing but give her drugs that will make her insensible. I became my own physician and studied up on it, and no less than three authoritative Hypatian texts speak of the wonders dragon blood can work on even severed nerves. Beyond that, I've heard stories. You wouldn't be the only dragoneer to get a little blood out of the stones of the Serpentine."

"Setting aside . . . setting aside v-violating my oath, I've never even seen the stuff, at least bottled as medicine."

"I'm certain there will be some in the camp that the engineers are outlining even now. As soon as the dragons arrive, I'll send you there. Under conditions that you do nothing that will imperil your safety or ability to return with the blood. No flying about on dragonback and getting yourself killed."

Governor Raal was a man of intriguing depths. He might not be a master of coup on the board, but in real life he played admirably. All the pieces were in place. Dragons. A campaign. Even her.

"But if I do this, I return to the Serpentine."

"With my thanks. And the Name Raal, if you want it."

Ileth took the plunge. "I promise nothing. I don't know if your plan is even feasible."

Raal's face hardened. "You have to do better than that. I'm not a governor for nothing. I can still spike the wheel. Without me, no campaign against the Rari."

"You wouldn't dare. It's the Republic."

"I could say the same to you. The Republic. The Serpentine. Against a little bit of dragon blood for a sick old woman. I want a definitive answer."

Ileth spent a moment assembling her next words: "I would see

Lady Raal's health restored, if it were in my power to do so. If she must have dragon blood, I will do my best to get some."

There it was. She was committed to betraying the trust the Serpentine had put in her. But the campaign had to go forward.

"Then I will see about arranging transport for you. You've no objection to another visit to the Sag, I trust? They'd seem a suitable family to look after you for me, and they're right in the thick of it."

Ileth nodded, unable to tell if she anticipated or dreaded seeing Astler Aftorn again.

PART THREE

A SWIFT AND FURIOUS CAMPAIGN

"I never won a battle in my life, sir.
I only survived them."

—CAPTAIN-GENERAL GARAMOFF

7

As spring finally warmed the chilly north in earnest, Ileth wondered if the campaign would ever get under way. Her seventeeth birthday passed, unmarked and uncelebrated, save by Ileth to herself with the promise that even if she failed to acquire the forbidden blood, only time would keep her from the Serpentine's dragons. She waited in agony until one day a message arrived by express rider, then next a carriage, really more of a sturdy, enclosed cart, to get her first to Stavanzer and then to the Headlands.

Back at the Stavanzer house, Ileth learned that the carriage wasn't the only thing Raal had prepared. He had letters of instruction and thanks to the Aftorn family, letting the family know that Ileth would take them up on their invitation to visit and asking they allow her to reside at the Sag "for the duration," but he did not make explicit the duration of what exactly in writing. A second letter he gave to her written in ink that would only become visible if the paper was painted with vinegar, concealed with some other blank sheets of paper, pen, and ink in a portable secretary-case he presented to her. He told her this one was to the dragoneer encampment with instructions to them that she was to represent his office in Stavanzer strictly as an observer to give him an accounting once the campaign was concluded for good or ill. The third thing he gave her was all the information he had gathered about how dragon blood was bottled and labeled, and the old

Hypatian alchemical symbols she was to look for. She was to then return immediately using a third order for her transport on dragonback, using as an excuse a prewritten note that Lady Raal was very ill and called for her. If a dragon to convey her was not available, she should go to a fishmonger's near the Sag and arrange for a crate of oysters on ice to be sent to the Governor's Residence in Stavanzer and lay the bottle within among the ice before the crate was nailed shut and sent by express. Raal had a connection there who would arrange matters for her.

She wondered just how long this plan had been in the works.

So she went in her cart to the Sag and the hospitality of the Aftorn family. Gandy was visibly taller and Ileth tried not to look too long at Astler, who'd put something in his hair in an attempt to tame the cowlicks.

They welcomed her, complimented her on her new clothes, but it seemed the Sag was nothing like the heart of an armed camp. She even had a guest bedroom of her own. The road to the Old Post had been improved, but she saw no other changes. There was no one about other than a gardener and the shepherd for the family sheep. Ileth wondered if the whole affair had been called off, failed in the Assembly or what-have-you.

"Your dragoneers are in the Chalk Cuts, just north of the bog," Comity said, privately, over tea and oat porridge poured on toast, dished out in order to restore her from the fatigues of travel. "The Old Post is simply too near the village. They won't be brought up until the campaign begins."

Ileth had heard of the Chalk Cuts as a child; hunters of pheasants looked for them there in the brush and small trees. It was supposed to be the next thing to uninhabited, something to do with the soil being poor and only fit for goats and plagued by great swarms of mosquitoes and biting flies.

She confessed to Astler and Gandy that she wanted to get back among the dragons. She even missed the familiar old oily reek!

"There's only paths going there," Astler said. "You'd spend a day

walking there. A horse isn't that different as there's no direct road, just easier on the legs."

That night, Gandy showed her where she could arrange her things, but she didn't feel much like unpacking.

"You'd rather be among them." She didn't phrase it as a question. "Astler will be disappointed. Are we that poor company?"

"It's not that," Ileth managed to say, fearing that she'd misstepped with people who'd been kind to her. "Yes, I miss the dragons, but Governor Raal gave me a few notes to deliver. It's duty that takes me away."

Gandy smiled with her eyes. "You and my cousin are so alike. He's had the word *duty* on his lips more than once this week. I'll let you in on a secret, since no duty binds me: I think he's a little disappointed we have spare rooms, and he's no excuse to creep in and talk to you." She giggled.

He wasn't the only one who was disappointed. Unable to sleep, Ileth purposefully rose twice in the night with ready excuses about forgotten gloves or a cat crying outside her window, hoping to run into Astler mooning about, but the house was quiet.

The next day, Ileth helped with cleaning the kitchen and arranging firewood and charcoal, then took a walk in the hills to exercise her body after being cooped up in the carriage. Happily tired, she sat by the fire with a book on natural science—it was difficult, and after carefully puzzling out five pages, she mostly looked at the illustrations—but Astler never appeared. Gandy said he was with a pair of workmen at the Old Post putting in new lamps.

The next day was more like summer than spring, even for the windy Headlands. Ileth felt restless. She couldn't shake the sense that she was missing something important.

"It may be a question of you going to the dragons or the dragons coming to you," Comity said quietly as Ileth helped her set out the breakfast things, forcing herself to full wakefulness with activity. "Astler told me that Taskmaster Henn is at the Old Post, working like mad with last-minute stores."

Astler appeared at last, smelling of his father's shaving soap, and

announced that he would take her to the Chalk Cuts the next day on horseback if she wished. Everything that could be done to ready the Old Post had been finished.

They packed baskets of food and extra meats and cheeses just in case. Ileth put her small bundle of necessities and letter case on her loaned horse. Astler carried the food and his sketchbook. Comity read off a list of advice and prohibitions for the trip that seemed to stretch on and on like the codicils in her apprenticeship contract, and Gandy offered her the red-and-white scarf Ileth had admired. "You never know this time of year."

Ileth was grateful. It was of the softest and highest-quality wool. Finally, they set off for the Chalk Cuts, a final warning from Comity ringing in their ears:

"Turn back if it looks like snow!"

The hills came in sight as bumps in the distance and patches of trees, with little slivers of white where the soil had worn away revealing chalky ground. No sign of dragons that Ileth could tell.

They stopped as the sun rose to midday, unsaddled the horses, and set up a picnic. They talked about the weather for a while. Ileth asked if Astler would draw something for her, pointing out patches of spring wildflowers, but he said there wasn't time to do them justice if they were to reach the Chalk Cuts by dinner. They got into a small, distressing argument about the Rari. Astler believed that the pirate captains were already breaking up; they'd been so long without much commerce to raid that some of the captains had taken their ships out to the Inland Ocean to try their luck against the Galantines and the others on the Inland's western shores.

"They'll be back to a nuisance in a few years," he opined.

"The Republic might not be here in a few years either," Ileth said.

"We'll muddle through. We've lived through hard times before."

"So we sit on a stump and do nothing? Lose a few dozen fishermen and a ship or two every year?"

"It's better than war," Astler said, tipping his head back a little as he tended to do when arguing a point.

"How do you know?"

"I've studied history at school. A military academy. Wars are like dogfights, you never know who's going to join in. Suppose the Galantines back the Rari?"

Ileth thought it best to change the subject. She didn't like hearing Astler pick apart Annis Heem Strath's plan to suppress the menace. "You went to an academy? Your mother allowed it?"

"She didn't have a choice. Family tradition. From eight until fourteen at the Navigator's. Basic education for two years, straightening out the weak bits from our tutors when I was little, two years classical art and education, and then the last two in cadet uniform, supposed to toughen me up and all that. One year being made miserable, then another making the boys under you miserable. I hated those years. One of my class went on to the Serpentine. Boy named Sleng. You know him?"

"Pasfa Sleng? Big sideburns?"

"Glad to hear he finally grew them. He tried for years with bucket to show."

Ileth smiled. "I don't really know him but I have a friend who is mad about him. I didn't know he was from the north. He doesn't sound it."

"He's not. He was kicked out of all the others."

Astler leaned toward Ileth. "It's a lovely warm day. There's a spring breeze with wildflowers on it. I'm picnicking with a beautiful girl and talking politics." For a moment she thought she was about to be kissed, but he plucked a stem of bluebells and handed it to her.

She'd never been called beautiful. Well, never by any boy she wanted to hear that kind of talk from. What did you say in reply? *Thank you?*

"These are nice," Ileth finally said. "If I had the right sort of pin, I could use them to close your cousin's scarf."

"She must like you. It's her favorite."

"She's a . . . a favorite of mine. She and-and her cousin b-both." Leave it to her cursed tongue to intrude on such an exchange!

Astler looked puzzled. "You met . . . oh, you mean me."

"Y-yes," Ileth said.

He looked uncomfortable. Ileth wondered if she'd misjudged.

"I'm sure you're eager to be back at work among your dragons," he said.

Ileth stretched. The riding and the lunch had worked on her. She reclined, settling her head against Astler's outstretched thigh. "A brief rest. I am . . . I am too happy now to move."

Astler tested her hair between his thumb and forefinger. He picked up one of the blue flowers by its stem and gently brushed the petals on various points on her face. "Spirit. Mind. Body. Soul," he recited.

The litany left her confused. "You lost me."

"A lover's four tells. Hair: spirit. Chin: mind. Mouth: body: Eyes: soul."

"Still lost."

"Just some rot out of poetry books. Her hair reveals how her spirit feels about you, her chin what she thinks of you, her mouth how her body fee—well, you get the idea."

She looked for soul in his eyes. All she saw was that same gentle regard. So different from that hot, hungry look she was used to from men near enough to smell their breath.

Maybe it was best that they get back on the horses. She had an increasingly irresistible urge to put her hand on the back of his neck, pull him down, and test what his weight would feel like atop her. The blanket and the empty meadowlands were too much of a temptation.

"I don't want to go, but . . . but we should," she finally said.

"Yes. The moment's over anyway."

"What moment?" she asked.

"The moment when you weren't thinking about your dragons. It's only the second one we've had."

"What was the first?" She thought she knew, though.

"That night when I came looking for my pencil case."

She got to her feet.

He sighed. "I'm sorry. You've been odd this whole visit, like something is weighing on you. I don't like seeing you unhappy."

"I'm not unhappy!" she said. "This was . . . this was very nice. I could spend all day with you and not care about anything else."

"Something is working on you."

She had to say something, it was difficult with a boy who read her like a child's copybook text. Perhaps she could laugh it off. "I—you know what they say about girls in military camps. They're not gripping sword hilts."

Astler knew her well enough by now to know when she was joking. "I might have to go into service myself." He turned serious. "If this is a last chance for the Republic, I want to do my part."

"I . . . I know it will work. In my gut. I trust my gut more than my head. It's fate."

"Fate? Then I wish I could be part of it. Maybe they'll let me make soup for the Auxiliaries," Astler said. "Though my mother probably wouldn't allow me even that distinction. Might burn myself. You know, there's a philosopher who thinks you will outcomes into being, positive or negative."

Ileth, who had been gloomily thinking all morning about the consequences of a theft of dragon blood being discovered, stayed silent.

He waited for her to reply. When she didn't, he said, "Well, if we're fated to win, perhaps I can give you something to look forward to. Our biggest warehouse, up the Hyacinth Canal, just outside Stavanzer—has been all but empty for years now. Both inside and outside are being repainted and new glass is going in. Why do you think that is, Ileth? Will you guess?"

"You think opening the straits will bring the warehouse into full use?" She tried to think of other possibilities an intelligent young woman of business might consider. "Is it to be sold and you want the best price? Wait, it is going to be the armory for the campaign?"

"Good guesses, but no. It is to be used for a celebration when the campaign is over."

"Even if it is a failure?" Ileth asked.

"I thought your gut declared that an impossibility."

"It's still fighting with my head about it."

He took her hand. She felt her pulse quicken at his touch. "Would your gut and your head agree to leading the first dance with me?"

"Why would I lead the first dance?"

"Oh, so I must explain my reasoning now? First, I do know you enjoy dancing. Second, you're connected to Governor Raal, and we will invite him. As his wife doesn't appear socially, you would be attending with him. In Galantine phrasing, the *Ancialia*—the princess prime. You and your dancing partner would be the first couple for as many dances as you chose to lead."

"I don't know social dances well enough to lead."

"Well, you should choose as a partner then one who would carry you through on the skill of his lead."

With that he took her by both hands and began saying, in a musical fashion, *"aaand-beat-beat-beat aaand beat-beat-beat"* while first pulling her toward him, then pushing away as he stepped away, then crossing one arm over the other and twirling her, then breaking off one hand's grip to step forward in parade, holding her hand and repeating the whole thing again *"aaand-beat-beat-beat."*

Dancing there, on the hillside, with the horses nosing about in their feed bags and watching the humans curiously, she forgot about Raal and the coming campaign.

Astler finished and bowed, out of breath from dancing and verbally keeping time. "I think you must go, and you must make the Governor buy you a decent party dress," he panted. "This will be your introduction to northern society, so you should look your best. Fifteen is the traditional age for an introduction dress, of course, but you're a smallish sixteen so I doubt anyone will be the wiser."

Ileth had just turned seventeen and had never owned a social dress of her choosing. What would it be like, to have one made by a seamstress to your size, rather than trying to improve on an overdress out of the slop bin?

"I should like to be there. I'm not promising anything about lead-ing dances."

"Then do I have at least the opening dance?"

"Some hero of the coming campaign might ask me. It's very hard to turn down a brave man in his country's uniform."

"No one else knows about it. All part of my stratagem."

"Maybe you should have taken a greater part in planning this cam-paign."

"I would have, and would ensure its success, just so I can see you in a party dress."

"I'll tell the dragoneers that your mind is made up: we must have victory."

Ileth still had enough of her religious upbringing to wonder if she wasn't tempting the Celestials to send a disaster by spinning fantasies with blood still waiting to be shed. Astler turned to the nose-bagged horses, a new assurance in his step. "I feel different. Like I'm under a different will. It's not some Galantine witchery, is it? A spell using your eyes?"

"The only thing Galantines do with their eyes is decorate them so that they might flutter them at their husbands when they're ready for another baby."

"Well, then flutter away. That'll make my mother happy. Gandy wants me to set up with you, but all my mother cares is that I reestab-lish the family. Father so many children the gods will pant from breathing life into babies like they've run up a mountain."

"You're quite ahead of me, you and Gandy and your mother. Stop it, the lot of you."

He swung up into his saddle. "We'd make a splendid couple. You, practically the Governor's daughter, me the last male of my Name with all my family's hopes resting on my shoulders, or perhaps I should say features farther down."

"I'm beginning to think I should have slept with a mounting-hook that night I was in your room."

"Those things that are half shepherd's staff and half pry bar? I'm

glad you didn't. You still haven't answered my question about the first dance."

"I didn't? The answer is yes. Don't be surprised if you find your partner hiding at the very back where no one will notice her, however fine a dress it is."

The horses weren't happy about being in motion again, and Ileth sympathized; things felt too much in motion. Astler, the Governor and his ailing wife, secret papers with invisible writing for the dragoneers, and looming over it all the coming campaign. She resettled the scarf about her neck and wished she could be Gandy for a few days, with nothing to think about but matchmaking her cousin.

A s they approached the Chalk Cuts, they were met by three provincial militia men roaming the tufted heather.

Astler recognized one of them.

"Militia been called up, Loak?"

Ileth decided they were still boys under the dirt and woodsmoke odor. "Astler Aftorn, it's been some time. Good to meet you again."

"You've picked a bad place to picnic," an older militia man said, looking at their basket. "There's plague in Yarth and Break Even Roads. They say it's carried by bugs from the bog. Or is it rats that carry the bugs? It's bad. Stavanzer ordered in some dragons to burn the swamps."

"Yes, well, this young lady is actually a dragoneer and has a message from the Governor. I really need to see the Captain. Is it still Patkers?"

"Yes, but it'll take hours to find him in this mess," Loak said, looking around.

"She needs to get through."

The older militia man scratched his chin. "Loak, as you know the young Aftorn gentleman, you take him to the Captain. Have to warn you, sir, you go past us and you could be subject to Republic Quarantine. The Quarantine Camp's not the most comfortable place. You want to be sure to see your bed again, you turn back for the Sag now."

"If you get quarantined it'll lay your mother out," another boy said.

Astler frowned. "I know."

They found an officer of the militia pickets who passed them on to the Captain, who summoned a dragoneer with a red studded pauldron and dueling saber who turned out to be Roben, Falberrwrath's dragoneer.

"Yeah, she's one of us. Message from Governor Raal, you said, Ileth? May I see it?" He had several gold teeth, and they flashed as he spoke.

"Won't do you much good, s-sir," Ileth said, showing him the paper with the secret ink so that the others could not see.

"Ahh. Yes, I won't fiddle with it. You may pass."

The Captain of the militia also knew Astler and extended an invitation to dinner. Astler offered Ileth the use of the horse while she was in camp, but Ileth declined. "I know the distance and the landmarks now."

They said a halting good-bye.

"It feels all wrong. It's the woman who should be seeing the man off at the edge of an armed camp," Astler said.

"It's just some mosquitoes that need suppressing," Ileth said with a wink. "I shan't be involved."

"Still. I feel upside down about it," Astler said, taking her hands in his. "Be safe, Ileth. Don't get . . . don't get sick."

If she were seeing him off at the edge of a camp, she would kiss him. She drew herself up to her full height, went up on her toes, and gave him a kiss that covered as much of his lips as her mouth allowed. She hoped she didn't kiss him like a signpost.

The kiss didn't make her swoon, or weak in the knees, or make her feel weightless. It did make her want another, however, and made her wonder what his arms would feel like about her.

"See you at Sag House," she said. He looked shocked.

"Lucky boy," Roben said. "She's a rocket, that one."

Roben escorted Ileth to the Chalk Cuts. She ignored his comments about her not being the only dragoneer sampling the local produce. A full dragoneer with a pauldron could say what he liked to a

lowly apprentice. She consoled herself that not every man could be a Dun Huss, but Roben was supposed to be good in a fight.

At first, Ileth thought she'd become lost, as she couldn't make out tents or campfires as she approached the white scars in the hillsides that must be the Chalk Cuts. The dragoneers had made good use of the many folds and furrows of the landscape to hide their tents. Her first clue that she was approaching an armed camp was the smell of cooking.

Then they broke out over a hill and saw tents scattered in the folds of the earth. Ileth marked dragons sheltering under great screens with cut brush tossed atop them and heard the clamor of work being done on wood and metal.

The expression *spectacle and beat of war* drifted through her thoughts as she followed Roben into the warrenlike camp, a mass of tented alleys and cut-brush pathways that already had her confused. What was going on in the Chalk Cuts was certainly a spectacle, most of it seeming to be related to feeding half the dragons of the Vales and the small army of men and animals in attendance to them. Even the local birds were getting in on the action, drawn to the piles of garbage.

The camp smelled of dragons. Roasting meat, tobacco, and sweating men were part of the odor, but it was mostly dragons.

She received more "oh, hullo, Ileths" and friendly nods than she ever had in the Serpentine. She wondered if it was her more distinguished attire or just the fact that very few of the Serpentine's women and girls were in camp, making her stand out. She spotted Garella in the mix, smoking a pipe on a camp stool and content to direct an apprentice in filling a suspended stewpot, using the pipe-stem as a pointer, and a wingman she met on one of the paths informed her that Shatha and Fyth had been set up in an old shepherd's hut.

"Falberrwrath is here?" Ileth asked Roben.

"Of course. Sleeping, mostly, which is why I'm walking the perimeter. I think he'd rather face war than his hatchlings." Roben greeted a pair of wingmen walking the camp.

"Aurue?"

"Yes, this is his first campaign."

Ileth would have to visit.

"There are some dragons you haven't met, too," Roben said. "The Auxiliaries are here with the Duke and Duchess."

Ileth had read the names stitched on memorial victory banners hung up in the Great Hall. They were a mated pair. The Duke and Duchess went back to the Troth, or before it, back when humans didn't use their actual names for whatever reason but called them by a Montangyan word. They were aged and no longer flew, or only could fly for a very short period, something like that. As they were both uncommonly fierce, they had gone off and joined the Auxiliaries. Or rather the Auxiliaries had grown up around them, as they were the original Auxiliary dragons.

Were they here just to cheer on old comrades? Annis Heem Strath's estimate of the campaign to suppress the Rari called for flying dragons. Perhaps they were here just for advice, like veteran commanders who'd seen a hundred battlefields and could be trusted not to lose their heads.

"Who should I present the Governor's letter to?"

"Watch the mud there, girl," Roben said as they walked. "Garamoff's in overall charge with the temporary rank of Captain-General, and doing a proper job of it. His chief of staff is your Dun Huss friend. You can give it to him, he's in the middle of camp." He pointed into a group of tents wrapped around the base of a low, chalky cliff. "I have to see what new messages and errands have piled up. You might want to put on your belt, apprentice."

Ileth had brought her novice brooch and apprentice belt all this way, and forgotten to pin them on. Silly. She rectified her clothing. It didn't look quite right on her Stavanzer-pattern overdress, but then she wasn't quite part of the camp. Officially.

She asked directions, became lost, asked directions again, met someone as lost as she, then ran into one of the apprentices from Horse Lot who was here at the express request of a dragoneer because he was a northerner as well. He brought her to the tent of Hael Dun Huss.

The tent was about the size of a two-cow shed, strung in a circle around what she assumed was a central tentpole, tall enough for men to stand up inside. Once it had probably been whitish, but it was weathered and stained now. It had some sea grasses tied to the top so from a distance it might be mistaken for a chalky cut.

Grumbling and swearing came from within. She recognized the voice of Dun Huss's wingman, Preece. "That'll hold it."

"Sir, it's Ileth, may I enter?" she called.

"Ileth? Ileth, yes. Enter."

She opened the tent. A dark figure hung there, arms out and reaching. She startled. Her eyes adjusted to the dimmer light inside and made sense of the patterns. Dun Huss had his flying rig hung up inside his tent on a crossbar. He was fitting armored bands and fine steel chain about it. She'd never seen his flying rig readied for battle, apart from the customary single pauldron identifying him as a full dragoneer.

"This is a welcome interruption," Dun Huss said.

"Good to see you again, Ileth," Preece said.

Her first duty was to hand over the letter from the Governor, so she did so, explaining the need for the hidden ink.

"At least he's careful about keeping secrets," Preece said.

"That is my impression as well," Ileth said.

There was plenty of vinegar about the camp, of course, and Dun Huss wetted the paper lightly and the letters appeared, faint but legible.

"Governor Raal has put strict terms on your presence," Dun Huss said, reading over the letter. "You're to stay with the household at the Sag, visit the encampment only in your ordinary clothes, no uniform. You're not to perform any hazardous duty. You're not to dragon-dance. In the event of any fighting or the likelihood of fighting in the Headlands, you are to return immediately to Stesside. He wants the Captain-General's word that you will be supervised to ensure that you abide by these rules."

Securing Garamoff's word wasn't difficult; his tent was just around

a set of bushes and a camp cooking-wain from Dun Huss's. He glanced at the now-dry letter. "Eyes and ears, then. Well, I'm glad you convinced him, Ileth." He turned to Dun Huss. "There's plenty to do around camp that doesn't involve breaking this. Ileth will be kept safe, but we won't have her idle in the Raal family tradition."

Ileth didn't think that was quite fair; Raal was many things, but idle wasn't one of them.

"There is the matter of her staying at the Sag," Dun Huss said.

"We'll have her go back once the thing gets under way."

Dun Huss scratched a note on the Governor's letter and handed it to Preece. "One for the archives, I suppose. Send him a letter saying that Ileth and his terms are accepted."

Dun Huss smiled again. "Have your novice pin, Ileth?"

"Always, sir, I keep it on my sheath, right above my heart."

"They gave you one of the nicer ones, I recall, symmetrical as an arrowhead. You really should show it off. The sunlight here is so bracing, I think it would catch it well."

"Is that—"

"It's not a uniform, or an apprentice sash, is it?"

"No, sir."

"Then you should feel free to wear it. But better take off the sash."

Ileth warmed as she pinned the bit of dragon scale on her breast. Ileth was glad she'd kept her novice pin. It was like her secret promise to herself that she was still of the Serpentine and not Raal's "ward." She felt suddenly lighter, knowing what to do.

They returned to Dun Huss's tent. Ileth heard a sort of muffled metallic banging in the distance. She supposed it was some bit of blacksmithery taking place under a blanket to hide the noise.

Once back in his tent, Dun Huss looked around as if gauging if he could fit another folding sleeping pallet in the place. "Ileth, I am curious to hear the story of just how you engineered your return to us."

"I can only explain the matter in p-private."

Preece wrinkled his nose. "Ileth, we're old campfire smoke."

"It's a . . . a feminine matter, Preece."

"Oh." He glanced at Dun Huss, who nodded.

"Find us some dinner. It's about that time."

"Sir," Preece said, in the tone Ileth had learned was an acknowledgment of an order. He stepped out. A campaign camp was a good deal different from the Serpentine, Ileth was learning.

"How may I be of service, Ileth?"

She lowered her voice. "I don't know what to do, really. It's Governor Raal. He says he'll release me back to service in the Serpentine . . ."

"That's good," he said, covering the gap where she groped for words.

"He wants dragon blood," she whispered. "Not for him. For his wife."

"Ahh. Did you agree to supply him with some?"

"I said . . . I said I didn't know how I'd manage it. But given that we're expecting battle, I expected I could try. It was the only way he'd let me come."

Dun Huss's face tightened. "Follow me," he said.

"Am I . . . am I . . ." Ileth almost cried.

"Heavens no, Ileth. I'm glad you took this trouble to me. I'd just like a few witnesses about while we decide what to do."

"Witnesses?"

Dun Huss chuckled. "Don't worry, you know them."

Dun Huss found them in Dath Amrits's crowded tent, playing cards. The Borderlander had set up his own camp within Amrits's, as he had no wingmen and apprentices on staff to help him.

"Ileth, good to see you. Are you back?" Amrits asked, looking up from his hand.

"After a . . . after a fashion."

"You know, Santeel never did let me see her in the dress I bought in that jade palace. How did she look in it?"

"Positively the part."

The Borderlander nodded at her. His great sword hung from the peak of the tent like a warning. "Good, I need some help with Catherix. All the talk of mosquitoes and mites and rats has her convinced her scale's infested."

"Well, go scrape it, then," Amrits said, throwing down his cards. "I'm tired of losing to you. How am I supposed to cut a figure in Stavanzer if you cheat me out of my money."

"It's not cheating! I've told you, over and over, that you mouth the card you draw half the time."

"Snuff and dash. If you know what card I have, that's cheating."

"You could at least change things up by mouthing a different card than the one you draw and bluff me, but no. I don't think you even know you do it."

"I just say a gentleman wouldn't look, is all. Keep your eyes on your own cards, not my mouth. Even if I have lips that are the envy of half the women in Vyenn."

Dun Huss closed the tent flap and put his back to it.

"Tell them what you told me. About Governor Raal and his request."

Dath Amrits sat back, with the air of a man expecting to hear an excellent joke and ready to laugh at it. The Borderlander, as always, waited with the same indifference to her he always displayed.

Ileth told them, feeling as though she were confessing to a jury. But she'd always felt better after being honest with these men.

"At least it's for his wife and not him," Dun Huss said.

Amrits snorted. "Ha. I've been in club rooms with the man. Priest-in-the-parlor-and-a-whore-in-the-garret type, by rep—oh, I'm terribly sorry, Ileth."

Ileth shrugged. "He's claimed me as his daughter. I never said he was my father."

"Well, I apologize regardless."

"Is it a crime for him to get dragon blood?" Ileth asked.

"Not at all. All the risk is on your part," Dun Huss said. "I imagine he knows that. It might have been wiser for you to refuse him and sit the campaign out with Lady Raal."

Amrits snorted. "Dun Huss, don't be such a stick. I'd have robbed highways to get myself free of Stesside."

The Borderlander scratched his chin. "Forget the blood. There's a priest here somewhere. Your idea about marrying her—"

"That wasn't serious," Dun Huss said.

Amrits's bulging eyes bulged even more. "I should say not, Ileth. Don't think—look, we were just talking about how to get you away from the Stesside kitchen and washtub. It wasn't meant as a romantic gesture. All my dealings with women are lecherous. I just thought if all that was standing between your service was a seal on a piece of paper and a few words from a priest, well, I don't mind getting dribbled and dusted."

Ileth laughed. "You just want that silver whistle back. I told you, Fespanarax ate it in the Baronies."

"That's it, boys, she's found me out. It was a very good whistle." He fingered the replacement's lanyard speculatively. "Never quite found another like it. The fellow who originally made it died. Damned impolite of him to do a thing like that to his customers."

"Ileth," Dun Huss said, after a single chuckle for appearances' sake, "what's your estimate of the situation? Does your—errr . . . father mean to give dragon blood to help his wife? He's telling the truth about that?"

"I believe so. I can see the pain on her face, and on his face when he watches her struggle. He doesn't want it as some sort of—" Ileth groped for a word fit for mixed company.

"Good enough for me," the Borderlander said.

"I say we get her some blood, then," Dath Amrits said. Dun Huss nodded.

"You're not going to—"

Amrits cut her off. "The situation has come up before, Ileth. Somebody with influence over the Serpentine pressures us."

"Let's see how things go with the Rari," Dun Huss said. "We might all be dead in a month."

The Borderlander rubbed the back of his neck. "True enough. They have more aerial defenses than the Scab, even if they looked rusty. So where do we put Ileth?" the Borderlander asked.

"Ileth, please take my tent. Bore, you don't mind sleeping rough?" Amrits asked.

"I can bed down by Catherix. Save my legs."

"Sir—" Ileth began. "It's your tent."

"It smells like mold. You're doing me a favor, Ileth. I can bunk up with Dun Huss. At least he has the courtesy not to look at my cards."

"Your mouth," the Borderlander said.

"I fail to see the difference."

"Sir, really, I can't turn you out of your own tent," Ileth said. "I just need a corner and a mat."

"No, wouldn't be proper. Unless you want me to set up that marriage ceremony after all," Amrits said, doing something with his tongue and cheek that might have been meant to be obscene.

"You'll sleep with me, Dath," Dun Huss said. "Ileth's not allowed hazardous duty on this campaign."

8

Ileth's first council of war took place the next night, outdoors. The dragons formed a tight circle around a dimple in the ground— there were no shortages of those in the Chalk Cuts, and this one wasn't even that soggy—and the dragoneers assembled within. For this assembly, there were no wingmen or apprentices, save for Serena and Ileth, who sat together off to the side. Serena opened a secretary that fit even her smallish lap and scribbled notes on sheets of paper bound together by a horse harness ring.

Serena represented the Charge and Ileth the Governor. When Dun Huss told her that she was, in effect, standing in for the entire civilian structure of the Republic, she wished she had found somewhere to bathe. The Chalk Cuts managed to be dusty, even with winter wet lingering everywhere.

"Dragoneers," Garamoff said, "this campaign will be one for the historians. So I suggest those of you with diaries commit a few pages to it. We want them to get it right.

"The historians will want to know about it because this campaign will be as short as it is furious. We will finish the fighting before any foreign king and court hear of it. There is another reason. The Serpentine made a study of the relations with the Rari pirates. When the Vales took wing and ship against them in the past, it was an act of reprisal, the destruction of a single troublesome ship, or clearing a single

inlet where the pirates brought their prize. After each reprisal, the Rari would send over their emissaries, offer proposals to make amends, restore a ship, or return a few mates to their families. Their goal was to always make peace when we had an advantage, and threaten when they saw their star ascendant. What happened when the dragon garrison in these straits was vacated? A brief season's peace and then new outrages, and after each outrage, negotiations, assurances, demands for this in exchange for promises of that.

"That was the past. We've planned a campaign of a sort of warfare the Rari have never experienced. We intend to use the natural advantages of dragons to bring the war to their coast and not give them an hour, a moment, to breathe.

"As I speak, a three-ship convoy is being put together in the Freesand. The cargo was well guarded—wains protected by a company of professional soldiers. We know the Rari have eyes in the Freesand harbors; no doubt messengers are even now hurrying the Rari fishing boats, boats that do little fishing but a great deal of sniffing about for rich cargos. Soon the Rari coast will know that a fat, well-guarded prize is in the offing."

This was new to Ileth. There'd been nothing in the Annis Heem Strath plan for any sort of decoy.

"Those ships will set out heavily laden, yes, but inside those heavy, well-guarded chests and barrels are weapons and armor. The merchant ships and their escort vessels will run the straits not with gems and silks and spices from the Azure islands, as the Rari are imagining right now, but soldiers.

"The Rari will have to come out in force if they want them. That's where we come in. We intend to catch as many Rari ships at sea as possible. They haven't had to contend with dragons in a generation. We'll teach them to remember why their fathers watched the sky in the direction of the Headlands."

Ileth liked the sound of that. How many times had she heard a widow wonder why the Assembly didn't return with the dragons and burn the pirate ships?

"For years," Garamoff continued, "the Rari have had the advantage. Excellent position. Plenty of gold to buy aerial defenses and professional soldiers to work them. Our latest spycraft says they've neglected their dragon defenses, but we won't find out for certain until we are over their harbors. Highpoons, bombards, rockets, who knows what we'll have to contend with. It is fortunate we have so many dragoneers with experience in the attacks on the Scab."

"It couldn't be worse than the Scab," a dragoneer said to the one next to him. "It just couldn't."

Captain-General Garamoff gave no indication that he'd heard.

"You've been divided into four groups and have been practicing in those groups in cold-weather flying over the Skylake and returning. We've heard the complaints from dragon and dragoneer, but there's a reason for effort. Once battle is joined, one group will always be in the air or in battle with another approaching to take its place. Battle group, when it has loosed its fire and set the Rari on an uproar, will be replaced by Aerial Reserve group which will be replaced by Rested group which will be replaced by Resting group, with each Battle group returning to Resting and so on in rotation for the three days we estimate it will take to complete the campaign."

"Three days? A campaign of only three days?" Roben muttered to his wingman in disbelief. Falberrwrath just behind looked delighted.

"Our duty role is destruction of Rari aerial defenses, pirate craft, fortresses, and shipyards in that order. While carrying this out, we will have the support of the Freesand militia and the Republic's Auxiliaries in the recovery of as many Rari slaves as possible. Whatever the nationality. We have constructed a special ferry the likes of which the world has never seen to carry them back. Anyone: Daphines, Galantines, Hypatians, even Rari who wish to give themselves in surrender, even if they're covered in blue-green ink from forehead to toes. One of the jobs of the dragoneers in each Battle group, after their dragons have loosed, will be to drop leaflets carrying a hopeful message to the slaves, and instructions on where to assemble so that they may be

conveyed back to the Headlands. What was that you said, Amrits? 'Newssheet hawkers'?"

Amrits half rose. "A small joke, sir."

"You're righter than you know. The newssheet publishers in Sammerdam have done wonders, in great secrecy, with next to no typesetters and inkers and other workmen, printing these for us.

"Dragons and dragoneers! Eat hearty and rest well. As soon as weather serves we will depart for the Old Post to write our names into the Republic's history. Dragoneer Dun Huss will stay to answer questions."

A few of the dragoneers asked questions about the Rari. Someone asked about how they would tell Rari ships from those of the Vales, and Dun Huss explained that they would have broad white stripes painted across the decks.

Ileth looked at the cryptic notes Serena was taking.

"What sort of writing is that?"

"Asposis notehand. It's a great time saver, if you're trained to do it properly. You need to use a marking pencil, there's no time to dip your quill."

"Hard to learn?"

"It's not a quick lesson or two. But it is worth it, Ileth. Being able to do this has saved lives. I mean that in a strict literal sense. I've brought my notes in front of a jury."

The address broke up and the dragons went off to a great meal prepared, a feast to fill their fire-bladders. They would relocate to the Old Post tomorrow, unless the weather prognosticators read the clouds and winds as turning unfavorable. Ileth didn't think it would change; she'd grown up here and sensed spring warmth on the air with a change of the prevailing winds.

Garamoff and a few key dragoneers, plus Serena and Ileth trailing behind as Governor Raal's representative, went into the command tent. Much of it was taken up by an improvised table made out of what looked like an old shed roof with a map atop it.

Ileth had seen the coastline before, but this was a new map on a larger scale than the old one she'd seen exploring the many sliding drawers of the Captain's map chest. She knew from Annis Heem Strath's report that back in the days when the Old Post had dragons and dragoneers, the pirates had been adept at hiding their ships in waters where you could hardly hide a rowboat—the Captain told her a story once of a small Rari two-master they'd somehow figured a way to haul up out of the water and under a cliff overhang to hide it from the dragons.

Dun Huss reviewed the history of the fortifications that were to be the dragons' first targets, for the fortifications protected the harbors. Hundreds of years ago the Rari lands had been an outpost of the Wurm, and they built fortifications to control the straits on their southern border. The Wurm faded as a great power and the Rari settled there, gradually taking over from the Wurm like spiders taking over a half-empty barn. At first they were mercenaries manning the forts and pulling oars on the ships, then they were running the docks and collecting taxes, and finally the tiny crust of Wurm society at the top either dwindled out or took on Rari culture themselves. Supposedly, there was still one Wurm regent in the throne room of the Citadel at Lengneek, a sort of figurehead where the last gold flag with black dragonhead still flew.

It made the plan a daring one, for the Wurm could consider it an act of war. Their flag would remain unmolested, but the Lengneek Citadel would be cleared of the Rari soldiers, as it commanded the town and the Rari's principal ship-harbor. It was the only place on the Rari coast with yards and fittings for the repair of oceangoing vessels. Lengneek had to be burned, reduced, or taken.

"From a distance the fortifications look formidable," Dun Huss said. "But they're hollow as a dead tree. The Rari have fallen victim to their own success."

"How's that?" an Auxiliary officer asked. He had a dragon-scale-decorated bandolier.

"Nothing to pirate. Shipowners don't see the point of the risk, and

what little there is bribes the Rari potentates. When everyone else is poor, pirates will be too. The Rari are like parasites who killed their host and are now starving. They've lost some of those fine mercenary companies and gentleman adventurers and specialists in fighting dragons—I expect the Galantines hired them away, as we learned to our discomfort in the late war. They've resorted to grabbing fishermen and turning them into slaves. Not as lucrative as plundering merchant ships, but it hurts the families of this coast more than shipping losses."

Ileth remembered Astler saying something about a few captains seeking better plunder elsewhere.

An officer in a militia uniform spoke next. "We've sent three missions in the past three months over to Lengneek to negotiate for the return of captives, but the real purpose has been counting Rari ships. Those with vessels suitable for long journeys are out on the Inland Ocean. Of course this could be completely wrong; all we know is their biggest ships aren't in their usual places in Lengneek. Paid spies are unreliable, and the Rari are famous for paying spies bonuses to turn against their paymasters."

Garamoff studied the map.

"Your friend from the Borderlands gave us an excellent close reconnaissance," he told Dun Huss. "They've let their harbor defenses go to pot. Only one highpoon manned at night in the Harbor Fort. Unless they're being very clever about it."

"I'm not yet at ease about the Sea Fort," Dun Huss said, pointing to a fortification outside the main harbor. "No light shows at night—ever, it seems—but there are often boats about. If it is still manned, we have yet another target to reduce or the removal of the captives might be impossible."

Garamoff thought for a moment. "I will conduct a close reconnaissance myself and swim Nephalia in. I'd like a look at Lengneek myself before things get under way."

"Is that wise, sir?" Dun Huss asked. "It's not 1550. We don't need a warlord in the vanguard. A Captain-General's place is at headquarters. Let me go."

"Give me this, Hael I've swum Nephalia more times than I care to think about. Just doesn't feel right for me to go to war dry. For the rest of the campaign Nephalia and I will be conventional, in reserve on the ground or observing from the air."

"Very good, sir."

Garamoff rolled up the map. "The plan is in place, the rosters are made. If I don't come back, we just need to adjust to securing the Sea Fort, then the Harbor Fort, then the Citadel. My gut says it's empty, or just has a few men unhappy in the cold and wet there to signal an emergency. I think I can find out by having Nephalia use her neck and elevate me to something wide enough for me to climb in."

The conference moved on to logistical matters of sleeping and feeding the dragons upon their return from the Rari coast, and Taskmaster Henn covered that. Ileth filed out at Dun Huss's heels.

"Sir, wait. I'll go," Ileth said.

"Keep quiet, apprentice," Dun Huss said.

"Who's that back there?" the Auxiliary officer asked.

Ileth fought to get the words out. "Sir, do you know how cold the bay is in spring? I enjoy swimming in cold water; I was brought up on it. I've read maps; if he's been around the Azures swimming his dragon, he's not used to this."

"Ileth, I have to tell you no on this, just as he told me," Dun Huss said. "Good of you, but part of the discipline at the Serpentine is following orders. You forget that we gave the Governor our word that you would remain at camp."

"Even when your superior is about to do something daft?"

"Even then."

"Well, could I talk to him?"

"He's the Captain-General, you're in his camp and one of his dragoneers. Of course you can speak to him."

She returned to Garamoff's tent and found him studying the rosters. For once, Dun Huss trailed behind her.

"Sir, I really must speak to you."

"I'm busy, uhhh . . . Ileth," Garamoff said. "I remember you from Vyenn."

"Yes. I was the girl who didn't order anything. The tablemaid didn't care for that."

"It's because she gets a share of what she sells. I'm too busy to—"

"Ileth wants to volunteer for that reconnaissance of the Sea Fort," Dun Huss said.

His eyebrows went up in surprise. Something that might have been a smile crossed his face, making a quick trip of the journey. "Excellent, apprentice. Thank you, most commendable. Denied."

"Sir, I'm not sure you understand those waters."

"I don't have to explain myself to an apprentice, but I will to the Governor's representative: Nephalia is a strong swimmer. I can hang on to her; whatever the currents and tides, she'll get through them."

"It's not how strong your dragon is, it's how cold the water is. I know I can take it."

"I realize I'll be chilled. I'll be sure to return all the quicker and warm up."

"It's just I'm used to this, sir. I grew up on this coast. We used to swim in these waters, winter and summer."

"No. This is a reconnaissance of an enemy fortress. I'm not sending an apprentice on that, even if she's got ice in her veins."

Something in Ileth refused to let the matter go. Besides, Dun Huss had been right, they couldn't afford to risk the overall commander of the campaign before it had even begun. "Apprentice or no, I'm better qualified to do this."

"Then, Ileth, rise to my station and you can give the orders. These stand. Let's have no more of this. Any more arguments and I'll send you back to Stesside."

"Yes, sir."

"Still, I'd like to hear what you have to say about survival in cold water. Any advice?"

"Breathe deeply when you're in the water. Try to relax. It'll be painful at first. That's the key, the breath. Deep, steady regular breaths."

Garamoff turned the matter over in his head. He nodded. "Be off with you now."

Ileth bobbed and backed out of the tent.

The good weather held.

It took a day of mad activity to relocate the camp to the Old Post. They moved everything but the dragons, who would stay in the Chalk Cuts with the wingmen and a few apprenticed feeders and grooms until the last moment. Ileth missed most of it, bearing a message back to Sag House that the campaign was about to get under way.

Back at Sag House Ileth tried to lie down and sleep but she was too anxious. Garamoff had departed on Nephalia and she had a strange sense of foreboding. She was tired, but her gut and her brain teamed up on her tired muscles and forced her out of bed. She made the trek to the lighthouse and stood beneath it.

She found the Borderlander there, smoking those odd long, thin tobacco roll-ups he liked, looking out across the channel. Catherix had been one of the key dragons sent ahead to the Old Post.

"Those mountains get so much snow, it melts past midsummer, and that fort is where two bays meet the straits . . ." Ileth said.

"Nephalia will get him through. She'll get him to a bare bit of coast and light driftwood on fire if she has to."

Ileth searched the horizon and the sky above. Lights flickered on the Rari coast like distant stars.

"He's not going to fly in anywhere near the lighthouse, you know," the Borderlander said. "Too much chance of a Rari boat spotting his dragon. He'll head straight for the Headland cliffs and come in low overland. Watch there," the Borderlander said, pointing off to the north-northwest.

He was right. After what felt like hours of being sure that various shadows her eyes imposed against the dark clouds were dragons, she

finally spotted what had to be Nephalia by the faint reflective gleam of her wet scale.

She hiked up the blanket she had wrapped around her shoulders and ran. Nephalia was down, and her rider dismounting.

He had water in his hair and his face was dark with grease so the whites of his eyes seemed unnaturally bright.

"Hullo, Ileth," Garamoff said tightly. "Here to get me to admit that I was wrong?"

"Of course not, sir."

"It was a rare bad business. But the Sea Fort is a tomb. Nothing there but rubbish and birds' nests. Pulled-apart war machines, only the rotting wood and some pegs left."

"That's good."

"The breathing trick helped. Thanks for that. If you make wing-man, girl, you are welcome to do the next wet reconnaissance. I put a finger on the promise." He cut the blade of his hand across his index finger. Ileth hadn't seen the gesture before.

"Maybe a toe, sir, you're down two already."

"You wouldn't have any of that local lifewater on you, would you?"

"No."

"Oh. It'll have to be tea, then. Does no one drink coffee up here?"

Coffee? He was mistaking the Headlands for Sammerdam. "No, too expensive."

"Well, if this thing comes off, maybe prosperity will return. Come along, you can help me get the seaweed out of Nephalia."

Ileth returned to the Sag, warmed herself, and slept at last. She woke late. Comity grumbled about her already acquiring governor's daughter habits.

Gandy was at her heels, as usual. Every time she turned around, at meals, at tea, asking about soap and a basin, Gandy was there. Perhaps she was just happy to have another of her sex near her own age around. It just made her feel Astler's absence. He'd gone down to the Freesand

coast to see the bait ships being prepared in harbor. Naturally he was interested; the Aftorns were part owner of the shipping line whose flag they flew.

Ileth felt cooped up in the Sag and suggested they follow him.

"Why do you want to go down to the coast?" Gandy asked.

"I grew up in the Freesand. I miss it." That was the biggest lie she'd told since crossing the Blue Range.

"Nothing to do with my cousin?" Gandy gave her a knowing smile.

"Haven't spoken with him since we said good-bye outside the Chalk Cuts." Ileth would have added that she didn't feel right, not knowing he was safe at the Sag. She was turning into his mother.

"*Said* good-bye. *Said.*" Gandy practically leered.

"Is there anything keeping us from going now?" Ileth asked, looking for anything to break the tension of waiting for the campaign to get under way and not being able to be involved except as a supernumerary.

"No, of course not."

"Then let's get dressed."

"But I want to fix your hair. What a strange way you keep it. Do the dragons break all the mirrors at the Serpentine?"

"It's easy to clean and I don't have to do much with it."

"Well, still, it's a challenge. The back is a horror."

"Yes, I sort of guess when I cut the back."

Gandy went to work. They talked a little of wigs; Ileth told her about Shatha in the Dancers' Quarter and how wigs solved so many hair problems. "You've been south of the Cleft too long," Gandy sighed. "Wigs! They'll call you *fancy*."

They shared a smile. In the north someone who was fancy was sort of a cross between disreputable and useless. Used on a woman it could have additional connotations. That outfit Santeel had worn for her arrival at Stesside would be labeled *fancy*.

It was nice to just talk with someone like her in accent and word-play. Their sympathy in language and sensibilities eased them into friendship.

Gandy therefore didn't ask direct questions but let Ileth talk freely

about her upbringing and how she made it to the Serpentine and on dragonback, so to speak, probing her in the most agreeable sort of manner. On a different person some of her chat might sound like flattery, but Gandy was the type who liked to look for the best in someone she liked and ignore any flaws. She never mentioned Ileth's stutter, showed no signs of impatience when a word wouldn't quite come; she just fiddled with her thin daggerlike scissors while Ileth reconciled herself with her tongue.

"Mind if I get a bit daring with the back?" Gandy asked, breaking away from talk about whether the town girls from Vyenn mixed much with the dragoneers.

"I never see the back. Feel free," Ileth said.

"I have a book in my bedroom, fairy tales. There's a woodcut of this woman. Evil, a sorceress. She had short hair. It sort of angled up toward the back. I always thought she was striking. How's that sound?"

"Think it would upset Governor Raal?"

"I've never met him, but I'll say yes."

"Then yes."

He hadn't put anything in his letter about her getting her hair cut, after all.

When she was done, Gandy found her a mirror. Ileth was shocked at how short it was in the back, but at least she wouldn't be mistaken for a shepherd boy in need of a haircut.

She tried a fierce expression. She almost regretted the metal pins above her eye. She could curse the Rari out of their slaves. "So that's my spirit, is it?" Ileth said.

Gandy looked worried. "I don't understand. You don't like it?"

"Just something your cousin said. I do like it, truly."

Ileth went to her bag and got out her small supply of cosmetics. She showed Gandy how to line her eyes, darken her lashes, and add some shadow that brightened them.

Ileth added a little to her own face. She tipped her hair back, glared, and intoned: *"I curse you and three generations of yours to despair and sudden doom!"*

Gandy laughed. "That's better. You were so serious the first time you were here. I told Astler that you acted like you had a dragon claw lodged somewhere hard to get at."

"Was I really like that?"

"Well, you could match Comity frown for frown."

Ileth tried different angles in the mirror. "I'm not sure about these bangs."

"I'll fix the front with a pin and a bit of green creeper. It'll look like springtime and go with your eyes. Then we'll be done."

They had to saddle the horses themselves. Comity had said everyone at the Sag had their own work, and if they wanted to ride down to the Freesand for the day, they'd have to saddle their own horses. And not forget feed, the horses would need to eat while they visited.

It was not much of a delay. Soon they were riding through the little village Ileth had flown over that winter. Gandy rode very well, Ileth poorly, but the practice would do her good. The place seemed to be crawling with soldiers.

"You want to take the crest road along the hills or the coast?"

Ileth didn't much feel like riding by her old Lodge, and the coastal road took you past its doorstep. "The hills. I'd enjoy the view."

"It's longer. We wouldn't be back until dark."

"You spent half the morning fiddling with my hair."

"I wanted to make you look nice for my cousin."

Gandy had to hold her horse back on the trip, as Ileth's seemed content to proceed west at a pleasant amble. The horses weren't saving them much time, just effort.

They passed a trio of shepherds just where the road started to drop from the Headlands toward the muddy flats of the Freesand Coast. Or rather, men pretending to be shepherds. For one thing, they only had five sheep. Ileth, in all her years in the north, had never seen three shepherds watching over five sheep. Three tough-looking, young male shepherds, with an older one giving commands to the others, and

"shepherd's" clothes cut from blankets and draped over and wrapped about their other clothing. She suspected they were soldiers, watching over the road, there to encourage wanderers heading into the area of the Headlands around the Sag and the Old Post to travel elsewhere.

Ileth was glad the hills obscured the Lodge, yet she fought an urge to ride to the highest familiar hilltop so she could look down on its roof.

They came into Yalmouth town midafternoon, hungry and tired. Ileth couldn't say whether she was pleased or displeased that no one noticed her. Several young people called out to Gandy and inquired about her. Gandy used the same response: "Don't you know Ileth?" and even that didn't bring a smile, or frown, of recognition.

Well, she'd never made much of an impression on the Freesand Coast.

They asked if anyone had seen her cousin but had only one helpful answer, and even that one wasn't very helpful; a priest who knew the family said he'd seen him hanging about the docks.

What they did see was the most active Freesand harbor Ileth had ever witnessed. The subterfuge with the ships had been well carried out. They'd finished loading them with the fake cargo, going so far as to accidentally drop a barrel and have it leak whale oil all over the wharf. Ileth thought that clever. Whale oil was a rich cargo, sure to attract the interest of the Rari and their spies, who were no doubt already pulling across Pine Bay with the news of the laden convoy. They chanced the docks but there was no sign of him, just men loading supplies and gear. The boats had thick rope webs piled about the sides; they'd been pulled up to the masts to keep boarders off. Ileth wondered if he'd gone on board one of the ships.

Walking her little Freesand town of Yalmouth, little of her face visible between high collar and pulled-down riding hat, she felt just as much a stranger as she had been in the Baron's Galantine village, even if every painted door and brick chimney wasn't a familiar sight. The markings seemed like the faces of old friends.

The town was the same as ever, with the little sundry shop with the

sweets in the window she'd hungered for as a child, the ship-chandler and the bootmaker, and the tea shop that opened early with cheap pies for the fishermen setting off to their boats, the tinker and his pots and tureens and kettles. The houses where the front rooms were devoted to hair-cutting and wigs, or pulling and replacing teeth, odd little hovels with secondhand furnishing and clothes long out of fashion that could be bought cheap for their material and buttons or recutting, herbalists with their ointments, poultices, and infusions.

And there was the sign for the Standing Gull, the old warehouse that had been turned into a grog shop where the old men mixed with the young when the boats came in, where the beer was a chancy business depending on which farm had offered the best price, but the singing and playing were the best the little village had to offer.

They stopped by a smithery and stable. A few militia messengers and their horses stood about, probably waiting for orders. Gandy thought it a good place to ask; Astler had friends there from his summers training with them, but none had seen him. Gandy whiled away some time in flirtation and they received an invitation to dine with the militia.

Ileth looked at the sky. There were low clouds. It had been a warm day, and at this time of year, a warm day was often followed by rain or fog off the cool gulf.

"We might want to head back, unless you like riding in fog," Ileth said.

"It usually stays low and close to the bay this time of year," Gandy replied. "We'll be above it once we're out of town."

They ate a short dinner with the militia youths in the beer garden behind the Two Lanterns, the town's only inn. The one who sat next to Ileth stared at the scar over her eye and said that she seemed very familiar, but Ileth didn't explain herself. It grew darker, but Gandy ignored her hints about leaving. The youths dropped cryptic hints that they knew a great secret but didn't dare let on. Gandy, who probably knew more than any of them, did her best to draw them out.

"Perhaps we should stay in town," Ileth said, looking at the now-dark sky, wondering if that had been Gandy's aim all along.

Gandy now looked worried. "Or we missed him on the way back, if he took the shorter coast road, sensible fellow that he is in all matters not having to do with his heart."

In the end, they resaddled their rested and fed horses. The militia was only to happy to help out an Aftorn and her friend.

As it turned out, it wasn't much of a fog, more of a mist, with the three-quarter waxing moon showing off and on through the clouds. They were just starting up the hills outside town when Ileth heard a bell ringing from the harbor and a distant crack—the sound of a meteor being fired.

"Hold up," Ileth said.

She could make out the Yalmouth rooftops, but the mist obscured the water. She saw a mist-muted flash on one of the ships and heard that faint cracking sound again.

"Sure, that's a meteor!" Ileth said. She'd heard them now and then in the hills above the Serpentine as apprentices learned about the weapons.

She and Gandy gaped at each other. Some terrible confusion must be—

No, it had to be the pirates. They'd heard about the ships and rather than risk letting them slip by in the straits had come right into the harbor to take them.

Ileth, like everyone else in the Freesand, had always assumed that the shifting currents, sandbars, and rockpiles of the shallow, southern end of Pine Bay made a raid by boat impossible. The Rari had done the impossible.

Ileth reached over and grabbed Gandy's wrist. "Dragoneers need to know of this."

"Yes. We must return at once!"

"You must. You're the better rider and speed is everything. I could never keep up. Go. Ride as fast as you safely can. If there was ever a time to put yourself and your horse to the test, this is it."

Gandy gulped, her eyes wide and staring.

"Ileth! I don't want to leave you alone with Rari attacking the harbor!"

"I grew up here. I know hiding holes and lookouts. They're after the ships. Just go. Get to the Old Post and scream that the Rari are taking the decoy ships in Yalmouth and don't stop screaming until the dragons are up."

"But you!"

"Go!" Ileth said, striking Gandy's animal on the haunch. It took off, Gandy standing in the stirrups. Her horse wanted to go with its friend but she wrenched it around and, using her heels as hard as she could, urged it back into town. She jostled down the main street, hearing the alarm bells ring. The horse didn't like the noise and kept shying this way and that.

Where were those militia? They should be out.

Her mind couldn't have been clearer, continually sorting and re-sorting things to do as if she were a busy housewife with a long list of errands in the village. She felt oddly divided from herself, watching with amusement this odd collection of limbs in riding leggings steering a horse, badly, into the chaos of a pirate raid.

She found their militia dinner partners at the stables, saddling their own horses.

"Militia!" Ileth shouted, riding up. "I'm a dragoneer," she said, hoping to put enough authority in her voice to stretch the truth, tapping the bit of dragon scale she'd put on.

"You two." She pointed at two already on their horses. If she'd learned one thing supervising the littles in the Lodge, it was that you had to be clear about who was to do what or nothing would be done. "Ride as fast as you can to the Headlands, the Old Post. As soon as you find anyone with authority, tell them the Rari have attacked the ships at Yalmouth."

That was in case Gandy fell or failed. She told the rider with the biggest horse—that counted for something, didn't it?—to ride the long road to Stavanzer and spread the alarm at every village and crossroads. Governor Raal and whatever Vale Republic forces were there would need to know as well. She supposed it was as good a way as any for the north to learn that a war had started.

"There have to be soldiers, not militia, real soldiers about some-where. Do you know where they are?" Ileth asked. "They were to go on the decoy ships."

The remaining two glanced at each other, wondering how this stut-tering girl knew so much.

"I know what you've been hinting at dinner. If you know where they are, go to them. They have to be near the harbor. My guess is they're at Cross Landing, they could take boats all the way to the ships from there, but you may know better."

They spurred their horses for the hills, in the direction of Cross Landing. So she'd guessed right. Ileth smiled, thinking of all the times she'd been called an idiot because of her stutter.

She had time to enjoy the sensation for two breaths before Yal-mouth fell into chaos.

Dogs barking, screams and crashing, and in a sudden swirl of heads and legs a gang of Rari appeared in the street, blocking the main road leading up into the Headlands, six or so with some stragglers be-hind. One already had a screaming child under his arm; another had a basket full of silver and plate.

They saw Ileth, or perhaps the horse, or perhaps both. They loped toward her in a bandy-legged charge.

Ileth was not enough of a horsewoman to trick-ride through this gang. She wheeled the horse in the opposite direction and broke into a trot as she slipped her boots out of the stirrups. The trot led to the wharf and more Rari, equally interested in her and her horse.

She sacrificed the Aftorns' saddle horse and jumped off, running into an alley, listening to the bare feet of the Rari behind. Her heels sounded like a carpenter's hammer in the alley as she ran—they could follow her through the dark by sound alone.

But she knew the town and they didn't. She'd played in these alleys and back rows and gardens all her life. She knew where there was space between a chicken coop and a wall to hide, or who had a wooden panel you could remove to get under the back steps, or where there was room under a fence to crawl.

Perhaps most importantly, that shelf on the spear-fisherman's chimney that let you access his roof. A few frantic dodges, ducks, twists, and turns and she was on the roof, with the Rari calling to each other from backyards. Ileth slithered over to the darker side of the roof.

From the rooftop, lying on her belly, Ileth peered down at the street she'd just made a confused loop to come upon again. There was another party of Rari moving down the road toward the harbor, six herding a throng of captives.

The Rari wore their wealth. She'd never seen so much gold, silver, and gemwork on anyone, man or woman. They wore it in rings for finger and ear, in twisted silver snakes about their necks, set into thick girdles, on bracers and bracelets, and every weapon hilt gleamed with precious metal and gems, some now slick with blood. Instead of art hung up in their homes, they carried it about on their own skin, for wherever there wasn't clothing there were intricate blue designs, or bonelike icons, perhaps letters or a code.

She watched a Rari, with a fistful of chains and shackles dangling, raise it and flail the painted design of a door three or four times, apparently out of pure spite, scarring the paintwork.

Ileth groped around on the roof for something to hurl but came up empty. Oh, for her old sling and a few good stones. She searched the peak, maybe there was a loose brick atop the chimney—

She realized she had an excellent view of the bay, the docks, and the waiting ships, the small boats the Rari had used to row into the harbor all about the ships like ants attacking a beetle. Patches of mist drifted across the bay like spirits. Was Astler on one of those ships, bleeding on a deck, or herded below with other captives? She searched the bay as though she could spot him by force of will alone. But in that moment's searching clarity she spotted lights leading out of the harbor, widely spaced—the most distant one disappeared even now as new mist blew in.

The Rari had planted channel markers so they could sail the ships right out in darkness. Clever. Very clever.

She slipped off the roof and, stepping carefully and shifting in and out of yards and alleys, made for the waterfront, stopping to listen at every corner and alley.

She crept about in the shadows in an unlit wharf filled with fishing traps and nets hung to dry. She hunted until she discovered what she wanted, a little service craft that could be rowed by a single person pulling at the oars. It was tied so you couldn't see it from the main harbor area.

Checking and listening, she hurried out onto the dock and dropped into it.

The boat was a small, flat-bottomed thing, very much like the one the Captain had sent her and the twins out to Dragonback Reef on so long ago. It was probably towed behind a larger fishing boat and used to row about and check traps or open and close nets. It had a pair of big buckets in it, empty now but probably meant to hold lobsters or crabs.

"Hssst!" A hissing voice startled her. "Whaty're doing? That's my boat."

She saw three men shivering in the water under the dock. "Get in here, miss. Chill's not so bad once you get used to it."

One seemed intent on continuing the argument she interrupted: "We should try and sneak up the coast in the water a bit. They might occupy the town. They're after people. Look, there's another lot being taken on to the ship."

He was right, a boat full of captives was being rowed out to one of the captured ships at anchor even now.

The biggest of the three, a powerful-looking man with a short beard, said: "No. They'll fill those ships and go."

"I want to get out on the bay . . ." She pointed to the first of the signal poles used as channel markers. At first she was just thinking of dousing a lantern or two. With the help of these men she could cause much more confusion to the Rari.

"Are you mad, miss?" a man with wide, watery eyes said. The sorting and cataloging part of her mind noted they'd been calling her "miss" rather than "girl." Probably the doing of her good riding clothes

and high collar. "The Rari boats are everywhere, pulling in with captives."

"We'll be out beyond them." Ileth looked around, then untied a line. "I'm game. You afraid to get them back for this?"

Watery Eyes shook his head. "Not worth the risk. There's bound to be boats of them, rowing back with loot."

The biggest sucked in his cheeks as he thought. "Best you can do is delay them, miss. They can nose their way out, towing with boats."

"That's all we need. Delay. The dragons will be on them."

"Dragons?" the big man asked.

It wouldn't hurt to tell them; even if all of them were taken, the Rari would find out soon enough.

"The Headlands are full of them."

"Someone said they had a couple at the Chalk Cuts. Burning swamp," said the man who wanted to move up the coast.

"She's barmy," Watery Eyes said.

"No," the big man said, as though a key had turned in his mental lock. "They're there. I heard Klinker sold his whole flock of two years off and I said, 'To who,' and he said, 'I don't know, Governor's agent wouldn't say,' and I've seen pigs driven to the Headlands so I believe the girl. I'll row you out to those poles, miss."

"Do you know how to sound?" the man in the back asked.

"Not really," Ileth said. It wasn't quite a lie, she hadn't done it since she was eleven or so.

"Then you'll need help." He moved to join them.

"Well, Royf, afraid to do what the girl's not?" the big one asked Watery Eyes.

"Seems to me you're taking as big a risk with dragons as you are with Rari. I'm staying dark and wet."

Her volunteers climbed into the boat. She took the tiller. The big man took off his wet boat cloak and draped it over the buckets. He took the oars in a confident grip. Ileth cast off and sat down.

He pulled hard. At a distance they might be mistaken for another Rari boat, quick to make a getaway with valuables.

"To love and havoc," she whispered to herself, the old dragoneer toast.

"M'name's Drod, not that I'm likely to keep it beyond tonight if we meet a Rari launch," the bulky fellow at the oars said.

"Ileth."

"Ileth? Galantine name. The Old Captain had—" Another key unlocked a memory. "You're the one that ran off and joined the dragoneers!"

Ileth tried not to smile on this grim night.

The boat pulled past a long pole, such as a boatman would use to move a punt along in shallows, with a keg tied to it so the keg floated upright. A lantern stood fixed to the weighted keg. It was a brilliant arrangement; the keg would rise and sink on the loops with the tide, the light atop it rising and falling like a mobile lighthouse.

"Aren't you gonna move it?" Drod asked.

"This one's in sight from the ships."

The men exchanged shrugs. The wind was fresher out on the water now, blowing sheets of mist about like laundry loose on the breeze.

The men muttered words about the depth. "Yeah, we're in the channel."

Ileth knew the fluky channels at the southern end of the bay, sand shifting with the seasons. As much as a dragon-length or two would ground the boats on a sandbar, or leave them hopelessly lost at night.

They heard oars ahead. Drod hissed at everyone to hush.

The Rari hadn't left the chain of lights unguarded. It was a small boat, just a rowboat, really, with two Rari rowing watch on the signals, probably making sure none had gone out.

It occurred to her that in the dark, from a distance, the hogsheads in the boat would look like people. She rearranged them and the wet boat cloak to look like a huddle of people.

"Cry. Sob. You're slaves," Ileth said. "Help, oh help," she sobbed loudly by way of encouragement. "Help us!" she called to the Rari boat, in her thickest northern Montangyan.

The man at the pole hunched down and let out a halfhearted moan.

"That's not loud enough," Drod said.

"I'm not acting, that's my back. Rheumatism. I haven't been on a sounding pole in years."

The Rari boat didn't challenge them, didn't even change course. It kept rowing for the ships. Maybe it wasn't a watch, maybe it was a Rari captain wondering what was taking so long.

They reached the next marker. This one she tried to pull up. It was weighted, but with the help of Drod she got it into the boat.

"Which way?" Drod asked.

"East, toward the rock ridge," Ileth suggested.

"The Captain did his job teaching you these waters," Drod said. "It shoals fast there."

They pulled hard. Ileth found comfort that they were headed toward the shore.

"Drop it here," the man in the bow advised, leaning tiredly on the pole. "I can barely see the next."

They repeated the process with the next, moving it from west to east. This time, they found a muddy bank.

"Told you, rock ridge," Drod said, though Ileth had been the one to suggest it.

She figured out how to get the pole out of the weight and they dropped it into the mud. Then she jumped out of the boat, dragging the poled lantern.

"I'll line it up with the other," she told them. "If you hear oars, just pull for shore."

Even without the weight, the marker was heavy thanks to the pole and lantern. Ileth dragged it along the sandbar about sixty paces and then splashed out into the shallow water. It was chilly enough to start her breathing hard. She planted the signal pole, digging it deep into the soft mud, and hurried back to the bar.

Leaking water from her boots, she sloshed back to the edge of the bar. The boat was gone. She thought she heard the creak of an oarlock, but it might have been her imagination.

"Hey!" she said into the night air in a ridiculous sort of breathy cry. She nerved herself. "Drod!" she called.

At any moment now one of the captured ships might be run aground and the sandbar could be filled with very confused and angry Rari. There was nothing to do but swim for it. She ripped the tear in the overdress farther to give her legs more room, then tied her muddy boots together and put them around her neck. She waded out into the water.

The danger was losing her direction. She'd swum out to sandbars more times in her youth than she could think of. The Freesand had a lot of shifting mud flats, but no ripping currents or whirlpools or sharks. About all you risked was a pinch from a disturbed crab.

As it turned out, wading was good enough for what felt like a considerable distance. Using the first of her false pole-lights as a guide, she struck out, breathing deep in the cold water. Every forty strokes or so she tested the depth with her feet, treading water and resting.

Lights again, lanterns on ship masts. The Rari were taking their captures out. Full-rigged ships, even empty, would be as valuable as the cargo. She treaded water again, watching one approach the marker, hearing orders carried over the water in the Rari tongue. They were probing the channel with a line to be sure.

They passed her false light and she heard a Rari astride the bowsprit say something over his shoulder. She didn't understand the tongue but he spoke again, more urgently. Someone else pointed to her next light, the one near the bar, and the ship stayed on course.

Another followed behind, she could now see, guided by the mast-lights of the first. It was not exactly on the same course, perhaps a boat length or two off to give plenty of room to veer if the first ran aground. One couldn't fault the Rari for their seamanship.

The first struck, hard enough so the stern rose and the lanterns in the masts swung like pendulums. Even Ileth heard the thumps and shouts. The ship's bell rang a warning, and the vessel following behind turned. The Rari of the second boat, though proceeding slowly, took

in sail and turned and still shuddered to a halt in the same muddy reach.

Ileth searched for the third. Perhaps the Rari were satisfied with just two.

The two grounded ships settled into quiet. Ileth didn't know if the tide was rising or falling. She hadn't examined the sandbar that closely but she suspected it was on the rise; the Rari weren't so stupid as to try to take out ships in the dark on a falling tide.

"We call it the Freesand for a reason," she whispered. She swam gently on her back away from the ships.

Her hands brushed into sea grasses and she was able to stand again. She waded toward a hummock of muddy weeds; it couldn't be the Freesand Coast as there was water beyond, so another sandbar, a more permanent one, it appeared. She squatted in the grass and watched events. The Rari put their crew into boats and started working the ships off, dropping anchors and using the power of capstans to drag the ships off the muddy bottoms. She knew it was tough work; a ship well stuck in mud would be held on as though gripped. More and more details of the ships stood out; the wind had shifted and the fog was clearing.

As the mist cleared Ileth saw the lights of the Freesand harbor and the third ship still at its moorings. The sails looked odd and the spars hung at a strange angle, as though damaged in battle. Had the soldiers arrived in time to retake it?

Ileth heard a rustle overhead and then there was a dragon, flying low and fast enough that its wingtips splashed in the bay. It didn't use its flame—it dragged its tail through the water, struck one of the ships' boats at work with the anchor line, and staved in the side. The bow flew into the air, turning over like a pan-flipped egg. Ileth saw Rari sailors thrown into the chilly waters.

Another dragon dived, white or silver, she couldn't be sure. Perhaps Catherix. The dragon went at the ship's masts from the bow, grabbing the bowsprit cable and dragging its tail through the rigging. Ileth

heard wood crack and lines twang and pop as they parted. The bowsprit was completely snapped and the mainmast sagged sideways in a mass of tangled lines and a crashing sound like a treefall.

She couldn't help but stand up and cheer for all she was worth as chaos erupted all around. She didn't care if every Rari in the Freesand heard her.

Something did. She heard a hard flap, felt a gust of wind, and the next thing she knew she was redoused as a green dragon splashed down six paces out into the water.

"Hullo, Ileth," Dath Amrits said from his saddle. Etiennersea displayed her teeth in a draconic grin. "Would you care for a ride, or do you wish to swim back to the Headlands?"

"I'll ride and thank my luck all the way," Ileth said, wading toward her rescuer.

"Luck has nothing to do with it. I was looking for you out here," Amrits said, offering an arm for her to hook on to.

"Really?"

"Of course. Town in an uproar, two stolen ships aground, alarm bonfires burning, soldiers chasing Rari through the alleys like loose chickens, bells ringing, pirates in boats pulling this way and that, confusion everywhere. I told old Tinny, 'Ileth has to be in the middle of this,' and to keep an eye peeled, didn't I, dear? And I was right."

The dragon tilted her head up so she could look back at them, staring through upside-down eyes. It was an unsettling move Ileth had never seen a dragon perform. Leave it to Amrits's dragon to be unconventional. "No, it was that human girl from the house crying and begging that you look for her. Now that your promise is fulfilled, I thought we might want to do something about the pirates, as they're threatening our Republic's good citizens."

"You could follow those lanternlike lights out to some Rari ships, I'm sure," Ileth said. "They sent the boats in from somewhere."

Flames shot up on the sea, far out beyond the sandbars. "A dragon got there ahead of us."

Dath Amrits contented himself with gathering news. He managed to find the captain of the soldiery who'd rushed down to the harbor at news of the Rari attack and determined that more dragons weren't needed. The five others who flew out with him were ample to turn the Rari's daring raid into a first-class disaster for them. The prisoner count was in the hundreds already, and they were still finding more hiding in alleys and trying to swim out to the sandbars.

Ileth engaged in her own hunt, for Astler or any news of him. No one in Yalmouth had news. Captives were still being ferried off the crippled ships, now floating again under guard in the calm waters between mudbanks.

Amrits tore her away from the search and they caught a fortunate wind. Flying back to the Old Post was only a matter of the time it took for the moon to set.

In the new, much more obvious and concentrated dragoneer encampment Garamoff's body had gone jerky in his excitement. He limped about gesticulating like a madman, pointing with his remaining fingers. "They say there's no such thing as luck. I don't believe it. Our luck is in for once. Damn! Damn! So much to do. Damn!"

He went about the camp shouting orders. "First wing, on the line! To hell with the moon, we'll go without it."

Dragoneers and their retinues rushed about, buckling themselves into their flying rigs, gathering and checking gleaming weapons with fresh strings, hanging religious icons about their necks or wrists or tucking them into their boots . . . their dragons shaking out their wings and having last coatings of salve applied, nostrils opening and shutting and *griff* rattling in excitement.

Ileth wished she had something to do other than keep out of the way.

Dragoneers Roben and Vor Rapp appeared out of the darkness. Vor Rapp had apprenticed under Roben. He was supposed to be a good fighting dragoneer. Roben grabbed her arm, pulled her along, and shoved her toward Vor Rapp. "Don't stand there, apprentice, go help with that gray. Aurue. He's asked for you."

Garamoff was shouting at one of his wingmen: "No choice, there's always the chance they've heard dragons are about. I'll lead the second wave myself. Their defenses will be organized by that time. Mark the dragons that flew into Yalmouth as 'resting.'"

The dragons formed a rough line on the flat ground near the light-house. It was a good spot to take flight; there was a cliff to add speed. Ileth hurried along with Vor Rapp toward Aurue and then Garamoff was beside them.

Aurue was at the very end of the line of dragons, standing stiffly. He nuzzled Ileth. "I'm glad you are here," he said.

"Aurue and Vor Rapp," Garamoff said, once he was where the gray could hear. "You'll have to marker-burn instead of Catherix; she and the Borderlander are still out. Our target is the Harbor Fort. You've both seen the sketches, above and beside. There's not much light from town and no moon. The first wing will need that marker to attack accurately so there's no time wasted over target, getting shot. You have to burn something in the Harbor Fort. If it's a launcher, all the better, but don't be picky. Approach by stealth, low, start as large a fire as possible, and return. A great deal depends on you."

Vor Rapp looked as though someone had drained the blood from him through a tap in the ankle. His lips were white. "Understood, sir," he said, turning his signet ring over and over again on his finger in thought.

Ileth helped Sifler, who looked splendid in his sword and sash and perhaps just a little like a boy playing dress-up with his father's uniform, adjust Aurue's saddle. She checked and double-checked cinches and fastenings. Vor Rapp stood with his foot in the stirrup, ready to mount. He couldn't get his flying gauntlets on over the ring so he handed it to Sifler.

She passed around the front of the dragon and felt Aurue's nose.

The dragon's head trembled against her. "I'm no battle dragon, Ileth." Ileth wanted to cry. She soothed him as best as she could, stroking him under the jaw where she could feel the little hearts assisting with moving the blood up his long neck. They were pounding furiously.

"Ileth, my dragoneer asks for you," Sifler said.

Aurue sniffed at her.

"You have a soothing air about you. I feel . . . better."

"Whatever's the matter?" Sifler said.

"Fear," Aurue said. His pronunciation of Montangyan has regressed to what it was when Ileth first knew him, and she had some difficulty understanding him. "I in difficulties moving."

He'd had to be talked into going out that night after the eggs too. Well, not every dragon was fierce.

Sifler stifled a laugh. "A sheepish dragon. Who would have thought cow—"

"Shut up, Sifler," Ileth said tightly.

"First wave: mount," Dun Huss called across the line.

Mnasmanus made a deep tone sound. It felt like it traveled through the ground and up Ileth's legs.

Vor Rapp climbed into the saddle and Sifler checked that his crossbow was secure, slung neatly under and around Aurue, and double-checked the safety tether to Vor Rapp's thick, furry flying girdle and main saddle girth.

"Ileth, I want you to know . . ." Vor Rapp said.

Aurue clacked his teeth. Ileth had never heard him make that sound before. She turned away from Vor Rapp. The dragon looked wide-eyed and anxious.

She caressed the dragon, felt his neck-hearts beating furiously behind his *griff*. "You're so fast, Aurue. They won't see you coming and you'll be gone before they know you've been."

"Aides, retreat," Dun Huss shouted once to his right, once to his left.

"See you . . . see you when you get back," Ileth said quietly in Aurue's ear. Then to Vor Rapp: "G-good hunting, dragoneer."

She hurried off, following Sifler back to the line.

"I can't believe this is happening," Sifler said. "Can you?"

It had been happening all night for Ileth, so she said nothing.

"Make ready!" Dun Huss called.

The dragons and dragoneers exchanged words. Ileth watched Vor Rapp give Aurue a reassuring pat on his shoulder, and calls of *ready* came back. Aurue's head and neck were unnaturally stiff and pointed forward. Ileth felt physical pain as she read the dragon's fear and balled her fists against it.

This time Dun Huss shouted: "First wave: dragons up!"

Ileth couldn't help but wonder what she'd be feeling, in a dragon's saddle and with an armored pauldron on, hearing that ancient call.

Mnasmanus opened his wings like a whip; a resounding crack broke across the line like lightning had struck the ground.

The dragons scuttled forward. Aurue hesitated for just a moment and then rushed off with the rest. Faster than the rest. Lighter and younger than the rest. He was first in the air, as it turned out, and climbed fast.

The night turned quiet. Perfectly ordinary late-spring night, chilly but the wind caressed rather than reaching for your bones.

The second wave readied with less chaos than the first, as they'd had time to prepare, and Roben on Falberrwrath lined the dragons up as Garamoff walked the line issuing last-minute orders with a good deal more *if-then* to them. Ileth had no duty, and though she wished to return to Sag House to see if there was news of Astler, she climbed the lighthouse steps to watch the opposite coast. A green-sashed apprentice wearing a uniform that looked as though it had been put together from odds and ends at the last minute watched the eastern horizon through a telescope. She recognized him as one of the clerks from the Masters' Hall.

The telescope stood on a tripod. Wheels and counterweights helped aim the thing, or perhaps hold it steady. To Ileth, the shore opposite was a smear with faint flicks of light from distant fireflies.

"Hullo, Ileth," the apprentice said, tapping a marking stick against an open page on a notebook. "You found your way back to us."

Taskmaster Henn was suddenly beside her. He was breathing hard.

"Mad beginning," Henn said. "At dawn you should—"

"Ahh," the apprentice at the telescope said.

A light, brighter than the rest, flared up, faded, but it could still be distinguished on the horizon like the Evenstar, twice as bright as any of the others. Could it be Aurue's fire? The apprentice studied matters through the telescope, then jotted something down.

The apprentice spoke without taking his eye away from the telescope. "Ileth, do me a favor and uncover that lantern. Don't move it, just uncover it." He waved behind.

"I've got it," Henn said, who was nearer anyway. He touched the conical shield carefully to check if it was hot, then lifted it. The lantern had a protective panel to keep it from disturbing their night-eye, but it shone brightly out toward the dragoneer camp. Ileth heard a cheer go up. Someone blew a hunting horn, and more cheers answered it.

Ileth ignored the noise. Sparks of dragon-flame could just be distinguished on the far coast, like fireflies glimpsed in a meadow. Ileth felt a cold thrill. It had begun.

The second wave called *dragons up* and took off.

She saw two dark objects, as big as the biggest ship she'd ever seen, shaped like oval floating rocks, moving toward the far coast across the straits. At first they seemed to be moving by, well, magic, but then she spotted a wave burst a dragon-length or so in front of one of the craft. That was no whale breaching, it was a dragon head.

"What are those?" she asked, but she had already guessed. Some kind of covered barge.

"We call them the 'sea turtles'—it's something we've been working on for a while." Taskmaster Henn became animated. "The idea came from those Galantine barges with the ladders they designed for taking the Scab. These are bigger versions built for sea use. They're like a turtle shell, hollow inside, with iron plates like scale on the top and sides. Barrels full of coconut coir lashed outside for extra buoyancy. Almost unsinkable. There are pumps inside for pumping out or spraying water across the top shell to wash off burning projectiles. The timbers are thick and reinforced and angled in such a way that most missiles—

stingers and heavy meteors and things of that nature—will bounce off. Or just miss, they ride so low in the water. Try and ram them and they'll most likely just bounce a bit, something to do with the oval shape. Try and board them and you'll have to axe through the top timbers while being poked with pikes from below. In theory the troops inside can make them spiny as a porcupine. The dragons solve the maneuverability issue. They pull them through the water and then push them up on shore or near enough, so you only get your feet wet."

Ileth nodded. She'd "plunked," as she'd once heard Annis Heem Strath style it, the night of the egg theft. But this was something new. The plan Annis Heem Strath had laid out provided for the transport of ships with fishing craft, coasters, things of that nature.

"They're taking troops over. That's the King's Legion going in."

"King's Legion?"

"I know, it's the Montangyan Legion now. Or just the Legion. Traditions die hard. A lot of us still call it the King's Legion."

Ileth, who sometimes grew confused about this or that guard company or even the more famous Battalions of the Republic, knew about the Legion. It was a formation mostly made up of those of foreign birth, or convicts of minor crimes who wanted a fresh start under a new name.

"They will come back with our people?"

"You have the idea. Bring soldiers over, bring the Rari captives back. If we can keep the Duke and Duchess from joining in the battle. We went over the plan with them again and again, but when the anvil chorus starts, no plan is safe with those two."

"I should like to meet them."

"Easier said than done. They hardly speak a word of Montangyan. The Duke says he's too old to learn another damned human tongue. The handlers use Drakine, or sort of a pidgin that's mostly Drakine, anyway."

She tried to share the Taskmaster's excitement at the new ships or barges or whatever the turtles were, but failed. Ileth wouldn't be easy until she saw Aurue again. She descended the lighthouse and passed

through camp as the third wave assembled. If it hadn't been a disaster, the first wave would be returning just at first light.

It wasn't a disaster. They didn't suffer anything worse than scattered meteor fire, and Mnasmanus had holes in his wings. Aurue landed first, somewhat blackened by soot clinging to the oily residue about his snout. Ileth danced and ran as she went to him.

"Overdid it making sure a storehouse was well alight," he said, examining his wings.

Vor Rapp's battle rig was splattered with vomit. His eyes were white against oily soot. "He's an acrobat. I suppose you know that," he said to Sifler and Ileth, who helped him out of his harness and tether.

So it went, wave after wave going out and returning. It became a blur to Ileth, which wing was landing and which was taking off. They had a great wooden board, weirdly like the job roster in the old Manor under the Matron, complete with wooden nameplates hanging from hooks, organizing the three wings and the reserve.

She knew there were other maps, a large one and multiple smaller ones, where the sketches of the Rari strongholds, docks, and walls were annotated, and updated by the nearsighted Gruss, who took reports from returning dragoneers and made fresh diagrams according to the reports, rapidly filling sheets of paper with quick sketches to be used by the following waves.

The cooks, both Serpentine and those impressed from the Auxiliaries, worked like mad. Meals, everything from fish to whole chickens, were doused in rough flour and fried using metal grids plunged into kettles full of cooking lard. Everything possible was done to add fats to the dragon diet to keep their fire-bladders full. The dragons returning from their flight stuffed food down their throat and moved off the landing fields to collapse, ignoring the weather and the usual desire for enclosure. Dragoneers and the ground staff snatched food and sleep when they could, working on their dragons even while the great creatures slept, sewing up rends in wings, pulling broken scale and slapping on plaster, then fixing a bit of stiffened leather as a temporary cap,

and applying salve to muscles and ligaments. It was organized, exhausting madness.

When the dragoneers ate and slept Ileth couldn't begin to guess. Perhaps they did it in the saddle on the way over and back. No one had time to bathe, and soon a thick layer of greasy dirt and soot built up, leaving the famous Vale Dragoneers looking like a team of chimney sweeps.

Ileth worked until her hands were raw and painful. She hauled food, wing repair gut, tankards of ale, and baskets of bread, anything the dragoneers called for, sleeping wherever she sat down until the next watch kicked her awake.

But it had its intended effect. The Rari were driven from point after point. Ileth heard that even fishing craft without a single armed man were able to "go over" and bring back freed slaves, who were taking advantage of the chaos to slip away, following the crude maps and instructions on the dropped leaflets.

It was close to dark on the second day when Sifler pulled Ileth to her feet from a dry patch of ground on the side of the lighthouse.

"Aurue and Vor Rapp, returning." Sifler was dark-eyed with exhaustion.

Ileth groaned to her feet and they trotted to the open field where the dragon wings took off and landed.

Aurue circled the field an extra time; he seemed to be talking over his shoulder to his rider. Finally, he landed, very gently, taking extra wingbeats and rearing up a little, like a butterfly alighting on a flower.

There was definitely something wrong with Vor Rapp. He sagged in the saddle, held by stirrups and safety harness.

They ran to Aurue's landing spot, keeping clear of other dragons coming in. Aurue wearily walked to meet them. He looked fresher than the other dragons—it wasn't as exhausting for him to fly this frequently, thanks to not having to haul scale into the air.

Ileth moved to soothe Aurue, but Sifler pulled up short.

"Stars, his head's off," Sifler said.

A dead dragoneer. A dragoneer who died because Ileth chose him.

"I knew something was wrong," Aurue said, craning his neck back. "Poor man. I hope there's not some superstition about your head being buried apart from your body like there is with the blighters, because I think it might have been smashed by a stone or ball. They were shooting projectiles at us."

"Guess you're a dragoneer now, Sifler," Mattin, the shaggy-haired apprentice, said. He was bringing wine in a little pull-cart for the dragons. It helped them sleep. "Congratulations."

"I felt a splatter before he went quiet. I thought it was vomit again."

"Aurue," Ileth said.

"We'll need to log this," Sifler said, mechanically. His eyes were fixed on the corpse. "It has to go on the board, so someone doesn't put his name up by accident."

"Steady there, Sifler," Ileth said.

"Could he be removed?" Aurue asked. "Him bobbing around back there feels unsettling. I need to walk by myself."

Others were gathering now, as word spread that a dragoneer had been killed. Ileth concentrated on inspecting Aurue for piercings. The way he was acting he might be injured too, blood loss fogging his brain. She couldn't remember the last thing Vor Rapp had said to her before he set off for this flight. They'd been talking about the local cheese he'd been eating, she knew that. The fact that she couldn't recall his exact words troubled her for some reason.

They set about removing his legs from the harness stirrups and unseating him from his crisscross safety lines. Between Mattin, who'd been press-ganged in because his dragoneer was still out with the second wave, Sifler, and Ileth, and with the slightest tip from the gray dragon, the humans got the body out of the saddle and laid it out on the ground. It looked like some sort of horrible practical joke getup to Ileth, something from a Feast of Follies where someone resolved to keep their head in a crisis. She giggled at the thought and the two young men looked at her in horror.

She blanked her expression. "Sorry."

"No apology needed," Sifler said. "Lots of people react to a shock by laughing. Completely natural. I have to . . . I have to attend to my comfort." He hurried off.

Ileth found a bucket of water and used it to take the blood off Aurue.

When Sifler returned from the toilet slits, he pulled a clean dressing sheet from his satchel and laid it over Vor Rapp's chest and onto the grass where his head would have been. It was a ridiculous act, but it struck Ileth as proper. Ileth wondered what Sifler was feeling at the moment. Triumph? Regret?

"I suppose we're flying together now," Aurue said. "I'm sorry, with all the confusion, what's your name?"

"Sniffler," Sifler said, lost in thought as he looked at Vor Rapp's corpse.

Four hours of rest and Aurue had to go up again. Sifler spent the whole time pacing and worrying at his nails. Ileth tried to find one of the senior dragoneers to encourage him, someone like Dun Huss, but none were awake.

Finally he disappeared into his tent and came back in his flying rig. It was such an ill-fitting assortment of odds and ends that Ileth hardly recognized him. He looked like an overstuffed scarecrow someone had decided to rig out dragoneer-fashion as a joke.

"We're doing message duty, giving notes from the previous wing to the next. You know how to pass messages?" Aurue said, flatly, while Ileth took over the wingman duties of adjusting his harness. He didn't seem quite as tired as the other dragons, except around the eyes, which were haggard and bloodshot. Interesting to learn that dragons could get bloodshot eyes too.

"I've done it in training. Once," Sifler said, from behind his face protection. It was an old full-face party mask, cracked and repaired, probably cast off from the Feast of Follies. A thick scarf was wound about his neck and there were two hats on his head, a tight skullcap beneath a tight fur riding hat.

"You know how it works?"

"You have to fly under the wave leader. He drops a line, I secure it, he drops the note canister on a ring, I get it, I release the line. Then we locate and fly above the next wave leader, I drop my line, he secures it, I drop him the message. Lets the wave leaders concentrate on their wave so they don't have to hunt around for each other."

Ileth knew the wave leaders had their dragon wings marked.

"Don't worry. We'll stay clear of the highpoons. I've learned my lesson," Aurue said.

They went through the takeoff routine with the rest of the wave. It had nothing like the snap and precision of the first, but the dragons and dragoneers all looked calm and alert. Ileth felt almost sorry for the Rari. What must it be like, dragon attacks day after day at all hours, throughout the day and overnight? If she was wrung out and exhausted, what was going on over there?

Out the wing went with Sifler. This time, Ileth couldn't sleep. She wondered what that little shopgirl would think, if she could see him taking off on dragonback. Which made her wonder, what was Rapoto Vor Claymass doing with himself? He was a wingman, and a good one, as far as she knew. Why had he been left behind at the Serpentine?

The wing returned a terrible, anxious stretch of time later. Ileth counted—all of them. Sifler landed, head firmly on shoulders.

She touched Aurue's snout; he passed his tongue across her sweaty palm, and then she went to Sifler.

Sifler slid out of his saddle. He moved stiffly. Ileth went to assist him; he waved her off, but she went anyway and she smelled the problem. He'd fouled himself.

"Let's get you to the wash-tent," she said.

"Keep away!"

"My first flight, on Vithleen, I came back the same as you. I didn't even have the excuse of war." While true enough, she left out the key detail that Sammerdam's water had given her terrible diarrhea.

"It was horrible," he said, tears in his eyes. "They had our people in

wooden cages. Warnings painted on the streets with whitewash. They burned them as soon as we attacked. I smelled people cooking."

"You have a dragon to tend to. He might be wounded. Should I look him over?"

"I'm well, Ileth. We stayed up out of range. Mostly," Aurue said.

"They're not even fighting anymore," a wingman said. "It's just vengeance now."

Sifler wiped his nose. "Nothing's worth this. It's mad. No order. Dragons coming down like crows on nests. Can't see for the smoke. I think they're burning wet rubbish to make it so we can't see. Explosions. Howling stuff flying through the air. They were supposed to be broken by now. All broken up."

"They are broken up. It's just that spot around the Citadel," Aurue said.

"Get cleaned up and have something to eat. You'll feel better," Ileth said, as if she knew. It was what they always did when new girls came into the Lodge, scared and overwhelmed. Cleaned them up, put them in a fresh sheath, overdress, and socks, and put food into them.

They were at the wash-tent. Sifler was saying something about wind directions and waiting for a good blow to attack so the smoke would be dispersed, but he seemed to be thinking out loud; his statements weren't organized in his usual intelligent fashion. Ileth couldn't just leave him, so she helped him undress. She doubted his underwear would be fit for much but rags ever again; the filth had started to dry. She'd worry about his attire later; she had to get his body cleaned up.

Another dragoneer, the one with the gold teeth, Roben, checked the confusion around Aurue.

"Knew he wasn't ready for this," Roben said. Ileth rounded on him, ready to spit curses, but his expression was sad and sympathetic. "Poor kid. That was a bad one. Bad luck."

"I can hear you," Sifler said.

Ileth got some fresh water to rinse off the soap.

"Too bad we won't be here long enough to build a proper sweat

lodge. Maybe they can add one to that garrison hole below the lighthouse," Roben said to no one in particular. He watched Ileth set the bucket down by Sifler. "Can I be next, dancer?"

"She's the Governor's daughter," Sifler said.

"Just having a joke, comp'ny."

"Ileth, go look after Aurue. I can get myself dressed again. This is . . . improper."

She left the wash-tent.

Aurue had his nose in one of the canvas feed troughs, eating greasy fish, slowly and without appetite or enthusiasm. Ileth waited until he finished. Someone had had the sense to loosen the girth before he ate. She reprimanded herself for forgetting that.

"Are . . . are y-you all right, sir? Was it bad?" Ileth asked.

"Cruelty is ugly. Are these your people? The ones they're killing?"

"Maybe," Ileth said.

At a word from Roben, Aurue and Sifler were put in the reserve for the rest of the evening so they could get some sleep. Dun Huss tiredly rearranged the rosters on the wooden board to give them the extra measure of rest. The third day of battle dawned clear, with a full moon visible in the sky.

Not that the numbers meant much anymore, but Sifler and Aurue were posted to Garamoff's second wing, following up on Dun Huss's strike at the Citadel, the last redoubt the Rari held in their main harbor of Lengneek. They started lining the dragons up for takeoff. There was some excitement; Garamoff was going to fly out himself to assess the situation.

"Sifler late?" Aurue asked, joining his new wing.

"You should check the tent. He had a bad night," one of the wingmen checking a crossbow before securing it to his dragoneer's saddle said.

Ileth rushed to what had been Vor Rapp's small tent. As a dragoneer, he had the option of having his own tent or sharing with his wingmen. Vor Rapp had opted to share, and now it seemed extra spacious.

Ileth paused outside. "The d-dragons are at the line. Aurue's waiting. You have to hurry."

"Come in," Sifler said.

He was seated on his cot. His boots were on his feet, but otherwise he was just in a long undershirt. "I'm frozen. My body won't work."

"Let me help you up."

"I can't do this, Ileth. I can't. You go for me."

"I don't have my flying rig."

"Wear mine. I've always been undersized. It'll fit you, close enough."

"I'm not a dragoneer, or a wingman."

"But you've flown on Aurue before. He likes you. Better than he likes me, I'm sure."

Ileth heard the first whistle for lineup. If he wasn't there by takeoff, there would be trouble.

She decided.

She flung herself into his rig, thrust his cap over her head, and buckled into the flying mask. Her hair wouldn't give her away. She hurried for the tent flap, ignoring a last-minute good-luck or something from Sifler, and ran to the flight line, still buckling herself into the flying girdle. The sword—the one that had belonged to Dun Klaff before she'd given it to Sifler, felt an awkward burden.

She just made it into the saddle as Aurue shook out his wings. Aurue sniffed her and his eyes widened. She shook her head.

"Now that girl Ileth's gone," another wingman said as he checked the saddle and safety tether. "What's she playing at?"

Ileth shrugged.

Garamoff walked down the line of his dragons and dragoneers. "Flight. Listen up. Nephalia'll lead, usual order to follow. Aurue and Sifler, you'll find Mnasmanus and get any observations and orders from Dun Huss and report back to me. Black and yellow stripes this time, they were concentrating their fire on Mnasmanus when he had the red and white. We'll strike at dawn. We're not expecting much resistance; this is cleanup. The only boats you'll see are ours. The barges

pulled by the Duke and Duchess are supposed to be on their way back now. They're to be defended at great hazard."

"On the line?"

"On the line."

"All secure?"

The dragoneers checked their safety lines and weapons. Ileth looked at Sifler's cheap little secondhand crossbow. Vor Rapp's had been dropped when he was killed, no doubt.

"All secure." Ileth didn't feel secure. She wished she'd been able to wear her own rig. This mess felt like it was going to fall off at the first hard wind.

"Then dragons up, and to glory!"

Fortunately for her, Dun Huss crossed his arms, looking down at her, giving the signal that there were no messages. Mnasmanus had a new hole in his wing and was having a hard time staying level.

Ileth got her first look at the Rari coast. There were blackened ruins everywhere. Bundles of dropped laundry had been lined up in a couple of the ruins for some reason. Ileth suddenly realized they were corpses when she saw a couple of militia carrying one out of the street on a litter.

Ileth turned her attention up. The flag of the Republic was waving over the Rari Citadel, flying jointly with the black dragon of the Wurm. Garamoff waved Aurue over to land next to him, where he hung from the widest part of the redoubt tower wall.

The dragons hung from their wing claws. Like bats, only head side up. Ileth clung as best as she could as Garamoff gave orders, thinking that she'd finally seen the great claws on their wings used—sort of— as nature intended. But it meant the humans had to hang on for all they were worth with their fingers and toes, or they'd fall out and be hanging from the safety tether.

"Sifler!" Garamoff shouted. "We saw a group of slaves gathered in the inner harbor, under heavy guard. Could be valuable hostages.

They're gone now. See if they're on the road. The mountains behind are filled with caves and overhangs; if they get them up there, there's not much we can do to get them back. If you see a long file of people, report back."

Ileth admired him, clinging there easily in his saddle, balancing on his stirrups, like a boy up a tree.

"Yes, sir," Ileth said, with a cough.

"Are you quite all right, young man?"

Ileth nodded.

"Aurue?"

"Might be hard to see. Trees," the dragon said, looking at a forested cut headed up the mountainside.

"Fly low northwest, go up, come back down the road from the mountains. They might not be keeping a close watch in that direction. Use your head and your skin. Now hurry!"

Ileth made a fisted pulling-down motion across her face, the flying mime for "order understood."

"Hold fast, Il—Sifler," Aurue said. "I'm going to roll off."

He waited until he felt her gripping with all the strength in her legs and arms she had, then dropped lightly off the tower backward, extending first one wing to start his turn and then the other, and he went shooting off across the rooftops of the inner harbor as Ileth's senses and guts rearranged themselves. It was a gut-rearranger of a stunt. It was just as well she hadn't breakfasted.

Aurue gained altitude fast, moving close to the trees parallel to the mountains. Up ahead Ileth saw a naked spur with a little bit of a wall and platform and a pole for hoisting signal flags, probably an overlook. It had a good view of the sea lanes to the west, where ships would appear making for the straits and the Inland Ocean. The pole was black and burned—someone had scorched it in one of the earlier attacks and nothing had been re-rigged, or she might have urged Aurue to get it again.

She saw a head bob behind the wall. Maybe they had crossbows.

"Avoid that," she shouted. "Rari."

Aurue didn't respond, but turned toward the trees and beat his wings harder. The updraft was stronger closer to the coastal prominence with the man or men hiding from the dragon.

They rose and Ileth had a better angle. The men were hiding around a soup pot. She was just thinking that they chose an oddly exposed location to cook a meal in the middle of—

Three sensations hit in quick succession. Ileth felt something like a gust of wind—a more appropriate sensation was that of a rock thrown at your head passing by. Aurue rocked her in her saddle.

Aurue lurched, beat his wings harder. He lurched toward the sea, caught some wind. She heard and then saw what was wrong, rends torn in his left-wing skin. They were wide and tearing wider, like sailcloth in a storm.

"It winged me," Aurue said.

He added something in Drakine; Ileth thought one of the words was *try*.

He partially closed his left wing, trying to protect the damaged area. They spun around and headed straight for the mountains. She saw the cut of the road they'd been following; it rounded a corner here in a switchback as it climbed toward a valley pass to a valley beyond.

Aurue tried to land on the road but fell short. Beset with his own difficulties, he didn't pay attention to branches or anything but his own limbs. She lunged forward and held through a quick succession of blows like she was passing through the Long Bridge gauntlet again.

Then they were down with a jolt that sent her into his neck-bones.

Aurue snorted and stood up. He started singing, of all things. In Drakine.

Ileth blinked. She felt like everything inside her body from womb to brain had shifted upward in the impact, and she needed a moment to adjust to the new configuration of her innards. She groaned.

"Ileth. Ileth? Ileth!"

"Still with you," Ileth managed to say. She tasted blood. She ran her tongue experimentally around her teeth. No gaps. Oh, there it was . . .

a cut in her lip. She probed it and felt a sting that flamed into mild pain. If that was all, then she was lucky.

They were on a steep slope just short of the road.

"What were you doing with that noise?"

"What noise?" Aurue asked.

"The singing!"

"Oh, I was just thanking the trees for supporting me, just in case they used to be . . . um, oh, what's the word. I can't think of it. Forest-people."

"You didn't strike your head, did you?"

"You have twigs stuck into you," Aurue said. "Let's have a look at my wing."

Ileth climbed off him, passed around under his neck—he flinched a little and she reprimanded herself; dragons were twitchy about their necks—and stood by his head.

"What was it, you think?"

"A bombard or an aerial trap."

There was a museum of sorts in the old Charge's residence. The cellars of it were full of projectiles and hooks that had been removed from dragons. Whatever they'd fired at Aurue hadn't left anything behind to add to the collection.

Ileth checked the cases on the saddle. There was a kit with some thread—that didn't look to be nearly enough for the festoon of wing skin—and a needle. The sooner the bits of skin were joined the better. She set about going to work when Aurue looked down the road.

A long file of people, mostly in brown or gray work tunics, shuffled along, linked neck-to-neck. Ileth, having grown up in the Republic, had never even seen convicts linked in that fashion, but knew it must be the slave train Garamoff had mentioned.

"That's who we were supposed to find," Ileth whispered.

Aurue lowered his head and wings. He was the same color as the spring pinewoods and brush. "We have to hide. If they don't kill us, they'll run for help and come back with enough to finish us."

Ileth saw one of the slaves, a little boy with hair in his eyes. He held

a woman's hand with one hand, a bit of tied-up rag that might be a toy or doll, or perhaps just a bit of food, in his other. Could she hide, let him walk by, spend the rest of his life under whips?

Ileth did her best to evaluate them. She wanted to fly reconnaissance, make estimations of the enemy—what could she learn from such close observation?

Well, they certainly weren't anything like the Rari who'd come ashore in the Freesand, for all the red-and-black they wore. Those had been scarred, heavily armed, dripping with gold. She looked at how they were dressed. Bracers with metal studs. Two were barefoot. Their weapons were whips, clubs, ordinary knives. Rags and cloth to absorb sweat and keep out the wind. One carried a savage-looking boar-spear with a crossbar—that might be a serious threat to Aurue, but more likely it was meant to intimidate a protesting slave.

The one in the lead was heavy; he had a silk scarf and head-wrap and carried a short whip. He had a shining gold necklace with a gem at the center of golden squares, obviously the leader and the only one showing real wealth or status.

Not the fiercest and best of the Rari. These were men who had others win their fights for them, then bought and sold the captives taken.

The Rari like to stop wars as quick as they start 'em.

Still. Six men. Six men were an impossibility, not without help from the dragon. She might get one with her little crossbow, if her nerve didn't fail. The dragon couldn't use his flame without striking the line of captives. Still, on a coup board, a single foot soldier with a dragon behind it would not easily be taken. The soldier could prevent the dragon from being surrounded and destroyed, and as for the dragon, it could kill whatever it moved against.

"We have to do this together or it'll never work," Ileth said, moving away from the column upslope, staying hidden. For Aurue, "staying hidden" was as much a part of his makeup as his breathing.

"Are you mad? Six paces deeper into the woods. They'll never see us."

Ileth unhooked Sifler's crossbow. She didn't bother to cock it, just

cradled it in her arm in the manner of some of the men she'd seen in camp. It rode easily enough there. She stuck a couple of bolts in her boot—just in case.

They made it to the bend and Ileth climbed onto the road. "Just look formidable. Fold your wings. Just don't run unless I do, and don't attack unless they . . . unless they hurt me."

Ileth took a step down the trail. It wasn't quite a road, but it had been filled and improved to the point where you couldn't call it a path. Three men could walk it shoulder-to-shoulder. Could she use Aurue to frighten them back down the road? No, they might fight an attack, or start slitting throats. She needed to play the part of a dragoneer, yet not provoke violence. What sort of dragoneer would the Rari expect, at her age? Some young scion of wealth and power. A valuable hostage, no doubt.

Her attire might give her away. Well, they shouldn't know a dragoneer from the scarecrow she resembled. She hoped.

The column halted in confusion at the sight of the dragon and its rider blocking the trail at the switchback. The Rari clumped up behind their slaves, using them as a living shield. So they were aware that the Republic was seeking to restore their freedom.

The fat Rari with the short whip—it was as gray as Aurue, so Ileth wondered if it was one of the sharkskin whips the Captain used to talk about—kept his face firm, giving away nothing. The man next to him twisted his fingers in his beard nervously as he spoke into the leader's ear. The leader held something in his hand, perhaps the size of a stone, but concealed it.

"Does anyone speak Montangyan? You?" Using a crossbow bolt like an accusing finger, she indicated the leader. "You, you must speak it."

Aurue did his part. He extended his neck toward the man like a dog pointing out a pheasant in a bush.

To his credit—if he was acting, that is—the leader looked confused and a little frightened. He opened his mouth and his hands.

"One of you must speak it," Ileth said.

"I do," the man who'd been tugging at his beard said. "What your honorable say for him?"

"The fighting is over." She tried to put conviction in her words. "You're safe. My dragon won't harm you. The fighting is over."

Several of the minders perked up, ceased crouching behind their captives.

"There are conditions," Ileth said. "I must take these people from you."

He passed that along to the heavy man, but by the way his eyes narrowed when she spoke, she believed the leader understood her every word.

The leader said something to his translator. A few of his men shrank away from him.

"Why should men take orders from a girl?" the translator asked.

Ileth thought for a moment. "Your . . . your men are not taking orders from me. They're taking orders from you." She pointed again with the crossbow bolt.

The translator held up his hands and made a little gesture to Ileth as he spoke. "Slower. Please, Captain." He spoke again to the one with the short whip. The leader went over to the side of the path and sat on a boulder. He slipped whatever had been in his hand back inside his black tunic and wiped his brow with a scarf of blue silk.

Ileth wondered what the Captain would say if she'd told him a Rari pirate had called her "Captain." It gave her inspiration to form her next words. "Tell your captain I only tell him information. None of you are in danger, provided you"—and here her tongue aided her as she had to slow it to be sure to be understood—"surrender my people."

She wondered if she should climb onto the dragon to make a more impressive figure as she developed her bluff. Instead, she made a show of counting them, nodding for each one and speaking the numbers aloud.

"You may keep any weapon a man can carry by himself. You may keep your wealth. You may not keep any slave or hostage; those are to

be surrendered." Ileth was vastly overstepping her authority with this bluff, but she needed convincing-sounding terms, something that would suggest that the Rari had accepted defeat but kept a few conditions plucked out of those histories she'd been wading through.

With pauses so the translator, now squatting at the feet of the short-whip man, could keep up, Ileth said, "Any man who wishes to make a claim about other property will have it examined to see if it shows signs of being used for piracy. Whoever wishes may return to the Citadel with me as well to make his claim. Do you own a ship, Captain? A house?"

The translator practically tore out his beard as he kept up with Ileth's speech. The leader spoke again.

"My master says he owns a house. It was not yet burned by your— your companions when he quit it."

"Then he may return with me and those under my supervision and claim it." Ileth tried to make it sound as though the slaves being turned over to her was already a settled point in this talk.

The man with the boar-spear had moved to the head of the file, ostensibly checking the line of neck-bound slaves and passing a water flask so that the thirsty might drink. But he was coming ever closer to Aurue. Could a spear like that be thrown? Perhaps by a very powerful man.

The man with the boar-spear reached the front of the file. He was perhaps a dragon-length from Aurue.

Ileth stood, cocking the crossbow with its lever and laying her pointing-bolt in the groove.

"Far enough!" Ileth said, putting her front sight on the fat seated man. The guard with the boar-spear made no attempt to ready to throw it. If he tried to run at Aurue, he'd get a faceful of fire. The file of slaves shrank away.

Aurue crouched, back curved and tail twitching like a cat ready to spring. His skin had gone a bright orangish-red with hints of dark stripes that reminded Ileth of the Lodger. Ileth felt a sudden pang. Aurue spoke:

"I think they were about to break the truce. Do you want me to tear the big one up as an example? Don't want the rest getting ideas."

The leader stood up and made placating motions with his hands toward her. He did understand some Montangyan.

She took her hand away from the trigger, showed her palm to the leader. He spoke. The boar-spear dropped with a rattle.

"Tell your captain I want him to cut the line on the first prisoner," Ileth said, worried that her stutter was making the men think she'd lost her nerve.

The translator spoke and the leader took out a small knife. For a moment she wondered if she'd have the nerve to shoot him if he started cutting throats, but he severed the first of the neck-lines, a strong-looking man, powerful like the lead horse in a team. The freed man tested the cut in the neck-line with his thumb, like he couldn't quite believe it.

The head Rari glared evilly when the freed captive snatched the knife away from him.

The rest of the group were freed quickly. Ileth heard a few thank-yous and a "The dragoneers did come!" in her own tongue, and a smattering of what might have been Daphine.

"Any of you coming with me to claim property?" she asked the Rari. "Start now. I will follow with the dragon."

None did.

She risked further delay—delay gave the Rari time to think—and ordered everyone to drink from the Rari waterskins. It was what someone certain of their advantage would order. She told the Rari they could keep the empty skins, but she wanted her people watered for the trip back to the Citadel.

"Go now. Pass the terms to any you meet," Ileth said.

The Rari moved off up the road. Their leader strode with head held high, as if the loss of his slaves were a matter of indifference. They passed the spot where Aurue had crouched. A couple of them checked the ground. Perhaps looking for dropped scale.

"There's blood on the ground there," Aurue said quietly.

The tailmost Rari looked back at the dragon thoughtfully. They ran to catch up with their leader.

"We should get our people moving," Ileth said.

As the column moved off, she noticed that perhaps a third of the freed prisoners had a serious limp.

"Have you been long on the road?" she asked the powerful man. He had picked up the boar-spear and carried it across his shoulder as though used to having a weapon there.

"We left in the dark this morning. I think he wanted us up by full light, but it was a slow trip because of all the hobbles."

"Hobbles?" Ileth asked. The man had a Daphine accent, and she wasn't sure she'd heard correctly.

"Bargun would lame anyone who tried to run away. The Rari put the fear of pain into you. They drown you if you try to steal a rowboat. Look along the lines, you'll see missing fingers, too. That's Bargun's favorite punishment: take off a knuckle or two and burn the stump. I wish you'd shot him."

"I didn't . . . I didn't want to break the peace," Ileth said. She hurried over to Aurue, at the front of the column. The dragon fascinated the few children among them; they'd hurried right up to his tail and were touching it experimentally.

Aurue said, "The sooner my wing is stitched, the better."

"Let's get out of their sight," Ileth said.

Ileth was neglecting the first duty of a dragoneer, care for her dragon. Weighed on a balance of pure reason, the dragon, even a scaleless gray like Aurue, was worth more to the Republic than any group of prisoners, but Ileth could hardly call herself human if she didn't want these wretched souls freed.

They passed a ridgeline with a path going down the spur to the signaling lookout with the bombard or whatever it had been that wounded Aurue. Ileth kept her crossbow cocked and pointed at the path. Ileth was tempted to take the dragon down and destroy the thing

and the crew, but the Rari might have other surprises in store, and she wasn't an experienced warrior.

"Difficulty?" the powerful slave asked.

"There was a Rari post down that trail, on an overlook. They shot at the dragon."

"How many?"

"Two, three, four. I'm not sure," Ileth said.

"You should be sure, dragoneer. You had a good view. I'll deal with them, if you want."

Ileth called a halt. The freed slaves were tiring from the downhill trip faster than she'd thought. Of course, they'd been on the move for the whole morning, probably without anything to eat. She went to work stitching the wing, crossing over the lines, as she'd once seen Annis Heem Strath do on Agrath.

Ileth saw Aurue wince. She started a conversation with the man with the boar-spear to give him something to think about.

"Who were you, before the Rari?"

"Watch Chief Tirut, Daphine Naval Armsman," he said. "They didn't get me in battle, but a shipwreck. They pulled me off a reef after a storm."

"I'm . . . I'm Aurue's dragoneer. This is Aurue." She took her time with the stitches, tying off each one with sure fingers. She could still hate the Captain for his shouts and cuffs and thank him for his hours of practice and examination over her knotwork, couldn't she?

"I should confess something to you, Watch Chief," Ileth said, quietly. "There's no truce."

"Thought it might be a ruse. You didn't have white streamers on your dragon or a signal flag." So the Daphines taught their men something of the Republic's dragoneers. Ileth felt a glow of pride.

With the bleeding stopped on Aurue, they moved the column of prisoners as quickly as they could down the mountain road.

Ileth heard hoofbeats.

"I feared that," Tirut said.

Ileth felt miserable. "We shouldn't have stopped."

Tirut shook his head. "Another two or three marks* down the road wouldn't have made a difference. No, you did the right thing. Take the children. Ride the dragon to the Citadel. I saw the Republic's flag above it yesterday. You can at least avenge us."

He gripped the boar-spear. "They can't come at us more than two abreast, not on this path. I'll get a couple before I'm done."

Ileth stepped next to him, holding her crossbow. Perhaps if she knocked a horse down, others would fall. It might not take much to make the Rari think the slaves weren't worth the bodies, given what the dragon would do to them.

She saw heads appear above the horizon of the road, bobbing on horseback.

Tirut smiled. "Well, if it isn't old Bargun come to get his property back. That poor horse."

Ileth made out the slave-master, looking awkward atop a mountain mule. He was gesturing and shouting at a spearman atop a horse with a basketlike helmet on his head of a type Ileth hadn't seen before.

"Do you see any meteors or crossbows, Ileth?" Aurue asked. "They won't be able to disperse on that path."

"I think they were hoping you would have flown off," Tirut said, apparently forgetting that he'd just advised her to do that very thing.

Archers dismounted and clambered for the rocks. They meant to get above them on the mountainside.

The former captives began to wail. One asked for Ileth to cut her throat before the end: "You can't know what they're like. I won't go back."

The archers had the mountainside to contend with. If they stuck to the path, they could stay ahead of them.

"Everyone, get moving," Ileth shouted. "We stay ahead of those bowmen, we have a chance."

The column rose to their feet and shuffled into motion.

---

* A sailor's measure of distance, about a quarter mile. What exactly a "mark" is in reference to has been lost to history.

"Looks like they're retreating too, Ileth," Tirut said.

The archers weren't just retreating, they were running for their horses.

"It's the reserve," Aurue called.

Ileth surveyed the sky. One . . . two . . . three . . . four . . . five dragons, almost wingtip to wingtip, were coming in from the sea. They wheeled briefly over the lookout where Aurue had been struck by the bombard. Two dived at it—one was purple, definitely Mnasmanus—and Ileth heard a distant *whump* of an explosion through the trees. Ileth held her breath until she saw the two rise again.

Three other dragons of the reserve headed for the mountain trail. The sharp-eyed dragons or their riders must have spotted the file of horses.

"Aurue—spread your wings," Ileth said. "Make sure they see you."

"I can do better than that," he said, rising. The retreating bowmen ran a little faster, a couple throwing away their weapons as they scrambled.

Ileth could not think of a more definitive gesture that meant victory for her side.

Basket Helmet whirled his arm around his head and the horses turned on the narrow trail. Bargun shook his fist at the sky in frustration, then turned his mule.

Tirut snatched the crossbow out of her hands. He raised it to his shoulder, sighted, and fired.

Bargun slumped atop the mule. As he slowly toppled off, she saw the shaft in his back. She started to look away, then steeled herself. If she wanted to be a dragoneer, she should harden herself to such sights.

Or should she?

She wished, futilely, that she had the Lodger to talk to. Would he have called that warfare or murder?

"That is not a bad crossbow," Tirut said, as though he'd just tested it on a Sag House gourd. "That blackhearted bastard's maimed his last. May the birds have his eyes and a dog his tongue."

The five dragons of the reserve formed up again. Aurue flew up to

meet them. At this distance Ileth couldn't see any holes in the stitching. She hurriedly put Sifler's mask and double-hats back on.

They passed low over the column. Hael Dun Huss signaled. She saluted in return.

"I think we can move back down the mountain at a more leisurely pace," Tirut said, shouldering the boar-spear again. "You want to set pace, or shall I?"

"Be my guest, Watch Chief," Ileth said.

"You ever get sick of the smell of dragons, look me up," Tirut said. "Food's very good, even by landsman's standards. You wouldn't be the first woman in breeches we've passed into the rolls with a wink. Brains and nerve matter more than whether you squat or stand to clear your bilge."

PART FOUR

MANY HAPPY RETURNS

"Glory comes with a bill attached.
You must be willing to pay it."

—SAYINGS OF THE SERPENTINE

9

After turning over the freed people at the Harbor Fort for transport back to the Headlands—she stayed to watch them being loaded and say farewell to Tirut, who was already making himself useful at the Harbor Fort by shouting instructions to Rari prisoners in their own tongue—she decided she'd fly back to the Headlands. Her wounded dragon needed to be examined by competent physikers rather than a single undertrained apprentice.

She saw the prisoners clamber into the sea turtle and the Auxiliaries pass the towing cables through the loops on the Duke and Duchess's swimming harness. The Duke was an old, heavily scarred copper dragon who had something very wrong with his wing—it dragged from the forehook joint out and was held in place on his back by strapping—and a gimpy leg; the Duchess was an equally aged green who lovingly nudged him along as he hobbled to the water.

She watched one of the Auxiliaries, standing chest-deep in the chill water as he attached the towing lines. But it wasn't her usual idle examination of shoulders and the muscles in the back working this time—she knew this youth. It was Duskirk! Yael Duskirk! He'd been sentenced to the mines for his part in the poisoning of Vithleen and the egg theft, but it seemed he'd made it out. Maybe they took volunteers from the convicts, especially if they were young and had experience with dragons.

"He's a sneaky one, the Duke, for something his size," an Auxiliary at the Harbor Fort gate said. He spoke as proudly of the broken old dragon as any Serpentine dragoneer. "See the marks there on the drawbridge? While the towers were shooting at the flying dragons and sending up rockets and such, he rolled around in some mud and crept up on the drawbridge from the water. Climbed up the side and popped it loose with his legs easy as you'd shove a door open with your foot. The Duchess used her fire to get the door good and hot, then smashed it open with her tail. Then they were inside like a couple cats loose in a rat-killing pit. The Rari ironmongery, they only had one that could swivel to cover the inside of the fort. They're both a bit mad—expect you to address them with all the old royal lingo like they were a king and queen of earth and sky itself, but they get the job done. Isn't one of us in the Auxiliary dragon teams that don't love 'em same as you in the Serpentine hold yours."

"That one getting washed about, working the harness, do you know him?"

"Shaggy hair? Convict volunteer. He's on the dragon team, though— that red wool shirt tied about his waist means dragon team. Tough little mutt, working in that sea."

Duskirk was departing with the Duke and Duchess, so she wouldn't have a chance to speak to him. He looked very thin. Maybe she could bring some food from the Sag into the Auxiliary camp, once safely back in her own clothes.

The man she was talking to went on to say something, apologizing for not giving proper credit to the dragoneers, but Ileth thanked him and went back to Aurue.

She flew back to the Headlands with her flying cap, mask, and scarf pulled well up, set down, pointed at Aurue's wing-skin and grunted, "Physiker, now," and hurried to the toilet pits. At the edge of the field she passed some men doing a "field oiling" of their swords by passing them over dragon-flame breathed into a sand pit by Nephalia. She now knew it was a quick way to get off the wet and preserve the steel.

Nephalia was belly down, resting limp wings, listening to a

wingman rattle off figures from a table, two dozen this and a hundred-weight of that, when Ileth passed. Nephalia sniffed idly, then perked up her snout and ears, looking at Ileth in confusion.

Ileth dived into the warren of tents.

The camp seemed quiescent, though she smelled food from a tantalizingly unlocatable source and heard snores. Three days of intense, round-the-clock battle had exhausted the dragoneers and Auxiliaries alike.

She found him settled behind a peg-screen for hanging armor and equipment.

"At last!" he said. "I feared you were both dead. What on earth kept you?"

She told him, briefly, about the slave train and Aurue being wounded.

"I got my nerve back, you know." He didn't seem happy about it.

"I'm glad to hear it."

"If you hadn't been so quick to climb into my rig and go off, I might have made it."

Was he really about to make this her fault? "You could have run after me."

"That's just like you, Ileth. Anything to draw attention to yourself."

"That—that doesn't even make sense."

He said something about her knowing exactly what he meant and he turned away. "Now please leave."

"Whatever happened today, you flew Aurue over the Rari coast. Think of the stories you'll have for Miss Caribet." She left him and his scarecrow flying rig.

Back in her usual plain camp attire, Ileth returned to work. It was the best way to get the memory of those dropped bundles of clothes on the roadside out of her mind.

Aurue's injury was minor, but Ileth wouldn't be at ease until one of the dragoneer physikers pronounced it so. With Sifler's permission—he played the part of an exhausted dragoneer needing sleep—she took Aurue into the Old Post along the cavern wharf.

The Old Post was crowded with spent dragons. Most slept, with evidence of vast, oily meals all about. A tub full of broken and damaged scale that had been pulled out sat between two grooms, both sleeping with backs to the stony wall. Ileth lent a hand in washing medical instruments in the seawater—the great starfish had fled—and helped haul dirty dressings up and out of the canyon to be burned outside. They didn't take chances with dragon blood.

She found Gift—Threadneedle was too old for a campaign camp—and had to wake him to look at Aurue. He gave her the caustic side of his tongue for waking him for something so minor and pointed out where her stitching could be improved. She accepted without thinking, then backtracked and gave credit to Sifler.

"Sifler did that? He's much improved," Gift said.

Aurue narrowed his eyes at her and glowered as she lied and elaborated on her lies.

The dragon turned away. "I'm for a meal and a long, long nap."

Ileth knew she should be exhausted, but she felt gloriously alive. She'd braved shot and a downed dragon, even though the shot had passed before she knew what happened and as for her dragon going down, there'd been bucket she could do about it other than hang on.

She wanted to shout, dance, be kissed. There should be an enormous party. Astler was wise to have thought of such a thing so far ahead of time. She remembered the promise of the victory ball in the warehouse. It would be fun to shop for a dress to wear to it. Perhaps she should take Gandy. She minded her less and less. She liked all of Astler's family, come to think of it. Even the widows seemed better on acquaintance. She wondered if she needed permission to return to Sag House.

Aurue was already asleep with his nose in the remains of a greasy dinner. He wouldn't need her for a bit, and there were a few grooms about. She went up to see who was about to ask permission.

The Borderlander was in charge of a reserve of himself and Catherix. He stood at the assignment board, trying to organize a sheaf of

papers on the ground before him with rocks atop them to keep them from being blown off in the wind.

"Hullo, Ileth. I'm trying to figure out if Auguriscious is on the wounded list or not. I've been told he is, but he's still active on the board and there's no physiker's report. Seen him about?"

"The physiker, or Auguriscious?"

"Either would suit me."

"The physiker is trying to get some sleep. You're a brave man, so you can wake him if you wish. Me, I'm exercising the privilege of being the Governor's daughter and going back to a tub and a real bed in the Sag."

"It's been a gargoyle's ball, hasn't it?"

"You think it's over?"

"Every item of Garamoff's target roster is scratched off. The Rari have been meeting under a flag of truce. A Daphine boat just brought them in."

If it was over, they should hear the news at the Sag. It would be good to see everyone.

The path back to the house was so different now, not just because of the weather. There'd obviously been coming and going. Bits of twine, bottles, a bootheel—there was litter of coming and going, as passing by the Sag was the fastest way to get to the nearest village.

A servant admitted her. The house was quiet. Comity was in the kitchen, at the open back door, looking out at the Old Post.

Ileth asked how she was.

"Perfectly fine."

"And everyone else?"

"I expect you're here to see Astler."

Ileth sensed something awful looming. "I would like to."

"You want to see Astler? Well, you should."

She led Ileth to a small, dark room on the first floor near the main entrance she hadn't been inside before. She'd assumed it was a big cloakroom for guests. It had only a single stained-glass window with a

priestly star design, and air came in through baffled shutters from the outside.

A long shipping box—Ileth had seen big fish come out of the ice-house in similarly rough-hewn containers—lay within. With growing horror, Ileth realized it was a coffin. A figure in a militia uniform lay within, packed with straw. Something had been written on his hand with ink and partially rubbed off again. He had Astler's build and hands, except the hands had gone fleshless like an old man's. The head had a bag on it. Even so, the way the bag lay on the head gave away that there was some terrible injury to the skull.

As was the custom in the north, the box rested tilted up. Ileth had heard stories that propping the corpse up encouraged the spirit to remain before departing forever, so that it might be touched by the fare-wells of those close to it before the funeral.

It felt as though she walked in a dream. This was some joke—a joke in very poor taste. Astler would yank the bag off his head, and she could be mad at him for days and days and days for horrifying her and his mother until he apologized, first through his cousin and then in person and she'd make it seem like she'd never forgive him but not really, she'd forgive him the instant he tore off that horrible bag and said *surprise* and why wouldn't he? Did he want her to suffer?

Everything felt cold and far away. Was she going to faint?

"What happened?" Ileth wasn't sure if she asked or shouted the question; it had to travel miles to this dark little room, didn't it?

"The man who brought back the body was the militia commander himself, with that taskmaster you met here. It's all in one of the letters they brought." She pointed to a small round table with some corre-spondence atop it in a careful hand. "There's one, a commendation, and another. He wrote it. To you. Left with the militia priest for safe-keeping, with all the others."

"I'm—how? He wasn't even in the battle—"

"He's my son, you little piece of nothing. You riser. You temptress. Now he's gone, my heart's dead—I thought losing his father was bad, but that was nothing, *nothing*!"

"He was—he would . . ."

"Yes, exactly, he was. All the family's hopes centered on *would have been* and now he's just a *was*."

"May I read my letter?"

"You may not. I'd burn it if it weren't the last thing he wrote. You've ended a family that's been part of this land for five generations. Now get out of this house and never set foot on our land again."

Blinded by tears, Ileth found the door, made the quick turn to the outside, made it three steps, and sank to her knees and pressed her hands to her face. Something shook her body. It was sobs coming out in silence.

She suspected Comity was watching and rose to her feet. She walked back toward the Old Post, no, she turned, then walked the other way, toward the Chalk Cuts. Was there some magic she could work by going to the last place she saw him? Wake from this dream? Warn Astler and Vor Rapp and even Sifler in time . . .

The old man was on one of the grassy, hummocklike hills around the Sag, tiny in a tentlike black overcoat. Ileth wondered how he made it up there. She saw other heads moving about. She should say farewell to him, so she started the climb. Horrified, she realized that the heads—and now torsos—she was seeing were a pair of men digging a grave. There were markers all about.

He looked up from his contemplation of the hole in the earth. The ground was a little too sandy; it kept collapsing on the diggers. "Oh, it's you . . . uhhh . . . never did manage your name."

"Ileth, sir."

"Oh, Ileth, yes. Connected to Governor Raal. Or was it the dragons?"

Ileth didn't bother clarifying. "I . . . I came about Astler, really. I'm so sorry. I didn't even know he was over there."

"None of us did. It seems he left a note, but he always has so many papers and drawings about, it was shuffled up by a servant. He joined his old militia friends. The Harbor Fort was secure, they said. The Legion cleared it. It was secure. The militia was just there to open and

bolt the doors. But there was a hidden passage the Rari used to come in and cut throats. They fought. In the end, they won, you could call it. They held them off long enough for the dragons to come."

"They just sent him over?"

"He pleaded with his captain to be allowed to be with his friends. He wasn't entirely untrained. So the captain agreed. He's grieved. He's grieved as much as my granddaughter. It's chance, I said. Same chance as my sons. Our family just seems to have nothing but bad chances."

"May I see him put in the ground?"

"Everyone but that Ileth is welcome."

"I'm Ileth."

"Oh, yes, you are. Well, his mother won't allow that. She's having a hard time with it, naturally. Thinks he wanted to have a uniform to impress you. Best you go back with your people. Your dragons, I mean. His mother is distraught."

"I, I can't just say good-bye this way."

"Oh, you often don't get choices with good-byes, girl. I'm at an age where it's mostly good-byes. I'm good at them. Good-bye, Ileth. Visit the grave, someday, when it's all faded. See to the flowers. He'd like that. Flowers would make him happy—he made such a study of them. He liked to draw, you see. I wonder if there's drawing in the other world?"

Maybe the old man was as broken as Comity.

What had she wrought with that stupid commission? "It wasn't for nothing," she said, perhaps more to herself than to the old man. "With the straits open again the whole north will thrive."

"You don't need to tell me that, girl. Got a letter just this morning about a shipping concern needs money to get going, and the man who handles the timber, he's desperate for workers. I told him to offer a hiring bounty."

She asked if there was anything she could do before she left. He sent the workers on a break and asked for a bit of her hair to bury with Astler, as they were close. "Not that you have a lot to spare."

Touched, Ileth agreed, and he chose one of the longer bits on top and removed it with a pocketknife. "This'll be between me and Astler. Comity has this idea that he went off with the militia to impress you. Comity knew him as a son, but I know men, or I'd never have prospered as I did. He wanted out on his own for once, to risk it all, after a lifetime of not being allowed to scrape a knee. I've heard it suggested he was after vengeance for his father and others of our Name, but that boy . . . well, vengeance wasn't admitted into that heart where it might crowd out all the good there. No. It was a last trick of Fate played on the Aftorn bloodline, girl."

He nudged one of the grave-soil clods of grass, broke it up with the side of his foot. Ileth saw a gleaming worm pulse as it moved back into shelter. "You'll have your chance. They've been waiting on me for a while now. Not the only ones."

Ileth saw the gravediggers exchange a look. The loose soil of the Headlands kept sliding back into the grave. Ileth felt her heart tumble down with the pebbles.

Peace came with the same suddenness as the war. The Daphine king, perhaps the friendliest of all the royal houses to the Vale Republic, offered his ships to keep the straits free and acted as mediator with the Wurm. It seemed the Wurm were as happy as the Republic to see the pirates chastised and effectively removed. Ileth heard that Watch Chief Tirut helped establish and organize the first garrison in the Harbor Fort under the Daphine Naval Armsmen; Ileth received a short letter from him some months later thanking her for her bluff that rescued him from service to the Wurm king.

Governor Raal agreed to help finance a garrison of three dragons in the north, decreased to two during the wild winter months when there was less shipping anyway. They would patrol the straits, from the Headlands to the widening past the Daphine coast where the straits met the Inland Ocean.

The dragons dispersed, back to the Serpentine for the most part,

where they could enjoy a long rest and be properly cared for. Ileth had been losing her sorrow in the endless work of runs between the Chalk Cuts and the Old Post, setting up the new station, watching the dragoneers make toast after toast to victory.

Serena was kind. She seemed to have an inkling of the curtains around Ileth's heart.

Ileth was offered the dignity and estate of an aerial return by Hael Dun Huss and Mnasmanus. Dath Amrits had been among the first to leave—Etiennersea thought it wise to take two dragons at her wing and do a quick tour of the border with the Galantine Baronies and other borders, to let the eyes on the other side know that whatever power had been concentrated in the north, there was no laxity in the south. The Borderlander had asked for a short leave to visit his home mountains west of Pine Bay; it had been granted, and he and Catherix promised to return to the Serpentine with a barrel of elk and moose livers.

"He'll spend his leave in some hunting lodge drinking distilled forage rye and dealing cards and come back with a barrel of cow livers," Dun Huss predicted, watching the Borderlander fly off.

"You three are so different, sir. How did you ever fall in together?"

"It was just chance posting that turned into habit. Usually when they station three dragoneers together there's a very experienced older one, a dragoneer in his prime who is being tested with a heavy burden of responsibility, and a younger one in need of experience. But a mix-up of orders and names, three fresh dragoneers off in search of glory. Makes a good tale for a winter evening and a heavy dinner to settle. I'll tell it sometime, when there's less to do. I believe we need to settle up with our good governor."

Ileth said a few good-byes in camp as she prepared for her return to Stesside. There was still her bargain with the Governor. Dun Huss told her that she needn't concern herself with it any further. She wondered if that meant she was to remain at Stesside until her eighteenth birthday.

With leisure to choose good flying weather, they left on a fine clear morning. It was a good flight and they made it in a morning's worth of air.

Governor Raal, by arrangement, was at Stesside to welcome her back. As she and Gandy had predicted, he disliked the way her hair looked. "Ileth, what did you do to your hair? Were you ill?"

She had an explanation ready. "There were lice at camp."

"Did you try a sulfur preparation? You look a fright."

"It'll grow back," Ileth said, which settled him.

Dinner was quiet. Lady Raal, usually the moderator of conversations, sat quiet and ate the way Ileth had taken her wine at her first Stesside dinner, a fair amount of moving of food with utensils but very little eating. Her husband helped her to her room early, with Ileth bearing a tea that was mostly warm milk.

"It was a brilliant campaign, I understand," Raal said over his own Stesssource lifewater in the dining room after dinner. Ileth noted that though she'd spent the whole campaign there as his "observer," he'd only inquired about her hair and her health.

"From the Serpentine's perspective, it could hardly have gone better," Dun Huss said. "Not a single dragon lost or crippled." Ileth didn't know if it was usual to speak only in terms of the dragons. She'd seen, now, the Academy's method ensuring that a lost dragoneer could be replaced quickly. But she'd never forget Vor Rapp's corpse, still saddled.

"I hope those odd ships the Auxiliaries wanted turned the battle in our favor. They cost enough."

"I'd say the loss of four hundred of their most cunning and experienced raiders and their most daring captains right at the outset made the greatest difference in the fighting," Dun Huss said, refilling Ileth's glass. Ileth imagined a game of coup where your opponent lost his captains and cavalry at the opening. The rest of the game would be a steady progression of picking up pieces. "Those ships were supposed to be a decoy, but we had no idea how well it would work. Their best

ships and crews go out, and what comes back? Dragons, organized for war. Lucky there."

"There's already talk of a parade in Sammerdam. I expect the governors will agree with the Assembly. It has my vote. Weather should be lovely for it, if you in the Serpentine can get your dragons organized soon enough. Don't want to delay too much; good news goes stale fast."

"We have a few dragons who are always in the mood for a parade. Will you allow your, um, daughter to attend in her role as a member of our company?"

"I could not deny Ileth the pride of taking part. She and I have come to an understanding about her hopes with the dragoneers. Or has seeing war up close made you appreciate the quiet hills and woods and views around Stesside, my dear?"

Ileth collected her words. "Your conditions limited my exposure to it. I hardly missed a meal, so at least I proved myself your daughter in that respect."

"You should be careful with that tongue if you want to ride a dragon in Sammerdam under the Archway."

"I don't deserve to ride a dragon," Ileth said. "That's only for people who fought."

"That's not quite true, Ileth," Dun Huss said, leaving open which part of her statement wasn't true. "Governor, it's a lovely evening and the summer twilight is worth a few insects. I like to have a short walk after dinner," Dun Huss said. "I've heard there's an excellent path up to the source of the Stess, and I should visit before departing. Everyone who's been there has told me it's worth the climb."

"Watch your step in the dark," Governor Raal said. "Would you like a lantern?"

"You don't wish to point out the family history yourself?"

"My old legs would only slow you down. No, I will catch up with Ileth. It's about time my observer offered me the benefit of her experience."

"Oh, I don't think that's necessary. My eyes are still reliable. Ileth,

look in on Mnasmanus before it gets too dark. His dressing may need changing."

"Was he wounded?" Raal asked.

"Only slightly."

Dun Huss departed.

"Excellent!" the Governor said, after watching Dun Huss from the door where he'd seen him out. "This is your chance, Ileth."

"Yes. But I should like to hear more about my mother first. I've already guessed you aren't my father."

"We don't have time for—"

"Lies are what take time. Truth can be out in a moment."

Raal considered.

"You are correct. I'm not your father. Yet, Ileth, I feel, no, that's not quite right, I am responsible for you. After you were born, I never did work my way back and determine anything other than that there was enough doubt about the wheres and whens that it's not an impossibility. You don't favor or resemble me, other than that you seem to be very good at getting your way when you set your mind to something."

"Do you know who my father might be?"

"Only from rumor. I never attempted to find out the tale in full, from your mother or anyone else. To seek an answer seemed— desperate. Or pathetic. There was a dragoneer connection. I don't even know his name. Part of the garrison at the Old Post. Your mother—I think she had designs about something or someone from her childhood. She arranged a journey in great secrecy with the dragoneers there, maybe having to do with her own birthplace. Perhaps they even flew her back to the Baronies. She was away some months. So your mother and father may both be Galantine. She never spoke to me of it; I found out what I could on my own. I don't know what she intended to do, if it was love or if it was—was a transaction. There was a period where I didn't see her or know what had happened to her. One day she appeared again at my door, ill, heavy with you, asking for my help. You were born a few weeks later, in this very house."

"What did you tell Lady Raal?"

"The truth, of course."

Ileth wondered if the Governor wasn't able to make the truth dance better than Ottavia could direct a novice. "She still took my mother into her house?"

"Which do you doubt, Ileth, Lady Raal's charity or her sympathy?"

Ileth lowered her face.

"You didn't ask for an explanation from my mother?"

"Ileth, among my—the way I was—if a woman, round with child, appears at your door some months after she's been in your bed, you don't interrogate her. I helped her as best as I could. As . . . after . . . once you were born and the infection took hold, she told me what she wanted: her child to keep her Galantine name and be raised in a Directist house. I forgot if Captain Congrave was born Galantine or just had parents who fled, but I did know he kept a Directist house, though he took his charges to the local priests to make sure they would fit in with Montangyan traditions. I asked him, as a special favor, to take you and said that one day I'd see you happily situated. At that point he was fairly reliable, despite the loss of his ships and flags."

"You must have heard gossip."

"Very little. The dragoneers were always high-handed with me. I did have one of my secretaries make an offhand comment about the dragoneers treating government property that properly belonged to the province as their own and a few of the clerks snickered, so I called the youngest clerk who'd laughed into my office and he confessed that there was a rumor that a dragoneer was involved with my own jade—sorry, it's a coarse term and it shouldn't have been applied to your mother, but he was a coarse young man and it slipped out."

"I wish Ignata were still here." Ileth was sick of being a coup piece, moved this way and that. Ignata had been the only one who'd been honest with her from her first word.

"She's set up comfortably in Stavanzer. We can talk about her after you fulfill your part of the bargain."

Ileth nodded and left.

Mnasmanus was out in the paddock, on the far side where the

fencing came up against the forest. He was itching himself with a branch plucked from a tree.

"What are you doing out here, sir?"

"They forgot to take the horses out of the barn," the dragon said. "The poor things are terrified. I'm trying to stay upwind. They won't listen to reason. Silly brutes."

She trooped over to the barn, did her best to calm the horses, and after achieving little except the knowledge that her best wasn't good enough, she grabbed Dun Huss's little kit of grooming supplies and its attached back with spare dressings and sticking plaster for Mnasmanus's battle wounds.

A non-horse sound from behind startled her. She squeaked.

It was Dun Huss. "You scared me, sir."

"I'm not our mutual friend but I can be quick and quiet at need. I wanted to make sure you weren't followed."

"I thought you really had gone to the source."

"I've never been much of a believer in the virtues of this or that lifewater. It's all just drink. I have that blood for you." He held out a camp bottle. It had a label on it but it was too dark to read the small letters.

Ileth waited perhaps just a moment too long before taking it.

"It must be very carefully used. There's still a great deal you don't know, apprentice."

"Yes, of course."

Dun Huss smiled at her. "Better be off. The longer a conspiracy proceeds, the better its chance of failure."

She returned, concealing the bottle of dragon blood in the bib of her overdress.

"I have it."

Raal let out a breath in a way that suggested it had been held in his lungs for months, if not years. "You look nervous. Don't worry, it's just us. I've sent the servants off to bed."

She nodded.

Raal touched her, gently, on the elbow, in the way he supported his

wife when she moved. "I . . . I understand this is hard for you. I know you're running a risk."

For the first time in the months she'd known him, he'd shown some regard for her feelings. Ileth thought it odd that it only appeared now, after he more or less admitted that there was little chance of his being her real father.

"Mnasmanus didn't notice anything. He wasn't even looking at me."

"The sooner she drinks it, the better," Raal said.

"I'd like to see it prepared," Ileth said. "You say you've consulted experts?"

"I don't even want her to know she's getting it. I brought the subject up to her once or twice and she said she'd rather die than take it. She's listened to too many old wives' tales. I've spoken to experts. They believe it will help."

Another conspiracy. Well, best carry it out quickly. "We could pour it in a meat pie."

"I have just the thing. Cold tomato soup. She loves it on warm summer days."

He brought her the tray. Ileth tasted the soup, added the contents of the phial, mixed it, and tasted it again.

"Do you have some pepper?"

"Aren't you afraid of taking dragon blood?"

"I've had so much on me one way or another, more than that has gotten into me," Ileth lied. Why was lying such a sin when it made so many matters easier?

He reached for a thick bowl with a pestle in it. "There's pepper in that."

Ileth ground it further, then added a generous pinch. She tasted it again. "That helps."

"Take it to her, then," Governor Raal said.

"Shouldn't you?"

"She'd like to see you."

Ileth wondered if he was afraid of the dragon blood or wanted to avoid a direct act if matters went ill with it. Ileth was indifferent. She carried the tray upstairs and went down to the farthest bedroom.

Raal knocked on the door and they were admitted. Lady Raal was sitting up in bed, books and needlework about her. Both inquired how she was feeling.

"Other than being tired of being in this bed, well enough," Lady Raal said. "Tomorrow I must get about more. It is often so, a good day follows a bad."

Ileth set the tray down. Lady Raal sniffed it. "How nice, Ileth. I was just thinking I wanted something sharp; just because I'm idle my palate doesn't have to be. I was going to ask for summer peppers and onions but this is better."

She tried not to watch too closely as Lady Raal ate, and instead occupied herself with a tapestry of a wedding procession. The faces were very good. It made her think of Astler. She'd gone almost the whole evening without thinking of him.

Lady Raal set down her spoon. "Delicious. I love a good cold tomato soup in summer. Did you have some, Ileth?"

"I tasted it. I like it with cucumbers and mint in the summer, and I thought I saw some in the kitchen. I can make my own."

Lady Raal smiled. "That's how the Galantines take it. I always say, blood will out."

She picked up the spoon again and ate with enthusiasm and relayed the humorous story from her novel about a man escaping a dull marriage because he'd fallen in love with a model who sat for a famous portrait, only to find that while the portrait did the subject's features justice, she made his life miserable. "Normally that wouldn't be funny at all, we're talking about lives being ruined, but when it's written in an entertaining fashion—oh dear."

She dropped her spoon on the bedsheet and sank back on her pillow.

"Dear!" Raal said.

For one dreadful moment, Ileth's mind seized on the idea that Raal had poisoned his wife and would use the dragon blood in the soup as an excuse.

Ileth grabbed her hand and squeezed it. She groped for a pulse as she'd seen physikers do but couldn't tell if her heart had ceased to beat or she was just bad at finding the blood vessel in the wrist.

Lady Raal's eyes fluttered open. "That was—odd. I felt faint there, like, well, dizzy like after drinking lifewater. How very strange. I don't usually react so to pepper; did you put a great deal in?"

Ileth stammered a bit about liking pepper, and remained long enough to be polite and slipped out, using getting the dishes clean as an excuse.

As she passed down the now-dark hall, the Governor caught up with her.

"You didn't tell me it would have such a dramatic effect," he said.

"I didn't know. You're the one who consulted with experts. Didn't they . . . didn't they warn you?"

"They only said the effects began to show almost immediately."

Lady Raal was the first one up the next morning, other than her new cook, Eloana. Ileth delighted Eloana by speaking in her native tongue as they made breakfast together, though she annoyed Ileth a little when she pointed out that a sure cure for a stutter was to carry a pin with you and prick yourself with it so the pain would draw the attention of the evil spirit in your body causing the stutter.

"The Lady is much better this morning," Eloana said.

"I'm happy to hear it," Ileth said, hoping that Eloana wouldn't start poking Lady Raal as she slept to draw out spirits.

"I never see her so well."

Ileth decided to see for herself. Lady Raal was dressed in more finery than Ileth had ever seen, on her feet, walking with the aid of a cane. She was pointing out moldings in the dining room to Severan.

"You and Eloana can't just wipe them off, Severan. Really go over them with a cloth, little circles, that's the only thing that gets the dust

out of this beading. Oh, Ileth, I see you look surprised. You didn't know I could walk unaided, did you? Well, I can, though lately I haven't felt up to it. This morning I decided I really must force myself more."

"Don't tire yourself, madam," Severan said.

"I know my limits. I am simply expanding them, Severan. Ileth, would you walk with me in the garden a little? I'd like your support if I tire."

She seemed so energetic Ileth could have taken her for having been taking Santeel's snuff, but she puffed a little and slowed once they passed over the back threshold.

Out in the garden and alone, Ileth feared a questioning about the tomato soup, but the lady of the house had other concerns.

"Ileth, I have what I hope you will consider good news. I've spoken to my husband and he agrees, a companion closer to my own age and interests along the lines that the young Dun Troot suggested would be better. I've spoken to him about returning you to your dragons."

She seemed to be expecting thanks, but they'd pulled her away from the Serpentine by means fair and foul. Of course she didn't know her husband's real purpose. Then again, Lady Raal had been kind to her mother, and to her. She could thank her for that. "Thank you. You are the best of women, Lady Raal."

"I should think you would want to leave the north. We understood you were forming an attachment to Astler at Sag House. I know you've never said anything about it to either of us, but some in that house were convinced enough of its existence to let us know in an approving fashion. I am sorry, for them and for you."

"He was . . . kind. I'd just as soon not talk about him." The emotion in her voice was real this time.

Lady Raal turned toward a bench and they sat. "That's better for both of us." She let Ileth collect herself before proceeding.

"We are thinking of perhaps adopting a boy, so as to carry on his Name. My husband likes you, but, how did he put it, he says you're like a wild bird that would fret and die in a cage. He'd hoped you might grow to like it here, take up a new life, and allow him to fulfill a promise

he made to your mother, but it seems you've found your destiny else-where. Can your mother look down, and see her daughter comfortable and happy in those smelly caves?"

It was Ileth's turn to feel faint. She was a good woman. Worth the risk she and Dun Huss had run. "Comfortable? No. It's not often com-fortable. But happy. Very, very happy, Lady Raal." Laughter mixed with her stutter as she spoke.

"All he asks of you now is that you and he present yourselves before a magistrate and agree on paper that as there seems to be not the slightest similarity between the two of you, a blood connection is im-possible, and both of you quit any claim to one. All those other letters shall be forgotten. Destroy them. Even old scandals sometimes stick."

Ileth's mood turned sour. What a coward that man was. Letting his sick wife carry out his dirty business. She wondered if that Galantine Baron hadn't had a point when he talked about republics being gov-erned by graspers rather than nobles who were expected to behave, well, nobly. At this point she'd happily swear out a statement that he wasn't her father and sign it with her own blood. Gods, the Captain was a better man sloppy drunk and crying over his lost ships.

"I hope you will visit now and then. Once you have your own dragon," Lady Raal said. "Perhaps if you accommodate my husband in his wishes to let this connection wither, he could exert himself on your behalf and show an interest in your advancement."

Ileth felt dirty at the suggestion. She'd come this far on her own, no help from Governor Raal or anyone else. "There's no need of that. I'm happy enough to return to my duties." She wondered if she'd be kicking herself for those words in four more years as her apprentice-ship began to run out. Well, four years was a long way off.

She begged an extra day or two at Stesside from Dun Huss so that she might take care of this statement of the Governor's.

"Mnasmanus doesn't mind mutton and is enjoying the change of scenery. He's trying to win over those horses, and once he sets to something, he likes to see it through. But are you sure you want to sign

something like that, Ileth? We're ankle-deep in letters from him about claims to 'his daughter.' You might wish for an inheritance of money, even if you don't have one of blood."

"I don't know how all that works, but couldn't he just declare that none of his property was to go to me in the event of his death?"

Dun Huss wasn't the sort of man to shrug, though he gave the impression one had occurred. "I suppose he could."

"Or we could just fly off on Mnasmanus and let him twist in the wind."

"Maybe you are his daughter after all. I would think the Serpentine would like to have a little leverage over a provincial governor, particularly this one," Dun Huss said.

"Do you know which dragoneers were here when he sent them off?"

"Almost twenty years ago? I wasn't even an apprentice then. I was digging ditches for the gas lighting system as a novice. Someone else will have to help you with that."

She decided to leave it at that, for now. As a change of subject, she brought up Lady Raal's recovery. "Where did you get that medicine? I thought you were going to give him a plausible fake. It wasn't a powerful stimulant, I hope."

"It was dragon blood, of course. Straight from Mnasmanus's neck-vein."

She tried to form words. It wasn't her stutter this time, it was shock. Hael Dun Huss, the best exemplar and upholder of the traditions and laws of the Serpentine—giving out dragon blood?

"Ileth, do you really think I'd let a sick old woman suffer? Give flavored tinctures of nothing like some back-alley Sammerdam quack? When dragon blood can do wonders? I talked things over with Mnasmanus and he thought the risk minimal enough. She's beyond childbearing age, at least as I understand such matters."

"I . . . I . . . I don't know what to say. But why tell me?"

"You'll understand, someday. You're the future of the Serpentine. I'd like to leave it, as we all must, in the right hands. With the right ideals."

With that, they quietly packed up and left. Ileth placed a note thanking Lady Raal for the hospitality of her table and grounds, explaining that Mnasmanus felt he should be looked at by one of the Serpentine physikers, as one of his wounds had recently opened up again.

As she and Dun Huss took their things out and attached them to Mnasmanus, it made Ileth think of Galia's elopement from the Baron's estate.

Now that the matter of the dragon blood had been resolved, Ileth had one last duty in the north that was much on her mind. She didn't know quite how to bring it up . . .

"What is it, Ileth?" Dun Huss asked, interrupting her imaginings of how she could request such a favor from Mnasmanus and his dragoneer.

"How did you know I wanted to ask you something?"

"Your mouth tightens and your lips disappear when you're working up to a speech."

"Do they really?"

"Truly." Dun Huss smiled. "It's a tell. Not as bad as poor old Dath, but I'd advise you not to gamble over cards. Let's have it."

"It's like this. Last summer, I had a conversation about flowers with a gentleman . . ." It all came out. The silver coin. Beggars. Her promise that she hadn't kept. Flowers for a dance. Astler and the grieving Comity.

"Hear that, Mnasmanus? She's forbidden to set foot on the soil of Sag House ever again. Presents a difficulty."

Ileth counted out the coins in her purse. Governor Raal had given her a travel allowance for going about the north, and Lady Raal had sometimes given her pocket money during her stay at Stesside, not realizing just how cheaply the Governor's daughter was used to living. "Is this enough, you think?"

"More than Mnasmanus can carry from the Sammerdam market."

Ileth bowed her head. "I feel terrible asking you two for such a service. So much flying."

Dun Huss put his hands on her shoulders. "Ileth, look at me."

She met his gaze.

"I've known you, what is it? Has it been three years? Through a duel with a man twice your size who wanted to kill you, through a fire in the Serpentine Cellars, over a year as a Galantine prisoner, a disfigurement . . . I could go on. I've never once been of real service to you, though I've wanted to do you some great favor since you battled your way through your oath with the whole Serpentine staring at you. Nothing would please us more than to finally be of assistance."

Dun Huss looked at the dragon. "What do you say, friend?"

"He seemed a fine young man," Mnasmanus said. "I would be happy to oblige."

Ileth sniffled. Growing up, Ileth had been jealous of the little girls who could go running to their fathers and sob out their troubles into a comforting chest. She'd gone seventeen years now without that, so she could, with pride, go on for the rest of her life without.

But she was sorely tempted at that moment to give in.

Instead she took a deep, refreshing breath of the Stesside air. "Thank you, sir. Thank you both."

The flowers on Astler Aftorn's grave the next morning became a matter of local legend in the Headlands, with the story being told as far away as the Freesand and south beyond the Chalk Cuts. Like most legends, every year it grew a little. How exactly someone managed to get what was practically a cartful of fresh blossoms of every type and color, none of which could be found within dozens of leagues of the Headlands, atop the fresh mound of soil without leaving a print or track anywhere near was a matter of much conjecture.

The supernatural was suspected. Perhaps a token of esteem from the gods. A message that prosperity would return, that no more families would be torn apart by slave-hungry pirates. Everyone had their own conflicting explanation. It didn't help that the Sag House girl, the dead boy's cousin, agreed that each and every version she heard was true.

If Ileth had been pleased and proud the last time she saw the Serpentine from dragonback, this time she had to blink away tears. How could gray be such a lovely color? She put her arms around Dun Huss from behind and pressed her face into his muscular back. She even cried a little.

"Thank you. Thank you, sir," she said.

"Thank Mnasmanus. He's probably set a distance record in the last day or two."

"I'll devote myself to dancing for him full time, if he wishes."

"Wouldn't do me any good," Mnasmanus said over the wind. "I've next to no sense of smell."

"Your hearing makes up for it," Dun Huss laughed.

Mnasmanus didn't try for a cave landing. Like Dun Huss, he was doctrinaire. He landed on the Serpentine road just short of the Pillar Rocks, as ideal a landing according to Serpentine doctrine as one would wish.

It was coming on toward dinnertime and the Long Bridge and road had groups of twos and threes heading to the up end. They paused, moved to the railing of the Long Bridge, and solemnly turned left or right to face the dragon as he walked to the Beehive, Dun Huss walking beside and Ileth trailing behind.

"Eyes on Mnasmanus of the Serpentine," a dragoneer shouted across the Long Bridge. Those standing drew themselves up. "Render victory honors!"

As Mnasmanus walked past, the assembly to either side saluted one by one as the dragon's head broke their precise noseline. Ileth was suddenly unsure if she should join the line of people to either side. She just tried to measure her pace and put on a solemn expression, but a smile kept breaking out.

Home.

Of course she had to report to Traskeer that she'd returned. She washed up, changed into her ordinary overdress, and went to dinner in the Great Hall. More than a few welcomed her back. She was

no Name, yet many of the apprentices and wingmen seemed glad to see her again and inquired about her health and the north. It made her flush with pleasure.

She asked about Traskeer and heard he was catching up with his index, having only just arrived yesterday after reporting the events of the campaign to the Assembly.

Ileth filled a tray with soup and bread and brought it to him.

She knocked, he answered, and she found him on a two-seat couch that had been added to his office since she'd last visited. The fabric on the seats was worn and he couldn't stretch out comfortably, but he did have his feet up. He had that greasy-sweat, washed-out look Ileth remembered from the first time they met.

"Ileth," he said flatly. "Run away again?" he asked.

"Released, sir. I brought you soup."

"I know some of our company get flux every time they visit Sammerdam. I seem to be the only one who reverses the complaint. I feel healthy as Master Justice in the city, and then as soon as I return here, I'm stricken anew." He sniffed at the soup, tasted it, and went to work with the spoon. "Thank you. Is there salt?"

"Sorry, sir, forgot it."

He moved the letters and notes he had on the table so Ileth had room to set down the tray.

"It can't be the water, I'm careful to drink spring water in copper pots. I wonder if it's the cooking lard. My digestion seems sensitive to grease."

"You could commission your next new apprentice to a study of the kitchens."

"Not a bad idea. The Committe of Public Health had a fellow who maintained that bad food kills more people in the Vales every year than accidents. Speaking of commissions, did you learn much about Raal's role in the Republic's order of things? Any new insights into the powers and limitations of the office?"

"Hardly, sir. He had me keep his wife company at the family home."

Traskeer dipped some bread in the soup and chewed thoughtfully.

"Yes, I remember Santeel saying something about that. She had a very clever idea, by the way, and harried Dogloss like a crow about it. Something about that old striped dragon naming you his heir and therefore having adopted you. You were legally his daughter and the Governor therefore couldn't have actionable cause or whatever the legal term is because of precedence. Dogloss said you already being at his residence would make things difficult. She was trying to get money together to bring a case."

Ileth didn't know what to make of that. Of course once Santeel got her teeth into something, she was like a wardog on a sword arm.

"I did learn coup."

"Did you? You know, the Charge and Dun Huss play a decent enough game, and that wingman, the one with the art patch of the thistles on the back of his riding rig. If we could just get a few more, we might set up a league. I believe Captain Tellence of the Guard plays. We'd need a league secretary to record positions at the finish. You'd do admirably, you're prompt and accurate. Salt excepted."

"Couldn't I play, sir?"

"In a competitive sense? Women don't go in much for coup, I've found."

"Let's have a game, then."

He smiled. "Excellent suggestion. That would clear my mind of the cobwebs of updating the index. As visitor, I'll let you have the first move."

They set up their array. Traskeer tut-tutted at her captain/tower ratio when she revealed it when the starting screen was pulled away. "Three towers, Ileth? You'll find it limits your attack."

The game began. She'd had plenty of time to brood over arrays at Stesside. She had set hers up defensively, in Lady Raal fashion. But you had to conform to your enemy's array too if you were to play the grinding game Lady Raal favored, and there was always a weakness. Ileth, with first move, nudged some infantry forward to defend her forward tower in the triangular array. It was the obvious defense against his now-revealed array. Traskeer, taking advantage of their placement

next to his lone fortress, moved his cavalry and a captain far forward to exploit the side that wasn't covered by Ileth's war machine.

Ileth brought out her dragon from its position next to a fortress and destroyed a cavalry piece. Traskeer's eyebrows shot up in surprise. "That's no way to play the Hedgehog Defense, Ileth. You'll need your dragon at a crisis to counter mine. He's way over that side of the board now."

He brought up more cavalry to lock her dragon down, surround it, and destroy it. She sent out her cavalry to support it. He brought up the war machine that would doom her dragon next turn.

And she sprang her trap. Her cavalry, instead of protecting her dragon, swung around to his now-exposed flank and took a captain and some infantry, unmoved from their initial position in his array. He had no choice but to use his war machine on the cavalry. Her dragon escaped the not-quite-closed vise and took his lone fortress. Now he had to bring up his dragon to attempt to trap her dragon again so the war machine could get it next turn, and her infantry came up in relief of the dragon, using the mobility provided by starting their move adjacent to a fortress, and destroyed the captain he'd initially brought forward with the cavalry that remained next to it.

"Coup, sir," Ileth said.

Traskeer gaped. "Coup! In six moves."

"Is that unusual?" Ileth said.

"I did . . . I did not expect such aggression from a girl of sixteen."

"Seventeen, sir—just."

"I think perhaps you were born with a strong masculine aspect. Your favoring of short hair reveals it."

"If only a strong masculine aspect prevented a woman's monthly flux, sir. I could do without that discomfort."

"Ileth! A decent woman doesn't talk of such things to anyone but her mother or husband."

"I'm sorry, sir, it's my masculine aspect. I'm also sorry for taking advantage of a sick man. This one was so short, I don't feel as though we had a decent game."

"I'm not *that* ill, just . . . I haven't played in a while. Rusty."

"Then shall we have another game?"

He cracked his knuckles. "With pleasure, now that I know you are a challenge."

"Yes, sir. I'd enjoy a challenge after that first match."

He recovered his destroyed pieces and placed the screen between them. He took his time setting up his array. "It's my turn for first move."

He went again with two captains and one fortress. Ileth did three captains this time, which favored her normal aggressive, slashing style. Though she had some initial success, managing to take his fortress, it turned into a grinding game where her dragon couldn't be used effectively because there were few open areas for it to operate, as he had spread his array and she had difficulty getting a solid punch formed against it.

"You know the social newssheet in Sammerdam," he said conversationally. "They're dreadfully careless. They were so slow in announcing Vor Rapp's promotion to full dragoneer that it appeared in the same issue as the announcement of his death. His poor family."

If it was an attempt to throw Ileth off her game, assuming she had an emotional connection to him that led her to choose him as Aurue's dragoneer, it didn't work. But it did bring up the memory of his headless body lying in the torn soil of the Headlands landing field. Ileth struck back on the board with her dragon, taking his war machine, and promptly lost it when the dragon was surrounded and destroyed. She didn't recover from the loss.

"Coup," he said, taking her last captain. To his credit, there was no triumph in his voice. He might have been pointing out that her bootlace was untied.

"Two out of three?" Ileth said, replacing the screen.

This time she tried his two-captains-and-one-fortress mix, and her favorite array, with the dragon forward and next to her war machine.

They settled on flipping a fig for first move. Ileth lost.

This one was more a brawl than an intellectual duel. Ileth tried to detach and look objectively at the game, but Traskeer seemed intent

on hammering her in his quick, methodical fashion. He could move quickly and not make mistakes. His quick certainty unnerved her.

"I had to . . . to observe the campaign for Governor Raal," Ileth said, conversationally, as she chose her next move. "I was able to attend every meeting. The overall plan was very like the one from Annis Heem Strath I put in my commission." Ileth moved a captain and infantry together, as his dragon was within a distance to counterattack.

"Yes, I suppose it was," he said, moving his dragon sideways instead of forward. Oh well, her war machine next to the fortress would get another chance, hopefully.

"The one variation was those 'turtle' craft," Ileth said.

"Yes, something our tinkers have been working on since that interesting maneuver the Galantines used to assault the Scab."

"Clever. A floating fortress."

Traskeer stared at the area around his fortress. He was down a captain, and he couldn't afford to lose it.

"Still," Ileth continued, "it was interesting to me that you were described in that same newssheet you mentioned as the author of the plan."

"I was."

"Not Annis Heem Strath," Ileth said, shifting her dragon around his right flank.

"I did mention her plan in my written report to the Assembly . . . and that you did staff work. I'm not unfair. I acknowledged your contribution."

"Could I read the plan you submitted to the Assembly? I'd like to learn how it improved on Heem Strath's."

"Those papers were marked 'Most Secret' for obvious reasons." His hand shook a little as he moved his war machine to cover Ileth's dragon.

"I suppose my commission no longer exists." Her dragon came forward again and took an infantry piece, forcing him to choose between surrounding it and potentially losing his war machine.

He chose to retreat his war machine next to his remaining captain.

"Yes, as a precaution I burned it, along with my initial notes and draft. Can't have that sort of thing lying about with an operation so dependent on surprise."

"You should have warned me there was such need of secrecy, sir. My hand is very bad. My first draft is still in the Serpentine. You only burned the fair copy. The draft really should have been destroyed too." Her dragon gobbled more infantry. He had very little left.

"My innards are in an uproar, Ileth; you must excuse me." He rushed out of the room, giving Ileth a chance to admire the paintwork on his coup set up close. It must have been painted using very small brushes and a magnifying glass. Traskeer had a steady hand and an eye for detail. Even his use of color was striking; every piece had one small bit of boldly colored detail.

Traskeer returned. "We may have to suspend this match, Ileth. I will be—ahem—in and out of my office tonight, I fear." He looked at the board. "Did you change a piece's position?"

"I admired them. I was careful to put them back on the right cell." Had she been careful? She looked at the infantryman and was suddenly doubtful. It had been inadvertent, but would he think that?

"Sir, p-perhaps you are right: that infantryman. He w-was just ahead of your captain. I was careless."

"So was I," Traskeer said. "We share more than one fault."

"We do?"

"We both give too much rein to our ambition," Traskeer said.

"My ambition has never been to be anything other than the best dragoneer I can be."

His shoulders sagged, a rare giveaway. "You should know it doesn't work that way. Credit me with some concern for the traditions here. They seem slow to someone your age, but they work. The Serpentine is a great war machine, full of gears and triggers and tension points. You aren't ready. You aren't even ready to be a wingman. Even if you have me draped over the proverbial barrel, I can't just promote you to dragoneer, Ileth. I don't have the power."

"I suspect you do have it in your power to put me in the Guards."

"The Guards?"

"I'd like to indulge my masculine aspect, sir. I have Dun Klaff's hat and it looks very smart on me."

"If I walk into Charge Deklamp's office and say, 'I'm putting Ileth in the Guards because she has a hat,' he'll send me for six months' rest in an asylum."

"Sir, you m-might try 'I'm putting Ileth in the Guards as her rew-reward for bringing my attention to Annis Heem Strath's excellent plan.' It's not just ambition. I need a place to sleep. I've lost my bed in the Dancers' Quarter."

"You? Sleep surrounded by boys? The Sanitary Commission would go mad."

"Oh, I'm sure . . . sure I can figure out something to preserve the niceties, sir."

"Speaking of niceties," Traskeer said, looking pained. His stomach gave an audible gurgle.

"I'll leave you. Thank you for the lesson in coup, sir."

"You're a formidable player, Ileth. I think you're right: you *would* look very smart in one of those hats. I look forward to seeing it on you for the next match," he said, moving swiftly out the door.

Ileth returned to the Dancers' Quarter to find preparations for the parade in Sammerdam occupying the whole troupe. So they were to travel again. Which was just as well, she'd lost her bed in the Dancers' Quarter to a promising girl from the '67 draft. Ottavia put her, temporarily, on a cushion near the warmth of that little stove (Ottavia took a second look at her hair and said something about easily sneaking her into one of the men's dormitories in the walls).

A grand review was being organized in Sammerdam. News had already spread across the Serpentine, and the fortress was hard at work polishing dragon scale in preparation for the review. Even the cooks and reclusive tinkers were put to work with cloths shining up the dragons who'd been on the campaign.

Ottavia also handed her a letter that had been waiting for her on

her desk. The letter was in a good, clear masculine hand from Taskmaster Henn and sealed with wax using the wheel sigil of the Auxiliaries. That was a curiosity; she'd barely seen the Taskmaster the whole campaign. Ileth tore it open as soon as she could find privacy and good light to read.

Ileth,

Gandy, your friend from the Headlands, writes you here. I am sorry it is just marked as originating from the Stavanzer Post Station, but I did not want to mail it from the village for Comity Hears All, so I entrusted it with our good friend Taskmaster Henn, who knows you and believes that you deserve some measure of my cousin's regard. I trust this letter catches up to you at the Serpentine and finds you well.

I heard that my aunt treated you most unfairly and I apologize for her words and actions though she still would not wish me to. Astler is dead in this family full of death, and I am in grief as well but cannot blame you. I believe you grieve too. I asked my mother to let me read Astler's letter to you and she went to Comity, who relented at last, but she watched me every moment I read it and immediately had me hand it back, elsewise I would have copied it word for word for you.

This is my memory of what he wrote.

He said his affection for you was strong, so strong at times he felt overwhelmed by it, but that you were following a fate that would not let you align yourself to him without breaking your fate and perhaps your heart. He thought your devotion to the dragons and the Serpentine beautiful, and as you knew my cousin you must also know that expression encompassed much more than a young man's praise of his heart's desire. My cousin could no more destroy something beautiful than he could fly by beating his arms. It was not in his character. But I get away from the content of his letter by adding my own thoughts.

He joined with the militia on this campaign because he weighed your words about all of us in the north wishing to be rid of the depredations of the pirates. As he had some of this at school and trained with

the militia as a condition of his attendance, he was admitted to the campaign and allowed to take a man's part. This made him proud and I think he said happy. Or perhaps he said "be happy for me."

I am very sorry you do not have his letter to keep. One day it should come to me in the natural order of things if my life is vouchsafed, and then it will be sent on to you without delay and I hope it will still mean something to you even if we both have gray (or our fates allow, white) hair on our heads.

You must write to me care of Taskmaster Henn, who will be our secret postal commissioner, and tell me of you and your dragons. He expects to be in the Headlands for a year or more at least in order to see to the restoration and improvement of the Old Post. May the dragons never depart and their watch never fail (and give you an excuse to return! Bring one of the handsomer young dragoneers, if you can persuade one to visit a lonely northern girl with you in a house full of widowed women). I shall never forget the night we escaped the Rari!

As this letter is a secret and Comity may discover me at any moment, I must close it here. I am sure you think me a very silly girl to write the above with her cousin fresh in his grave, but I have gone a bit mad like grieving Dannsa in that play about the dead prince.

Your friend,
G. A.

Ileth reread it and then sealed it back in the envelope by warming the wax seal with her reading candle. She wished she had a way to repay Gandy, assuming the introduction to a handsome dragoneer was a joke. Though maybe it would do Gandy good to lose herself in a romance. But she wondered exactly what Astler had been thinking. If only she could read his exact words, instead of Gandy's memory of one hurried reading. The idea that any boy—well, young man—would be so impressed that he'd want to emulate her took some getting used to.

She tried to imagine circumstances where she would be admitted to Sag House again. Probably not until the death of Comity, if ever.

Gandy would have to visit her if duty called her to the Old Post—or whatever they were going to rename it once it reopened.

It was a solace, a small solace, that Gandy didn't blame her for Astler's death. Whether Ileth didn't blame herself was another question.

The fact hardly had time to sink in before Ottavia called her troupe together. The dragon-dancers would all join in the parade, mostly dancing, with the newer, less experienced dancers carrying baskets of flower petals and throwing handfuls of them about to fall on the dragons as they walked down the Archway. When they weren't rehearsing, they were working on their costumes, as dancing sheaths wouldn't do for Sammerdam. Even in a victory parade.

What Ottavia had in mind for costumes was a sort of wrap that went over the shoulders, reminiscent of a ship's sail, belted with cording that crossed the dancer's chest and tied at the waist in classical Hypatian fashion, with a tight dancing sheath beneath in whatever shade best matched the dancer's skin tone. Ottavia had "run out the bank" for buying costuming materials, having begged Shrentine to fly her down to Tyrenna to purchase material and cording and having them flown up from Tyrenna. She had Santeel model her prototype. Just standing there it had nice lines; Ileth couldn't wait to wear it. The shoulders and upper bust were bare or covered in cording, depending on who was opining, the girl who would wear it or her mother, and as Santeel moved it seemed very daring and provocative.

"The Charge is going to get angry letters or a visit from the Committee," Ileth predicted.

Ileth was posted with the petal throwers.

"Well, Ileth, you've been away for so many months. I'm afraid you are out of practice. There's no reason you can't do angle lifts and backouts and full turns as you throw your petals, though. If only it were a month later!"

There were three reasons for the timing, according to Dun Huss, who, having been Garamoff's chief of staff, now had to work himself ragged at the few seams that weren't already frayed by the campaign arranging the victory review. First, news had just reached the city and

excitement was at its peak. The people were in the mood to celebrate. Ileth thought it odd that the review was taking place in Sammerdam instead of, say, Stavanzer, because the north had done most of the suffering from the difficulties with the Rari.

Second, new ambassadors from both the Galantine Baronies and Daphia had arrived. The Daphine dignitary was of particular interest, as he was a minister plenipotentiary, whatever that was, who would work out how the Rari ports would be supervised to ensure no return of pirate vessels and that the Rari that remained were limiting themselves to peaceful use of the straits that connected Pine Bay with the Inland Ocean. It never hurt to remind the kingdoms surrounding the Republic that there were battle-hardened dragons just a short flight away from their borders who'd just carried out a campaign of singular note for its brevity and ferocity.

And third, and perhaps most important in his opinion, the Exchange and Bankers' Row would soon close for the traditional Six Weeks' Suspension at the end of summer, and would be setting up policies to keep businesses going while no shares were being bought or sold and changes in the percents made. On these matters Ileth also had to confess ignorance, but apparently how things were set up at the summer break could sometimes carry over through the Six Weeks' Suspension through the fall and on into the new year. Confidence in the Republic's future could cause the financial crisis to subside, and there were shipbuilders and warehousers looking to expand in the north needing capital for improvements to her roads and canals.

As preparations for the parade grew to a climax, Ileth found herself back with Horse Lot learning to load pack horses and mules for the trip. After vacillating for a day, she told Quith about Astler.

"I have no happy news either," Quith said, and commenced her usual mooning about Pasfa Sleng.

The Serpentine sent some of its complement overland for the parade in the form of a group of novices and apprentices to help tend the dragons and participate in the parade. Ileth had the impression that the novices were mostly important Names and the apprentices those

who could easily "be spared" for the festivities. Charge Deklamp gave a speech in the Great Hall to those who would remain behind, with him, that they were to act as if those who went to Sammerdam were lost in a great battle and it fell to them to carry on the Serpentine's traditions without them and care for the remaining dragons. They would hold their own victory feast and throw open the gates to Vyenn. She saw fewer downcast faces after that.

As the Horse passed down the line of departing dragons and riders, someone did ask him (Ileth was later told) why he wasn't going to participate in the parade. He smiled and said, "I've done my ride. You young people enjoy yours."

Of "her dragoneers" Amrits and Dun Huss would be in the parade, but the Borderlander skipped it. "Crowds make me itch," he said, repeating the sentiments of his Stavanzer farewell to her.

"That's just your fleas trying to jump off and move to a juicier accommodation," Amrits said.

Ileth found satisfaction in seeing Sifler say good-bye to Eswit. She didn't hear what was said, they were too far away and she had no business taking them near her, but he looked put-together for once and he'd learned the knack of walking with a sword so he didn't trip himself or bang an admiring young woman in the shins. The only thing that disturbed her was the sight of an overlarge golden ring on his finger. It seemed familiar. But he took a faster route to Sammerdam, being with the dragons, and she didn't have an opportunity to examine it closely.

Ileth alternately walked and rode with her fellow dancers in a slow-moving wain. A single young dragon led the procession, the copper Cunescious who had watched Ileth take her oath three summers ago, so that everyone might have a dragon to cheer as they passed through villages and small towns. The summer weather was fine and they were rained on just enough to refresh themselves and wash off the dust. In the only sizable town on the road to Sammerdam before they reached the coastal flats, the boys and men gallantly slept in barns and stables so the girls and women could have beds.

Ileth learned on the trip that word had spread about Astler. She was no longer the girl who was kicked out of the Manor after being caught in a stall with Vor Claymass; now she was the girl who'd had hopes for a young man of property from the north but he'd been killed in the Rari Suppression. It wasn't the outcome Ileth wanted—she thought it would be nice to have Astler's story woven into the tale of the Serpentine through dragoneer folklore—but she accepted it. Astler would have offered his shy smile and said that he was happy to be of service in changing the gossip about her. But then, at night, lying alone in the cart and remembering the smell of that shaving soap, she decided she'd happily be reputed the worst jade in the Serpentine if it would only bring him back.

They reached Sammerdam in five long, slow days of travel and set up camp on the festival grounds near the famous Archway. Ileth, having experienced Sammerdam's water before, had taken the precaution of filling a glass bottle with vinegar from the kitchen stores and mixed vinegar with a little honey to soften the taste to protect her innards. She didn't want to be in distress when walking in the parade.

There would be three guests of honor that the review would pass by: the Speaker of the Assembly, of course, who had managed to organize the vote for the war without word getting out (how he managed this was told to Ileth but she did her best to forget it within minutes of hearing about various select assemblymen representing various constituencies and a secret meeting of those involved in Asposis), Governor Raal, and the Serpentine's own former representative at the Assembly, Master Traskeer.

Traskeer passed through the dragoneer camp but once, mostly to receive congratulations on his brilliant plan. He didn't camp with the rest. Instead he stayed at the Speaker's house to catch up on all the Assembly gossip he'd missed.

Dragoneer Garamoff would lead the review atop Nephalia. Last in line would be Taresscon, the senior female of the dragons, and young Cunescious, posing as the Duke and Duchess, pulling a mock sea turtle on wheels with Taskmaster Henn at the reins. Of course a real sea

turtle didn't need a driver or reins, but the crowd didn't know that, they just wanted to see the object that so many were talking about. Ileth learned that the sea turtles for some reason had excited the imagination of Sammerdam's designers—turtle-skin boots and bags and lo, a bit of polished shell were the thing to have this summer.

The dragoneers would ride atop their saddles as the dragons walked down the Archway, their wingmen either walking along next to the girth or just behind the dragon's head.

Sifler stood beside Aurue in one of the groupings. He looked a little pink. Maybe it was just sunburn.

"Did they promote you to dragoneer? I thought only dragoneers could ride in this parade," Ileth said. She glanced at his hands as soon as he looked away. He wore no ring or band.

"Still just acting dragoneer. They said the matter is under discussion. I have a lot of coursework to complete still, and my survival. Were it wartime they'd promote me, but they're stricter about the formalities in peace. My, that's quite a costume. Good thing it's warm today."

Aurue stared straight ahead.

"I don't understand why I feel guilty," Sifler said quietly. "A difference of a moment—just a moment or two—kept me from being on his back on that last flight."

Ileth patted Aurue and the dragon nuzzled her hair. He didn't snuffle, it was pure affection. "I know. Too many humans," she whispered in his ear.

She continued down the line. Dun Huss was issuing some orders to the grooms who'd be walking along the dragons' sides. There was no danger of the dragons venting in the middle of a parade; the grooms were there to keep children from running up and touching the dragons and possibly being trod upon. His voice was tired and hoarse.

"I didn't see my name in the dancer groupings, sir," Ileth said. "Am I first, second, or third group?"

Dun Huss closed his folio. He took Ileth firmly by the arm and walked her forward. First group, then.

At the other end of the wide avenue Ileth could see a great

rectangular arch, its two legs astride the road. It looked part temple, part mausoleum. She didn't know enough about architecture to identify it, but she recognized some flourishes similar to some of the newer halls in the Serpentine.

"Have you ever been under the arch before, Ileth?" Santeel asked. "It's really impressive, up close. Much bigger than it looks at this distance."

"Is it safe to go under? It looks like there are cranes and scaffolding."

"Until the Academy, I'd lived in Sammerdam my whole life," Santeel said. "It's always having one part or another of it built and rebuilt. We joke about it. 'I'll pay you back when the arch is complete'—that sort of thing."

Dun Huss cleared a frog out of his throat. "The arch is like the Republic. It's never done. A labor for each generation—"

Ileth thought there were layers to those words worth investigating, but a senior female dragon pushed up along the edge of the street. Her scale was oiled and gleaming, her pop-eyed dragoneer already bowing to the crowd from the saddle as he took his place. He looked down at the flower girls.

"Santeel Dun Troot, what are you doing walking on the pavement with your leg hardly healed?" Amrits said, late as usual and only now getting his dragon into position in front of Mnasmanus.

"I judged her sound, sir," Ottavia said, rapping her walking stick on the cobblestones for emphasis.

"What, Ottavia, are you going to make a broken-legged girl walk the whole Archway? I knew you were a hard woman but never thought you cruel. Well, except for that night in Asposis when you dropped a flowerpot on me when I begged you to let me climb up and enter through your beautiful rear balcony."

"You call a bold line, sir, but you've never unbuckled and pierced me with anything but your wit. Climb on up, Santeel. He's harmless. Sorry to deprive you of your partner, Ileth."

Santeel passed her basket of flowers to Ileth and scrambled up nimbly enough. Ileth suspected she'd been exaggerating her limp. Ileth

wondered if the Dun Troots would try to make this the capstone to Santeel's career at the Serpentine. Joai had once told her that society girls joined the Serpentine to ride a dragon a few times, be in a parade down the Archway, and then retire their sash to an advantageous marriage and the ability to entertain other society women with stories of their years with the dragoneers. Somehow she didn't think that would be the case with Santeel.

Ottavia eyeballed Santeel's skirt. "Keep your knees constant companions, young lady. Your mother and father will be able to see you up there, and we don't want the canalers shouting anything too lewd. The Dun Troots will be proud of their namesake. Ought to be worth thirty votes the next time funding for the dragoneers is before the Assembly."

"Well, now my roster is unbalanced," Dun Huss said, looking at his folio sadly.

"Parades are like battles. They never go according to plan," Dun Huss's wingman, Preece, in his best gray uniform, said from his position at Mnasmanus's head. The dragon wore a victory garland of yellow flowers woven together by some Academy or other about his upper neck. The yellow looked very well against his purple scale.

"Well, it's a minor change to the order," Dun Huss said. "But Ileth's never shrunk from duty just because she has to do it alone."

Ottavia smiled and nodded at him. Ileth got the sense that some secret plan of theirs had just been executed.

Retaking his hold on her arm, Dun Huss marched her up to Nephalia at the front and set her firmly before the dragon.

"Sir?" Ileth said.

"I hope Nephalia doesn't object to only have one girl in front of her." Dun Huss waved to the trumpeters, who evened out their array on each side of the street and readied their instruments. Garamoff stood beside her in a brilliant uniform that looked fresh from the tailor. He wore a matching decorative pauldron on each shoulder for the ceremony, green with gold braid threaded through the edges.

"Better this way. One girl ahead of one dragon," Garamoff said, ready to swing up into Nephalia's saddle. "You'll be active, Ileth. Be

sure to wave to both sides of the street and set an easy pace for the walkers."

Ileth flushed. This was a bit much. She didn't like being the center of attention, whether it was running across the Long Bridge as tailer or—here she swallowed her nerves with a physical effort that might as well be a gulp—leading a parade up the Archway. She wished she were wearing armor, with what felt like every citizen in Sammerdam staring. She turned when she felt the dragon breathing down her neck. "Try not to get flower petals in my eyes," Nephalia said, giving her a gentle nudge forward with her snout.

Ileth relaxed a little. She had a simple duty to attend to, to keep her mind off the gauntlet of the spectators. She was just a flower girl. Garamoff would draw all the attention.

Captain-General Garamoff, Dragoneer and Victor of the Rari Campaign, looked back over the line of glittering dragons behind him, then put his fists together toward her. He didn't exactly smile, but he gave her a friendly nod. Ileth did the best she could responding in kind, as the basket of petals she carried made for an awkward burden.

"We move out at your command, Ileth of the Freesand," Garamoff said loudly from the saddle. Ileth felt a chill run up her spine.

Ileth took a deep breath, then started her internal music box playing a parade step in her head. She grabbed a handful of pink and white petals, remembering to judge the wind so they wouldn't float into Nephalia's eyes.

She stepped out, throwing the fistful of petals into the breeze. They spun and danced in the air to the sound of trumpets.

CAST OF CHARACTERS

IN THE SERPENTINE ACADEMY

ILETH, a new apprentice and "tailer" of her draft

SANTEEL DUN TROOT, Ileth's fellow dragon-dancer of renowned family

QUITH, Ileth's former roommate in the Manor

SIFLER, an apprentice from Ileth's draft

RAPOTO VOR CLAYMASS, a young wingman from a wealthy and important family

VAREEN DUN KLAFF, a wingman of the Blacktower group

VOR RAPP, another wingman and friend to Dun Klaff

HEEM BECK, another of Dun Klaff's group

FINILA, a new apprentice in Ileth's training lot

GOWAN, the archivist's apprentice

GRUSS, a talented artist who provides topographic sketches

AT THE SERPENTINE FORTRESS

CHARGE ROGUSS HEEM DEKLAMP, in overall command of the Serpentine's humans

OTTAVIA, the Charge of the Dragon-Dancers

MASTER TRASKEER, responsible for the Serpentine apprentices

THE HORSE, the Master in charge of Ileth's training lot

KESS, the archivist

DOGLOSS, wingman and assistant to Charge Deklamp

SERENA, wingman and Charge Deklamp's eyes and ears in the Republic atop his dragon, Telemiron

ROBEN, Falberrwrath's dragoneer

JOAI, a nurse and cook and informal counselor to the Academy youth

VELLEKER, Taresscon's nominal dragoneer

GARAMOFF, Nephalia's dragoneer, recently arrived from the west

THREADNEEDLE, a physiker

GIFT, Threadneedle's apprentice and principal assistant

SHATHA, the senior dancer in Ottavia's troupe

VII, a dancer who helped Ileth when she was new to the troupe

PREEN, another dragon-dancer

HAEL DUN HUSS, Mnasmanus's dragoneer, leader of the trio of dragoneers who aided Ileth her novice year

DATH AMRITS, Etiennersea's dragoneer, another of the trio

THE BORDERLANDER, Catherix's dragoneer, provided Ileth with her flying rig her novice year

IN THE NORTH PROVINCE

GOVERNOR RAAL, elected leader of the province

LADY RAAL, his wife, who lives at the family estate

SEVERAN, a long-time servant at Stesside

IGNATA, a Galantine cook

GADIKAN AFTORN, the eldest of the most important family in the Headlands

COMITY, his granddaughter

ASTLER AFTORN, his great-grandson and heir

GANDY AFTORN, Astler's cousin

TASKMASTER HENN, a military engineer

WATCH CHIEF TIRUT, a Daphine soldier and slave to the Rari

OTHERS

COMMISSIONER-GENERAL NAVARR, a staunch republican suspicious of the aristocratic dragoneers

FALTH, a servant of the Dun Troots and Ileth's correspondent

ESWIT CARIBET, a girl from Vyenn

ACKNOWLEDGMENTS

The Cold War nuclear horror film *Threads* (1984) begins with these lines: "In an urban society, everything connects. Each person's needs are fed by the skills of many others. Our lives are woven together in a fabric. But the connections that make society strong also make it vulnerable." Writing acknowledgments for a book with a pandemic snipping those threads tempts me to break tradition and acknowledge my grocery shelf stocker, Amazon delivery people, the corner pharmacist, plus the truck drivers and food industry workers, none of whom I know but who are currently keeping me and my family alive at various levels of risk to their health. I never thought myself important, but what's going on outside the door in the spring of 2020 does make me feel unimportant to a new and disturbing degree.

That being said, this book has its own network of threads supporting it stretching from the author's chair to your local bookshelf. I'd like to thank my wife, Stephanie, always my first reader, not just for the benefit of her diligence but for all the encouragement and support through the ups and downs of an author's life. A great deal of credit goes to Miranda at Ace, who took up this volume when the series was orphaned when the acquiring editor, Rebecca Brewer, was let go in the course of publishing upheavals and cutbacks. Of course, John, my agent, has spun a global net of financial support for my writing over

the years. Then there's Alexis and Jessica in marketing and publicity who worked so hard to get Ileth and the Serpentine Academy in front of readers. Finally, I'd like to thank all of you who buy books and then pop by on social media to visit or write a review recommending it to others.

You're all threads in the web. Stay joined.

E. E. Knight was born in Wisconsin, grew up in Minnesota, and now calls Chicago home, where he abides in domestic felicity with his family and assorted pets. He is the author of the Age of Fire series and the Vampire Earth series.